I0746190

this story is for those of us who ultimately cycle back to tragedy.

there is beauty in destruction and devastation. in inevitability. in the darkness.

(just remember, there's beauty in redemption and rebirth as well.)

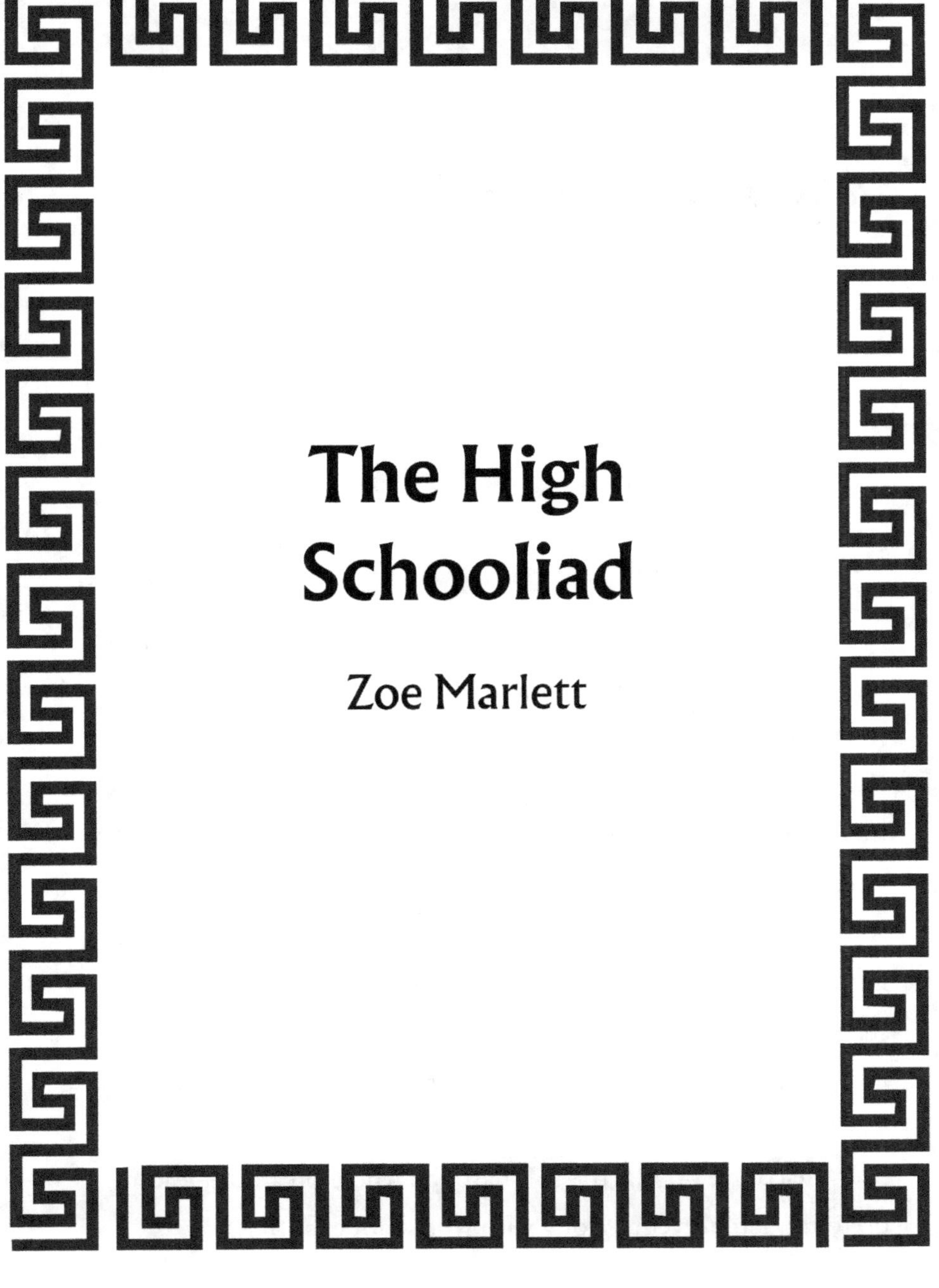

# The High Schooliad

## Zoe Marlett

# Author's rambling

**Beginning Note:**

Hey everyone! This story idea has been in my head for a looong time and here it is. Finally. (Ahahaha.) I just wanted to start it off with a little context. I got super obsessed with the Iliad over... that gross time between 2020 and whenever the gross time ended, and yes, it's a terrible story. Terrible in the way that it's violent and male–centered and very sexist. Essentially, it's a story about the fragility of the male ego, which is always interesting. In my version, I've modernized it, keeping as much of the original story in there as I could. Obviously, I had to change some things. Many pieces of the ancient poem just... aren't acceptable in any way, shape, or form in the modern word. (The Iliad also takes place over the course of 52 days, so I have the whole preamble, leading up to the actual events, along with what happens after.)

I wanted to make this story more accessible, because not every-one wants to read a 456 page book in a weird type of (often stunt-ed) poetry about men beating each other to a pulp and *not* being consent kings. (Interesting fact: it's usually men who do transla-tions of the original text, so they often changed the descriptions of the female characters to fit modern beauty standards. *shakes head disappointedly* BUT that's changing now.) After reading the poetry version, I read some more recent adaptations, and then spent hours looking through fanfiction sites. Sue me I'm a bit of a nerd. I really really wanted to find a high school alternate–uni-verse fic that stayed true to the original story, but alas, I couldn't. (Maybe I didn't look hard enough. So if you wrote a fic like this, I apologize for my inadequate searching skills. AND SEND ME THE LINK.)

Eventually, I decided I would write the story myself. This is it. So I thank you for picking up this weird little story. Like I mentioned before, the Iliad is such a male driven legend. I took some liberties with the female characters because they have *zero* character development in the original. Helen of Sparta has a single monologue, explaining who the Greeks are to King Priam of Troy. Briseis talks once. Iphis is *mentioned* once, and not in every transla-tion. Very frustrating. (And Achilles and Patroclus were totally to-gether. Would you call your platonic dude–bro bestie your beloved companion who you loved as much as your own life? I don't know. Seems a lil... fun.) Seeing as it's not acceptable to kidnap women, or to keep a dead body with you for days on end, I've changed things to make them more akin to modern times. Before actually considering this for six seconds, I wanted to say that the world was no longer like the one of this book, but unfortunately, horrific things still happen everyday. I hope that one day, humanity can sort itself the fuck out. Seriously.

The story is also, at its root, a tragedy. It deals with some difficult themes, like drugs. alcohol, loss, grief, death, homophobia, violence, not awesome parental relationships, and the human mind at its worst. Please take care and be kind to yourself.

Anyways. Thanks for reading my ramble. I appreciate you :)

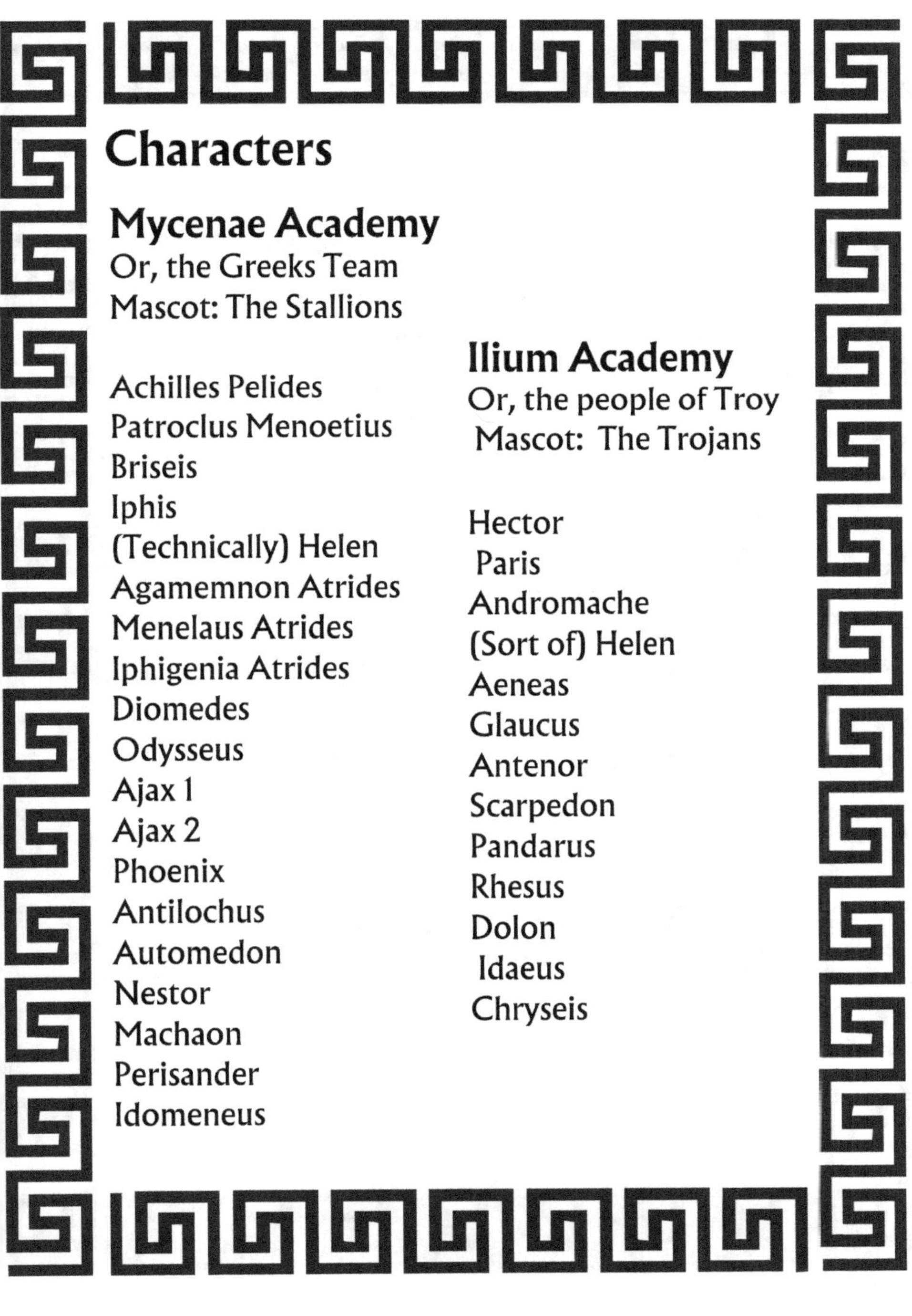

# Characters

## Mycenae Academy
Or, the Greeks Team
Mascot: The Stallions

Achilles Pelides
Patroclus Menoetius
Briseis
Iphis
(Technically) Helen
Agamemnon Atrides
Menelaus Atrides
Iphigenia Atrides
Diomedes
Odysseus
Ajax 1
Ajax 2
Phoenix
Antilochus
Automedon
Nestor
Machaon
Perisander
Idomeneus

## Ilium Academy
Or, the people of Troy
Mascot:  The Trojans

Hector
Paris
Andromache
(Sort of) Helen
Aeneas
Glaucus
Antenor
Scarpedon
Pandarus
Rhesus
Dolon
Idaeus
Chryseis

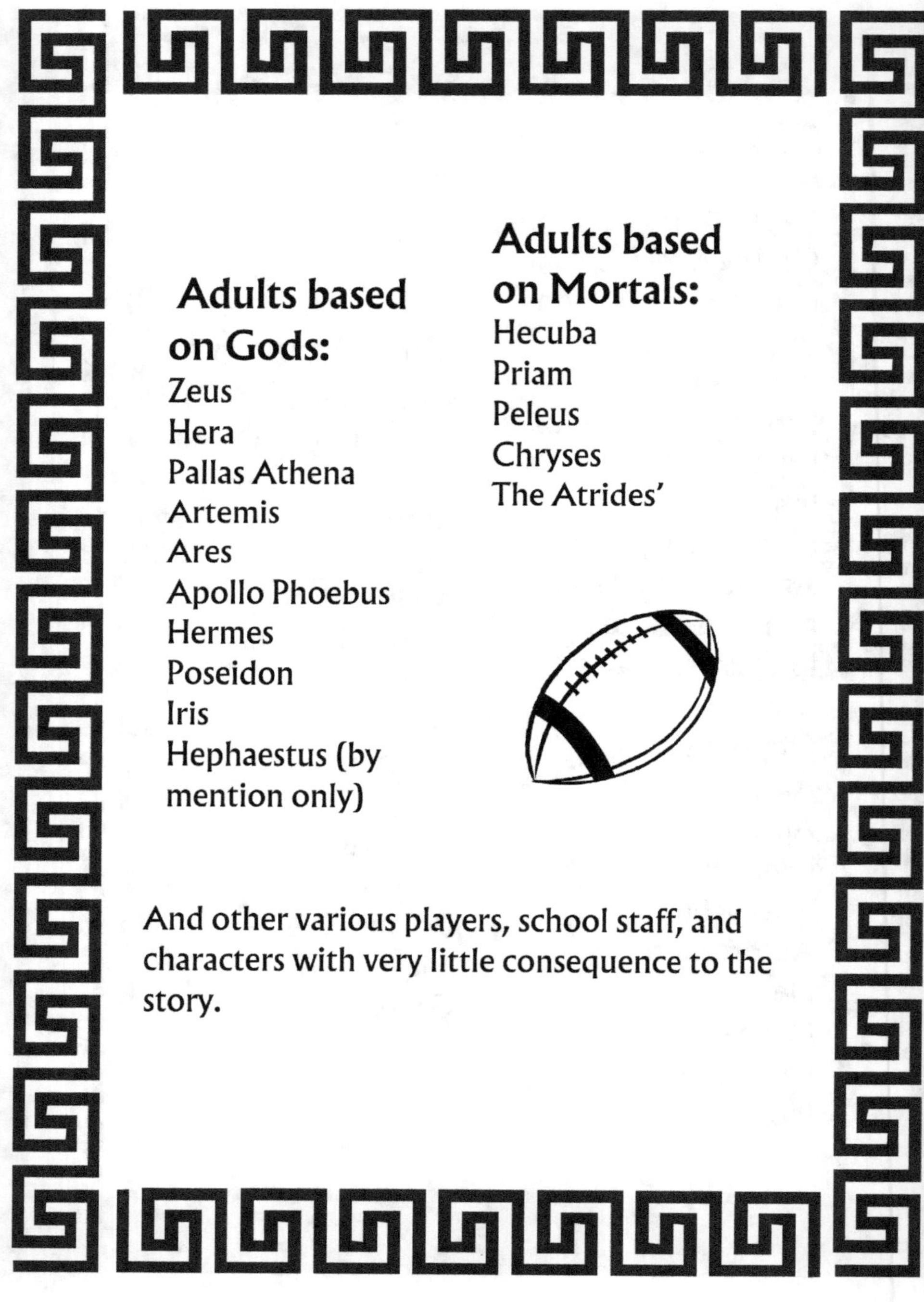

## Adults based on Gods:
Zeus
Hera
Pallas Athena
Artemis
Ares
Apollo Phoebus
Hermes
Poseidon
Iris
Hephaestus (by mention only)

## Adults based on Mortals:
Hecuba
Priam
Peleus
Chryses
The Atrides'

And other various players, school staff, and characters with very little consequence to the story.

# Prologue

REALLY, IT WAS PARIS' fault, but no one blames it on him, because... well, no one even remembers. And he was so young at the time. It started at Achilles' parents' wedding. They got married on a hot day. Not pleasantly warm, and definitely not temperate. The day was *boiling*. The tent where the ceremony was supposed to take place felt like wearing a sleeping bag in a hot tub. Peleus, the groom, had taken off his suit jacket before his begrudging bride had even finished getting ready.

But the temperature was the least of their problems. Thetis didn't want to be married, which was one fairly large issue. By this point, their son, Achilles, was five, and so was Paris. His brother, Hector was six, and serious as a drill sergeant already. Priam and Hecuba, Hector and Paris' parents, were the two people there that might have been having a good time. Except for maybe the kids, who were playing tag, despite the heat and their fancy clothes.

Thetis watched Achilles from her window as he ran around screaming and laughing with some boys she'd never seen before.

Her little blonde cherub chucked a football that was the same size as his torso, at Peleus. It hit her soon–to–be–husband in the back of his head, and Thetis laughed. She hardly ever laughed. She was trapped, and unhappy, with a strong hatred towards her family. Thetis had gotten pregnant in a situation neither she or Peleus enjoyed discussing. (On a vacation. They were both a little... intoxicated) and finally, her parents had enough. Hence, the horrible, backyard wedding that probably cost her parents more than the house was worth.

Thetis had a huge family. They had plenty of their *own* problems, but they were together on one thing. Eris would *not* attend the wedding. Eris was that chaotic aunt who *would* object to a marriage, just for the fun of it. She'd be the one to slip a sleeping draught into someone's drink, or hide a dead mouse in the cake. She was admittedly insane. Zeus, one of Thetis' old... friends, had sanctioned this exclusion, but Eris, being the crafty, slightly demonic person she was, showed up anyways. She entered with the dramatic flair of an escaped convict in a broadway show, right during the the first waltz, if it could even be called that. It was more of a fight between Thetis and Peleus, with red cheeks and sweat dripping from damp hairlines. Thetis was the kind of woman with a permanent sneer on her face, that just oozed disapproval, but in this moment, she was livid. Peleus, who was hardly ever upset, was *definitely* upset. A muscle pulsed in his clenched jaw.

The wedding guests smiled politely, but whispered rudely behind delicate hands, to shield the unhappy bride and groom from their gossip. Zeus, and his own resentful wife, Hera, sat in chairs near the unpleasantly warm punch, both with rod straight posture. Hera curled her lip at the whole affair. She was a wedding planner, but she hated weddings, and people in general. Zeus, on the other hand, was eyeing the crowd, trying to find his next... infidelity. He hadn't wanted to marry Hera either, but his coping mechanism was much less socially acceptable than hers. He didn't get bitter. He became an opportunist, seeking out any woman who would sleep with him. Zeus left long a trail of devastated young women, saddled with fatherless children.

Occasionally, he would send monetary aid, but more often than not, he just disappeared. One would think that this behavior would be stopped, or even discouraged, but Zeus supported those he was close to, so no one complained. And he *did* offer help to people, every now and then. When he lent a hand, it was so monumental that the people who had previously disliked him sung his praises from the rooftops. After all, Zeus owned the biggest oil empire in the North West. No one wanted to be on his bad side.

Zeus had just spotted a woman speaking with a young girl when Eris dropped by. Her entrance was grand, with lights and stage fog. The whole shebang. No one knew what was happening for a time, and the tent fell completely into a silence, confused and uncomfortable, until Eris started coughing. A concerned mumble arose from the fog-shrouded onlookers until the smoke cleared. Eris was doubled over, hacking away. Zeus stood up so fast his chair fell to the floor with a clatter. Even the kids stopped running around, instead gathering at their parents' legs uncertainly.

It was Thetis who said what was on everyone's mind. But she said it with glee, rather than concern. "Eris, why on earth are you here?"

With that, Eris stood up, clearing her throat. Everyone there could see the gleam in her dark eyes. She was chaos, wrapped into human form. The wild lady ignored Zeus as he made his way across the tent, discreetly shoving people out his way.

In the still air, her hoarse voice rang out. "For the most beautiful," she cackled gleefully, producing a golden apple from her strange assortment of shawls and skirts.

Carefully, Eris placed it in the middle of the makeshift dancefloor and backed out of the tent. Even Zeus stopped advancing at this point, his steely brow furrowed. It took a moment for the chatter to explode like a statue brought to life. Hera leapt to her feet, practically throwing people out of the way, to get to the center of the newly formed circle around the apple.

"It's mine!" she cried, suddenly possessed with the pressing need for the golden trinket, which glinted dully in the humid afternoon.

"Not so fast," Aphrodite, a bombshell of a woman who was a distant relative of some sort, declared, stepping out of the crowd, pointing a perfectly manicured nail at Hera.

People were whispering again, and backing away from the two women who had taken on the air of hungry lionesses.

"*Wait,*" one last voice cut through the crowd, silencing everyone, yet again. Athena, Zeus' daughter, who was (debatably) with Hera made her way inside of circle. She wore an extravagant dress, styled to look like an avant–garde suit of armour. Even Priam and Hecuba, who were always opposed to such dramatics, peered over the shoulders of guests, trying to understand why the wedding had descended into a contest.

(Both Thetis and Peleus were secretly relieved. They had split from their dance the moment Eris arrived. Thetis was inside, sitting in a bathtub full of cold water, still in her dress, and Peleus was absentmindedly tossing the football that had hit him on the head earlier back and forth with Achilles, who was doing less catching, and more falling over. Neither Peleus nor Thetis cared for this drama.)

The three women stared at each other so intently that the hair on the back of Zeus' neck started prickling.

"Hera, dear," he said tentatively, when she rounded on him.

He flinched backwards as her mood changed visually. "Zeus, darling, would you be so kind as to decide? Who should get the apple?"

Athena and Aphrodite stared at him with such heat that the day began to feel cool. Hera smiled sweetly. Zeus loosened his yellow tie, struggling slightly, to breathe. The woman he had been eyeing earlier stood near the front of the crowd, her arms crossed, brow furrowed.

He shook his head uncertainly, before picking up speed. "No. I cannot choose between my lovely wife and my clever daughter, and I cannot offend the wonderful Aphrodite."

Hera looked practically homicidal. (And she felt it too. She hated Zeus more than ever in that moment, which is really saying something, seeing as her husband was a man who had somewhere between twenty and fifty affairs during their fifteen years of marriage.) Zeus could feel it too. He inconspicuously eyed the crowd, trying to find a way to avoid his wife's rage. And he found it.

Young Paris stood right at the front of the throng, his eyes wide with excitement. Even as a five year old, Paris enjoyed watching people argue, disagree, and snap at each other. He loved conflict and he loved drama, which, later on, would cause him and his family a lot of grief. Priam and Hecuba had even debated bringing him to the wedding, but because Hector was going, Paris went too. (They were strongly regretting that choice now, as Zeus walked over and crouched down next to their son.)

In a fatherly way, Zeus put his hand on Paris' tiny shoulder. "Hey son, could you do me a favour?"

Paris nodded eagerly. Priam hid his face in his hands. Hector glared at his little brother, who loved the spotlight more than anything. *Gods. That kid,* he thought, annoyed, though he was only a year older.

"Good man," Zeus said, looking back up at the three indignant women. "Young Paris here will decide who the apple goes to," he said confidently, standing up again. "He's a good kid."

"He's five—" Hecuba started to say frantically, knowing that this couldn't possibly go well.

Zeus raised a harsh finger to his lips, shushing her with a sharp look. (He'd never particularly liked the two of them. They were so bland, with their happiness and common sense.) Priam put an arm around his wife's shoulder.

"Paris is such a trouble maker," she whispered to her husband, ducking out from under his comfort. "It's too hot dear, I'm sorry."

He chuckled silently, even though he was just as concerned as she was. "All good. But yes. That kid. He'll bring ruin to our family."

Hecuba shook her head at the joke as Hera, Athena, and Aphrodite gathered around Paris, crouching down like Zeus had.

Paris had never been surrounded by strangers like this before. But he didn't mind. He crossed his arms, trying to imitate how Zeus stood. A little bug buzzed around his brown curls. He *didn't even move to swat it away.* He felt so old and important, even though he didn't quite know what was happening. Athena handed him the golden apple that had been the cause of all the problems, as far as Paris could tell. Well, that and the lady with the smoke. He took the apple in his little hand. It seemed like something he could eat, but it didn't *feel* like he could eat it. It was heavy, and somehow cool, even in the heat. Paris was entranced by it.

"Hi," Aphrodite whispered.

Paris looked up at her. She was very pretty.

"If you just hand me that little apple there, I'll make sure you can have a very nice girl to be your girlfriend," she said softly, nodding all the while.

Paris had been playing with a girl named Helen earlier. He thought *she* was very nice. Aphrodite winked, then held out her hand.

"Ah ah ah," Hera cut in, smacking Aphrodite's hand away. "Paris, if you give *me* that apple, I'll make sure you become president of the entire country," she said with very wide eyes, and a tiny smile that reminded Paris of his mother when she made cookies.

That bug by his head was getting *very* annoying now, and he didn't even know what half those words meant. He scrunched up his nose. He wanted cookies now.

"Paris," Athena sang quietly. If she offered him cookies, he would give her the apple. "I offer you endless wisdom. I'll help you with anything you want, and teach you whatever your heart desires."

That didn't sound like cookies to Paris. He shook his head, looking back down at the heavy apple in his hands. It was actually a bit too heavy and his arms were starting to hurt.

"Here," he said, handing it to Aphrodite, not necessarily because of what she offered, but because she was sitting right in front of him, still holding out her hand. (In truth, he didn't even remember what she said she would give him.)

Hera growled under her breath as Athena stood up, a cold expression spreading across her face like frost. Aphrodite smiled.

"Why thank you, Paris," she cooed, brushing a stray curl behind her ear, before getting to her feet. The apple, when held above her head, glinted dully in the smoky sunlight. "*I* am the most beautiful."

Paris watched her. Zeus watched her. Hera watched her. *Everyone* watched her. They watched her warily, with jealousy, awe and despair. They watched her, unsure what she would do next. The air in the tent was as taught as a lyre string about to snap.

Until the beautiful Aphrodite giggled. "Have fun with your party," she smirked, turning on her sparkling stiletto heel and marching out of the circle, which parted for her as she clicked and clacked away. Everyone stood in complete silence. Except for the buzzing of the horrible little insects that seem to multiply when it's hot.

Achilles continued to laugh and chase around the football, but no one paid any attention to either of those things for a long moment. Nobody knew what to do, until Zeus started the music back up. The tense silence dissolved into nervous chatter. They would turn into rumors, that would spread across the entire county, because no one had anything better to do. The gossip was nearly as bad as the heat.

Paris wove his way through the legs of all the adults. He brushed his hand along a dress covered in beads. The people who noticed him all discreetly shook their heads, muttering to each other conspiratorially. The common opinion (which would *not* leave the wedding) was that Aphrodite didn't need anything to boost her ego, and young Paris had given her... just that. The little brown haired boy finally made it out of the stifling crowd, and found his way over to a goat statue (that Thetis hated with a burning passion). It was tucked in the very corner of the gigantic yard, beneath a bush, positioned so only its head could be seen.

Paris sat underneath the stone goat's gaze to get a bit of shade. He didn't feel like playing with the kids anymore. As the wedding started up again, without the bride *or* the groom, Paris felt a little strange, like he didn't fully understand what had just happened.

And he was right. He didn't know how monumentally his simple little choice would affect his life eleven years later. Like the first rock of a landslide, that choice would push something tragic into motion.

# Before

Eleven years later:

# I

"Well..." Menelaus sat with his head on the picnic table, numbly watching the dirty river.

"*Well what?*" his older brother demanded. "What do you *mean,* dickhead?"

"Gods, Agamemnon, no need to be rude—" Odysseus, who was not related to either of them started, feeling a bit bad for the distraught sounding redhead who was studying the stream with a staggering intensity.

"Shut up, Odysseus," Agamemnon growled. (He was always growling. Or yelling. Or snarling.)

"Sorry," Odysseus replied, putting up his hands.

It was that time of summer where going back to school loomed on the horizon, but not close enough for anyone to *really* care. The air was hazy with humidity, but all the guys at the picnic table were wearing letterman jackets, except for Odysseus, because he didn't think the jackets were proud at all. Last week, he had finally caved and told Agamemnon why he hated them.

(It was, *"Because in university, no one's gonna think it's cool to have a high school jacket, so I'm not paying $500 for something I'm gonna use for what, two years?"*) (Agamemnon had plenty to say about that, but Ajax 1 had made some joke about *'Odysseus tryna follow in Achilles' footsteps and be different from the rest of the team,'* which made no sense, but Odysseus had paled and agreed to buy a 'stupid fucking football jacket' when they went back.) (Essentially, Ajax was jealous of Achilles' abilities, and therefore took every opportunity to make fun of him that he could. But only behind Achilles' back.)

"Menny," Agamamnon said, attempting to be gentle, even though he considered toxic masculinity to be the height of style. "What *happened*?"

Menelaus sighed. He had only blurted what he had blurted to shut up his older brother, who was back to the rant about Achilles going away for the summer, which was apparently 'breaking the brotherhood of the football team.'

"She said she's transferring to Illium," he muttered, trying not to sound as defeated as he felt.

"No fucking way!" Diomedes exclaimed, hitting the table with a bony fist that had a shocking amount of force behind it.

Menelaus felt the weathered wood creak against his face. A plastic bag drifted down the river, which was really more of a muddy stream. It made Menelaus feel slightly better, because at least that plastic bag looked like he felt. Discarded, left to float down the dirtiest puddle of a river in the whole damn world. He related to that bag. Sadly. Hilariously.

"I mean…" he started, not even sure why he was talking. "She said she didn't *want* to go."

Agamemnon was on his feet in record time. "Then why is she going?!" he demanded, stomping around the table and crouching at the front, where Menelaus was avoiding all their eye contact.

Menelaus was scared of his brother. Agamemnon was a short, but sturdy guy, with wild black curls that he hadn't cut in years. They reached his shoulders now, but he tied them back most of the time. Menelaus remembered, a few months ago, that Agamemnon thought they made him intimidating. He was right, but it wasn't *just* the hair.

"Menny. This is ridiculous," his older brother growled.

"You can't let people walk all over you like that!" Diomedes offered, from the opposite end of the table.

Menelaus wanted to say, '*they do anyways*,' but restrained himself.

He sighed, blowing a fly away from his face. "Helen can do what she wants. I don't care."

"Clearly," Odysseus said, a hint of his signature sarcasm drizzled over the word.

"But why is she going to Illium?" Ajax 2 asked. He was a scrawny kid, who, annoyingly enough, was always with Ajax 1. They were easy to tell apart though. 1 was pretty much twice the size of 2. But yelling at people gets annoying when they have the same name, Agamemnon had said. Hence the 1 and 2. Agamemnon called them Greater Ajax and Lesser Ajax, but that hadn't really caught on.

Menelaus shrugged, silently praying that his brother would go back to his seat. "Said something about a crazy aunt. Aphro... something."

"Achilles probably knows her," Odysseus offered. "I could text him?"

No one responded. Odysseus rolled his eyes. Everyone was stupid, in his humble opinion. He pulled out his phone and shot a message to *Achilles The Buttery*, even though he probably wouldn't respond for a few hours. (The contact name had come from Ninth Grade, when Achilles had first come to the Mycenae Academy. They'd been fooling around with nickname generators during a math class, and both thought that one was hilarious. They weren't as close as they used to be. Not after Odysseus had threatened to spread rumors about Achilles.)

Odysseus:

> You know some crazy lady called Aphro... something?

*Sent 11:46 am*

Odysseus stared at his phone for a moment, before shutting it off, satisfied with Achilles taking a while to respond. While he was on his phone, Menelaus had sat up. There was a red mark on his face from where it was pressed against the wooden table. He was the youngest of the lot, going into his junior year. Agamemnon was sitting beside Diomedes now, across from his younger brother.

"And so she broke up with you because she was changing schools?" Diomedes asked, his thick brows furrowed.

A cool wind blew briefly through the dusty park. All the grass was dead at this time of year, although, it was supposed to start raining before they went back to school.

Menelaus nodded, scrubbing his hands over his pinkish face. Odysseus was boiling hot, and Ajax 2 was getting the beginnings of a burn on the back of his neck.

"Can we talk about this somewhere cooler?" Odysseus suggested. "With a cold drink, maybe?"

"Good idea," Ajax 1 said, getting up from his spot with some difficulty. He was the tallest player on the team, about 6ft 8', and a solid 275 pounds of muscle. "I'm done out here."

They had been sitting at the picnic table for about an hour and a half, arguing about the next school year, what they would do for tryouts, and what they should do tomorrow. They had gotten exactly nothing done. Ajax 1 lumbered around the table and pulled Menelaus out of his seat by the back of his jacket.

"Let's go. There'll be other girls, y'know," he said, pulling the significantly smaller boy along with him.

Ajax 2 ran after the two of them, leaving Odysseus, Diomedes, and Agamemnon behind. Diomedes nodded, getting up and throwing his letterman jacket over his shoulder. His badly done stick–and–poke tattoo showed from under the sleeve of his white T-shirt. It looked sort of like a fish, but everyone had seen the lumpy mermaid in the change room. Diomedes thought it was hilarious. Agamemnon crossed his arms, watching grimly as the Ajaces threw their arms over his younger brother's shoulders and started singing an obnoxiously loud song that the humid air sort of swallowed.

"There's something he's not telling us," Agamemnon said matter-of-factly, scratching his neck.

"Give the kid a break, man," Diomedes chided, starting towards the parking lot where Agamemnon's convertible was parked. "He's just had his heart broken. She was his first girlfriend, right? They were together for a hell of a long time."

Agamemnon jogged to catch up, his white Nike hightops crunching against the brown grass. "It's not *that* impressive to be with someone for a year."

Odysseus followed the two of them, a few steps behind. "Dude. That's like four times as long as any relationship you've been in."

"Fuck off."

"He does have a point," Diomedes laughed.

Agamemnon growled something under his breath, but didn't argue.

"Hey!" Ajax 1 yelled from the parking lot, making the three of them glance up. Menelaus was already in the car, lying across the backseat of the open convertible like he'd been dropped there from fifty feet up.

"What's wrong?" Diomedes yelled back, walking quicker.

Ajax 2 pointed to the stream/river/muddy water. Agamemnon stopped and squinted towards where 2 was pointing. He couldn't really see for a moment, because he was staring into the sun, which was glaring off the water, but when his eyes adjusted, he saw a little boat. A dingy, more like it. But it was kitted out with an umbrella. And a cooler. Agamemnon couldn't see the people inside the... floaty, so he started walking towards the Ajaces, squinting as he went. He didn't really understand why the *'boat'* was so important, or why he should even care about it, but he went along with his teammates anyways. Odysseus and Diomedes followed him, like they always did. Agamemnon got a rush of satisfaction knowing that they were scared of him, and that they respected him. Being captain of the best private school football team in the state paid off.

He stepped over the wire dividing the parking lot from the grassy area, coming to a halt beside Ajax 1. That's when he caught the glint of blonde hair in the raft. He understood immediately after that. Helen draped herself off the side of the dingy, trailing her hand in the water. Under the umbrella sat... Paris. Fucking *Paris*.

"What. The hell. Is that manwhore doing there?" Agamemnon hissed.

"Again, captain, don't think *you* can use that word as an insult," Diomedes snickered to Odysseus, who covered his mouth with the back of his hand.

"They're a couple," Menelaus groaned from the back of the convertible, "okay?"

Agamemnon started marching towards the river, fists clenched. "I'm going to fucking tear that—"

Ajax 1 had to hold Agamemnon back before he marched into the river and killed Paris. The five of them watched the little boat drift lazily down the filthy river–like–body–of–water. Agamemnon was seething, his tanned skin flushed with an undertone of red.

Menelaus sighed. "She said she didn't *want* to go out with him."

"Hey genius!" Agamemnon snarled. She may have is *said* that, but there she is! She's going out with that pig of a soccer player! She's dating him! And flaunting it! In your fucking face!"

"Dude," Diomedes interjected, sounding offended, even though he wasn't the one being yelled at. "It's not his fault."

Ajax 1 slowly released Agamemnon from his grasp. Agamemnon took a few steps towards the river, craning his neck to see Helen and Paris disappear around the bend in the stream. He was furious. He was *always* furious. There was anger bubbling just beneath the surface. It exploded out. This made Agamemnon even more annoyed. He couldn't *control* the things he did. That's why he played football. Not *soccer*. *American* football. Aggressive. Slightly dangerous. It was his game. The summers were bad, because they didn't play as a team. Sure, he played on his own, or with the six people around him now, but it wasn't the same. He craved the crowds and the lights. The excitement. The feeling of being *alive*.

"I might quit the team," Menelaus said quietly.

The five of them watching the river whipped around faster than should have been possible, all demanding in unison: "*What?*" "No!" "Menny, what the hell?" "You can't!"

"I'd have to play against him," Menelaus continued, unphased. "And watch her cheer for him..." he added, a tiny bit of strain in his voice.

Agamemnon slammed his palms against the trunk of the red car. "Nope."

Menelaus sat up, frowning. "What do you mean, *nope*?"

Agamemnon meant so many things in that one word. Football was the only thing he and his brother shared. He wanted to help soft little Menny learn how to play the game. He was grooming him to be Team Captain after he left. He wanted Menelaus to love the game like he did. He wanted his brother not to be afraid of him. But he didn't say any of that. Obviously.

"Look," he began sternly. "This isn't just about fucking football anymore. It's about your godsdamm *honor*, Menny. Do you want that tiny snivelling manchild to take away the girl you love *and* the game you love to play?"

"Love is a bit of an overstatement..." Menelaus said under his breath.

Agamemnon went on as if he hadn't heard his brother. "So you lost the girl. Whatever. But you can clobber that idiot on the field! Maybe show Helen that she went with the wrong guy."

Normally, Menelaus didn't fall for his brother's bullshit, but today... he just needed something to believe in. Helen had broken up with him the night before, in an alleyway beside a diner. It was *their* diner too. They always went there together, because none of Helen's 'posse' as she liked to call them, would ever be caught in the same room as onion rings. Or a deep fryer. Helen though they were hilarious. Menelaus thought they were... intimidating. And maybe he *could* rough Paris up a little bit. Not badly, of course. And maybe, *just maybe*, Helen would see some sense. Menelaus shrugged at his audience of five seniors, who were watching him like they would watch a ticking bomb.

"Couldn't do me any harm to try," he said, sounding far glummer that he felt like he ought to.

Ajax 1 cheered as he hopped over the closed door of the convertible, landing in the backseat. He gave Menelaus a firm pat on the back that felt like it might break his bones. "Atta boy."

Menelaus disguised his *oomph* as a cough, squishing over as Diomedes and Ajax 2 climbed into the backseat as well. Agamemnon slid into the driver's spot, jamming a pair of old aviators over his eyes. Odysseus rolled his eyes when Agamemnon told him to hurry up and get in the damn car, and proceeded to enter the vehicle with the speed of Helen and Paris' boat. (Which was *very* slow.)

When they were finally pulling out of the gravel parking lot, Agamemnon looked into the backseat. "Y'know what this means, fellas?"

Diomedes indulged him. "What does it mean, Cap?"

"Paris means to start a rivalry."

"I don't think that's what he meant—" Menelaus tried to interject, but stopped when Ajax 1 elbowed his side hard enough to knock the wind out of him.

Someone honked at them, but no one in the red convertible really payed attention. Everyone's eyes were locked on Agamemnon.

"This season's gonna be crazy boys," the driver continued, as calm as the sunrise before a rainstorm. "You know, why?"

Again, Diomedes was the one who responded. "How come?"

"Because Paris doesn't know he's gonna get a whole damn war."

# II

THE LAST WEEK OF Helen's life had been... well. Like hell. She hated every moment since her aunt once (or twice) removed waltzed into her living room, sporting low cut designer blouse and the tightest jeans Helen had ever seen. The woman's strawberry blonde hair was curled to perfection and her make-up was flawless. Normally, Helen would have been interested in talking someone who looked like this, but... now she resented the fact that she had even said hello, because the beautiful woman had stormed her house, forced her to switch schools, *and* break up with her boyfriend, all because some kid had given her a golden apple at a wedding Helen didn't even remember attending.

To be completely honest, Helen didn't remotely understand the whole situation. She only understood that this Aphrodite woman thought Helen was the prettiest girl in the county, and that Helen's parents were receiving a large sum of money to allow Aphrodite to screw up their daughter's life. And the rest was determined by a five year old boy. Who Helen would have to... date. He wasn't five anymore. Helen had been very confused when Aphrodite explained this to her, because she forgot to mention the detail of the boy being sixteen now. *That* was a relief at least.

Breaking up with Menelaus had been the hardest part of all of this. Before him, she had been in a bunch of short lived flings or *things* or crushes, but they had been together for a long time. Since the middle of Sophomore year. He was the first person beyond her family that she had actually loved.

When she broke up with him, they went out for dinner, to their favourite place. Hestia's Diner, where the air smelled of grease and the staff knew them by name. No more. Helen had cried. She said they couldn't be together anymore because she was switching schools. And then she had spilled the whole story out into his shoulder. About this stupid kid, Paris, who gave her aunt the apple. About how this wasn't her choice. About how she would miss him. He had listened. He always listened. That's why she loved him. He was her break from the cheerleaders, the AP classes, and the demanding parents.

But now he wasn't hers and she wasn't his. She was with Paris. The Mycenae Stallions football team had always made fun of Paris. He was a stuck–up kid who thought he was better than everybody, but had never stepped onto the football field. One thing that couldn't be argued about was his vicious looks that rivalled even Achilles. He had a sharp chin and dark curls that fell over icy blue eyes. Where his brother Hector was just cruel–looking in general, with wide shoulders and a shaved head, Paris was a deceiver, lithe and reserved.

In Helen's opinion, that kind of beauty was cold. It was withdrawn and untouchable. Achilles was sort of like an aggressive golden retriever, but Paris was like a hawk. A... cowardly hawk. And Menelaus was perfect. He wasn't like Achilles, and he wasn't like Paris. He had a kind face and freckles across his back. He had red hair and quiet smile and was a surprisingly good dancer...

Helen didn't want to torment herself anymore. She leaned backwards out of the stupid dingy that Aphrodite had driven all the way across the state, insisting that they just *had* to float down the wonderful river, which turned out to be... sludge. Helen wasn't grossed out by a lot of things. In fact, she loved backpacking, but when a half decomposed fish floated past, she sat back up so fast that she almost tipped the raft. Paris watched her from under the pink umbrella that Aphrodite had provided. She offered him a bitter smile, which he returned. Aphrodite has taken Helen to Paris' house yesterday. It felt like a seven hour drive, which was absolutely horrible, because Aphrodite loved country music, and Helen was... not a fan, to say the least. (The drive was maybe an hour and a half. At the very most.) That wasn't even the worst part though. Being in the car with a woman who thought she could jump into Helen's life and shake everything around until it was unrecognizable far surpassed the woes of country music.

*At least he doesn't have awful music taste,* Helen thought numbly, dragging her fingers through the filthy stream. She gave up on being disgusted. It was pointless, unless she just... waded out of the stream. It might be funny to tip the boat. She sighed. Menelaus loved folk music. Anything with a banjo and harmonies, he'd be up on his feet, dragging Helen after him. Gods, they laughed so much together. Paris was playing some kind of melancholy string quartet at the moment, which suited Helen's mood perfectly.

"So," Paris said, breaking their hour long silence like he was about to start a business meeting.

Helen disliked him *immensely.*

"Are you looking forward to school starting?" he asked, sounding as bored as he would be *in* a class.

Someone wolf–whistled from the river bank. Helen sat up straight, finding the culprit almost immediately. A man way too old to be acting so immature, for sure.

"That's not a compliment, you uninformed patriarchal supremacist! It's gross and creepy and no one appreciates it! Leave people alone!" Helen yelled back. (What else could she say? She was feeling wronged *before* he had thought to dampen her horrible day.)

She watched his eyes go wide. He walked away from the 'river' and Helen slumped back down, crossing her arms tightly. Paris smirked at her, ever so slightly.

She scrunched her nose at him. "Don't look so shocked. It *is* gross."

He nodded in seemingly sincere agreement.

"And yes," she added grumpily, "I will yell at everyone who even looks at me the wrong way. Also, I do kickboxing when I say I'm at the hair salon, so I *will* fight you."

Paris gave her a small round of applause, causing her to roll her eyes, cracking the tiniest smile.

"That's more than I can say," he said with a shrug.

Paris was nervous. This whole situation was weird. He didn't even really have time to comprehend and agree to this plan of Aphrodite's, but here he was, with his new... girlfriend. Helen. She wasn't impressed. She didn't try to make conversation or keep conversation going. It made him uncomfortable. He could tell that she was upset. And it was hot outside. The river was fucking disgusting too. He said so. She laughed.

Helen begrudgingly admitted that Paris was better than she and her friends had thought back at Mycenae. Only a smidge, though. He still seemed stuck–up, and emotionally distant. But that might have been because they had only known each other for what, a day and a half? Or maybe it was the fact that they were floating down a puddle of what looked like sewage. Helen sighed, pulling her phone out from the back pocket of her shorts.

"Do you know how long this float takes?" she asked absent-mindedly, opening her phone.

Paris nearly fell out of the boat. She was *talking* to him. "Uh... I can ask Aphrodite. She said she's picking us up at the end?"

Helen nodded, her lips pushed forwards as she read a text message over and over again. She'd been reading it all day.

Menny <3 :

Let me know if you ever need anything  okay?

*Sent 12:45 AM*

She hadn't replied. She didn't want to hurt him (or herself) more than she already had. Helen sighed. The melancholic strings drowned out the buzzing insects for the most part, but it didn't drown out Paris' voice.

"Are you excited for school?" he asked again. "I didn't hear your answer before."

*Maybe because I* didn't *answer before?* Helen snapped inside her head.

"I'm... I guess it'll be interesting," she replied lamely.

Helen hated the thought of leaving Mycenae Academy. She liked the dorms and the classrooms and the teachers and the uniforms and the people and the library and everything. Illium Academy, though an hour and a half away from Mycenae, was supposed to be just as good a school, but all of Helen's friends were *also* an hour and a half away. Helen didn't have her license, and it was *far* to long too bike. Aphrodite has driven them back to the town that housed Mycenae Academy, because of the 'wonderful river.'

"Yeah. Ilium is fun though. You'll get used to it," Paris offered, trying to be helpful.

Helen didn't *want* to get used to it, but she shrugged anyways. "C'est la vie," she muttered under her breath, the message from Menelaus burned into her mind.

Achilles hadn't had reception for two and a half weeks, and the moment they got back into cell service, his phone had exploded with *drama*.

The bane of my sorry existence aka Agamemnon:

> Menelaus and Helen broke up. Get your ass back here you cowadrly deswerter.

*Sent Wednesday*

Odysseus:

> You know some crazy lady called Aphro... something?

*Sent Wednesday*

Cornerback ginger:

> Okay Helen and I broke up so just... well I'm fine she's just going to Ilium next year. And apparently she's dating Paris but its not her fault

*Sent Tuesday*

He stopped caring about the messages after that.

Patroclus had been reading them over his shoulder. "You were gone for like... fourteen days. That's ridiculous."

"Bound to happen, though," Achilles replied, shoving his phone in the pocket of his sweater.

He closed his eyes, leaning back against the velvety bus seat. The air conditioning was blasting freezing cold air across his face, which was really dumb, in his opinion, because it was literally raining outside. He didn't want to go back to school. He wanted to keep running around the woods and singing around campfires and laughing like there wasn't a single problem in the world. The summer was his escape. Those two and a half weeks at Camp Pelion were pure bliss. He could be himself there, with no freaking expectations. Patroclus slumped against his shoulder, and Achilles tried not smile.

"It's freezing in here," the other boy muttered, sounding as perturbed as Achilles felt.

"I wish we didn't have to leave."

"You say that every year," Patroclus laughed. "We'll be back in eleven or so months. It'll be fine. We always survive."

"Pffft. Don't be so optimistic," Achilles said.

"Don't be so *pessimistic*," Patroclus countered playfully.

Achilles shook his head, opened his eyes and glanced out the window. Rain streaked across the filthy surface, urgent to get to the other side of the glass pane. As a kid, Achilles had always pretended that the rain drops were racing across. When he was old enough to sit in the front, he and his dad would pick raindrops and compete against each other. But that was before Patroclus. Achilles was probably about eleven when they met in school. Patroclus was this quiet kid, who was always late, because... no one knew. No one even talked to him. Until Achilles did.

He had innocently asked why Patroclus was late, and the brown haired boy had looked up at Achilles with giant eyes, like he was surprised that someone was talking to him, let alone sitting with him at lunch. Eventually, Patroclus, who was used to being ignored, shyly told Achilles about how his dad refused to drive him to school, so he had to walk.

When Achilles' dad, Peleus found out about Patroclus, he insisted on picking him up, but the boy had refused. Achilles didn't understand why, so he kept hanging around. Patroclus had been confused at why someone as popular as Achilles would spend time with him. He was afraid that it would turn out to be one big joke.

But Achilles was different. Persistent and friendly and someone to talk with.

Finally, a month and a half into winter, Patroclus confessed that he didn't want his father to know someone was driving him to school. Peleus started picking him up a block away from his house, and they were friends from then on. Patroclus started spending more time with Achilles and Peleus than at his own home. When Peleus sent the two of them to Camp Pelion on the summer of eighth grade, Patroclus' father didn't even care. One of the counselors, Chiron, took an instant liking to Patroclus, and took him under his wing. Achilles had never seen Patroclus talk as much as he did that summer. And they were still going to the camp every year. Achilles loved it. (He was an escapist at heart.)

"I didn't know you could play guitar so well," Patroclus thought out loud, pulling Achilles out of his head.

Achilles looked down at him, frowning. "*How?* I play all the time. My mom thinks it's annoying."

"Ah. That must be why," Patroclus said, his voice slightly tense. He and Thetis had a mutual... dislike for each other. Patroclus never went to her house. They tolerated each other purely for Achilles' sake, but preferred not to engage otherwise. "You don't play much at Peleus' house."

"Yeah because you're there. When I go over to her house you don't come with me and I have nothing better to do."

Patroclus laughed softly.

"Helen and Menelaus broke up," Achilles said after a moment, unsure of how to continue their previous conversation. "Because of Aphrodite. She knows Thetis and Dad. I think she was at their wedding. Though... I don't understand how she could make Helen switch schools. That seems kind of weird. And now she's with Piddly Paris?"

Patroclus snorted at the nickname.

"She and Menelaus were happy. At least... I thought they were?"

One thing the two of them had bonded over was their enthusiasm for peace. Achilles had always been surrounded by drama, at home and at school. Patroclus had been around for most of it, so when Thetis had wanted to send him to public school, Peleus had paid for Patroclus' tuition to Mycenae Academy. They held each other up. (Achilles had begged his mother to let him have this one thing.) (Eventually, she caved.) (She always did eventually.)

"Guess I should respond to people before we get back," Achilles sighed.

"You very well may get attacked if you don't."

"I could take them."

"Yeah right."

# III

T HE HALLS OF ILIUM Academy were more or less the same as
Mycenae's, except for the colours. The halls Helen used to
inhabit were covered in red and black, with accents of gold. Here,
it was all purple and grey. And of course people used to stare at
her, but now people were staring at her in a way that made her
uncomfortable. She already hated this place. The uniforms were
uglier, she had no friends, and she wasn't allowed to wear her
own shoes. It didn't make things any better that she had every
class with Paris. Aphrodite must have arranged it that way, which
made Helen want to get herself expelled. But she didn't think
that menace in designer clothes would let her off that easy. Or if
Mycenae would even let her back *in* if she got expelled elsewhere.

Somehow, Helen ended up in the same dorm with Paris' brother's girlfriend. Andromache. Helen had brought in her stuff on
Sunday and she still hadn't met her yet. She hadn't actually talked
to Paris' family very much, which was odd, seeing as she had been

at their house for the better part of two weeks. She had only seen Hector once.

All around her, people were laughing with their friends, hugging, smiling… all Helen could think of was everyone at Mycenae. Menelaus, Patroclus, Achilles, Ajax 1 and 2… her cheer friends… she wasn't even sure if she would join cheer here. She was already wearing a purple blazer. She wasn't sure if she could betray her old team so easily. Not that it was her fault. But still. Even if she had time to explain the whole situation, Agamemnon wouldn't believe her, and she didn't owe him an explanation *anyways*.

"Hey Paris!" someone called over the racket in the hall.

Paris had been trying to decide whether he should take Helen's hand. (He was so anxious. What was he even supposed to *do*? School stressed him out enough, and now there was Helen? Who he didn't know?) (He decided against grabbing her hand.) She was staring right above everyone's heads, her jaw clenched.

When Paris heard his name, he glanced up. Hector was leaning against a roughly cut, brown, stone wall, surrounded by a bunch of members from last year's football team. Apparently it had gotten out that he was captain. Again. Andromache was there too, an arm hooked through Hector's. Paris rolled his eyes, grabbed Helen's bag strap, and dragged her over to his brother. Helen did not appreciate this, so she yanked her strap back, crossing her arms. She almost didn't follow Paris, but then realized that she had no idea where the gym was, for the first assembly.

Hector had only yelled his brother's name because he hadn't talked to Paris' new girlfriend yet. As they walked (she sort of marched indignantly), Hector shook his head. Paris grated on his nerves.

"Hector, you look like you want to murder someone," Andromache whisper–yelled in his ear.

He snorted, attempting to look less homicidal. "Thanks."

"Anytime, darlin'," she said with a smile Hector knew she reserved just for him. "Wait, is that Paris' new... girlfriend?" She was staring at Helen, her green eyes wide. "Good Gods. She's really pretty."

Hector frowned as Paris shoved his way through the crowd that had gathered around them. "She looks thrilled to be here."

"Oh yes. I am *thrilled* to be here," Helen replied, her voice oozing pure sarcasm as she and Paris came to a stop. So this was Hector. She'd seen him before. He was huge, but not as big as Ajax 1. He *did* have a shaved head and two freaking lip piercings but still. Helen didn't judge based on appearances. Someone slammed into her from behind, knocking her a few steps forwards. *Godsdamn school hallways.*

"*Helen*," Paris gasped, his face a perfect rendition of incredulity as she slammed into him. "What the fuck?" He was more nervous than angry.

Hector laughed, ruffling Paris' curly hair, because he *knew* his little brother hated it.

"That makes two of us who can't stand it here," Hector said with a grin. And while Paris was occupied, muttering curses under his breath and trying to fix his hair, Hector held out a hand. "Hector. You must be Helen?"

Helen was trying not to giggle as Hector offered her his hand. Paris was attempting to preen himself in his reflection, on a rain streaked windowpane. He had been holding his blazer over his head, trying not to get it wet when they had walked inside. Helen, being fed up, had stolen it and danced around in the rain, holding it just out of Paris' reach, because why the hell not. He had given up and run inside before he could take it back.

She shook his hand. It was at least one and a half times the size of hers. "Yeah. I'm Helen. The one and only."

"Lovely to meet you," Hector said with a nod, letting go of her hand and draping a large arm around Andromache's shoulders. "This is Andromache."

"Oh!" Helen exclaimed, pointing at the willowy, red haired girl. "We're roommates!"

"Yeah. We are," Andromache nodded, sounding somewhere between intimidated and unsure. Helen was used to that kind of treatment.

Paris reappeared at Helen's side. She sighed. She was over this.

"Dude," Hector said, noticing the change in mood. "You guys should come with us to dinner tonight."

"Wait, you can leave for dinner?" Helen interjected, one eyebrow raised.

Hector mimicked the gesture. "What, you can't do that in the stables?" (That's what they called Ilium, because their mascot was the Stallions.)

Someone passing in the stream of people yelled, "Stallions suck!"

Helen fought the urge to break into the cheer routine for the Stallions fight song. She held back, but... just barely. Hector saluted to the crowd, though Helen wasn't sure how he could find the person who yelled. All she saw was purple. Purple banners on the walls, purple lockers, purple uniforms. The whole nine yards. The brown stone walls and the grey floors were a nice break.

"But yeah," Hector continued on, like nothing had happened. "We can go out between four and seven, so as long as you don't eat like a turtle, you'll be fine."

"*Finally*," Helen said, spinning around in a circle. "Something *good* about this place."

"It just gets better, baby!" Hector replied, chuckling.

"Hey!" Paris squawked, leaping in front of Helen.

Andromache snorted as she made eye contact with Helen, who was shaking her head, one hand splayed across her face in dismay. The height difference between Hector and Paris was almost comical.

"Paris. Man. Chill," a new person said as he joined the discombobulated circle. He was taller than Paris, with short coils of dark hair and brown skin. "It's an expression. And besides. He's got Andromache," the boy said, sliding an arm around Andromache for a quick side hug. When he saw Helen, he nodded. "Welcome to Ilium. You're Helen, right? Head of Mycenae's cheer squad?"

"Former," Helen said bitterly.

The newcomer, who Helen knew to be Aeneas, raised his hands. "Apologies. Of course, I meant no offense." He was know for his ability to talk people down.

"None taken," she replied with a gloomy shrug.

Paris was still riled up, but more quietly now. He wouldn't be able to take Hector in a fight, and he didn't even really want to, but Paris despised Hector's patronizing attitude. It didn't help how he flaunted their parents' favouritism in Paris' face. Everything that went wrong immediately was blamed Paris. He crossed his arms and hunched his shoulders. Andromache had wandered over to Helen, and the two were whispering about something. Aeneas and Hector were both leaning against the wall now. Hector pointed subtly to someone passing in the hall, and Aeneas was nodding. They were probably talking football.

That's when the bell rang. It was one of those brutally loud trilling noises. For a moment, Helen thought it was a fire alarm, but no one else seemed to react to it, so she didn't bolt for the door. Andromache looped her arm through Helen's.

"What classes do you have?" she asked as they jostled their way through the crowd, all heading towards the gym.

She watched as Helen furrowed her brow, then shrugged. "Whatever Paris has." The blonde girl paused. "Unfortunately."

Andromache shook her head. "He's not all bad. Just a little conceited sad–boy. With mommy issues. And the god complex that comes with being a mediocre soccer player."

Helen laughed, but it was lost in the clacking of the mandated Mary Jane heels. Helen missed her floral skate shoes. She disliked walking in heels and sort of resented Andromache for moving so gracefully in them.

"And yeah, Hector tried to explain the whole situation to me," she added, whispering in Helen's ear. "Aeneas is Aphrodite's kid, so he knows more than Hector did. They're not close, but he tried to talk her out of it. Sadly, that woman is stubborn as hell, so. We're here for you, okay?"

Helen grimaced. Andromache was slightly jealous that she could look pretty with such an ugly expression, but she didn't want that to show. She was supposed to make Helen feel like she wasn't a complete loner, with only Paris to talk to.

"Thanks," Helen said, grateful that she wasn't completely alone, with only Paris to talk to.

<br>

"Where the fuck is Peliedes?" Agamemnon demanded. He was fed up with everyone, because they were incompetent. It was already lunchtime on their first day back, and he hadn't seen Achilles once. The core players of the team had agreed to meet on the third floor, where the athletes' lockers were. Mycenae Academy took its sports program very seriously. A few people were milling about, but they were on the opposite end of the hall, for fear of Agamemnon.

Odysseus shrugged, glancing at Diomedes, who shook his head. Ajax 1 and 2 were playing chopsticks against the red and yellow lockers. Menelaus was sitting on the floor, his eyes closed, his head resting against the red brick wall across the hallway. Agamemnon had been trying to figure out how to make this football season go from a rivalry to a full scale war, ever since they had seen Helen and Paris on the river. He had recently come to the conclusion that telling the Trojans that stealing people's girlfriends was unacceptable, and therefore demanded consequences. But the football season didn't start for another week. They did have a week long tryout camp at the beginning of the summer where the team was decided, but they had to practice for two weeks during the school year before the first game. That had him in a bad mood, and the fact that his star player was late didn't bode well for the rest of the day.

"He's usually late," Odysseus offered, remembering how many times Agamemnon screamed at Achilles last year. It was an equal number of times Achilles had rolled his eyes and paid Agamemnon no attention. Actually, that number was probably higher. Achilles was always rolling his eyes and paying Agamemnon no attention. The only reason Achilles was still on the team was... because they needed him.

Agamemnon rounded on Odysseus, face flushed. "Do you *know* how many godsdamn times I've told him to be on fucking time?"

"Yessir," Odysseus replied, nodding. He was used to Agamemnon's temper. "You could call him, if you like."

⁂

Achilles was outside, avoiding Agamemnon. He and Patroclus sat under the stone arch over one of the back doors. Neither of them were eating. Just sitting. Watching the rain. They came to this spot a lot. No one seemed to be able to find them there. The steps were cracked, weathered from age. Achilles had already discarded his red blazer and grey sweater, loosened his tie, and rolled up his sleeves. A gust of wind blew a spray of cold water and they both winced. True, Achilles had played games on days worse than this, but he wasn't used to it yet. Patroclus had Achilles' blazer over his head in a feeble attempt to keep dry.

"You should go in before Agamemnon murders you," Patroclus said, glancing over at Achilles.

The blonde boy snorted, raising his eyebrows skeptically. "I'd like to see him try."

Patroclus shrugged, turning back to the rain. "I wouldn't," he muttered under his breath.

"And besides," Achilles continued, ignoring that last comment. "I'd rather stay with you."

On their second summer at Camp Pelion, they had discovered... their feelings for each other. It had been after a year of playing catch, laughing, staying up too late while talking about inconsequential nonsense, dreaming, accidentally catching the other staring, and listening to Peleus read Aesop's fables. One night, they were sitting outside, supposed to be drawing nature, when Achilles had tugged on Patroclus' dark curls.

*"This is awkward," he whispered, "but..." Achilles stopped, swallowing.*

*Patroclus turned to face Achilles, his dark eyes wide. He hoped he knew what Achilles was going to say, but there was no way that it was going to be that. No way. "What?"*

*Chiron, their favourite counsellor, who had been inspecting some other kids' drawings, started meandering towards where the two of them were sitting, facing each other now.*

*"Achilles," Patroclus hissed, jerking his head towards the man who was making his way over. "Draw. Nature."*

*Both of their pages were blank. Patroclus started sketching a pinecone, his pencil flying across the page with surety. He hated breaking rules, or getting told off by adults. That fear came from the fact that him merely being alive had pissed off a lot of people. Achilles watched his friend draw. Patroclus was better at art. Achilles couldn't art for the life of him.*

*"Well then," Chiron mused, peering down at Achilles' empty sheet. "Polar bear in a snow storm?"*

*Achilles nodded, smiling with confidence he didn't have. "Impressive you guessed it."*

*"You'd be surprised at how many of those I've seen," Chiron chuckled, walking around to where Patroclus had moved on to some kind of finch. "Wow. That's impressive. Better than I can draw."*

*Patroclus looked up, surprised, tugging the cuffs of his sweater over his hands. "Thank you?"*

*"No problem, champ," the tall man said with a grin, before wandering towards a red haired girl sitting on a log.*

*A gust of wind blew through the pine trees, causing them to sing a creaky song. Achilles was blushing as he watched Patroclus watch Chiron walk away.*

*"You know..." Achilles started again, heart pounding as he ran a hand through his hair. "I kind of..."*

*Patroclus reached across and quickly wrote on Achilles' blank page, before he could convince himself not to:* I kind of like you too.

"Achilles." Patroclus poked his head.

Achilles smiled. "What?"

"Go inside."

"Only if you come with me."

"The team doesn't like me."

"Then the team is an idiot."

⚶⚶⚶ ⚶⚶⚶

Briseis had gotten lost seven times in one morning. There has always been people to help her get to where she was going, but she had a sneaking suspicion that it wasn't out of kindness. She had flown in from the California Airport on the previous Tuesday. Mycenae Academy had sent a car for her, and let her get settled into her dorm room almost a week early. It was very strange seeing the school full of people. She was doing a six month exchange program that her parents had located online, much to her chagrin. They thought Texas would be good for their daughter, but she was already fed up with the people here.

The cafeteria was loud, and extremely overwhelming. Briseis ran a hand over her loose curls, taking a deep breath. Her friends back in Cali thought it was hilarious that she was here. She would have traded with any of them in a heartbeat. Fucking Texas.

The cafeteria had a gothic–esque vaulted ceiling, and was filled with long, stained tables. People kept running into her, so she moved away from the entrance, instead standing in front of a vending machine. She pulled out her phone, just to look like she was busy. Avoidance tactics. Which apparently didn't work in Freaking–Country–Nowhere, because someone sidled up to her. He was a stocky guy, with broad shoulders, bronze skin, and shoulder length hair tied back in a ponytail.

"Hey," the guy said, leaning against the vending machine glass, facing her.

Briseis glanced up at him from the game she had been playing.

"You new here?" he asked.

She had been getting this question all morning. Briseis sighed internally, whilst externally pasting on a wan smile.

"Yeah. I'm Briseis." She paused. The black haired guy waited. "And you are?" she asked begrudgingly.

"Nice to meet you, Briseis." She hated the way her name sounded in his mouth. "I'm Agamemnon. Care to join us?"

Briseis glanced around the room, feeling somewhat helpless. She kind of wanted to start on the math homework that had been assigned, but it was impolite to refuse an offer. *I could use some friends, I suppose,* she thought, though having a friend like Agamemnon wasn't awfully appealing.

"Alright," she agreed, hiking her leather satchel higher onto her shoulder.

Agamemnon's smile was somewhat unnerving as he nodded towards a group of guys standing by the door. They were attracting a crowd, and blocking the entrance. *Ugh. They're probably football players.* She had never understood football. Who wanted to watch giant men tackle each other for three hours? Apparently this school. And most of the country. She followed him through the dwindling crowd, seeing as it was about fifteen minutes into lunch already.

"Fucking Pelides hasn't showed?" Agamemnon demanded when they got to the center of the football jocks.

A guy with curly hair cut short on the sides shook his head. "And if he did, he's probably on the third floor, seeing as you left without him."

The guy beside the one who had spoken noticed Briseis. "Who's this?"

"Oh, this is Briseis," Agamemnon said, like he had known her forever.

Briseis waved awkwardly. "Hi."

The curly haired one nodded. "Odysseus."

"Diomedes," the guy next to him said.

"I'm Menelaus—" a tired looking ginger started to say, only to be cut off.

"Agamemnon!" someone yelled, over the lunchtime ruckus.

All the guys around Briseis looked towards the door. She leaned around one of the two people who hadn't introduced themselves, to get a better view of who had distracted the macho gang. Turned out to be more men. Briseis studied the two of them. They were walking beside each other, one with long, wavy blonde hair, half up in a bun, the other with dark curls that wreathed his head like a halo. The first guy wasn't wearing his sweater *or* blazer anymore, his red tie hanging loose, the sleeves of his white dress shirt rolled to his elbows.

Briseis noticed all the people staring at him. He didn't seem to care. He waved at a few, but didn't pay much more attention than that. The other boy had a red blazer thrown over his shoulder, but he was wearing one as well. Briseis frowned as they stopped in front of the clump she was a part of. Two blazers guy looked nervous, his olive skin sort of waxy, but the blonde guy clapped Menelaus on the shoulder.

"Hey guys," he said, beaming like he couldn't sense the animosity flooding off the black haired man/boy/child (Briseis couldn't decide). "I see you've found the only girl in the school who doesn't know your reputation, *Agamemnon*."

Briseis raised an eyebrow. Someone tapped her on the shoulder while Agamemnon strode over to the blonde guy. She whipped around, only to find the boy who had come in beside the blonde one.

"C'mon," he whispered, gesturing towards the door with his head, smiling slightly.

For some reason he was much less threatening than Agamemnon. He offered her a hand and she took it. The brown haired boy glanced over his shoulder, then started inching away from the circle. Briseis followed him, feeling adventurous for no reason. Agamemnon was still engaged in an argument with the blonde boy, who's eyes darted over to his friend and Briseis. He smirked knowingly before shaking his head at Agamemnon.

Briseis found herself being led out of the cafeteria, and down a hallway that she felt like she had seen, but wasn't sure about.

The guy let go of her hand with a kind little laugh. "Sorry about that," he said, sliding down a yellow locker and ending up on the floor.

She sat down next to him, arranging her skirt as she did so. "No worries."

"You *weren't* enjoying yourself, right?" he asked anxiously.

Briseis snorted, covering her mouth with the back of her hand. "No. I wasn't."

"Okay good," he said, relaxing a bit. "Well. Not good, but good that we didn't kidnap you from something you were having fun with. Some girls like Agamemnon. Weirdly enough. But. Yeah."

She laughed again, finally feeling okay for the first time since she got here. "I haven't laughed all week," she admitted, not knowing why she said it.

The boy frowned, placing the extra blazer on the floor. "That... I'm sorry. That sucks." He paused. "You *are* new here, right?"

Briseis picked an invisible piece of lint off her grey pleated skirt. "Yeah. Flew in from Cali last week."

"Oh!" he exclaimed, making Briseis jump. "You're an exchange student? The school's website was talking about their new exchange programs, so Achilles and I were wondering if anyone would come this year."

"Yep," she replied, pressing her lips together. "All the way from paradise."

"That's insane," the boy said, shaking his head.

A couple of girls walked past the two of them. They didn't even glance their way.

"Is Achilles the one who was with you when you came in?" Briseis asked, pulling off her bag and placing it on the floor beside her.

The guy beside her shook his head again, scrunching his eyes shut. "Yeah, sorry. I forgot to tell you who I am. Hah. I'm Patroclus. And yes. He is Achilles."

"Lovely to meet you, Patroclus," Briseis smiled, taking the hand he offered for her to shake.

"Heyyyyy," Achilles announced as he came careening down the hall, skidding to a stop like some kind of cartoon character in front of Briseis and Patroclus. "Sorry that took so long. Agamemnon is the bane of my existence, so. I tried to be speedy."

He sat down in front of them, creating a triangle. "I'm Achilles," he said. "Also sorry about that. I know it may have been weird, but at least you're not eating near Agamemnon, because he has a tendency to... I dunno. Be pushy. Also, what's your name? So I can thank you?"

Briseis raised her eyebrows. "Briseis. But you can call me Bri, if you want."

Achilles stood, and bowed deeply. "Thank you, Briseis-call-me-Bri, for saving me from a horrible team meeting that I did not want to be a part of."

Patroclus had his face in his hands, laughing.

"Thank you for *also* saving me from the horrible team meeting that I *definitely* did not want to be a part of," Briseis replied, trying to suppress a grin.

Achilles sat back down, nodding. "The thanks is mutual, though I do have to attend a team meeting tonight, seeing as I have practice, seeing as I've been driving between my house and school for several weeks of the summer to play pass with four people I hate. The positive in this situation is that the commute will be much easier now."

"That's some forced optimism," Patroclus observed. "At least we're not doing mornings this year."

"Wait," Briseis said, looking between the two boys. "*You* play football too?"

"That's an understatement," Patroclus snorted under his breath, before gesturing towards Achilles with his head. "This one here is pretty much the only reason that Mycenae Academy is actually *good* at football."

Achilles waved him off as Briseis' jaw dropped.

"He flatters me," Achilles said, like it cleared everything up.

"Your ego doesn't *need* my flattery," Patroclus insisted playfully.

Achilles sighed dramatically. "Okay *fine*. I can play alright."

Briseis cocked her head at Patroclus, who was looking at Achilles like he was endearingly annoying.

"Wait do you play too, then?" she asked, scooting out of the way so some guy could get into his locker.

"Gods no," Patroclus said, smiling.

"But he *could*!" Achilles interjected, smacking the gray floor with both hands. "Look at this guy! He hits the gym more than *me*."

"But I don't play," Patroclus countered, grinning like he was trying to hold back a laugh. "I'm a sports med trainer. So I attempt to patch them up. Machaon is a lot better at it then me, but—"

"Lies," Achilles interrupted. "All lies. Coach and I were talking about your medical prowess just yesterday!"

"What the..." Patroclus grimaced, slightly horrified. "Maybe don't... say that. Ever again."

"As you wish," Achilles said, completely straight faced.

"Is that a Princess Bride reference?" Briseis asked, leaning forwards.

"What else would it be?" Achilles demanded.

Patroclus nudged Achilles' foot, frowning and giggling at the same time. "No need to be rude." He turned to Bri. "But yes, both the book and movie are great."

"Thank you for saving me from football," she said again, not believing that she was sitting with people who had at least two common interests. (Those interests being The Princess Bride and Not-Being-In-The-Same-Room-As-Agamemnon.)

"Hold your horses, Briseis-call-me-Bri," Achilles said, suddenly serious. "I may not be a letterman jacket wearing dickhead, *but* I am very enthusiastic about the game, so if you're going to hang out with us then you need to get used to..." He did a set of extremely *un*enthusiastic jazz hands. "Football."

"Yeah," Patroclus said, looking over at Bri apologetically. "For awhile, we're the human embodiment of football. But you can come to practice if you want. Just to have something to do. You can save me from watching sweaty people run around in circles for two and a half hours."

Briseis shrugged. "That's fine. I have nothing better to do."

"Yayyy," Achilles cheered, tilting his head towards the ceiling. "You accept the not–jock–jocks."

"*You're* the jock here, Achilles," Patroclus said.

Achilles pretended to be offended. "I don't act like Agamemnon." He paused. "But fine. I'm wildly popular and good at sports. So sure. Call me a jock, for all I care."

"I don't think you're a jock," Briseis reassured.

Achilles gasped, holding a hand to his heart. "See Patroclus? Someone loves me."

"Mmhm. Her and three quarters of the girls in this school," Patroclus said, a textbook suddenly open in his lap.

Briseis nearly choked. "No one said anything about love."

"Sorry," Achilles winced. "I've known you for a solid..." He checked his phone. "A solid twenty five minutes and I've already made you uncomfortable."

"Good job," Patroclus said, his eyes darting across the textbook page.

"Patroclus. It's the literal first day of school. How do you have a textbook?" Achilles asked, his brow furrowed in concern.

He knew Patroclus better than anyone else, and knowing him better than anyone meant that Achilles had watched Patroclus continuously run himself into the ground, and proceed to apologize for it. Briseis bent at the waist, trying to read the cover of the book.

"It's Math," Patroclus said, snapping the book shut, and avoiding eye contact with Achilles. "Where's your next class, Bri?" Patroclus asked, tossing Achilles' blazer back to him.

"Um..." she started, pulling out her phone. "I think it's room 436?"

"That's a weird one," Achilles said, catching the piece of clothing deftly. "Wanna go there? We can show you where it is. And you can meet Patroclus by the field after school if you want to come to practice too."

Briseis nodded. "That would be... really nice." Not lonely.

Patroclus stood up, offering Achilles a hand and hauling him to his feet. They both offered her a hand, nearly throwing her info the opposite wall as they attempted to help her up.

"Thanks for that," she muttered, smoothing out her skirt and picking up her bag.

Maybe things at Ilium Academy wouldn't be too bad.

# IV

P RACTICE WAS ABOUT AN hour and a half after classes ended, which was supposed to give the players time to do homework or ask teachers questions, but Achilles always changed right after the bell. This was so he could avoid being in the changeroom with the rest of the team. He could then avoid unnecessary locker room drama. He usually had to go back in for shoulder-pads on scrimmage days, but they were working on cardio today, so he just changed into shorts and a black Mycenae Stallions T–shirt.

When he stepped outside, he was pleasantly surprised, because it had stopped raining. It was still humid, the grass damp, but it would dry as soon as the sun came out. Achilles ran around the school to the fenced off football field, enjoying the goosebumps that sprung up on his arms. A bunch of people were sitting on the steps of the school, books open, regardless of that fact that the year had barely started. The bleachers on the football field were empty, save for one dark haired person hunched over a book, because practices were mostly closed, except for coaches, sports med people, and some random people from various clubs who snuck in to take photos. Achilles wasn't sure why Investment Club needed photos of football, but who was he to judge?

Just because he could, Achilles climbed over the fence, leaping down from the top. The chainlink rattled enough to make Patroclus glance up as Achilles landed. He applauded.

"You weren't even watching," Achilles said, scandalized as he jogged along the fifty yard line and stopping at the bottom of the metal bleachers, a couple sets of benches below where Patroclus was sitting.

He shrugged. "But I'm sure it was wholly impressive, and therefore deserved applause."

"Okay, but what if I had actually fallen face first off the top of the fence?" Achilles asked, raising an eyebrow and putting his hands on his hips.

The sun peeked out from behind a cloud, flooding the field in late afternoon light. Patroclus squinted at Achilles before throwing his pencil at him. Achilles shrieked but somehow still caught it.

"See, that's why I know you *didn't* fall face first off the top of the fence. That, and the fact that you do it almost everyday. Did you lose your key again?"

Patroclus loved teasing Achilles. He always got defensive, only to realize that it was a joke, blush, and make some mumbled remark before hiding his face in Patroclus' shoulder.

"No!" Achilles exclaimed, only to purse his lips guiltily. "As a matter of fact... yeah. I did lose my key. Again. Coach probably won't give me another one."

"You can have mine," Patroclus offered, closing his textbook. "If you want to lose that one too."

"Hey!" the blonde boy yelled as he leapt up two rows of benches with seemingly no effort. "That's not fair."

"You're just proving me right, you know. If you want to convince me that you even have the slightest chance of falling face first off the fence, you need to stop performing athletic miracles."

Achilles plopped down beside Patroclus, leaning forwards on his elbows which rested on his knees. "Okay fine, you win."

They sat in comfortable silence for a few minutes. Patroclus closed his eyes, facing the sun. The few days between Camp Pelion and Mycenae were always awful. He stayed out of his house as much as he could, but every few months, he had to go back. His mother resented him for being away so much. Once, two years ago, he had tried to convince her to leave his father, but she was adamant that she could fix their broken family. Patroclus didn't *want* to be a part of it. There were too many haunted nights from his childhood to repair anything between the three of them. And now he was home. Achilles was next to him, and he was far away from the place he was tethered to, until he was eighteen. In less than two more years, he'd never have to see his parents again. Just two more years, and then he was free.

"Patroclus, dearest, can you braid my hair?" Achilles asked after a long moment of watching him.

Patroclus smiled, keeping his eyes shut for a second longer. "Sure, my angel." He laughed when he said it. Achilles snorted, removing the textbook from Patroclus' lap.

"Oh damn," Patroclus winced. "That was keeping my legs warm."

"Sorry."

"All good."

Achilles hopped down to the next row of metal bleachers, and in front of Patroclus.

Briseis finally found them like that, about fifteen minutes after the bell rang. The grass smushed under her feet as she walked towards the fenced square of grass. (It was more of a rectangle, but she didn't particularly care.) The gate was open and she could see Achilles and Patroclus sitting on the opposite side of the field. She wasn't sure if she was allowed to walk inside the white spraypainted border, so she started making her way around.

"What're you doing?" Achilles called to her. "You can walk across the field!"

She shrugged, walking across in a diagonal line. "Why isn't anyone here?" she asked loudly. "I thought practice started right after school?"

"Whoops," Achilles replied sheepishly. "No, it starts at like... four thirty."

Briseis pulled out her phone, checking the time. Three forty–five. "What, do you guys just... sit here?" she asked, frowning and stopping in front of the bleachers.

"Do you have an elastic?" Patroclus answered her question with a question, which was one of her biggest pet peeves, but this one was so unrelated that Briseis frowned, only to realize that Patroclus was braiding Achilles' hair.

"Wait..." Briseis said, squinting.

"Achilles doesn't have two," Patroclus replied sadly.

"I can't keep track of *keys.* Do you really expect me to be able to take care of tiny bands of elastic?" Achilles asked, sounding very disturbed.

"Are you guys dating?" Briseis asked, stopping them both in their tracks.

Achilles squinted at her, as if offering a challenge. "So what if we are?"

"Is it that obvious?" Patroclus asked softly, looking extremely nervous.

"No no no no, I don't have a problem with it," Briseis backtracked as fast as she could, frantically waving her hands in front of her. "California. Remember? It just makes sense. Not that I know you guys that well. But you seem to make sense together. I don't even know what I'm saying anymore. Here, have an elastic," she finished, ears burning as she held out her elastic to Patroclus, who was watching her like he had no idea what to say.

"Aw thank you," Achilles said after an awkward silence where Patroclus had accepted the hair tie. "I agree with you. We do make sense, but if my mother finds out, I am *toast.* Like, maybe even the burnt toast crumbs that permanently live at the bottom of the toaster...so. Maybe don't tell a whole bunch of people?"

"Or... anyone?" Patroclus suggested feebly, starting on the un-braided half of Achilles' head.

Briseis covered her mouth with a hand. "My lips are sealed," she mumbled.

They both relaxed a little bit.

"Did you text Iphis?" Achilles asked Patroclus, trying to look up at him.

"Stop moving," Patroclus replied. "And yeah. She's eating with us tomorrow."

"Who's Iphis?" Briseis asked, climbing carefully up the wet metal steps and setting down her blazer to sit next to Patroclus.

"Uh..." Patroclus had his tongue sticking out in concentration. "She's... my girlfriend. Not actually. I went to her house for dinner a few month back because we're both... rather queer with the need for a fake heterosexual relationship. She had a girlfriend for awhile, but they broke up over the summer. She said she wanted to meet you."

Achilles nodded, making Patroclus hiss at him.

"Sorry sorry sorry," Achilles blurted.

"Just sit *still*, for Gods sakes."

Briseis laughed.

"Pelides!" someone yelled from across the field. "Why didn't you meet Agamemnon at lunch?"

The yeller was a tall woman, but that was pretty much all Briseis could tell.

"He was being a right asshole," Achilles yelled back in a horrible British accent.

Patroclus snorted, tying off the end of the second braid.

"Wow. My team building didn't work very well, did it?" the woman replied, walking across the damp field.

She was intimidating, to say the very least. Broad shouldered and at least six feet, the woman was probably eye to eye with Achilles, who was sitting on the second bleacher. He hopped up to the third one, sitting next to Patroclus.

"This is Head Coach," Achilles said, looking over his shoulder at Briseis.

"Athena," she corrected sternly, though Briseis could tell that she had a fondness for Achilles. "Hi Patroclus." She exchanged a nod with the dark haired boy.

"Hi," he said with a brief smile.

"And you are?" Athena asked, turning her attention to Briseis.

"I'm Bri," she said carefully, trying not to stammer. "I'm the exchange student."

"Nice to meet you," Athena said curtly before turning back to Achilles. "You need to get along with Agamemnon. He's team captain. He calls the meetings. He calls the shots. He calls the plays. You may be the best, but that doesn't mean you're not a part of the team."

Briseis reached around Patroclus and smacked the back of Achilles' head. "Mm yes, you're *alright* at playing football."

"Hey!" Achilles yelped, ducking.

Athena crossed her muscular arms, raising an eyebrow at the blonde boy. "Have you been lying again?"

Achilles shrugged guiltily, still hunched over to hide from Briseis. "She's new. She would have found out eventually."

A commotion from the school made everyone abandon their conversation, startled. The ruckus turned out to be Agamemnon, the gigantic guy from lunch who hadn't introduced himself, and five other guys that Briseis didn't recognize. The huge guy was screaming some kind of fight song as Agamemnon and the other guys slammed him into the chain link fence.

That, for some reason, was the perfect cause for all of them to scream, "Let's GOOOOO."

"Good gods," Athena said, exasperatedly running her hand across her face. "Sorry," she apologized, before marching across the field, like she was heading into battle. "Those *idiots,*" Briesis caught her muttering.

Briseis was glad that she wouldn't be on the receiving end of whatever lecture was about to be administered.

"What the hell is wrong with them?" Achilles wondered under his breath, squinting at the guys like they were puzzling earthworms. "And *how,* in the *names of the freaking gods,* is Agamemnon *still* the captain of this team?"

"Probably because he's the most mature one here," Briseis suggested, nodding like she had finally figured out life's mysteries. Achilles snorted.

Patroclus put his forehead on Achilles' shoulder, pretending to cry. "Can we not have this conversation again? Please?"

"Okay fine. But only for you," Achilles said with a sigh.

"We've discussed this like, eight hundred times. You'd think that one would understand there's no logical explanation for this particular problem, *Achilles*, but oh nooo," Patroclus replied, ignoring Athena yelling in the background.

As a matter of fact, she didn't *stop* yelling for the entire fifteen minutes before practice. Those minutes were... essentially chaos. Two people from the offense line, Automedon and Nestor, joined Achilles, Patroclus, and Briseis, later followed by Machaon. They had a whole group sitting around them, chatting about strategy, classes, and anything in between.

Unlike Agamemnon and his crew, Briseis actually found these guys to be somewhat nice. And far less threatening. Some guys were playing catch in the middle of the field, while others were stretching. A couple of people who seemed to be running late were sprinting towards the field from the main school doors. The sun was fully out now, and Briseis took off her sweater. Athena had finally finished yelling now, and was talking to a few other adults Briseis assumed to be coaches as well.

"Warm up!" Agamemnon hollered, way louder than necessary as he started jogging around the field.

Nestor and Automedon waved as they leapt off the bleachers, rather gracelessly. Briseis wondered why they didn't wait for Achilles but he stood up. "Duty calls, my friends. See you on the other side," he said seriously, saluting to the two of them, and jumping into the stream of players running around the field.

"Perfect timing, huh?" Patroclus said, glancing up at the clear sky.

"I'm just glad it stopped raining," Machaon said gruffly, laying out the two giant first aid kits.

Briseis was watching Achilles.

"Slow down, Peliedes!" Agamemnon screamed, his face flushed with undertones of red.

"It wouldn't be a warm up if I went any slower!" Achilles called over his shoulder as he practically sprinted past the black haired boy. (Briseis had decided; Agamemnon was a boy. Not a man.)

Now she understood why Achilles' friends hadn't waited for him. Briseis was pretty sure it would have taken her ten minutes to run around the field *once*, but after about seven minutes, Achilles sat down and started stretching.

"He did a four minute mile over the summer," Patroclus said to Machaon.

"Really?" he asked, looking away from Achilles, impressed, as he glanced up at Patroclus. "That's kind of insane."

"*He's* kind of insane," Patroclus said, watching Achilles. "He was mad when Odysseus got chosen to be quarterback, but now he's runningback, so he scores most of the touchdowns, in scrimmage at least, because he's so fast."

Briseis couldn't wrap her head around how fast Achilles could run until the rest of the team finished their five laps of the field, ten minutes after he had started stretching.

For the rest of the practice, Briseis wondered why these guys even played football. Just watching all the cardio made Briseis sweat, although that might have been because of the sun.

"They don't do this everyday," Patroclus reassured her when she asked. "Mondays are cardio, but the rest of the week they run drills and plays."

The sun was setting by the time the team, which must have been forty five players strong, finished exhausting themselves.

"Alright, time to stretch," Athena called from the tent that was set up on the opposite side of the field.

They had been doing crunches, but when Athena spoke, a bunch of the guys collapsed onto the ground. Achilles sat up, looking unimpressed. He shook his head, making eye contact with Patroclus, who gave an exaggerated shrug. Briseis giggled a bit. The sky was stained pink as the sun began its journey to Australia. Achilles jumped to his feet.

"And he returns from battle," Patroclus whispered dramatically to Briseis, gesturing to the players laying on the ground. "Leaving no man alive. Look at the bodies behind him, so carelessly strewn across the bloodied plain—"

Briseis laughed so hard that she couldn't breathe, which seemed to make Patroclus laugh, which ended with them both wheezing, and gasping for air.

"It wasn't *that* funny," Machon said, looking up at the two of them like they were idiots.

Achilles slowed to a stop, his brow furrowed as he studied Patroclus and Briseis. "Are you guys okay?"

"Patroclus made a morbid joke," Machaon explained unenthusiastically as he packed up the first aid stuff.

"Morbid," Briseis repeated, through slightly delirious laughter.

"Oh Gods," Achilles said, hopelessly shaking his head. "Patroclus, you broke her."

Patroclus tried to calm himself, breathing in, and wiping his eyes. "Yeah, yeah. Sorry. Not on purpose."

Achilles shared a look with Machaon, who fondly muttered, "Idiots."

"Achilles!" Automedon skidded to a stop beside him. "Agamemnon says team meeting."

"And I say no," Achilles replied primly. "Tell him I have homework."

Patroclus stopped laughing. He raised his eyebrows at Achilles. "Is that a good idea?"

Achilles gasped dramatically, before exclaiming, "I never have bad ideas!"

"Care to see my alphabetized list? Of all your bad ideas?" Patroclus replied, pulling a notebook off the top of his pile of textbooks and waving it at Achilles.

Machaon snorted. "Better get going if you don't want to be steamrolled," he said, glancing at Agamemnon, who was with Menelaus and Odysseus.

"Library?" Patroclus suggested, gathering his stuff.

"Lovely." Achilles nodded in agreement. "Bri, there's a hole in the fence behind the bleachers that I'm gonna go out of, but you guys just leave through the gate." He started walking away, then turned, flagging down the player from before. "Automedon? Can you tell me if there's anything important I need to know about the meeting?"

The younger boy nodded. It was clear that he practically worshiped Achilles. "Sure thing."

Achilles gave a clicking sound of approval and a thumbs up before sprinting around the bleachers.

The restaurant wasn't crowded. Hector had driven Andromache, Paris, Helen, and Aeneas across the city to a place that Helen wasn't sure she could afford. It was stylised to look like ancient ruins, so there were plaster columns and half built walls interspersed between the tables. The columns had fairy lights and vines strung through them, which Helen thought was a nice touch. An elegant hostess led them over to a booth in a corner. She seemed to know the group, seeing as she had greeted them by name at the door.

"I'm assuming others will be joining you?" she asked as everyone was settling into their seats.

Hector nodded.

"Wonderful. Let me know when you'd like to get started on drinks."

Helen opened the menu, to distract herself from the fact that she was smushed up against Paris. At least Andromache was on her other side. Helen sighed when she realized she had been right about the menu. The dishes were ridiculously priced. Just a salad was astronomical.

"Helen," Aeneas whispered loudly across the table.

Her head jerked up at the sound of her name. No one else was paying any attention to Aeneas.

"Don't worry about the price. It's on the team's card."

It took her a long moment to comprehend Aeneas' statement. She leaned on the table, sure she didn't hear correctly. "What?"

"The team has a card. Hector's dad is a major donor to the school—"

"He's my father too," Paris announced, suddenly very interested in the conversation.

Andromache rolled her eyes as she read the menu.

Helen elbowed Paris' shoulder, a bit harder than she needed to. "Dude. Chill out."

"*Ouch*," was Paris' aggressive response.

The noise level in the restaurant seemed to climb at that moment, making Helen look up from the drink selection. A group of six or seven guys had just come into the stylish ruins, yelling at each other. An elderly couple who were sitting in a booth on the other side of the restaurant were shaking their heads at each other. Helen could practically hear them thinking, '*ugh. Teenagers.*'

Hector stood up and made his way over to the guys. He ended up shaking hands, shoving heads, and patting backs as they made their way over to the table. Helen had spent most of her high school years with Mycenae's football team, and she was sure she had been intimidated by them at first, but she was *also* sure that they hadn't been nearly as large. And she had had Menelaus with her too. She sighed, resting her face on her palm.

"You good, babe?" Andromache whispered in her ear.

Helen shrugged as they squeezed closer to each other in order to fit the latecomers.

"This booth is *not* meant for eleven people," Helen huffed, annoyed, and practically sitting on top of Andromache.

The red haired girl snorted. "Yeah, but you're forgetting that half these guys count as two people, so really, we're seventeen people at a booth for five."

Hector leaned over. "And the stupid thing is we've been sitting in this booth for three years."

"Ah, that must explain why it's so dirty," Helen joked.

This earned a laugh from Andromache. Aeneas was snickering beside Paris as well, but Helen wasn't sure if that was because of something the guy next to him had said. The booth's leather cushions were scuffed, but not stained. Paris shook his head as he put his menu in the center of the wooden table, which was *very* stained. He crossed his arms, and ended up even more cramped than before as Aeneas leaned forwards, laughing hysterically with the guy next to him.

Paris hated these dinners. The core of the football team had them quite often, but he wasn't even really a part of football. He preferred soccer. Hector wanted Paris to play, and Hector got whatever he wanted so, that was that. Paris hadn't even tried out for the team, but his father had paid way more than he should have to get him on. Lots of the team resented him for that, even though its not what paris wanted, nor was it his fault.

Hector smacked the table with both hands, sloshing water out of overfull cups. "Guys," he said, loudly enough that people a couple tables looked over before realizing that he wasn't talking to them. "This is Helen." Hector gestured to her with an open hand. "Paris' girlfriend... type person," he added off of Helen's dirty look.

"I heard you kidnapped her from Mycenae," one guy teased aggressively.

"Hey hey," Aeneas chided, "That's not funny. No one got kidnapped."

Helen wasn't so sure about that, but she didn't say anything.

"Anyways," Hector said, supposedly steering the conversation back on track. "You guys gonna introduce yourselves?"

"Yeah sorry," the guy who made the kidnapping joke said. "I'm Pandarus."

One of the huge guys on the outside of the booth waved. "Scarpedon."

"Euphorbus," the guy next to him said gruffly, more engrossed in his phone than the topic of conversation.

"I'm Idaeus," said a dark haired boy, who looked like he was going to fall asleep.

"Those are Glaucus and Antenor," Andromache told Helen when the guys next to Aeneas started talking before they had introduced themselves. "And that's pretty much all the important people on the football team."

Paris pulled out his phone, and Helen couldn't help looking over his shoulder. (She could literally see his phone no matter where she tried to move.) He was watching a video, which she didn't find interesting, so she tried to look away.

"Are we ready to order?" Aeneas asked, attempting to get himself some space, and failing miserably. "Castilla's here."

Castilla turned out to be the pretty waitress. Everyone ordered. Helen tried to get the least expensive thing, which turned out to be the thirty dollar green salad. She knew she would be hungry.

"There're snacks back at school," Andromache told her after everyone but Paris had ordered.

He got the most expensive item on the menu, which was a steak and lobster platter. He wasn't the only one to get that, but Helen rolled her eyes anyways. *Rich kids.* She had gotten into Mycenae on a full scholarship, and Aphrodite was now paying the tuition to Ilium.

"Oh my..." Paris muttered under his breath. "What. The fuck."

Helen once again looked over at his phone. He was holding down someone's Instagram story, which was full of text.

"What?" Helen asked, putting her chin on his shoulder.

Paris had *not* expected Helen to do that. He didn't really even like her, and his heart rate spiked to a dangerous level. (Or that was what *he* thought at least.) In fact, he started sweating, and almost, *almost* forgot about what Agamemnon had posted.

"What can he even do?" Helen asked, frowning up at Paris after scanning the paragraph.

"What?" Hector asked.

"What's going on?" Scarpedon leaned around Pandarus.

"Um..." Paris started, only to stop, looking nervously around the table. "Before I tell you, I'd like to start by saying that this is *not* my fault."

Aeneas cringed. "Yeah, it's probably my mom's fault, if we're being honest here."

Helen doubted that anyone would have believed Paris if Aeneas hadn't added on his piece. Technically, according to the story about the wedding where Aphrodite promised Paris the 'most beautiful girl in the world,' Paris *had* given the stupid apple to her. So it was his fault. Partially.

"Okay." Hector shrugged. "It's not your fault."

Andromache snorted, quickly hiding it behind her hand. "It's his fault, isn't it?" she whispered under her breath.

"Mine too," Helen replied, biting her bottom lip.

"Okay. So funny story, Agamemnon just posted this," Paris said, holding up one hand as if trying to pacify the team. "Okay. Here's what it says. All you thieving cowards..." He paused to clear his throat. "All you thieving cowards from Ilium had better be ready for war. We've had a rivalry in the past, but now you've taken something that is rightfully ours."

"I'm not a fucking *object*," Helen found herself growling to Andromache, who scrunched her face into a combination of annoyance and pity.

"You're a person, Helen, and should be treated as one," Aeneas said softly, nodding.

"And therefore, this season will be war. If we win this season, Helen comes back. If not, she can stay. I will do everything in my power to make this so." Paris took a breath that was more like gulping for air. "Let the war begin," he finished.

"Screenshot it," Aeneas said immediately. "Instagram will probably take that down. We need proof of him threatening us so we can get him kicked off the team."

"No wait," Hector cut in. "Helen, did you even *want* to come here?"

Helen grimaced, shaking her head slowly.

"But do you really want to go back *there*?" Andromache asked, her light eyebrows bunched together.

"I think this could be fun," Scarpedon said with a shrug of his huge shoulders. "If we only played Mycenae this year, we'd get to know our opponents well, and then we'd win."

"See," Hector said, leaning forwards, pointing at the ceiling, "I say we 'fight' them. I agree with Scarpedon. We've been neck in neck with Mycenae ever since ninth grade, when we were Freshmen. This is good, because we can prove we're better than them. And then that Agamemnon won't be threatening us again, 'cause we beat their team to a bloody pulp. And Helen, you can do whatever you want. No one's going to force you to do anything."

Helen made a noncommittal noise.

Aeneas had his arms crossed, looking between Hector and Paris. "Guys, do you really think this is a good idea? We could get them disqualified from the league for threatening us. That's another way of—"

"Well," Euphorbus said, putting his phone facedown on the table. "It's too late. They took it down."

"I'll bet Agamemnon will find a way to make sure—" Hector stopped, pulling out his phone from the back pocket of his black jeans. "Oh wait. Yeah. Dad just texted. Says there's been some adjustments to the game schedule. We have our own league now. County showdown, is what they're calling it, apparently. Damn. Agamemnon is efficient," Hector said, smiling a bit. "Don't get me wrong, he's brutal, but still."

Helen shuddered, wrapping her arms around herself. The expressions around the table ranged from annoyed—disguised–as–nonchalance to pure excitement.

"This is getting out of hand, Hector," Andromache said, her fingers pressing into Hector's arm. "Like. This is completely uncalled for. People are going to get hurt if you agree to play them as your only rival. You think this doesn't come with consequences? Like, what if he bribes refs? Into not seeing violence? You *know* that isn't beyond him."

"Darlin' dear, we've been trying to win against this godsdamn team for years," Hector reassured her. "It'll be very sportsmanlike. We'll be *fine*. Besides, we have another week or so before the first game."

"I'm sure it'll be sportsmanlike," Andromache said sarcastically, "Especially seeing as it started with dehumanizing threats."

"We'll sort it out, Andra," Hector replied softly, wrapping an arm around her and pulling her into him. "Though, I appreciate your concern."

"*You* should be concerned," Andromache muttered darkly. But she leaned on Hector anyways, because he was warm and no matter what she said, he was a headstrong dumbass, but at least he was *her* headstrong dumbass.

## V

Agamemnon's Instagram account got disabled after they took down his story, but it didn't matter. The Ilium team had seen it. Everyone important, except for Achilles, had seen it. This was *extremely* annoying. Achilles had missed the team meeting last night after practice, so that's why Agamemnon was waiting by the star player's locker. After eight fifty, students weren't allowed to leave their dorm buildings, so Agamemnon hadn't been able to track Achilles down. *Coward.* He wanted to be the one to break the news to Achilles, so the idiot didn't storm up on him demanding what the hell Agamemnon had done this time. He'd probably find a way to get Agamemnon kicked off the team.

People would still be eating breakfast in the cafeteria or in their dorm common areas, but Agamemnon knew that Achilles and his friend... the sports med trainer, usually went out running in the mornings. Agamemnon pulled out his phone. Eight fifteen. Footsteps announced the arrival of two people, about to come around the corner. The top hallway had windows that let in the early morning light. Classes didn't start for just over another hour. Achilles and his friend rounded the corner, both laughing at something.

Agamemnon faked apathy as he pretended to study the old fashioned photograph of a fencing society on the opposite wall, which was framed and placed in between two of the windows. There were photos like this all over the top floor. Apparently to show the athletes where the school had started, and how far they'd come. Agamemnon's photo was up here, on the wall of captains. If you captained a team, your face went up there with the greats from the past. Of course there was also a wall of exceptional players. Achilles' face was up there, which irked Agamemnon to no end.

"Dude, what're you doing here?" Achilles asked, finally, *finally* clueing in to the fact that they weren't alone.

Achilles' friend stopped, sort of behind Achilles, eyeing Agamemnon with caution.

"Odysseus needs a moment to get here," Agamemnon said, crossing his arms.

Achilles huffed, seemingly irritated. "Can I at least get into my locker?"

Agamemnon ignored him. Achilles started forwards, but his friend grabbed his arm, spinning him around. The two of them started whispering. Achilles was buzzing aggressively, while his friend was speaking sort of calmly. Agamemnon wasn't annoyed at Achilles' friend for once. (He was *usually* annoyed at Achilles' friend, because that meant Achilles would be sneaking off or laughing with him, and this made Agamemnon's life very frustrating, because without Achilles, the team was a little hopeless.) What *was* his name? Pat... something. Patra...?

"Patroclus," Achilles said, cutting the other boy off, just as Odysseus rounded the corner.

He waved at Agamemnon. Achilles glanced over, scowling. *Patroclus* was still gripping Achilles' wrist, looking up at him anxiously. Agamemnon pushed away from Achilles' red locker, joining Odysseus.

"So is this about the team meeting you *forbid* Automedon to tell me about?" Achilles asked gruffly as Patroclus let go of his arm.

The brown haired boy backed away from the conversation and began fiddling with Achilles' lock. Agamemnon knew he would still be listening.

"Agamemnon, Helen sent me a terrified text last night," Achilles said seriously, opening his phone. "She said something about you threatening the Ilium team? Something about doing whatever you can to make the season as aggressive as possible?"

Agamemnon shrugged. Patroclus stopped turning the numbers, his mouth in an uncomfortable line. The hallway was dead silent now. Agamemnon hadn't realized how much noise the lock had been making. He crossed his arms, straightening his back so he was almost as tall as Achilles.

"They took Helen from us," he said, like that explained everything. "Wait, Achilles, is Helen still *talking* to you?" Agamemnon demanded, Achilles' previous statement catching up to him.

Odysseus taped his fingers against the locker beside him to a rhythm that... couldn't actually be considered a rhythm. It grated on Achilles' nerves. The blonde boy gritted his teeth.

"Yeah. Helen and I are friends, no matter what school she goes to," Achilles said, dragging a hand over his face. "She's unhappy there, you know. She didn't *want* to date Paris. I know Aphrodite. She was there when my parents got married. The whole thing with the golden apple? Apparently Paris gave it to her, so she made Helen transfer schools to date Paris. Aphrodite's rich and she's got a lot of influence, so. Yeah. Helen didn't really have a choice. And you can't win her back—"

"That's where you're wrong," Agamemnon cut him off, grinning. "The Trojan captain, Hector... oh wait. You know him. Yeah, Hector messaged me last night. Said their team agrees. We came up with terms. Not to brag or anything, but I got this county its own league. It's us against them, all season long. And we're allowed to bribe refs."

"What the *fuck* is wrong with you?" Achilles spat, taking a step towards Agamemnon. "I'm not going to be a part of this. Helen is a *person*. Did *she* agree to this? You can't just—"

"Yeah, I can," Agamemnon said with a joyless smile. "It's called connections, money, and not giving a shit about what anyone thinks."

Patroclus bit his bottom lip, arms wrapped around his waist. "There's got to be a better way to sort this out," he said quietly. "One that doesn't involve threatening and bribing and hurting people."

"Didn't you hear me? Let me spell it out. I. Don't. Care. This is about honor. It's about not letting people walk all over us. It's about taking back what's ours. What's done is done, dipshit," Agamemnon snarled, taking an involuntary step forwards, glare locked on Patroclus.

"Oh don't you fucking dare," Achilles hissed, pointing a finger in warning.

Patroclus pushed in between them. "Guys. *Stop.*"

Someone was breathing hard, the sound taking up far too much space between the four of them. Odysseus was watching the whole thing happen, slightly concerned, and slightly amused. These guys got so riled up over the smallest things. At least, Agamemnon did. Achilles chose his battles with slightly more restraint, but still. Minimal. And Patroclus was the kind of guy who Odysseus would expect to step in the middle of a fight. He hadn't disappointed.

"Agamemnon, what do you want?" Patroclus said, sternly and passively at the same time. He seemed to be used to dealing with people who didn't want to resolve things quickly. Or maybe he just disliked conflict.

Agamemnon huffed, crossing his arms. No one stood up to him. This was another reason not to like Patroclus. He didn't know what was good for him. Agamemnon took a step back, still glaring, though unsure of who to glare at. Odysseus stood up from where he had been leaning against the lockers.

"I'm not going to be a part of this," Achilles said decisively, never taking his eyes off Agamemnon as he started backwards down the hall, his hands in front of him.

Agamemnon barked out a laugh. "That's where you're wrong, my friend."

Odysseus stepped forwards.

"If you're threatening me," Achilles said softly, "I wouldn't."

"Don't drag him into this," Patroclus said quietly to Agamemnon, who snorted.

"He's on my team," the black haired boy stated, "So he has to follow my orders."

"Maybe I'll quit," Achilles suggested loudly as he opened his locker.

"I'll tell everyone about how your mom wanted to send you to Nantucket Dance School because she didn't want you playing football," Odysseus said.

Achilles shrugged. "Go ahead, man. No one will believe you."

"How you've never watched anything rated R?"

"Again, no one will care." Achilles opened his locker door, stepping out of Agamemnon's view.

"Your love of classical music?"

"If you think that's embarrassing enough to get me to be part of this, you're very wrong," Achilles called back.

"The stuffed animals you still sleep with?" Odysseus tried. "What were their names? Achilles and Friend?"

"Wow, am I ever glad that I'm not *your* best friend anymore," Achilles said dryly.

Patroclus stared out the window, a hand on his face. He was completely done with this argument. Agamemnon cracked his neck. The pop jarred the quiet space with sudden anxious tension.

If Odysseus didn't come up with something that was bad enough to get Achilles to play this season, the Mycenae Stallions were fucked.

Odysseus sighed. "How about when your mom cheated on your dad?"

"Nothing to do with me," Achilles replied, though Agamemnon could no longer hear him rummaging around.

Patroclus held his breath.

"What about your half brother?" Odysseus probed.

Achilles slammed his locker door shut, the horribly loud noise echoing through the hall. Patroclus watched Achilles warily.

"And how he's already got two football scholarship offers? To Penn State and Notre Dame? In his freshman—"

"Fuck you," Achilles laughed, shaking his head at his locker door.

"Your dad was your mom's weakness, so she went and made something better, didn't she?" Odysseus said, though he hated himself a little, in that moment. (They *needed* Achilles to play for their team. Achilles' half brother may have been better, but he lived across the states.)

"Okay stop," Patroclus cut in, looking at Agamemnon and Odysseus with pure disappointment. "That's really awful and *extremely* immature. And also, how could you break someone's trust like that, Odysseus? More than once? You guys stopped hanging out *because* you threatened to tell everyone something. Haven't you learned your lesson?"

Agamemnon was holding back a grin, watching as Achilles made a fist and hit it gently against his locker, once, twice, three times.

"No, I haven't learned my lesson," Odysseus said, somewhat morosely.

"Fine," Achilles muttered.

Patroclus turned to face Achilles, his mouth hanging open, but only until his friend met his eyes. He looked helpless. Trapped. Achilles was terrified that he wasn't good enough. Odysseus just spat his worst fears in his face.

"Pardon?" Agamemnon asked, though he had heard perfectly. He just wanted Achilles to say it again.

Achilles took a deep breath. "I said," he whispered through gritted teeth, "Fine. I'll play."

"And this is why I haven't learned," Odysseus said, shrugging. "People always cave in eventually."

"Thanks, Achilles." Agamemnon nodded, smirking. "Looking forward to the game next week." To Odysseus, he said, "Let's go. Gotta talk to someone."

Odysseus saluted mockingly to Achilles, who didn't even notice because his eyes were shut, his head resting on his closed locker door. The two football players left, high fiving just as they turned the corner.

Patroclus hated them so much. He tried not to hate people. He really did. But when people were deliberately awful... well. There wasn't much to be said. Except that they were probably struggling with their own lives. But it still didn't give them permission to tear someone apart and expect them to obey you.

Checking that the hallway was still empty, he walked over to Achilles, wrapping his arms around his waist and resting his cheek against his back.

"Why are they hell bent on breaking me?" Achilles whispered, the pain raw in his voice. "I didn't do *anything* to them."

"Not to be rude or anything," Patroclus said softly, "But you're very intimidating." This made Achilles laugh pathetically. "And you're good at everything. Agamemnon is afraid of you. It doesn't make what they're doing right, but Achilles, darling, you're the spirit of the team. You're practically the school mascot, and some people have a god complex that you... disrupt, thereby, you invalidate their belief that they're superior to everyone."

"I'm not *trying* to be superior to everyone," Achilles complained, only to dissolve into a fit of quiet giggles. "That sounded really spoiled. And like I have a god complex myself."

"It's only me you're talking to," Patroclus said. "I understand that you only have *half* a god complex."

"Haha very funny," Achilles said sarcastically. They lapsed into silence. "Thank you," Achilles whispered after a moment, placing his hands on top of Patroclus'.

"Should we go eat?" Patroclus asked.

"I guess so."

Patroclus:

> Achilles is not having it today, so if he's weird, it's because of Agamemnon

*Sent 11:28 AM*

Briseis was in math class when she got the message. She was already on her phone, so she replied.

Briseis:

> what did he do now?

*Sent 11:28 AM*

Patroclus:

> He and Odysseus threatened him because he didn't want to hurt people.

> Whivh is dumb. Just thought i'd let you know because. Yeah.

> *Which

> He said he wants to explain it himself.

*Sent 11:29 AM*

Briseis:

fair. meet you in the cafeteria?

*Sent 11:30 AM*

Patroclus:

Yeah. By the door without the vending machines. So. Away from Agamemnon.

Achilles says hi by the way, even though we'll see you in like. Half an hour.

*Sent 11:31 AM*

Briseis:

i say hi back. see you later!

*Sent 11:31 AM*

She had been scrolling through Pinterest, because math wasn't very exciting. Briseis had a gift for numbers. The test on Thursday wouldn't be a challenge because she had learned the concept on the flight from California. She had actually gone over the entire math curriculum, only to discover that she had learned most of it already.

What baffled her more than linear equations was Achilles and Patroclus. They actually seemed to like spending time with her. Last night, when they had gone to the library, Patroclus had given her both of their phone numbers. The three of them ate dinner in between the tall stacks at the back of the dusty room, even though it technically wasn't allowed. A librarian had seen them sneaking back, but she had held her finger to her lips and winked. Achilles explained that the librarians loved Patroclus, because he was one of the school's most avid readers.

Apparently he had volunteered over a hundred hours last year, and that pretty much gave him a place heaven, according to the library staff. Achilles begged to differ, but he admitted later that he loved the library. It was beautiful place, with giant bookshelves that seemed to stretch on for miles. Like maybe one could walk in and never come out again.

When the lunch bell rang, Briseis packed up her notebooks that she hadn't opened and left the classroom. The teacher glared at her, but she didn't care. That would change soon. And besides, half of the class had been on their phones anyways.

Briseis yawned, covering her mouth with the back of her hand as she jostled her way through the hall. A bunch of people didn't carry bags, because there were five minutes in between classes, and everyone else knew the school. You could supposedly sprint up to the fifth floor in the east wing of the school to grab a book and make it back to the west wing before the bell rang, but Briseis didn't think that would be a good experience. She almost got hit in the face when someone flung their black locker open dramatically.

To dodge the door, she leapt out of the way, only to run onto someone. She apologized, but it was lost in the hallway chaos.

Briseis finally found her way to the cafeteria by following the masses. She would have pulled out the maps app, but it didn't have a guide to the school. There was an admissions package that had a map, but it was lost in her satchel. And besides, it was an aesthetic bag, so she didn't mind carrying it with her. Briseis stopped in the doorway to the cafeteria, frowning. Just as she was about to pull out her phone, someone tapped her on the shoulder. Her heart lurched as she looked over her shoulder, expecting Agamemnon or one of his cronies. Instead, she found a girl. A girl who was few inches taller than her, with a messy blonde pixie cut.

"Sorry," the girl said, her voice lower than Briseis had expected. "I couldn't help but wonder if you're... Briseis? Or Bri?"

"Either is fine," Briseis said quickly, hiking her bag onto shoulder. "Who're you?"

The girl laughed, running a hand through her hair. "Again, sorry. Not a stalker. I promise. I'm Iphis," she said, offering a hand to shake.

"Ohhh, you're friends with Achilles and Patroclus," Briseis said with a smile, accepting the girl's hand.

They shook hands for an awkwardly long time, which made them both laugh, though not uncomfortably. When they let go, Briseis brushed a stray lock of hair behind her ear.

"Um..." she started, unsure what to say next.

"C'mon," Iphis said, solving Briseis' problem. "I came over 'cause you looked lost. Achilles and Patroclus are over here."

Agamemnon and his crew were sitting in the middle of the high ceilinged room, laughing wildly about something Briseis was sure wasn't funny. She glared at them as she and Iphis passed the table.

"I somehow ended up on the wrong side of the cafeteria again," she said, noticing Menelaus staring at his food with no interest. The red haired boy sat at the end of their table, his posture slumped. Briseis felt like he didn't quite fit in.

Iphis laughed, though Brisies could barely hear her. "It's alright. This school is one hell of a maze."

Briseis found Achilles' head of blonde hair in the crowd. Patroclus waved at her, and she waved back. Someone dropped a tray of fries at the table behind the one Achilles and Patroclus were sitting at, spilling ketchup all over the checkered floor. Patroclus disappeared from view momentarily, until Briseis and Iphis reached the table. He was helping the girl pick the fries up. Achilles was shaking his head at Automedon, who was also at the table. Patroclus glanced up, smiled at the two girls, and continued cleaning up.

"Hi," Automedon said from where he was sitting alone on one side of the table.

Briseis thought it was weird that the lunch room had chairs instead of benches, but she sat down anyways. "Hi. You're Automedon, right?"

The boy nodded. "That's me." He looked rather serious.

"Loosen up, man," Achilles said with a brotherly grin. "She's not going to attack you."

Automedon shook his head, cracking a tiny smile. "I know. I've got to go. Have an English test next period."

"*Already*?" Patroclus asked, his head appearing from the other side of the table.

"Unfortunately," Automedon sighed, taking his tray off the wooden table and standing up. "See you at practice."

"Best of luck, soldier," Achilles said solemnly as Automedon walked off, weaving his way through the groups of people sitting down. Achilles leaned forwards, narrowly missing a spilled drip of sauce with his white shirt. "That kid is a fantastic player. Only Sophomore to make the actual team."

Briseis nodded.

"Nice," Iphis said, untucking her white collared shirt and pulling two protein bars out of the waistband of her pleated skirt.

"What are you doing?" Briseis asked in disbelief.

Iphis tucked her shirt back in with a grimace. "These skirts don't have pockets, so I'm forced to resort to other methods. Desperate times call for desperate measures." Iphis shook her head regretfully.

"Like... maybe a backpack?" Briseis suggested, still sort of confused.

Iphis smiled. "Nope." She offered Briseis a bar. "You want one?"

Briseis took the bar, because she didn't want to go wait in line for real food.

"Cheers," Iphis raised her protein bar and thunked it against Briseis', making her giggle.

Patroclus slid back into his seat beside Achilles, resting his head on his arms. "Today has been a day."

"Sorry," Iphis said, throwing her wrapper at his head. "I'm out of protein bars."

Achilles grabbed the wrapper out of the other boy's dark hair as Patroclus sighed. "What am I to do, Iphis? You're dumping me for the first pretty girl you see? I feel very betrayed."

Briseis suddenly found one of the folds in her skirt to be one of the most interesting things she had ever seen. Iphis reached across the table and smacked Patroclus on the back of the head.

"You know I love you," she said, though her face was a bit… pink.

"Let's not attack Patroclus," Achilles said, raising an eyebrow. "He's keeping me sane."

"While you're driving me to insanity," Patroclus muttered into his arms.

Achilles rested his head on the table, looking at Patroclus. "Am I really?" he asked so quietly that Briseis barely heard him over the burst of clamorous laughter from the table beside them.

"No, I love you," Patroclus said, pulling his head out of his arms. "In a *bromance* kind of way. Because we're *roommates. Bro.*"

Briseis looked across the table to find Achilles staring at Patroclus, his eyes wide, just before he burst out laughing. Patroclus shook his head, frowning in a happy kind of way.

Iphis stuffed the rest of her protein bar in her mouth, smiling fondly at the two of them.

"Oh. Hey Briseis," Achilles suddenly said, sobering quickly. "This is super super weird, so I'm sorry in advance—"

"Achilles, you can't ask her this," Iphis quipped. "You barely *know* her."

"What do you need?" Briseis asked sincerely, leaning forwards.

At this point, Briseis would do anything for the three people sitting at the table, (within sensibility, obviously). They took her in, *and* saved her from Agamemnon, which seemed like an odd thing to do for a complete stranger.

"Look," Achilles said, running a hand through his hair. "You can totally say no. I'll understand, because it's just... weird."

Iphis bit her lip, glancing over at Briseis. Patroclus swallowed nervously.

"So you know how we have a long weekend this week? Well... my mom, Thetis, is coming into town for those couple of days and... she really doesn't like Patroclus. And she also doesn't like Iphis. And she's slightly... um. She's a bit close minded. And she never sees my side of things," Achilles said, seemingly growing smaller with every word. "So I was wondering if you could come to dinner with me. And pretend to um. Be my girlfriend. If that's weird... which it is, it's fine I'll just tell her that my girlfriend couldn't make it. Iphis and Patroclus are going to be there too."

Briseis put her protein bar wrapper onto the table, right on top of the many carved initials. She finished chewing, swallowed, then nodded.

"*Really?*" Iphis asked, incredulous as she turned in her chair to face Briseis.

Patroclus frowned at her. "*We're* doing that."

"Yeah but..." Iphis trailed off before aggressively whispering, "Are you straight, Briseis?" she then proceeded to smack a hand over her mouth. "Sorry. That was a very personal question for meeting you like. Fifteen minutes ago."

"No. I'm bi," Briseis said, shrugging. No one cared back home.

"Heyyy same!" Achilles exclaimed, offering Briseis a high five.

She felt herself flushing as she smacked his hand. This was weird. But in a good way.

"Don't yell about that," Patroclus muttered, glancing around.

"Sorry," Achilles blurted, his eyes going wide. "Sorry. Forgot."

Iphis was scratching the wooden table with a pocket knife.

"Iphis, darling," Patroclus said, looking slightly concerned. "Where did you get that knife?"

She looked up, her eyes wide with some kind of false innocence as she folded the knife back up and hid it under the table. "What knife?"

Briseis raised her eyebrows at Iphis, who winked.

"Wait you have a knife?" Achilles asked excitedly, drumming his fingers on the edge of the table.

"Ooookay let's go to our next class, Achilles," Patroclus said, getting up from the table, and grabbing his satchel.

"Thanks again!" a girl who was probably in ninth grade said as she walked past Patroclus.

He glanced over his shoulder, giving her a quick smile. "Oh yeah. No problem."

"Why are you a literal angel?" Achilles asked, watching the girl go.

Iphis burst out laughing, only to stop very quickly. "Yep. Sorry. Yep. Literal angel." She turned to Briseis. "What's your next class?"

"Bye guys!" Achilles said as Patroclus hauled his chair away from the table with him still in it. "See you later?"

"Yeah," Iphis replied, standing up. "Ugh, I hate how my legs stick to these chairs."

Briseis snorted, only to realize that the stupid chairs were made of awful fake blue leather. "Yeah that's nasty," she grumbled, picking up her bag off the floor. "I have... um. Computer Science."

"Good Gods." Iphis shuddered. "I have math, sadly. But I think the rooms are close together. Walk with me?"

Briseis smiled. "Yeah."

# VI

Helen and Andromache hung out on the weekend. The first week of school had been confusing, with tensions running high. The Ilium Trojans had open practices, and Andromache had told Helen that Hector was screaming at everyone more than normal. Everyone was stressed about the first game on Wednesday against the Stallions. Achilles had told Helen that he had tried to convince Agamemon to stop, but it hadn't worked. Helen hadn't really expected it to, but she was glad he tried.

The two of them were sitting in Hector and Paris' living room on Sunday night, with their parents. The house was a monotone picture of suburban wealth, with a three car garage and fancy light fixtures. Helen sat on a leather couch that was made more for style than for comfort. Priam brought in a tray of drinks, which he assured Helen were non–alcoholic. She didn't know why he said that to *her* specifically, but she just nodded and smiled.

"So Helen," Priam said, setting down the tray of drinks on a rustic coffee table that looked like it was fresh out of Pottery Barn. "What do you think of our lovely school?"

She had many opinions, and none of them seemed to be the right answer to that leading question. "Well... it's definitely... different from Ilium. I do appreciate being able to leave campus in the evenings."

"Ah yes," Priam said, sitting beside Hecuba on a couch that looked like a very wide chair. "We're the only school in the area that gives its students such freedom on weekdays."

Andromache shifted from where she was sitting on the floor. She seemed like she belonged in this living room. With her willowy grace and simple, yet stylish outfit, she fit right in. Helen felt like an eyesore.

"Looking forward to the new football season?" Hecuba asked politely, trying to make conversation.

She was a kind looking woman, probably in her late forties. Her hair was dyed a mousy brown, and she wore an outfit that seemed very... motherly, with a knitted sweater and jeans on the looser side. She wasn't nearly as intimidating as Aphrodite. But when she asked about the football season, Helen stopped breathing.

"Oh, it'll be interesting," Andromache cut in, grabbing a drink from the table and sipping delicately. "It's exciting that we have our own league." She didn't agree with this statement, but she said it just to save Helen from having to talk.

Priam nodded appreciatively, taking a drink for himself. "We won't have to travel much this season, which is very nice. We got the schedule the other day. Most of the games are at Ilium, because we have a better field."

Helen smiled stiffly, nodding along with the conversation.

"I hear this whole thing is about *you,* Helen dear," Priam said, running  hand over his thick white goatee.

Andromache stiffened, inhaling sharply.

*How was this allowed if they* knew *the reason?* Helen thought frantically, all the while nodding with as much politeness as she could muster.

"Y–yeah. It was because I transferred schools," she said, cigging her new light pink acrylic nails into her palms. (She had gotten them yesterday with Andromache.)

Priam and Hecuba both looked at Helen, with matching expressions of pity on their faces.

"I know you don't love, or even *like* my son," Hecuba said kindly.

Helen's heart nearly stopped, regardless Paris' mother's tone.

"Helen, we know all about Aphrodite. At Peleus' wedding, she picked on Paris and she promised him something. We didn't think she would go through with it, but we really shouldn't have underestimated her. Aeneas, one of her sons, grew up with only his father, because she doesn't really think about the consequences of her actions," Hecuba continued sadly. "Helen, dear, even though Mycenae's Captain declared that this is about you, whatever you do is *your* choice. We're here to support you."

Andromache looked up at Helen and gave her a quick smile, squeezing her knee. Helen could feel her bottom lip trembling. She was so lost, and for a moment, she felt like she had been found.

"I'm afraid to see everyone from Mycenae again," Helen admitted, feeling incredibly small.

It didn't matter that she didn't know anyone here. Hecuba made her way over to Helen's couch and sat next to her.

"We tried to talk Aphrodite out of this," she said softly. "And you don't have to see them if you don't want to. You can sit with us."

"Yes," Andromache added, turning to face Helen. "Please. Sit with us. Don't go disappearing."

Helen ran her hands over her face, trying to figure out how to breathe properly. It didn't work. She was really, really trying not to cry, but that *also* didn't work.

"This isn't fair," she whispered. "You're being so nice to me, and I'll have to choose in the end. I don't want to leave, but I don't want to stay."

Hecuba pulled Helen into her, stroking her hair. "I'm sorry," she said softly.

***

Hector was starting to regret agreeing to Agamemnon's threats. It didn't help that, on top of everything, Paris was an inadequate *coward.* It was getting dark, the sun sinking below the horizon. They had eaten about an hour and a half ago. Not everyone went home on weekends, but Hector and Paris usually brought people back to their house. They had four extra rooms.

Scarpedon, Aeneas, Euphorbus, Glaucus, and Antenor were staying over for the long weekend because their parents lived hours away. Aeneas' dad lived on the same block as Hector's family, but he was away for work. The six of them had gone outside to play football after eating, along with Hector and Paris.

The grass was no longer dead, like it had been over the summer, and the air was humid. Paris was lying on the ground, complaining about being tackled. The Trojans had one of the best offensive lines in the state. They had made it all the way to the private school finals, only to be beaten by the Stallions, because of Achilles, their runningback. And the fact that their quarterback was smarter than a horsewhip.

"Paris," Hector said, barely containing his frustration. "That's part. Of playing. *Football*."

"C'mon man." Aeneas hauled Paris to his feet. "You gotta get used to that."

Scarpedon, the one who had bowled Paris over, crossed his arms. Hector tossed the ball to him, just to distract himself from knocking Paris over again.

"First game's Wednesday!" Antenor yelled, running down the soccer field as Scarpedon hucked the ball at him. "And we've gotta *crush* them!"

"I'm done with this," Paris muttered darkly. "Going home now."

With that, Paris jogged off the field towards the streetlights that had just flicked on in the twilight. Hector watched him go, biting one of his lip rings.

Euphorbus walked up to Hector, resting his elbow on Hector's shoulder. "Off goes the wuss."

"Finally!" Scarpedon bellowed from the other side of the grass. "We can have a real scrimmage!"

Euphorbus shoved Hector as he ran back to the game that would now have zero rules. Aeneas appeared next to Hector, his hands on his hips.

"He shouldn't even be on the team," Aeneas said, uncharacteristically blunt.

Hector ran a hand over his shaved head. "Yeah. Dad wants him to be though, so. Can't really retract a bribe."

They watched Paris disappear through the doorway of their house, the light from inside briefly spilling across the large porch. Hector sighed.

"I thought I could make him less of..."

"A soccer player?" Aeneas suggested, his eyes glinting gleefully in the dusk.

Hector snorted, shaking his head.

"Hector!" Glaucus yelled.

Hector spun around and caught the ball, even though he could hardly see anymore. The light from his house had stained his vision, making him mostly blind. He could make out Antenor, running down the field, so he threw to him, the ball leaving his hand a second before Aeneas rammed into him, knocking them both to the ground.

"Gods," Hector wheezed, rolling onto his back. "That was awfully aggressive."

Aeneas got to his feet, offering Hector a hand. "Couldn't be helped."

"Let's goooo," Antenor yelled violently, slamming into Glaucus in celebration. Hector supposed that his team had just gotten a touchdown. He looked up at Aeneas.

"Is it the anxiety that's causing this unbridled anger?" Hector asked, posing a serious question as a joke.

"Actually yes," Aeneas answered, pulling Hector to his feet, even though he was at least thirty pounds heavier. "Wednesday is freaking me out for some reason. Maybe it's how the season's starting out. Agamemnon doesn't... make me comfortable, if y'know what I mean. Mycenae's players are a bit unnerving. Slightly unhinged."

"And now we've made it more of a competition," Hector finished as they started jogging back to the field.

"The captain himself is having second thoughts?" Scarpedon demanded, shoulder–checking Hector playfully, but rough enough to send him stumbling into Aeneas.

"Nope," Hector lied easily. "Just getting hyped up for the war, as Agamemnon has so kindly declared."

Achilles was nearly having a panic attack. Dinner with Thetis had been weighting on him for three weeks now, but he didn't realize how nervous he was. It was Odysseus' fault. He was the one who brought up Phyrrus, Achilles' half brother that he had never met. Briseis and Iphis were waiting outside the hotel, where Patroclus had dropped them off. He was driving Achilles' used Toyota Camry, but now he killed the engine, looking over at Achilles with concern.

"I'm fine," Achilles said. "I'm fine. It's fine."

"I don't believe that for a second," Patroclus replied softly, turning in the drivers seat to face Achilles.

"This is a bad idea," Achilles blurted out. "You shouldn't have come."

Patroclus glanced out at the street in the rearview mirror, watching the weekend traffic rush by.

"I just want her to be proud of me," Achilles whispered, swallowing.

A group of nicely dressed people walked in front of the car, talking so loudly that Achilles could make out words from their conversation. They mixed in with his thoughts, making it almost unbearable.

"Hey," Patroclus whispered, offering Achilles both of his steady hands.

Achilles took them, trying to stop his own hands from shaking. The car still smelled like it was new, even though his dad had gotten it off Craigslist. That polished leather and chemical kind of smell that made Achilles' head ache. He exhaled.

"Look at me," Patroclus said, squeezing his hands.

It took a second for Achilles to clue in to what was being asked of him. He gritted his teeth and met Patroclus' dark eyes.

"Achilles, you're the most wonderful person I know," he started. "Breathe. You're not breathing. Achilles?"

They inhaled together.

"Whatever happens, I'm here, okay? And Briseis and Iphis too. You're ridiculously strong, and you're resilient, and you're funny. Last time you saw her was fine." Patroclus paused, as if realizing something. "This is because of what Odysseus said, isn't it."

Achilles was feeling slightly okay again. Less like he was going to vomit. "Yeah. I think so."

"Well fuck that idiot," Patroclus said aggressively, making Achilles laugh in surprise. "C'mon. But only if you're ready. We can sit here for a bit if you want."

Achilles shook his head. "We should go now. Before we're even later than we already are."

"It's not even six," Patroclus chided, squeezing Achilles' hands one more time before letting go. "We're meeting her at six fifteen."

"Yeah, I know. Just... she's always early."

Iphis and Briseis were whispering to each other as Achilles and Patroclus walked up to them.

"Shall we?" Patroclus asked, offering his arm to Iphis, who flipped him off, then took it.

Achilles took a deep breath, nodding. They walked up the stone stairs together, over the dusty red outdoor carpet. The man at the valet booth nodded to them as they walked through the automatic doors, into the hotel's entrance. Classical music floated through the air, tip-toeing around conversation and filling in the silences. Achilles knew it was Heinrich Ignaz Franz von Biber's *Battalia*, which he thought was a very strange piece to be playing, but he didn't mind. The four of them made their way across the lobby towards the restaurant. They'd had to drive an two hours to get here. Thetis was staying in Austin because she refused to stay within a fifty mile radius of Peleus, unless it was for football finals, or an emergency.

After waiting an antsy five minutes in line, a waiter guided them to their table. Like Achilles had expected, Thetis was sitting there, straight backed and looking like she just ate a lemon. She probably *had* just eaten a lemon. Achilles had forgotten she liked to do that. It made him smile a little bit.

"Mom?" he said as they reached her table.

Thetis looked up, her eyes widening at the sight of her son. She broke into a smile that Achilles genuinely didn't know if it was real, got up from her seat and pulled him into a hug. Thetis always smelled like sunscreen. But the good sunscreen, that was like oranges. The kind you wore at the beach. So she reminded Achilles of the sun and the sand and the waves. He forgot how much he missed her.

"It's so good to see you," she whispered into his hair.

She was a ridiculously tall woman with sleek black hair. No one knew where Achilles had gotten the blonde from. Thetis was at least six foot three, a whole four inches taller than Achilles. When she released him, Thetis turned to his friends.

"Good to see you, Patroclus," she said, shaking his hand. "And hello, Iphis." Briseis had begun inching around to stand by Achilles, but Thetis caught her in the middle of the act. "And who is this?" she asked, her perfectly shaped eyebrows raising slightly.

"I'm Briseis," the dark haired girl said, offering a hand to Thetis.

Patroclus and Achilles shared a quick glance as Thetis shook Briseis' hand.

"Achilles and I... are dating," she added, shaking her head slightly, her eyes wide as if she was trying to convince Thetis that she was telling the truth.

Thetis looked at Achilles, her eyebrows inching higher. "I... why didn't you tell me? Achilles! She's gorgeous!"

Briseis' dark skin flushed with red undertones as she took her hand back from Thetis.

"Oh, I'm so happy for you," Thetis said, pulling out her chair again and sitting down.

Achilles felt slightly guilty for the lie, but the last time they talked about dating, Thetis had proved to be very inflexible in her views. And she had said something about Achilles being such a late bloomer in the world of romance. He *wasn't*, but... this was something both he and Patroclus had agreed on. It would be better for both of them if their relationship stayed a secret, at least until they were older. Achilles sat next to his mother, who then insisted that Briseis sit across from her so she could get all the '*details*'. Patroclus slid into the seat next to him, giving Briseis a nervous nod as she sat down.

"She's not going to be our friend after this," Achilles whispered to Patroclus.

Iphis studied the menu like it held the answers to all her problems as Thetis tried to ask Briseis about something unsuitable for the dinner table. (Or really any public situation.) She glanced up at Achilles, who knew he was bright red, and mouthed *kill me now*. Patroclus stared at the ceiling, wincing every time Thetis started talking. That's when the waiter showed up, asking what drinks they would like, and saving them from further humiliation.

The rest of dinner went somewhat smoothly, except for when Thetis asked Achilles how he and Briesis had started dating, and it was a different story than Briseis had told. That caused a minor panic, but Briseis saved the day, by saying Achilles' story was when they had first *met*, not when they started dating. Iphis didn't say anything the entire time. Patroclus didn't talk much either, but not for lack of trying. Thetis usually just talked over him. She *had* promised to come to more of Achilles' games this year, which made it hard to stop smiling. The food was good, if not a little bland. The conversation was energetic, if not a little mortifying. The night was alright, if not a little stressful.

On the drive back, Achilles felt the need to apologize to everyone over and over.

"Achilles," Briseis interrupted after about three minutes.

He looked into the back seat, biting his bottom lip. "What?"

When Briseis said, "Thank you for taking me with you," he wasn't sure how to reply. He had been so sure that she was going to say something along the lines of '*I never want to see you guys again.*'

Iphis looked at Briseis curiously. Patroclus was smiling faintly at the road.

"I'm glad I could help," Briseis said earnestly, shocking Achilles again.

"You... what?" he asked, mystified.

Briseis smiled at him, though something akin to pity lurked in her gaze. "Achilles, I can see how much you care about her, and how much you want her to care about you. I'm glad I could help."

"Yeah, Patroclus, let's never do that again," Iphis cut in playfully. "No offense Achilles, but your mother has *zero* chill and that was awkward as fucking hell."

"You've *met* her before," Achilles insisted. "You *agreed* to come."

"Yeah, I know," Iphis said sullenly. "Will Peleus have snacks?" she asked, brightening up at the thought of food. They were driving to Achilles' dad's house, because it was the best place to stay. It was close to the school, and it was better than staying *at* the school.

"He always has snacks," Patroclus said, glancing over at Achilles with a tiny smile.

❧❧❧❧❧ ❧❧❧❧❧

"Sorry for the interruption. Agamemnon Atrides, please come to the office, Agamemnon Atrides, please come to the office. Thank you."

*Today is* not *the day for this,* Agamemnon thought grimly as he left his psychology class. The rest of the week had flown by, shocking him when Wednesday rolled around. He hadn't been paying much attention to anything in classes because he could just read the textbook later, but getting called to the office meant one of two things. The game tonight was cancelled, or he was... about to be in some deep shit. The hallways were empty between classes, and his footsteps echoed. The banners on the walls were for both athletic and intellectual competitions, all done in the school's loud colours. They mocked him. Especially if it was going to be his last day at school. What if he got *expelled*? Agamemnon came into the grand main foyer, wiping his clammy hands on his slacks. *Gods, why today?* His brain started listing all the things he had done that could possibly get him kicked out of the school and it...was *not* reassuring.

The main office was a large room with three desks up front. Mrs. Agafya, the head secretary, always gave out mints to people visiting the nurses office. She didn't look up from her computer as Agamemnon walked in.

"Ms. Artemis needs to see you," she said, trying to keep her voice even.

She'd never liked him. She thought he was arrogant and aggressive, which was always dangerous in young adults.

"Thanks," Agamemnon replied, smiling to himself as he walked to the misguided counsellor's office, down a short hallway on the left.

He knocked on a door with a simple golden name plate.

"Agamemnon?" she called from inside, her voice coarse like sand.

"Yeah, that would be me," he said, opening the door.

He expected to see Artemis sitting with one leg flung over the arm of her chair, smoking a cigarette (she was old school like that). Instead, he was greeted by two cops; a short woman and a stocky man who was a head and shoulder taller. The more surprising of the two irregularities was to see Artemis sitting properly.

"Someone OD'd on Speed, Agamemnon," Artemis said, her eyes narrowed.

"Adderall," the male cop corrected. "A member of your school community told us we may be able to find out more from you? Or a member of your family?" he asked, clearly hoping that Agamemnon would dig his own grave and lay in it, but he just shrugged.

Artemis gestured to the brown couch that Agamemnon knew had strategically placed throw pillows to cover the cigarette burns. He sat down, careful to keep his body language open. Not crossing his arms, keeping his feet on the floor, his face a perfect mask of concern and confusion... he would be fine. In and out of here in no time.

"When we searched your locker, we found this," the sandy haired man said, gesturing to several bottles of pills.

"What?" Agememnon asked, frowning. "I've... they aren't mine."

"This is a serious offense we're talking about, Agamemnon Atrides," the female officer said, crossing her arms.

*Fuck.*

He took a trembling breath, shaking his head slightly. "Can I... talk to Artemis for a moment?"

The cops shared a look, then the man nodded. "We'll be right outside."

As soon as the door swing shut, Artemis released a sigh. "You *had* to get caught today? Of all the effing days? It's the first game tonight."

"I know, I know, I'll be out for the rest of the season and probably expelled and also probably thrown in... it would be jail now, wouldn't it?" Agamemnon frowned at that thought. "But I didn't do it."

Artemis plucked a hair off of her beat up leather jacket, glancing skeptically up at him.

"I *need* to play this season," he hissed. "And besides, I've never touched those drugs."

"Then who's are they?" Artemis asked, crossing her arms.

Agamemnon huffed, his eyes straying from his councellor's face to the posters for metal bands and movies plastered to the walls. He wondered how much longer she would be employed. Hopefully until he was done school, at least.

"They're Iphigenia's," he said, meeting her eyes again.

She snorted. "Your little sister? What, is she like, nine?"

"Iphigenia is fifteen, and that's her prescription medication. And also, have you *seen* the people she hangs out with?"

"They're all nerds," Artemis said, exasperated, draping her head over the back of her black office chair.

"Exactly. It's Speed. Adderall. For the... extra focus? I think? The guy who..." He was going to say *'The guy who bought it from me wanted that,*' but the cops were right outside. "The guy who got it from Iphigenia wanted it for that."

Agamemnon's patience was starting to wear thin. He glanced up at the deer shaped clock. Two fifteen. Half an hour before the team was leaving to drive over to Ilium Academy. Or... maybe he'd go to jail for the rest of his life. That thought bothered him less than it should have.

The office chair squeaked as Artemis readjusted herself. "You know... that might actually work. Does she know your locker code?"

"She should," Agamemnon replied, crossing his legs.

Light streamed in from the open windows, making the dust in the small office very noticeable. Artemis spun around and picked up the phone on her desk, quickly asking Mrs. Agafya for something.

"Sorry for the announcement," came over the intercom. "Iphigenia Atrides, please come to the main office. Iphigenia Atrides, to the main office. Thank you."

Agamemnon sighed. His little sister was annoying. Hitting two birds with one stone, he supposed. Or if this didn't work... it would be like *getting* hit with two birds and a stone. He just *needed* to play this season. Hell, he'd even give up football if it meant they could crush Ilium once and for all. Go out on a bang. He found himself subtly pleading, as if there was an omnipotent being that could actually help him. He picked at a loose thread on the couch as the police officers and Iphigenia came into the office.

"Agamemnon, what's going on?" Iphigenia asked, her brown eyes wide with concern.

The female officer had her lips in a thin line. "Are these yours?" she asked, gesturing to the pill bottles.

"Yes?" Iphigenia said, looking between the cops, Artemis, and Agamemnon. "They're my prescription medication?"

"Have you been selling them?" the man asked.

Iphigenia opened her mouth and closed it again, before saying, "*What*?"

She looked to Agamemnon for help, but he just gave her a pitying look.

"These were found in your brother's locker," the man continued. "He denies ever touching them."

"I'm not a drug dealer!" Iphigenia exclaimed, slumping against the wall. "I... I store them in his locker because he's the oldest and he's supposed to... he's supposed to make sure I get the right doses. And so it doesn't get stolen."

Agamemnon felt the tiniest twinge of guilt as he watched the scene unfold. His younger sister slumped to the floor, looking tiny and lost.

"Do you have your brother's locker code?" the woman asked, not lightening up the slightest bit.

Iphigenia was trying not to cry now. "Four–six–zero," she said into her hands.

The cops shared a quick glance.

"Do you know Mr. Homer?" asked the male officer.

"He's a friend," Iphigenia managed to respond, gasping for breath. "He likes to write about the football team, in the school paper...?"

Agamemnon glanced up at the clock again. That Homer kid was so *annoying*. Ten minutes until he was supposed to be in the gym. Artemis was watching the whole thing with the slightest amusement, but she also seemed disturbed. Like she maybe... regretted her choice to go through with this. Agamemnon gritted his teeth, winding his finger around a stray piece of hair that had escaped his ponytail.

"We're going to need to call your parents, Miss Atrides," the lady said with a tinge of regret in her voice. "Mr. Atrides, you're free to go."

Agamemnon blinked. Was this really going to be that easy? Artemis shrugged discreetly when his eyes darted over to her. Iphigenia was still curled up in a ball beside the door, like she was trying to disappear.

"Thank you," he said, standing up from the couch. It creaked, as if glad to be relieved of its burden.

On his way to the door, he stopped, crouching down in front of his sister. She looked up at him, her face streaked with tears, her eyes bloodshot already. All the evidence pointed towards her. He had no reason to sell her prescription medication. If her friends has asked for it, which Agamemnon knew they had, then she could have just sold a pill or two. Besides, he never touched the bottles without gloves on.

"This really sucks, Iphy," he whispered. "I'll stay if you want."

She didn't say anything, instead meeting his eyes defiantly. He pulled her into a hug, just because it would look off if he didn't.

"You've gotta get to the game, Agamemnon," Artemis said from her chair.

"You play football, son?" the male cop asked as Agamemnon stood up.

"Yessir," he said, throwing a quick smile, which was returned.

"Good luck with your game," he said with a nod and a smile. "Go Stallions."

Artemis saluted to Agamemnon behind the officer's backs. He raised his eyebrows in lieu of a wave, and shut the door behind him. He stood in the hall for a long moment, not really understanding what just happened. What he had just done. But Artemis was right.

He did have to go get ready.

# VII

ACHILLES SAT IN THE hallway beside the change room, his bag next to him. They'd have time to change before the game. He wasn't necessarily *excited*, but he wasn't dreading it either. It would definitely be interesting, to say the very least. Agamemnon came running past him, barrelling through the change room door like he was trying to break a wall. Achilles laughed under his breath. Agamemnon was never late for games, but today, he had arrived the moment they were supposed to be leaving. (Athena once told Achilles that whatever time she said the team needed to leave was actually a half hour early, because the team sucked at time management.)

Patroclus poked his head out of the sports med lounge that backed onto the main gym. "Who was that?" he asked, looking between Achilles and the door.

"Agamemnon," Achilles replied. "Late for once. Maybe we can get him kicked off the team."

"Don't be so blasphemous," Patroclus joked, receding back into the room.

It was almost time for class change, which would mean people flooding into the changeroom for gym. It would also mean that Achilles would be trampled. He was just waiting for Patroclus and Machaon to get their stuff ready, then he would go to the main foyer. Achilles pulled out his phone, ignoring the fifty six notifications from the football group chat.

Briseis and Ipis had both texted him good luck. He replied to them, even though they had talked to him about the game at lunch. Ever since the weekend, the four of them had become... sort of a unit. They all learned that Briseis was a math genius, getting one hundred and two percent on the first quiz in her class. Patroclus had to ask about fifteen times to get her to say the grade loudly enough for them to hear. When she *did* say it, Patroclus and Iphis both freaked out, because they... all sucked at math. Worst class.

Automedon and Antilochus came out of the changeroom, chattering excitedly.

The two of them stopped in front of Achilles.

"You coming?" Automedon asked, waving his helmet at Achilles' face.

"Yes he is," Patroclus said, emerging from the sports med room once again. Achilles frowned. He sounded weird. "Let's go."

This was because Patroclus was carrying a huge blue cooler in one hand, a giant red bag in the other, and a roll of tape in his mouth.

Achilles got to his feet, throwing his red gear bag over his shoulder. "Do you want me to take anything?"

"No I'm fine," Patroclus replied, his voice muffled.

Antilochus and Automedon looked like they were about to offer the same help, but didn't after Patroclus refused Achilles.

"Go," Patroclus said, bobbing his head in the direction of the end of the hall.

Achilles took the tape out of Patroclus' mouth, tucking it in the pocket of his slacks. The four of them walked down the gym hall, through the English wing. Achilles always thought this wing was dustier than all the other wings, because...it just *felt* dusty. Like books that no one had read in decades. They emerged on the other side, coming into the main foyer just as the bell rang. Athena was waiting with her assistant coaches by the gathering of sleek gray couches to the right of the doors. No one ever sat on them. It was just a good meeting spot.

"You're almost on time!" Athena said with fabricated enthusiasm. She looked at Patroclus before frowning. "Where's Machaon?"

"He's literally on the football team," Patroclus said, setting down his burden of medical supplies. "He's a free safety."

Athena's frown deepened. "Why does he sit out with you sometimes?"

Patroclus touched a hand to his forehead, like he just couldn't handle anything anymore. "Because you and the defensive coordinator discussed this with us. It's so he can get in his training hours *and* play on the team."

"Athena?" the defensive coordinator said, stepping out from the group of coaches. "That's true. Machaon is a great player but also a gifted medic."

Athena let out a breath, nodding. "Alrighty then." She turned back to the coaches, signifying that their conversation was over.

Patroclus crouched down and started sorting through the red bag. "Can I have that tape please?"

"What tape?" Achilles asked, confused.

His friend sighed. "The one you took from me?"

Automedon and Antilochus were talking with the next person to arrive. Idomeneus. Decent player. Good for team spirit. Achilles crouched down next to Patroclus.

"Are you okay?" he asked, fishing the tape from his pocket.

Athena glanced over her shoulder. "Achilles, do you know where Agamemnon is?"

Achilles bit back a snarky response. "Yeah, he's in the change-room."

The head coach laughed through her nose. "Odd of him to be late." She paused for a moment, then went back to showing the other coaches her strategy book.

"Patroclus?" Achilles asked, tilting his head so he could look at the brown haired boy's face.

Light from the old fashioned chandelier washed everything in the lobby with a slightly yellow glow that mixed with the daylight from the huge windows. It made Patroclus look tired.

A draft of hot air flooded into the room as the front doors burst open with surprising force. A woman burst into the foyer, draped in glamorous clothing and perfume so strong that Achilles could smell it from ten feet away. Patroclus pressed the back of his hand to his nose, as if trying to block out the cloying scent. The man who followed her was barrel chested with a black beard and stern eyes that swept over the room, making Achilles feel inferior.

"Where is Iphigenia?!" the woman demanded shrilly.

Mrs. Agafya came hustling out of the main office, panicked. She was followed by a police officer with honey coloured hair, who strode over to the two people with confidence and a subtle air of sadness. He shook hands with the man, and gestured to the main office. They both followed, the woman's heels clacking on the concrete floor.

"That was...dramatic?" Antilochus said, breaking the silence.

Automedon laughed nervously.

"Weren't those Agamemnon's parents?" someone asked.

Everyone dissolved into anxious chatter, far louder than it was before. Players kept arriving in twos and threes, making the noise level rise even higher.

"Iphigenia's Agamemnon's younger sister," Patroclus said, placing the roll of tape Achilles had given him into the red bag. "It's weird that there are police involved. She's a nice kid, from what I know, at least."

Achilles had never met Iphigenia. He didn't even know she existed, until now. Someone tapped him on the shoulder. He looked up to see Menelaus, staring at the office with concern.

"Was that my mom?" he asked, deeply concerned.

Patroclus rubbed his thumb across his bottom lip, lost in thought.

Achilles got up, standing beside Menelaus. "Yeah, I think so."

"I just heard someone yelling about Iphy," the red haired boy said, running a hand over his head. "And then yeah. I know, it's definitely my mom. And my dad too probably. No one else would be able to yell at her. She's too innocent."

"Okay team," Athena called over the chatting. "Time to go. Is everyone here?"

Agamemnon, Odysseus, both Ajaxes, and Diomedes came out of the hall.

"Everyone's here *now*," Odysseus said with a wave.

"You'd think she would do attendance on the first game," Patroclus whispered to Achilles, hoisting his medical supplies off the ground.

Menelaus eyed his brother as Agamemnon's group jogged past everyone else to talk to Athena.

"Are you *sure* you don't want help?" Achilles asked as Athena started leading the team from the school, swarmed by Agamemon. He didn't understand how she could possibly stay calm around that jerk.

Patroclus sighed. "I'm fine, Achilles. I just didn't think Machaon would be playing this game. I've never been the *only* trainer before. There will probably be a sports med *doctor* anyways. I dunno why I'm nervous."

"You'll do fine!" Achilles said, bumping Patroclus' shoulder.

Patroclus rolled his eyes, but didn't comment when Achilles held the door for him.

The bus ride was long and annoying. They had a specific bus for the football team, where they could store their stuff underneath. But Patroclus kept the cooler full of ice, because apparently it melted when it was under the bus. So he was sitting sort of cross legged, with one leg braced against the seat in front of them. Achilles was half listening to a conversation Automedon and Nestor were having. Phoenix, one of Achilles' oldest friends, kept chiming in as well, but the conversation was mostly about school. And also girls. Iphis would enjoy it. And Briseis, he supposed. Patroclus had his head pressed against the window, watching the sparse trees whip past. Achilles *knew* he was upset, because Patroclus refused help when he was stuck inside his head.

It took maybe an hour and fifteen to get to Ilium Academy. Achilles had done this ride far too many times to count. He pulled out a math textbook and looked at the problems, almost expecting them to do themselves.

"Are you just going to stare at those, or are you actually attempting math?" Patroclus asked, leaning over to see Achilles' non-existent progress.

Achilles glanced up. "Well if you want to help me I might actually attempt."

Patroclus put his foot down on top of the cooler, his brow furrowed playfully. "That's really sad you're asking *me* for math help. I barely passed last year, my friend. You *could* ask Bri, because apparently she's a freaking genius."

Achilles had forgotten about that. He nodded thoughtfully, shoving his textbook back in his bag. So much for getting homework done before eleven thirty at night.

"Hey," Phoenix said, leaning out into the aisle and poking Achilles. "Memnon want us to… oh wait. It doesn't really apply to us. He was just talking about not doing zone D. And maybe running that Blitz play they've been working on." He shook his head as he said this, rolling his eyes like it was the stupidest thing he'd ever heard.

"He *what?*" Achilles demanded, agreeing whole-heartedly with Phoenix's reaction.

Phoenix held up his hands, as if washing them of all responsibility. "Not my choice."

"That's going to fuck with offense," Achilles groaned, dragging his hands over his face.

Nestor nodded, like that was obvious.

Achilles started to get up, but Automedon said, "Do you have to fight today? It's the first game. Just let him do what he wants."

"Yeah, but—"

The bus hit a speed bump, jostling everyone and halting conversations briefly. Someone's helmet rammed into the inside of the compartment underneath, making a loud clang. It *normally* took an hour and a half to get to Ilium, but their driver liked to speed. Patroclus muttered something under his breath about wasting time and energy, but Achilles didn't really hear it. He stood back up, leaning on the back of Antilochus' and Idomeneus' seat.

"Agamemnon!" he yelled.

Hardly anyone looked back at him. Half the team was wearing headphones, or talking to someone. The bus was very loud. The black haired boy looked over his shoulder, from where he had been talking to his crew.

"What do you want, Pelides?" he barked, annoyed.

"I want you to not run stupid plays on the first game of the fucking season," Achilles shot back, glaring daggers at the team captain.

Out of the corner of his eye, Achilles saw Automedon and Patroclus cringe, sharing a concerned look. He huffed, waiting for Agamemnon to come up with a response.

"Who's captain?" Agamemnon yelled. "You or me? In case you couldn't figure it out, it's me, so I make the Godsdamn calls alright, *soldier*?"

Achilles felt heat rush to his face. He dug his fingers into the faux leather seat, grinding his teeth together. Patroclus knotted his hand in the hem of Achilles' shirt, silently encouraging him to let go of the useless argument. (Achilles knew it was useless. But he pursued it anyways.)

"Look," Achilles said. He didn't have to shout anymore because everyone on the bus had fallen silent. Achilles wasn't sure when, but now it was so quiet that the hum of the engine and the gravel under the tires seemed deafening. "Fine." He heard Patroclus let out a breath. "Okay whatever. Expose your weapon before you're ready. Just put all your cards face up on the table for the Trojans. Let them know all our plays and strategies so they can practice specifically to defend against them. I don't care. We can lose to fu—to Ilium. Doesn't matter."

With that, he sat back down, feeling very smug.

Patroclus didn't let go of his shirt. "And that was important because?"

Achilles shrugged defensively. "He was gonna make us lose the game!"

"Mm," Patroclus said, releasing his grip. "And pissing him off was a good way to insure that we *don't* lose?"

"Well I thought that was fucking brilliant," Pheonix said, sounding impressed.

"Don't encourage him," Automedon muttered, shaking his head at Achilles, who was now grinning. "The fighting doesn't *help* his social standing."

"Social standing is for losers," Achilles announced insolently, waving a hand as if to brush away a fly.

Patroclus breathed out a laugh. "That's the first thing you've said today I agree with."

"Ouch," Achilles replied, clutching his hands to his heart. "That hurts."

Athena stood up at the front of the bus. All of the conversations that had once again reached peak volume dissipated. Achilles didn't really understand her coaching style. She hardly ever interfered when people were fighting, verbally or... physically, which happened with disturbing frequency. But she did have a good team, so he supposed that whatever she was doing must be working.

"We're playing a simple game today," Athena announced, her arms crossed. She was standing in the middle of the aisle with perfect balance. Achilles wasn't sure how she could do that. "No fancy plays, no dirty plays, just a match of basic skill against basic skill. We don't want them to realize how good we are until later in the season. As I've previously stated, we have a completely different season this year, only playing one team. It's a distance race instead of a sprint. I'm playing the starting lineup for the second and fourth quarter, as is the Trojan's coach. We're almost there, so be ready to get off. If you have any questions, come find me when we get there."

She sat back down. The instant she was out of view, the chatter jumped back to full magnitude. Achilles closed his eyes, grateful for her subtle intervention of Agamemnon's plans.

"See how she did that, Achilles?" Patroclus said, leaning forwards into the seat. "She did that with dignity, which is more than you can say."

Achilles snorted. "But which one... catalyzed the other reaction? I had to abandon dignity for the greater good."

"Why do I put up with you?" Patroclus groaned, pretending to cry.

"Because I'm funny and clever and devastatingly handsome?" Achilles suggested, flashing Patroclus a bright smile.

The brown haired boy ran a hand over his eyes, but Achilles could see his grin.

By the time they got off the bus, Agamemnon had at least calmed down enough to think properly. Sort of. The strategy talk had died after Achilles so kindly... interjected with his bullshit nonsense. Agamemnon had mentioned using that play *once*, before asking Odysseus to pass down the message about zone defense. Of *course* he wasn't going to use that play. It wasn't ready. And besides, it was more of a passion project that the defence had wanted to try. In a practice scenario. But Athena wanted them to run a simple game, so that's what he would give her. Hell, she was even playing the second lineup first. Agamemnon wanted to start off the season with a win, but it wasn't particularly necessary. Especially when this game didn't count. It was the calm before the storm.

Ilium Academy was a bit bigger than Mycenae. Diomedes got lost in the school last year and missed the whole first quarter of a game. Agamemnon never let him forget that. As they got off the bus, Diomedes eyed the brick building with suspicion, like he held a personal grudge. Odysseus bumped into Diomedes, distracting him from the school. They didn't even have to go inside. The school had a godsdamn stadium with change rooms, a concession, and *merch* booth, for Gods' sakes.

"Okay all," Athena announced. She rarely yelled. Just somehow... spoke much louder than everyone. The giant team came to a halt, about a hundred yards away from the stadium entrance, where people were already streaming in. "Let's change quickly, then go on a warmup run. Around the outside of the stadium. Then go onto the field and Agamemnon, lead the usual pre–game routine. After that, you're supposed to go back into the chute so you can run onto the field."

Agamemnon could tell that Athena thought the pomp was unnecessary and ridiculous. He wished he could agree, but running onto the field was the best part of playing at Ilium.

"All right, that's it. Three, two, one break!" Athena barked, as the entire team clapped at the same time. One clap. Supposed to make a team more... teamlike. Achilles seemed to be immune to that.

They started off towards the back door to the stadium, Agamemnon and Odysseus in the lead. Menelaus shouldered his way through the crowd, panting by the time he reached his brother. Running with the gear bag was tiring. Menelaus opened his mouth to say something, but Agamemnon held up a finger, watching Athena holding back Achilles to chat with him. How satisfying. He savored it for a moment, then they continued on.

"What do you want, Menny?" Agamemnon asked as he yanked open the heavy brown door to the back hallway.

Ajax 1 ducked through the doorframe, followed by some offense players. Ajax 2 walked beside him, his playbook open. Menelaus looked worried.

"*What?*" Agamemnon demanded, squinting so his eyes would adjust to the semi–darkness.

"What happened with Iphigenia?" his younger brother asked, his eyebrows pinched.

Odysseus inserted himself between the two brothers. "Menelaus, Agamemnon did what he had to do. He has a duty to this team as captain."

Agamemnon clenched and unclenched his jaw. He felt slightly horrible about what he had done. The bus ride had given him time to stew in the inkling of guilt. He kept telling himself that he would probably be in prison if he hadn't blamed Iphigenia, but the look on her face...

Agamemnon sighed. "Don't worry about it."

Menelaus was worrying about it.

"Dude, it doesn't matter," Diomedes said, making his way to the front of the group, talking to Menelaus. "Put it aside and focus on the game, alright?"

Menelaus didn't respond. He sped up, and disappeared into the away team changeroom. Agamemnon stopped at the door, turning to face the team. They stretched about halfway down the dimly lit hall, watching him expectantly.

"Remember guys," Agamemnon yelled, just to be heard. "Efficient."

"Coming from the guy who almost missed the bus?" Achilles retorted, from the back of the group.

Agamemnon was *this close* to strangling that idiot, but for once, he pretended he hadn't heard.

Shockingly enough, the team got ready in just over ten minutes. Even Achilles. Agamemnon had been pretty sure that he would go as slow as possible, just to spite him. (It wouldn't have been the first time.) Achilles even stayed with the team during their warmup run. He didn't do it *quietly*, but Agamemnon was glad. Achilles was the bane of his existence. Especially when he ran with Menelaus. Agamemnon hated it when they hung out together.

Odysseus wondered out loud about plays, and if the Trojans were going be overly aggressive. Lesser Ajax said that the bribed refs weren't coming until the real season started. So, two weeks from now. By the time they made it into the stadium, about half the seats were full. Some people from Mycenae were arriving now, seeing as a lot of them had left just after class. *Technically* students weren't supposed to leave without permission, but the wardens turned a blind eye to people sneaking out. Most of the time.

The assistant coaches huddled around the bench on the right side of the field. Athena was talking to a couple men at the 50 yard line. Agamemnon watched the Trojans warming up for a moment before jogging off in the direction of the bench. Everyone started arranging their stuff, and Agamemnon stared at the stadium. A grand beast, with some semblance to a city, surrounded by an imposing steel wall. There were steep sections of seating on either side, and less banked seats by either end zone. So many people. Just for a silly high school game. But none of the pros came to their towns. This was the best the people could get. The field was lit by floodlights that made the green turf more vibrant in the growing dusk. Agamemnon loved playing at night. He loved the roar of the crowds and the moment before a play started, staring at the player across from him right in the eyes.

Ilium's stadium held so many memories. Agamemnon was glad to be back. This year, they would win. They would crush those snivelling weaklings to the ground. He had a good feeling about this season. The Trojans interrupted the flow of his thoughts with a loud cheer, which spread through some of the spectators like a crashing wave. Agamemnon smiled. Odysseus joined him, right on the boundary line.

"You ready?" Agamemnon asked, looking at the crafty quarter-back.

Odysseus raised an eyebrow before shoving his helmet on his head. "Born ready, captain."

Hector watched the Stallions warming up, standing beside their team's head coach, Mr. Phoebus. The slight man had his nose wrinkled as he watched the Stallions' coach run over to her team, who were skipping aggressively. Hector knew Mr. Phoebus wasn't a fan of Athena, partly because last season, when the Stallion's team had beat the Trojan's in overtime. Hector was starting to question his decisions. Playing this team for the whole season might... take a toll on the team's morale. He crossed his arms, looking over at Mr. Phoebus.

"Evaluation?" his coach asked without taking his eyes off the field.

"They're probably gritty players. More so than last year, I bet. And fucking Achilles Peildes is back. He's an issue. Too fast."

"You're the only one who can beat him," Mr. Phoebus said, glancing over at Hector, who scoffed. "But it doesn't matter. This game isn't important."

Paris appeared next to Hector, peering at their opponents. "Who's that giant guy? He's taller than *you.*"

"We played this team last year, Paris," Aeneas chided, joining them. "That's Ajax."

"What? I thought *that* was Ajax," he said, pointing to a skinny guy running over to the Stallions' bench.

Hector sighed. "They're *both* Ajax."

Paris threw his hands in the air, exasperated as he walked away.

Mr. Phoebus shook his head slightly, frowning. "Gods, that... ugh." The Stallions erupted into deafening cheer that cut off whatever Mr. Phoebus had been about to say. When they had finished, the coach looked at his watch. "Coin toss time."

"Yessir," Hector said, glad for an excuse to leave his team.

When he looked over his shoulder, he saw Paris standing beside the stands, talking to Helen. She was sitting with his parents and Andromache, who waved. Hector gave her an overly enthusiastic smile and thumbs up, which made her laugh. He turned back to the field to see Agamemnon walking up to him. The Stallions' captain had a smug look on his face when he reached Hector, even though he was probably half a foot shorter, at *least.* The ref jogged over to the 50 yard line, but he didn't get there fast enough to stop Agamemnon from opening his mouth.

"Good to see you again," he said, his teeth gleaming in the odd light. "Glad we see eye to eye on our... issues. Can't wait to see how this ends."

Hector didn't have time to reply. Agamemnon was an unsettling person. Hector really wanted to punch him in the face, but he had *some* common sense, so he refrained from breaking the shorter guy's nose.

"Shake hands," the ref said, like this was the last place he wanted to be.

When they obliged, after an uncomfortably long moment of intense eye contact, Hector realized how much animosity could be conveyed in such a simple gesture.

The ref, who was a man with white hair and a permanent scowl, turned to Agamemnon. "Heads or tails?"

"Heads."

Hector watched the coin spiral, a glinting contrast to the darkening blue of the sky. The ref caught the coin, flipping it into the back of his hand. Heads. Hector hated losing the coin toss.

"Receive," Agamemnon said, still looking at Hector.

"Right endzone." The second line up was playing first. Hector preferred the left endzone.

"Alright. You've got three minutes until kickoff," the ref said dismissively as he walked away.

Agamemnon saluted mockingly. "Best of luck, *Hector*."

"Don't give me your luck," Hector called to Agamemnon's back. "If we're gonna win, we'll do it on skill alone."

Hector didn't even watch the first quarter of the game. He knew it was going to be a disaster. Their second lineup was... sub par. He spent the time talking with Helen and Andromache. Helen was antsy, and kept staring at the Stallions' bench. Hector felt bad for her, but he was short on patience. Agamemnon had a tendency to do that to him. When Mr. Phoebus called a quick team meeting between quarters, Andromache leaned over the railing to kiss him. Helen took a picture. Andromache shoved her good naturedly, calling out something about playing well to Hector. Mr. Phoebus was reassuring some tenth grader who was *certain* that the mess of the first quarter was all his fault.

"Dude, it's your first game," Hector said kindly, ruffling the kid's hair. "It'll only get better from here."

A buzzer went, signalling the second quarter was about to begin. Mr. Phoebus looked at Hector as the second lineup took their spots on the bench. Hector watched the offensive line run onto the field.

"When you go on, see if you can make this something better than a total embarrassment," he said as Hector grabbed his helmet off the bench.

"You got it," Hector said, cringing as Paris got bowled over three seconds into the play.

By halftime, the Stallions were winning 23 to 6. Agamemnon had excused himself from the team meeting to find the man Athena had been talking to at the beginning of the game. Not the

Trojan's coach. The grey haired man in the tailored suit. Zeus. He was a powerful alumni of some Ivy League school who liked to see the Stallions and the Trojans pitted against each other. For the last three years, he had been sending the football team he liked best an extra (undisclosed) amount of money to get new equipment, guest coaches, and supplies. Agamemnon was determined to convince the benefactor that Mycenae needed the money this year.

He found the man sitting right in the front row by the left end-zone, looking at his phone. Agamemnon had never seen someone sitting with such good posture while texting. He waited until the man noticed him. Zeus put down his phone, giving Agamemnon a professional smile.

"Is there any way I can help you, son?" he asked, crossing his legs and interlocking his fingers over his knee.

"I was just wondering..."

"If I'd chosen a team this year?" Zeus finished, one eyebrow slightly quirked. "Because the answer is almost."

Agamemnon nodded, unsure of what to do with his hands. The older man flashed him a quick, half–believable grin. "I wouldn't worry, Mr. Atrides. The fates are conspiring in your favor this year."

Zeus picked up his phone again, a clear dismissal. Agamemnon turned to face the field, holding back a gigantic smile. *Finally*. He was about to make his way back to the team, feeling like he was high, when the Trojan's cheer team ran past him, off the field from their performance. He hadn't even noticed them. (That was really saying something.) For Menelaus' sake, Agamemnon was glad Helen had the sense not to join Ilium's team. Maybe she'd join mathletes or something. (Agamemnon hated mathletes.)

He waited for the girls to pass him, staring after them with a smirk.

"Um… hi," one of them said, running towards Agamemnon and waving.

He sighed. She'd probably yell at him. Helen liked to do that. Thought she was a feminist or something. The girl came to a stop a few feet away from him, tucking a blonde curl behind her ear.

"Sorry to bother you," she started, smiling a little. "I was just wondering if… I could maybe… have your Snap? Or if you're free after the game for a bit? Maybe?"

Agamemnon raised an eyebrow. She was pretty. Kinda short. It was rare for a girl to ask *him* out.

"Sure," Agamemnon said, glancing up at the minute clock to make sure he still had time. "What's your name?"

"Chryseis. But everyone calls me Crissy," she said with another smile, brushing back a strand of hair that wasn't there. Cute. "And you're Agamemnon, right?"

"That's me," he replied, unable hide his smirk. "After the game?"

"By the back door?" she asked, her eyes shining in the floodlights.

Agamemnon winked, starting to walk back to the Stallions' bench. "See ya then."

Crissy giggled and ran back to a group of girls who enveloped her. Agamemnon didn't really pay attention to the rest of the game. Greater Ajax smacked him on the back of the head when he zoned out on defence, and Achilles yelled at him from the bench. Agamemnon was really starting to appreciate Patroclus, because he could generally shut Achilles up. He was also one hell of a sports med trainer. When Protesilaus cracked his ribs, the quiet boy taped him up as Athena called the actual doctor that presided over their games.

The Stallions won the game 48–42. Menelaus wanted to talk to Helen, but Achilles dragged him back to the bus. Agamemnon borrowed someone's girlfriend's car so she could ride back with the team. Then he went to meet up with Crissy.

# VIII

Hector was finished. Just completely done. The season had barely started and he was already fed up with his team, their team, and Paris, who *someone* had decided should play Center. At least they hadn't *tied*. There was nothing worse than a tie. Hector wanted to go to bed, but the Trojans were sitting in their lounge after the game. The walls were painted white, with a mural of their logo blazing across one of them. (The Trojan helmet. Very creative.) There was a TV on one wall, with a couch across from it.

Throughout the whole year, at any time, Hector knew he could find at least three members of the team in here; skipping, studying, hiding, impressing their partners. Among other things. Only people on the team had keys to the room, but it was hard to actually fit all forty seven members, plus the four coaches in comfortably. Helen and Andromache were beside Hector. He wasn't sure who had let them in, but he didn't mind.

Mr. Phoebus got up onto the table in the corner of the room, whistling to get everyone's attention.

"Alright boys!" he yelled, tying his long hair into a messy ponytail thing. "Tonight was a learning experience, obviously. Don't worry. The season hasn't started, and we now know how those fools play. And now we can improve. What do we need to work on, Hector?"

The entire team turned to face him. He sighed, scrubbing a hand across his eyes. This room always made him uncomfortable. It was like the pictures on the walls were judging him, whispering behind his back about how bad of a captain he was. But... it didn't matter. He was here and those champions weren't.

"Well first," Hector started, surveying the people staring up at him, tired, excited, defeated, eager for another try. "Let's give a hand to the second line, seeing as this was for most of them the first game. You all held your own."

Aeneas whistled, starting a generous round of applause that doubled in strength because of the echoes. Hector was glad his team at least had *some* spirit. He smiled at the guy from earlier, who had been about to cry because of the first quarter. The kid laughed, shaking his head.

As the excitement quieted down, Hector started again, "And with that said, we have a lot of improving to do if we want to beat them." It took all of his willpower not to stare at Paris as he said that.

Glaucus snorted from where he stood with Aeneas. "Understatement?" he muttered, so only the people around him could hear.

It was honestly true. The only reason the Trojans did as well as they had was because of their defence. And how the Stallions defence hadn't been up to its normal standards today.

"Tomorrow, and for the next week here, we're going to run a bunch of basic drills, to try and figure out the issues. Mr. Phoebus and I talked about this before." Hector looked around once more. "Any questions?"

"Next game is two weeks away?" someone called from the back.

Mr. Phoebus nodded, hopping off the table. "Correct."

"And that one counts?"

"Also correct. Anything else? There's class tomorrow," Mr. Phoebus said.

Hector was glad that he had taken over again.

"But I can get you excused if you come talk to me."

That elicited a few confused glances from the newbies. Bonus perks of being on the team. Condoned skipping after games.

"Okay, bring it in," Hector yelled, ready to leave. Best get a cheer done and go sit outside or go to bed or go cry in a forest. (Not the last option. There wasn't a forest by Ilium.)

The team, some still in their gear, clamoured to get up from where they were sitting and made their way to the middle of the room. Andromache tapped Hector on the arm. He looked at her, a question on his face. She pointed to the hall with her thumb. He nodded as the two girls slipped out of the room, then joined the team.

"Who are we?" Hector demanded, from the centre of the group.

Around him, voices rose from their defeat.

"The mighty Trojans!"

"Who are *we*?" he yelled, as the noise in the room started building.

"The mighty Ilium!"

"Who are *WE*?"

"TROJANS."

"WHO?"

"TROJANS!"

"WHO?"

"THE MIGHTY MIGHTY TROJANS!"

No one would understand the words to the cheer if they didn't know it. It was absolute chaos that dissolved into rollicking whoops that seemed to shake the very floor. Hector hated writing cheers, but that was a captain thing at Ilium. He was required to add a cheer to their arsenal. Stupid tradition.

"Have a good sleep everyone!" Mr. Phoebus yelled over the noise. "Remember, come to me to be excused from classes tomorrow!"

Hector barely caught the end of the sentence. He snuck out into the hall, Aeneas on his heels.

"That cheer always gives me a headache, man," Aeneas said. He smacked his helmet into the brick wall, gripping it by the facemask.

Helen and Andromache were waiting about twenty meters away from the lounge door.

"I agree, Aeneas!" Andromache called with a wave. "Why couldn't you have written a nice song, Hector?"

Helen burst out laughing, then quickly covered her mouth.

"What?" Andromache demanded, rounding on the other girl.

"Football is just... loud. A song wouldn't be a very good hype cheer *or* a consolation cheer. The best cheers are the ones that sort of... rile people up," Helen said confidently.

Aeneas nodded, contemplative, as the four of them kept walking. The team's chatter receded as they stepped outside, into the cool night air.

"You're not skipping tomorrow, are you?" Andromache asked as they paused on the damp grass.

Hector shook his head, draping an arm over her shoulders. "Seems kind of irresponsible."

"Then Paris will be doing just that," Helen muttered. "And he'll expect me to do the same."

Aeneas grabbed her arm as she started away. "Helen, you don't have to do anything you don't want to. I *will* talk to my mom if you need me to."

Helen stopped, the lights from the pathway reflecting in her eyes. "Paris won't actually skip class. He's kind of a nerd. And no, don't talk to your mom. I know it can't... be helped. It's not fair to you."

"But Helen, this isn't fair to *you*," Andromache said, stepping out from under Hector's arm.

He kind of missed her, for some odd reason. She was still right there.

"Yes, but now I'm complaining again and I shouldn't!" Helen replied, yanking on her hair. "It's okay. I'm fine. But I do have a test tomorrow. I'm going to bed."

"I'll be quiet," Andromache said, though Hector doubted that Helen even heard her.

Aeneas sighed, looking back at the two of them. "This is kind of hopeless, isn't it?"

Andromache said, "No," at the exact same time Hector said, "Yeah, pretty much."

The three of them shared a brief glance before bursting out into laughter. Aeneas was clutching his sides by the time they calmed down.

"My Gods," he wheezed, wiping off his brow with the back of his hand. "I am *way* more sore than I should be."

Hector nodded in agreement, though he wasn't any more tired than he was after a practice.

"Yeah, I'm going to bed," Aeneas said after a long moment. "It's nice out though. Too bad it isn't a weekend."

"Yeah," Andromache said, staring up at the navy blue sky. The air was warm, perfect for staying up all night outside with a couple of drinks and good friends. They had done that over the summer, before Helen showed up. It felt different now. Like more was on the line. Hector didn't know why.

"Anyways," Aeneas smiled, his teeth standing out in the dark. "See you tomorrow. For that English exam."

Hector resisted the urge to smack himself in the face, but just barely. "Right. The fucking exam. See you."

As Aenas left, Andromache turned back to Hector. They stood there for awhile, facing each other without really being able to see.

"Tomorrow seems so far away right now," Andromache whispered, looking up again.

She was beautiful. Hector didn't know how he'd been lucky enough to end up with her. He didn't quite understand how they worked, but he knew it was rare to have someone who felt like his other half. They were both complete, despite their flaws. Two wholes put together to make something bigger. She looked at him again and laughed.

"You have something against the stars?" she asked, her eyes glinting.

Hector tucked his hands in his pockets and looked up. "Y'know, Andy, I don't see any stars. I just see the glare of the pathway lights."

"You're not looking hard enough, you idiot," she said, appearing beside him. He could feel her arm against his.

She pointed up. "Can't you see that? The one dot up there?"

"You're expecting me to find a singular dot. In the *entire sky*."

"You're generally pretty smart," Andromache said, wrapping her arms around his waist. "And sometimes, that makes up for the fact that you pierced your lip. Twice. And got a giant tattoo of an eagle on your back."

Hector looked down at her, putting his arms on her shoulders. "You still mad about that?"

"I will *always* be mad about that," Andomache said, raising her eyebrows, unimpressed. "You owe me a thousand times over for that one."

Hector put his forehead to hers, eyes closed. "Then I guess I'm yours."

"Good," Andromache whispered. And then she kissed him.

He forgot about his English exam until his phone alarm went off the next morning, and he woke up next to a sparsely clothed Andromache, on the damp grass by the exit of the football stadium. She was wearing his sweater. And that was it. He gently shook her awake, unsure of how she would react. Luckily, she ended up laughing into his shoulder.

As they pulled on their soaking, rumpled clothes, Andromache shook her head. "Fine. I like your early alarm." The sun was barely rising. "Security would *definitely* have caught us if it wasn't for that stupid thing."

Hector laughed, handing her his sweater again as they walked back across the lawn.

❦

The bus ride back the night before had been miserable. Even though Agamemnon hadn't been there, and even though they'd won the game, Athena had ripped into them for a good hour. She'd been on about the flawed plays, but she never criticized Odysseus, because apparently he could do no wrong in the coach's eyes. Patroclus fell asleep, leaning against the window, and Achilles was suddenly horribly mad at himself for being afraid of what people would think. He needed to run, or play guitar, or *something*.

But now, light streamed through the white curtains in their dorm. Patroclus was still asleep, facing away from Achilles. The second bed in the room had just... become storage for Achilles' guitar, assignments that hadn't been done, and overdue library books, seeing as no one ever used it. When the monitors checked the rooms every night, Achilles just sat on the mess bed, or hid in the bathroom. They had figured this out a long time ago.

Achilles scooted over, hiding his face in the back of Patroclus' neck. The other boy exhaled sleepily. That's when the knock at the door came. Achilles sat up so fast that he almost knocked Patroclus to the floor. He wasn't quite sure what to do. All he could hear was his own heartbeat.

"Achilles?" someone whispered, so softly that he wasn't sure if he was imagining it. "It's Briseis. And Iphis."

He frowned, getting out of the bed, nearly tripping on his football bag, which he'd been too tired to deal with last night. When he cracked open the door, it was indeed Briseis and Iphis, standing anxiously in the hall. They slipped inside and Achilles shut the door behind them.

"How did you get in here?" he whispered incredulously, glancing over to see if Patroclus was still asleep.

"Well—"

"Shh," Achilles cut Iphis off. "Be quiet, you oaf. He's asleep."

"*Sorry,*" she replied with a roll of her eyes, sitting down on the mess bed.

Briseis kept standing by the door, her arms crossed. She looked worried.

"So what's wrong with you guys?" Achilles asked, locking the door. It wasn't a real lock. It was just a bunch of string, tied around the door handle and attached to a hook on the wall where a painting usually hung.

"Well we heard you won," Iphis said softly. "So good job. Is he okay?" she asked, her voice a little kinder than usual as she gestured towards Patroclus.

Achilles was still confused about why they were there, but he nodded. "Just tired. Had to fix like six people last night. Because Machaon was playing the game."

"That's not fair," Briseis whispered, staring at the window. "Maybe I could come and help."

"I don't know if they'd let you," Achilles said with a shrug. "But you could try."

Patroclus rolled over and everyone froze, falling silent. (Except for some idiot, running down the hallway and yelling something to a friend.) Patroclus opened his eyes, confused for a moment before bolting up.

"What the—"

"Shshsh," Achilles whispered frantically, waving outstretched hands.

The duvet cover rustled as Patroclus fell onto his back again, throwing an arm over his eyes. "Sorry," he whispered. "I'm not going back to sleep. Just. Headrush."

"Um anyways," Iphis whispered as Achilles sat across from her, beside Patroclus' legs. "We were out... um. Drawing..."

"Walking," Briseis said at the same time, with a curt nod.

"You were drawing walking?" Patroclus asked, a smile in his voice.

"*Yeah*," Iphis said aggressively. "It was an *art* assignment."

Briseis pinched the bridge of her nose. "Aaaanyways. We saw Agamemnon, right? And he's *just* pulling in to the student parking lot, this ugly smug expression on—"

"I think you've just described *all* his expressions, Bri," Achilles said.

Iphis smothered a laugh by bending over and shoving her face into her hands. Briseis rubbed her eyes.

"You really shouldn't talk about him like that, Achilles," Patroclus said, sitting up. "Yeah he fucking sucks, but still. Wait until the season is over to talk trash about him."

More people ran down the hall outside the dorm, making everyone hold their breath again. There were very serious consequences for having girls in a guys dorm and vice versa. Unless the doors were open, and it was outside of curfew. They were breaking both these rules, seeing as it was six fifty in the morning, and well. The door was closed. Not that anything was going to happen. But proving that to the dean would be a fun experience. Achilles didn't want anyone to have to do that.

"Okay," Briseis said, stepping further into the room and sitting down on the floor next to Iphis' feet. "No, we were just walking by the parking lot. And he waves us over. Iphis says that we should go just in case he challenges us to a fistfight, then we could beat him up—"

"Ah yes, good reasoning, girlfriend of mine," Patroclus said with scathing sarcasm.

Iphis flipped him off.

"Will you *listen* to me, *please?*" Briseis asked, exasperated.

"Yes." Achilles nodded once, leaning forward to give her his full attention.

"Thank you," she said. She actually sounded worried. "The reason we went over isn't important, but we *did* and he's now dating a fifteen year old." She used air quotes when she said dating.

"*Who?*" Patroclus asked, dismayed as he swung his legs over the edge of the bed.

"The sleaze wouldn't say," Iphis growled. "If she goes here, I'm going to have to... talk some sense into her." She paused. "Guys, did you notice how I didn't say *beat* some sense into her?"

Briseis reached up and patted her knee. "Yes, I'm very proud of you. Now. Is there anything we can do?"

Achilles ran his hands over his head, looking at the floor between his knees. There were all kinds of rumors about Agamemnon, including the most recent, where he blamed his younger sister for his drug dealing. Achilles had no doubts that most of the rumors were true, but it was absolutely pointless to brag about sleeping with someone. The thought... made Achilles feel a bit unwell. Patroclus put a hand on his lower back, anchoring him to the moment.

"Well," Achilles said, breathing deeply. "I guess we... I guess *I* could find out who it is. I'll just eat with them today."

"I'm coming," Patroclus said, walking his fingers up Achilles' spinal cord.

Achilles didn't argue.

"Okay," Briseis said anxiously. "Isn't that... illegal though? The age gap...?"

Iphis was now scratching the library sticker off of a book. No one said anything about it.

Without looking up, she replied to Briseis' question with no emotion. "Not if they've both consented. And we can't really... know that until we know who it is. And also... we wouldn't want to press her either, so whatever she says, we don't pry. If we even *know* her, that is. I don't think Agamemnon would be bragging so much if she went to the school, because *who in the Gods names would date Agamemnon Atrides.* He's already hooked up with every willing eligible bachelorette in the school. I'll bet she's from Ilium."

Patroclus sighed. "This is going to be a long day."

"*We've* been up since five thirty!" Iphis replied.

Briseis raised an eyebrow up at the other girl. "And whose choice was that?"

"What is going *on* between you two?" Achilles asked, looking up from the floor.

"Well we'd better get going," Iphis said, her cheeks flushing slightly as she got to her feet. "Seeing as we're not supposed to even be up here."

Briseis shrugged. "Out the window?"

Iphis already had it open and was surveying the drop. "Uh. Yeah it should be fine."

"Guys?" Patroclus asked. "You gonna ignore us?"

"I already do, most of the time," Iphis said without a backward glance.

"Good point," Achilles replied, getting to his feet. "But next time I see the art teacher, I'll ask about drawing walking. Best of luck getting out."

He walked into their bathroom and locked the door, ignoring their protests and grinning as Patroclus laughed. After brushing his teeth, Achilles listened. It seemed like the girls were gone, so he stepped out. Patroclus was by the window, pulling up a giant climbing rope that was tied to the leg of one of the two desks in the room. Of course, those didn't really get used either. Patroclus preferred studying in the library and chairs annoyed both of them. The desks were used as seats more often than productive work spaces.

"Where did you get *that*?" Achilles asked as Patroclus stowed the rope under the desk.

The dark haired boy looked up and shrugged. "People just give me things."

"Like fifteen meters of good quality climbing rope? Patroclus, do you realize how much we could have done with this?"

Patroclus raised his eyebrows skeptically. "That was a mildly concerning sentence."

Achilles covered his mouth with both hands, feeling his ears flush. "No not like that. I meant like. Um. Sneaking people in and out—"

"Because we need to do that *all* the time—"

"Or like, tying it to the ceiling—"

"Okay, yeah we need to do that even less than the first one—"

"Or rope jewelry!"

"Would you be the one wearing that, or would I have to?"

"No, I wouldn't wear that and I wouldn't make you wear it either," Achilles said, shaking his head. "I'm just saying there's plenty uses for rope other than what your *dirty mind* leapt to."

Patroclus shrugged. "Fine. Do as you please. What's mine is yours, including that rope. As long as you don't... cut it up to make rope jewelry."

"I solemnly swear that I will not use your rope to make rope jewelry."

"I... don't know if I believe you, but that's fine."

Achilles didn't even know what rope jewelry was. He had come up with it on the spot, in a stroke of questionable genius. And a stroke of avoiding a conversation about... being tied up. With Patroclus' mystery climbing rope.

Somehow, this semester Achilles had ended up in almost all the same classes as Patroclus, which was great because then he could help Achilles understand things. (Except for math. They weren't in the same math class, and Patroclus *hated* math with a burning passion.) Achilles had also opted out of sports med, but both those classes were in the afternoon. And they had Sports Performance in between those two classes. In the morning, their schedules matched. In all honesty, Achilles had two classes he was actually interested in, then chose all the classes Patroclus had. So he really did know how they'd ended up with most of the same courses.

Today, Patroclus fell asleep in World History, so Achilles took notes. He had never been more grateful that Agamemnon was a grade ahead of him. That meant no classes with that... that... *guy*.

Their teacher was talking about the American Revolution, and how it was caused by the British. Achilles glanced out the hall to see Agamemnon sauntering past. He almost chased after him to find out about this poor girl, but he decided against it. He gritted his teeth and kept writing. The teacher ended up assigning a bunch of questions from the textbook, due tomorrow. So they'd be in the library after practice. They'd probably eat in there with Iphis and Bri. Achilles reminded himself that he needed to talk to the art teacher about this so called '*drawing walking assignment*,' as they made their way to L.A.

The rest of the morning was like every other morning. Sometimes Achilles felt like he was living the same day over and over and over. That's what school was. Sort of a prison. A way to keep people busy from a young age to an age where they were supposedly more responsible. (Agamemnon being a prime example that this was *not* the case.)

When the lunch bell rang, they had one essay due on Friday, the History questions, and a whole coding thing that Achilles didn't understand at all. But that wasn't important right now. He grabbed Patroclus' arm and wove through the crowd. Their Computer Science classroom was on the opposite side of the school from the cafeteria, so Achilles felt like he had run half a mile by the time they made it. He let go of Patroclus with a quick apology. Patroclus just shrugged, with a little smile. It took Achilles approximately three seconds to locate Agamemnon and his crew. Partly because of Ajax 1. He towered above most people, even when he was slouched over.

Achilles rolled his eyes when he saw Agamemnon nudging Menelaus playfully. His younger brother was looking at an empty table on the other side of the cafeteria with such intense longing that it made Achilles feel sorry for him.

"Let us go forth," Patroclus said in a weird accent, gallantly taking the lead as he wove through the tables and chairs.

Jogging to catch up, Achilles slowed when he fell in step beside Patroclus. "Let me talk."

"You would anyways," Patroclus said. Achilles thought he was serious for a hot second, but then he caught the smile.

He bumped into Patroclus' shoulder. "Wow. Thanks for that."

"I *do* have a girlfriend," Odysseus was saying as they neared the table.

Ajax 1 laughed so hard that Gatorade shot out his nose. He started coughing. Ajax 2 pounded his back, though it would probably hurt the smaller boy more than it would help. Patroclus chuckled under his breath.

"Okay," Diomedes said, leaning over and pointing at Odysseus with a fry. "So what's her name?"

"You idiot! You all *met* her! Remember Penelope? She goes to the public high school!"

Achilles paused, enjoying the fact that Odysseus was being challenged.

"Oh yeah," Agamemnon said. "Totally. She just goes to *public school*. What's her school even called?"

And suddenly the fact that it was Agamemnon picking on Odysseus made it unfair. Agamemnon got to pick on *everyone*. Achilles grabbed an empty chair and sat himself with the captain's lunch group. Patroclus following suit, taking a chair from a different table.

"Hey besties," Achilles said, interrupting their conversation. "How's it going?"

Agamemnon narrowed his eyes, but no one else seemed bothered by Achilles' unexpected interjection. Except maybe Odysseus, who frowned.

"It's certainly going," Ajax 1 said through a cough. He was still laughing.

"I mean, that's good," Achilles said, leaning back and turning to Agamemnon. "So who's your new... woman?"

Agamemnon remained surprisingly calm, as if he had been expecting Achilles to drop a literal bomb. "Some girl from Ilium. Perky little cheerleader. Chryseis, her name is."

Patroclus cringed.

"How's it going with you, Achilles?" Agamemnon asked, taking a sip from his annoying squirty waterbottle. "Heard Athena was mad at you last night."

Achilles shrugged. "Said I shouldn't have held myself back. Nothing I can't fix."

Agamemnon didn't seem to like this answer. Diomedes grabbed the captain's empty red tray and left the table.

"How about you, Patty Cakes?" Agamemnon asked. "How's it feel being the single medic?"

Achilles could practically hear Patroclus' jaw clenching. Agamemnon using a name like that was... wrong. Patroclus hated it.

"It's good," Patroclus said with a dull smile. "Nice learning experience."

Odysseus opened his mouth to say something, but Achilles stood up. He wasn't ready for more Odysseus trauma yet.

"Anyways," Achilles said to the football guys. "Good game. See you at practice."

Menelaus nodded, though he seemed disappointed that they were leaving. Ajax 1 gave a thumbs up and Ajax 2 said, "Long live Achilles!"

"Thanks, Pelides," Agamemnon said, apparently not in the mood for a proper comeback.

Patroclus dragged his chair back to the table it had come from, a storm cloud practically thundering over his head. The metal leg scraped against the floor, making Achilles wince. He squinted across the cafeteria to find Bri, Iphis, Antilochus, Automedon, Nestor, and Phoenix at their usual table. When Patroclus looked back, Achilles pointed at the other table with his thumb. Patroclus nodded, going between a table full of cheerleaders and Diomedes' empty chair, Menelaus' chair, and finally Agamemnon's chair. Patroclus tripped right over the legs of that one, falling onto his knees. Achilles could practically feel the annoyance rolling off the usually peaceful boy. When he got to his feet, he turned to face Achilles, his knees covered in some kind of sauce.

Achilles didn't really think when he grabbed the side of Agamemnon's chair and proceeded to dump the idiot onto the floor.

"What the *fuck*, Pelides!" Agamemnon roared from his new seat on the ground. "This isn't fucking preschool!"

Achilles covered his mouth, walking around the team captain. "I'm *so* sorry Agamemnon! I didn't see where I was going!"

"I'm not believing that for one Godsdamn second, you fucking *child!*" Agamemnon roared, getting to his feet.

Shockingly enough, Agamemnon didn't come after him. He just righted his chair, sat down heavily, and growled something under his breath. Patroclus grabbed Achilles' arm and dragged him away from the table.

"Achilles, I appreciate the protectiveness, but you didn't really need to annihilate the chair, for Gods' sakes."

"Sorry," Achilles muttered. "I just..." hate to see you hurting. He didn't finish the sentence out loud.

"No, I literally could kiss you right now," Patroclus whispered as they reached their table. "You made my week, dear."

Achilles smiled, sitting down next to a disapproving Bri.

Iphis gave him a thumbs up. "Best thing I've seen all day," she said with an encouraging nod. "Violence solves problems."

Briseis glowered at her. People from the tables around them were staring at Achilles, like he had just... well. Flipped the football captain out of his chair. He didn't mind.

"The girl he's with goes to Ilium," Patroclus said, sounding defeated. "So there's not much we can do, really."

Briseis must've filled in the other boys, because they all shook their heads.

"That *creep*," Phoenix said, picking something out of his teeth and looking over at Agamemnon's table.

"We could... assassinate him," Iphis whispered, wiggling her fingers around like she was spreading pixie dust.

"Violence is *not* a reasonable option, Iphis, my imbecile," Briseis said, hiding her face in her hands. "*How* is that manchild the team captain?"

Achilles smacked the slightly sticky table with both hands, barely avoiding Automedon's yogurt cup. "That's what I've been asking every day of my life!"

# IX

WHATEVER BRISEIS HAD EXPECTED Texas to be like... was very incorrect. She honestly wasn't sure why her perceptions were so wrong. She was still worried about Agamemnon's girlfriend, even if she couldn't really do anything about it. Iphis told her that she should try to put it out of her mind. It took a couple days, but by the weekend, she was less upset about it.

Achilles and Patroclus went to Peleus' house. Iphis turned down the invitation. Briseis had been a little upset about that, but Iphis made up for it. They spent the weekend running around the mostly empty school, exploring the hidden nooks and crannies. Iphis showed Briseis the tunnels under the old brick building. She said it was because of the war, but she thought it was funny, because America didn't get bombed. Their laughter echoed through the dimly lit brick passageways as they wandered. They got lost down there, but luckily, Iphis had cargo pants stuffed full of snacks. Briseis had previously noticed that Iphis never wore skirts when they weren't required to be in uniform. When she asked about it, Iphis shrugged, offering a package of fruit gummies to Briseis instead of answering.

There was no cell service under the school, and after about four hours down there, the two of them sat down. Briseis felt like she was on top of the world, rather than hopelessly lost in a series of ancient tunnels.

"Are we going to talk about our walking drawing?" Iphis asked after a moment in the dead, dusty silence.

Briseis swallowed, her ears burning.

"Because if you don't want to... acknowledge it, that's fine with me," Iphis continued, closing her eyes and resting her head against the wall.

One thing Briseis would never understand was Iphis' ability to seem so calm. She was always making jokes, but nothing ever seemed to fluster her. Briseis was quite the opposite.

"Achilles is genuinely going to ask our teacher if it's an assignment," Iphis laughed, her composure cracking ever so slightly. "So just a heads up on that."

Briseis had never seen Iphis smile like that. It was the tiny, embarrassed child of a blush and a grin.

"I bet it *is* an assignment," Briseis said, hyper aware of how close to Iphis she was sitting. "In some class."

Iphis opened her eyes, letting her head fall towards Briseis. "We're going to die down here anyways, so, my conscience doesn't matter. I like you. I know you're *technically* not supposed to be in a relationship because of the um... exchange program so we could just be casual, if y'know what I mean." She wiggled her eyebrows.

Briseis rolled her eyes, wiping her dusty palm on her green pleated skirt. (Not the school uniform. Imagine wearing that on a weekend.) She shifted, so she was sitting cross legged, facing Iphis.

"Wow, you know how to sit in a skirt," Iphis said sarcastically.

"There's something called shorts," Briseis replied, yanking the sleeves of her hoodie over her hands. "It's kind of cold down here."

And before she could stop herself, she leaned forwards, stopping an inch away from Iphis' face. "Can I?"

Iphis kissed her by way of reply. It was the second time they kissed. The first time had been while they were out. Early that morning, walking. They were tired, but it was so nice out, and they went walking and just kind of... started making out against a wall. For a long time. (That was *before* they came across Agamemnon.) This time was different. It was faster and their mouths were confident and hot and oh... Briseis had no regrets—until Iphis threaded her fingers through Briseis' hair.

"Hey!" Briseis yelped, leaping away. "You have *no* idea how much effort I put into that *stupid* bun!"

Iphis burst out laughing, her head thrown back with wild abandon. Briseis couldn't help joining in. They laughed until neither of them could breathe properly. Wiping tears off her face, Briseis made eye contact with Iphis, who was holding her stomach and groaning as she tried to get the giggling under control.

"Yeah, Iphis, I like you too," she said, sitting in the middle of the tunnel, facing the short haired girl.

"Ah that's good," Iphis said, grinning. "Otherwise... it may have been very awkward trying to find our way out of here."

Both of their phones were dead by the time they emerged from the underground maze, through a loose manhole cover about three miles away from the school, in the middle of a residential street. It was almost dark when they made it back to Mycenae Academy. Briseis felt like it had been ten minutes, instead of eight hours. *Time is weird when you're with someone who makes you feel alive,* Briseis thought as they raided a snack cupboard in the girls' dorm.

Achilles and Patroclus found them in the library on Sunday afternoon.

"Aha!" Achilles shouted, leaping around one of the bookshelves.

Both Iphis and Briseis jumped. Briseis gasped against her will, her Women's Studies book falling off her lap. They had found a little corner of the library with beanbag chairs, and they had both been quite comfortable until Achilles had intruded. (Even though, Iphis had been whining about a math problem Briseis' had told her to solve herself.) Patroclus appeared beside Achilles, shaking his head.

"I've been informed," Achilles said, strolling down the aisle towards them, his hands clasped behind his back, "That drawing walking... is actually an assignment."

"Hah!" Iphis exclaimed, pointing at him gleefully.

"*But!*" Achilles said, holding up a hand to stop her. "I have discovered that it's an assignment in AP Art 30. I *know* that neither of you are in that class."

Patroclus sighed as he inspected the books at the end of the aisle. "I tried to tell him it wasn't important," he muttered, pulling out a volume that Briseis was sure she wouldn't even be able to lift. "But he insisted."

"I'm curious," Achilles said defensively, rounding on Patroclus.

"Mm," he said, not looking up. "Alrighty then."

A duck noise interrupted the conversation.

Iphis growled, dramatically leaning over the back of her bean-bag. "*Why* are you so attached to the duck ringtone?" she whined.

Achilles flashed her a brilliant smile. His eyes darted over to Briseis, who just shook her head.

"Because it's your favourite, of course," Achilles said, pulling out his phone. His expression turned stormy. "Um—"

"What?" Patroclus asked, tucking his giant book under his arm and walking over to Achilles.

On weekends, the library was empty, so Briseis could nearly hear the dust in the air as both boys fell silent. Patroclus read over Achilles' shoulder and ran his thumb across his bottom lip, his brow furrowed.

"Apparently dearest Agamemnon brought his little girlfriend into town this weekend," Achilles said. "Menelaus just told me."

"There's nothing we can do, guys," Iphis said softly, pulling a granola bar out of one of her many pockets.

On Monday, Agamemnon wasn't at school. Ajax 1 and 2 confirmed when Achilles asked. He was late to practice, grinning stupidly. On Tuesday, Diomedes accidentally set fire to his science lab, so the whole school spent the afternoon outside. Briseis found Patroclus and Iphis together with textbooks out. Achilles was with Menelaus, who later informed them that Agamemnon had left to get his girlfriend. On Wednesday, Patroclus failed a math test, which diverted Achilles' attentions away from Agamemnon. Briseis offered to help Patroclus for the exam, which he readily accepted. Iphis and Achilles spent a long time talking about an L.A. assignment instead of letting Briseis help them with math, which pissed her off a little, seeing as they both had the same test tomorrow. On Thursday… well. Shit hit the fan on Thursday.

Late Wednesday night, Agamemnon and Crissy stumbled into her father's house, an hour and a half away from Mycenae Academy. Agamemnon hadn't slept for most of the week, because he'd either been picking up his girlfriend after school, or driving to meet her. Crissy had texted him during fourth period. *My dad isn't home tonight.* That's why they were here.

"C'mon," she whispered, chucking her shoes onto the orderly rows in the closet.

Her house was huge. That kind of old modern house with beige stucco that Agamemnon always thought belonged in California.

She lived with her father, who seemed to be absent from most of her life. But Agamemnon didn't pry about personal details.

Crissy dragged him up the tan carpeted stairs. They had made out on the first landing on Monday, both skipping class. Later, she had laughed about the carpet burns on her back, making a joke about how glad she was that the school uniform covered so much skin as she pushed Agamemnon out the door, because her father was coming home. They had driven past him on the way back to Ilium, and Crissy had ducked down, giggling. This was all a big game to her. Agamemnon agreed. Dating was all a big game. It didn't mean anything.

Once they had made it to the top of the stairs, Crissy pulled him into her room. He shut the door behind him. He had never really paid attention to what the room looked like. It was pretty big, and it had its own bathroom, but that was the extent of his knowledge. Crissy yanked on his arm and they fumbled their way through the dark, falling onto the bed. That was another thing he knew. The bed was soft. They started kissing, her hands in his hair, her legs around his waist. His mouth on her neck, hands up her shirt—

And the lights turned on.

Chryses had been waiting in the basement of his own house. It was around twelve thirty in the morning. He had told his daughter that he wouldn't be home tonight. And it was just as he suspected. When he turned on the light in Chryseis' room, there was a man... boy... something in between. He *hoped.* This man (who was younger than he looked, Chryses prayed) was on top of his daughter.

It took a long moment for this to sink in. Chryses couldn't manage much thought. Just anger.

"*Out!*" he roared.

The man/boy leapt to his feet and ran out of the room. Chryses wished he would fall face first down the stairs. When the front door slammed shut, Chryses turned to his daughter, who was laying on her bed, one hand clamped over her mouth, the beginning of a hickey blooming on her neck. She was *fifteen.* He wasn't supposed to have to do this for another year, at least. He stood there, feeling like he had failed. Why wasn't he a bigger part of her life? Why hadn't he remarried? Why hadn't he asked how she was *doing*?

"Who is he?" Chryses asked, sounding like someone was pressing down on his windpipe, strangling him.

Chryseis started crying, curled up on her side. The bed dwarfed her, making her seem tiny. She was so *young*.

"Chryseis, who is he?"

"He goes to Mycenae," she choked out. "I'm sorry. Sorry. I... fuck. He's their team captain."

This was his little girl. He had made her like this. He hated himself, and he hated that boy. He had half a mind to pull out his shotgun and chase him down. Crissy buried her face in a giant stuffed dog. She still had that dog. Her mother had given it to her. *Gods.* She still had stuffed animals on her bed. Chryses didn't know what to do.

"Dad... I really like him," she wailed into the dog. "Please don't..."

He stepped out of the room, closing the door behind him. Chryses didn't understand his daughter. He didn't want to hurt her, but this couldn't continue. He put a hand on his forehead, staring at a family portrait hanging on the wall. Crissy was tiny in the picture. The three of them looked so happy, the sun shining over their heads. It may have been the last time Chryses actually felt joy. His wife had died a month and a half later.

The hallway was dark, a sliver light leaking out from under Crissy's door the brightest thing in the house. He sighed, slowly making his way down the stairs. He felt too old to understand, and too young for anything to make sense. That thought made him laugh under his breath. The paradox of being human. The idea came to him as he stood in the kitchen, unsure of how he got there. He was swaying, dancing with the ghosts of his past. It was the perfect idea, where Crissy would come to him for comfort, and this boy would no longer be a problem.

On Thursday morning, Chryses drove his daughter back to Ilium Academy. She didn't say anything. He didn't try to make her. This was their relationship in a nutshell, he thought sadly. It was his fault they were this way. When she got out of the car, he waited until she walked inside, then turned the car around. The hour to Mycenae Academy was a haunted, lonely hour, full of contradictions. *Should I? Should I not? Is there a better way to fix this?* He nearly turned back after half an hour, but then decided that he had come too far to stop.

Mycenae Academy was on the on the outskirts of a little town. It was just like Ilium that way. A little town full of retired people, rich people, and people who didn't like big cities. This school was just as imposing as Ilium, though it was wider and shorter. Chryses didn't quite understand why the private high schools had to look like knockoff ivy league universities, but that didn't even cross his mind today. He hadn't slept all night and he just wanted this to be over with already.

Chryses parked in the visitor lot and stepped out into the dry air. It was hot, and he was wearing a sweater with slacks. Too many clothes. Students were scattered across the lawn, lounging with their blazers and sweaters discarded on the lush grass. He figured, as he walked towards the doors, that most high schools were nearly the same, regardless of the student body's wealth. Teenagers would be teenagers. These private schools had all the problems that public schools had. They just did a better job of hiding it. Most of the time.

None of the students even acknowledged him as he climbed the front steps, pulled open the door, and followed the signs to the cafeteria. People were *everywhere*, sitting in groups on the floors, chatting in classrooms, wandering about on their phones... he had to jump over several legs to get where he was going. Chryses wasn't prepared for the sheer chaos of the cafeteria. He had to stop in the doorway to collect his bearings.

*Gods.* He was too old to be here. Students were laughing, talking at the top of their lungs. There was a group of kids all sitting on the table, instead of at it. Someone ran past him, holding a phone over his head. He apologized, stepping out of the way, only to be shouldered by the person in pursuit of whoever had the phone.

It took him a long five minutes to find the boy (thankfully) who he was looking for. Chryses wiped sweat from his hands and strode across the cafeteria, trying to ignore the fact that he had stepped in something mushy.

"Hey, you a teacher here?" one of the boys asked as he approached their table.

Chryses shook his head. He was now realizing that he didn't even know the black haired boy's name.

"Which one of you is the team captain?" he asked, feeling ridiculous.

"Agamemnon," said same, thin boy who had asked about him being a teacher.

"Me." The one who said it had been at Chryses house the night before. "Oh. What do you want?"

So *Agamemnon* recognized him then. Chryses squinted at the boy, who had his jaw set. "Are you dating my daughter?"

The boy raised an eyebrow. "Yeah. So what?"

"You're *much* too old for her."

Chryses hadn't planned what he was going to say. This whole plan was terrible, seeing as it was less than half of a suitable course of action.

"I'll do whatever I want, old man," Agamemnon growled, his lip curling.

The boy across the table from Agamemnon, who had red hair, chewed on his lip anxiously. Agamemnon didn't even notice when the boy got up and left.

"Agamemnon, I'm prepared to make you an offer," Chryses said under his breath, as quietly as he dared, lest his voice be absorbed into the noise. "Ten thousand dollars to break up with my daughter."

Everyone at the table fell silent, eyeing Chryses suspiciously.

Agamemnon snorted. "What if I say no?"

"Fifteen thousand," Chryses replied. He *needed* this to happen and he was willing to pay however much it took.

"Hmm," Agamemnon said, pretending to think as he tapped his chin mockingly. "But what if... I *love* your daughter? What if it crushes her heart?"

Chryses ground his teeth together.

"Agamemnon," the boy next to him hissed. "Just take the money and be done with it. There are other girls."

Agamemnon ignored him, getting to his feet. He was taller than Chryses, and definitely stronger.

"What if," the boy said, grinning, "I married your daughter? What if I took her with me, to Russia, or Japan, or somewhere she wouldn't have contact with *you*? What if we ran away and never. Came. Back."

"Fifty thousand," Chryseis offered desperately.

"Agamemnon!" someone yelled from the other side of the table.

Chryses looked over to see the red haired boy from before trailing behind a boy with long blonde hair, tied in a loose ponytail. He was the one who yelled. Agamemnon gritted his teeth as he turned to see the other boy.

"Achilles," he snarled, "This is none of your fucking business."

"This is ridiculous!" Achilles said, glaring around the table. "Are you all *idiots*?"

"I told him not to," one guy grumbled.

Achilles rolled his eyes, about to say something. He stopped himself, turning back to Agamemnon. "Why do you have *no* common sense? This man obviously knows that you're bad for his daughter, so just do what he asks! For fucks sake, he's even offering you *money*!"

Chryses glanced back and forth between the two boys, praying to whomever might be listening, that this would work.

Agamemnon turned to face Chryses again, his expression like a mask of stone. "Sorry, old man. Your daughter is mine and if you try and fuck up our relationship again, well, no one will care, will they, because you're just a meddling son–of–a–bitch."

He sat back down. Chryses stopped breathing for a second.

"Oh, and one more thing," Agamemnon said, looking over his shoulder. "Your daughter fucks like an animal."

Chryses didn't even absorb anything the boy said until much later. He didn't remember leaving the school. He didn't remember getting in his car. He didn't remember clenching his jaw so hard that it locked. When the town gave way to open fields, the red he was seeing cleared ever so slightly. The anger turned to purpose. He *hated* that boy. This was worse than he thought. It couldn't go on, even if it meant killing his daughter's happiness. She would thank him later, when she realized that this was a disgusting relationship bound for failure.

His knuckles were white on the leather steering wheel. A herd of cows grazed next to the road. Chryses had a friend who owned a big farming corporation. Started it from fifty cattle. Now it was practically an empire. *Apollo*. He coached Ilium's football team because he had nothing better to do. Apollo was a crafty, spiteful, and overly proud. If anyone would have a solution for Chryses little... problem, it would be this man.

X

A POLLO'S HOUSE WAS ABOUT twenty minutes away from Ilium Academy. Chryses filled up his tank when he got into town, avoided a conversation with an acquaintance whilst filling his tank with gas, and nearly spilled gas all over his shoes. Luckily that was avoided, just like the conversation he didn't want to have. He drove a BMW that was subtle but classy which, at the moment, was covered in dust from his impromptu road trip. Chryses debated washing the car, but decided against it, because time was precious, and he couldn't stand his daughter being associated with that bastard one moment longer. He was still seething under the surface. Who raised that boy? Chryses wanted to have strong words with them.

He peeled away from the gas station, leaving his acquaintance in a spray of dirt and gravel. He knew he'd have to apologize to the man, but that was a problem for tomorrow Chryses. Apollo's home was down a long, meandering road lined with trees that were unnatural to their prairie town. The leaves trembled in the hot breeze, a few shrivelled ones flying off their branches. That's why the trees weren't natural. They would pretty much die of dehydration or heat. But knowing Apollo, he probably had an irrigation system or something, seeing as most of the leaves were still green.

The lane wasn't paved, and Chryses cringed as the dust billowed up behind him. At least he hadn't washed the car. A herd of cows grazed in the distance as he pulled up to the refurbished farm house. It was a family property that Apollo had... fixed. (Meaning that he had completely changed it to suit his tastes.) Chryses stopped in the driveway and stepped out of his car. The damp heat hit him like full grown bull. He laughed a little, pushing his hair back. The long night was catching up to him in a wave of delirium. The house, now that he looked, wasn't the monstrosity he remembered. It was probably only two stories tall, though a sprawling mass of wood and brick buildings stretched grandly into the trees.

Chryses shook his head, locking his car and making his way across the stone walkway, up to the door. Bronze statues of animals that were placed artfully across the lawn glinted dully in the hazy light. *We're back in a hot spell,* Chryses thought. The air felt thick in his nostrils. He was about to press on the technologically advanced white doorbell, when the door swung open.

"Ah!" Apollo drawled with a smile, like he had been expecting an exhausted, infuriated Chryses. Maybe he had. There were rumors he was psychic. Chryses wasn't sure he believed that. "Welcome, my honored friend!"

"Greetings Apollo," Chryses replied, trying not to sound too gruff. "I seem to have an... issue that requires guidance."

Though the long haired man in front of him was far younger than he, Chryses trusted him. Apollo was nothing short of brilliant, and at Chryses' request, he smiled even wider. He loved being asked for help, *if* it was sensible.

"Please," Apollo said, stepping aside. "Come in."

Several minutes later, Chryses and Apollo sat at a rustic wood table in the kitchen, cold tea in hand. The air conditioning was on, and the floor felt cool to the touch. A relief from the aggressive heat outside. Chryses had removed his sweater in the car, and has still been uncomfortable in a T–shirt. But that was the price of living here. So be it.

"What seems to be the cause of your anguish?" Apollo asked, his southern accent disagreeing with the formality of his word. He plunked a reusable, glowing ice cube shaped like a sun into his glass.

Chryses stared down into the amber tea, swirling it around. "My daughter—"

"She's the cheerleader, right?" Apollo interrupted, resting his elbows on the table and leaning forwards. "Crissy?"

"Yes, that's her," he replied, taking a sip of his tea. It was hibiscus mint. Chryses couldn't say he'd ever tried it before. "Anyways. My lovely daughter..." *apparently... does things like an animal.* "Well. She seems to be in a relationship with the captain of Mycenae's team."

Apollo made a face of barely restrained disgust. "Ah."

"And today, I discovered that he's worse than I thought," Chryses continued, feeling the anger crawling up inside him. He took a deep breath. "I was simply wondering if you could help me free my daughter from such a dangerous situation."

The refrigerator turned on, making a loud whirring noise. Apollo drummed his fingers against the table, squinting into space for a long moment.

"You know I respect you," the man across from Chryses started, still staring at the air. "But I have to ask one question."

"Go ahead."

"Does your daughter *want* to be with him?" He paused. "Actually, no. Two questions. And what have you done so far to stop this?"

Chryses laughed humorlessly, taking another gulp of tea and wishing it was something stronger. "She wants to be with him. As for the second question... ah, well. You see, I don't want to ruin my relationship with Crissy. So I drove down to Mycenae Academy and offered him a *ridiculous* sum of money to break up with her. He refused, telling me that he would marry her and take her to Japan or some place like that."

Apollo raised an eyebrow. "Who raised this boy? I'd like to have a conversation with them."

"Yes, I thought that too."

"See," Apollo said, leaning back and crossing his arms. His wooden chair creaked. "I was about to suggest what you told me you already did." He sighed with false sorrow. "So this calls for more desperate measures. My friend. Please. Leave it to me. I *will* take care of this."

Chryses chuckled, relieved and a little bit concerned. "Thank you."

Apollo plucked up his tea and offered it to Chryses in a toast. Their sweating glasses clinked merrily in the afternoon light.

"To justice," Apollo said with a small smile. "That boy already had his chance."

The next Tuesday, Apollo let his assistant coaches run the Trojan's practice. That meant Hector would be the one doing everything, but that boy was an excellent player. He had potential. Some University scouts were coming later on in the season to look at him. And that Achilles kid. Apparently he was in high demand as well, even though he was in eleventh grade. Apollo didn't really care about the post secondary prospects for members of Mycenae's team.

He drove his yellow Tesla into town, slightly annoyed with himself that he hadn't gotten his road paved. But if it *had* been paved, it wouldn't have fit the aesthetic. Also, it discouraged people from dropping by, because they didn't want to get their own fancy cars dirty. Except for the brave souls who ventured beyond the threshold. Like Chryses. They had been friends for ages. Before the old man had been married. That must have been fourteen years ago, when his wife died. Apollo felt sorry for him. There was a reason he took lovers but was never in a committed relationship. Gotten hurt too many times. Hurt others too many times. Learned the same lessons too many times.

Love was a game, and games end. You win, or you lose. There's no such thing as a tie in real life. His father had taught him that. Zeus. Who seemed to be constantly cheating on his wife. Apollo and his sister, Artemis, weren't her kids. And neither was Athena. But he didn't have the same mother as Athena. Their family was a mess. Apollo preferred to ignore it, and everyone who was a part of it. Except when Athena took the Godsdamn coaching position opposite him. It was harder to ignore her now.

The Roadster growled down the highway, sending little rocks flying. Apollo frowned in disgust as a bug splatted against the windshield. But he would endure the bugs, because the one thing that was *more* unappealing than bug guts was Agamemnon. Decent Center defence man, but not good enough to warrant the kind of ridiculous pride the boy displayed. Sam Smith blasted through the speakers as Apollo rolled down the windows. He reluctantly slowed, meeting the town's speed limit.

The previous evening, Apollo had discovered that there were a disturbing amount of doughnut shops open just twenty minutes away. Krispy Kreme, Lola's Candy Doughnuts, Durkin' Doughnuts, Shipley's Do–Nots, Doughnuts for a Better World… it seemed obscene. He had ended up choosing one called Cione's Modern Doughnuts. The name seemed kind of familiar, though he wasn't sure why. When he had preordered, he had almost blanched at the cost. How, in the name of everything holy, could deep fried dough cost so *much*? But it didn't actually matter. He would spend five hundred dollars on doughnuts to help a friend. And to spite Athena. Just because he could.

He parked in the loading zone, went inside, was appalled by the amount of neon colours in the shop, got yelled at by an ex lover, (*that* was why he had recognized the name) and picked up the four dozen artisan doughnuts. All in all, not a lovely experience. The doughnuts were shockingly heavy. Apollo placed them in the front seat. He laughed as he sped back to his house, because the last time he had a passenger sit next to him... was someone who had died. The last *two* of his passengers. Daphne, who died mysteriously one night and was buried in a biodegradable sack, and then Hyacinth, who died in a stupid accident. Apollo looked at the doughnuts. They were a sub par replacement for the people he had loved more than anything. But it would be satisfying, what those doughnuts would accomplish. To some extent.

Once Apollo had deposited the doughnuts in his kitchen, he went out to the garden. Another reminder of the loved ones he lost. Daphne had planted the little trees there, by the fence. And Hyacinth had *hated* the hyacinth flowers, so Apollo had planted them everywhere. He couldn't make himself get rid of either. The heat didn't bother Apollo as much as it should have. He wore a T–shirt and jeans, feeling the sun soaking his neck as he gently uprooted some of the purple hyacinth flowers. The plants made him smile, however melancholy he felt.

Back in the kitchen, he detached the bulbs from the stems. He was wearing rubber gloves as he cut them into pieces and dropped them in a pot of boiling water.

Achilles was *not* looking forward to the game. His shop teacher pointed up at the clock, interrupting Achilles in the middle of sawing a piece of wood. Skipping the game wasn't a plausible option, but *man,* did he want to. He sighed, turning off the saw.

"I'll take care of it," his teacher called from his project.

"Thanks," Achilles said, trying to sound excited.

He pulled off his apron and goggles, hanging them on a hook by the door. The problem with playing games at Ilium's fancy stadium was that he had to leave his last class early, and that happened to be one of his favourite classes. He knew he shouldn't complain. Hell, he was one of the football team's star players. People would kill to be in his shoes. The thought didn't comfort him as much as he had anticipated.

He sighed, grabbing his bag and making his way through the empty halls. This game would have the bribed refs. So it would be aggressive. Probably beyond that. Achilles just didn't have the energy. And this weekend would be all homework, because he had been avoiding it. Even *he* could only get so many extensions on projects due three weeks ago.

When he reached the changeroom, he peeked into the sports med area to find Patroclus in there, hunched over his computer, sitting cross legged on an old wooden table that was pushed up against the wall.

"Hi," Achilles said, leaning in the doorframe.

Patroclus glanced up. "Oh. Hello Sunshine. Did I do something, or are you just generally upset at life?"

"Do I really look that mad?" Achilles asked skeptically. "It's been awhile since I got the sarcastic sunshine."

The other boy laughed through his nose, looking back at his computer.

"I really really hope that's my english essay," Achilles joked, walking across the room and sitting on one of the squishy sports med athlete bed things.

"In your dreams," Patroclus muttered, the clicking of his keyboard just louder than the ruckus of the locker room. "Shouldn't you go change or something? Or do you want me to give you crutches so you can pretend you got hurt in gym?"

"Alas, that wouldn't work, because our gym teacher is one of the assistant coaches," Achilles said miserably, hopping off the bed. "See you later then."

"Wait," Patroclus said, still looking at his computer. "C'mere."

"Remember last time I tried to edit one of your essays?" Achilles replied, walking over anyways. "It didn't go well. Because English is nonsense."

There was a moment before Patroclus replied. "Yeah, I'm not asking you to do that again. It was a literal mess."

Achilles stopped in front of Patroclus. "What dost thou need?" he asked.

Patroclus finally looked up, grinning. "Wow. That was atrocious. Can I kiss you?"

"Huh?" Achilles said, certain he was hallucinating.

"Don't make me say that again," Patroclus pleaded. "My heart is... going really fast."

Achilles' was too. He leaned over, pressing his lips to Patroclus'. Sweet and soft. And thrilling. They'd never kissed in public. Not that this was public. But it was close. Achilles stood up, feeling dizzy.

Patroclus smiled sheepishly. "Good luck."

A weird euphoric state carried Achilles into the changeroom, but as soon as he stepped inside, his crushing annoyance reappeared. No one was getting ready. The members of the football team were pretty much just fucking around, slamming each other into lockers, stalking girls on Instagram, yelling, and eating. They had to leave in... Achilles checked his phone. They had to leave in ten minutes. Agamemnon wasn't in here either. Menelaus was, sitting with a textbook on a bench away from the rest of the team. At least he was in his pregame uniform. Achilles wished Patroclus was on the team. It would just be *better*. And Patroclus was good too. He could easily play if he didn't pull out at the last minute. Maybe next year.

Achilles sighed, shoving his way through the team and responding to people calling his name. His locker was filled with his gear bag. He changed quickly, then yanked his duffle out.

Automedon tapped on Achilles' shoulder.

"What?" Achilles asked, barely preventing himself from snapping at the younger boy.

"Do you know where the doughnuts came from?" Automedon said.

Achilles turned around, frowning, more confused than angry now. "Doughnuts?"

At that moment, Agamemnon and his crew burst into the changeroom, yelling their classic, "LET'S GOOOO, BOYS!"

That made the changeroom erupt in some kind of messy fight song, that included people slamming their fists into the lockers to a beat that made Achilles cringe.

"I didn't hear about any doughnuts," Achilles had to yell over the noise.

Automedon shrugged, his eyes calculating. "Okay. Whatever. Maybe someone on the team got them."

"Who ate them?" Achilles asked, slamming his locker door shut.

"Most people," Atutomedon replied, hoisting his bag over his shoulder. "Not Menelaus, Nestor, Phoenix, Automedon, and me. But everyone else, I think. I can't imagine eating before a game." The younger boy shuddered. "Too many nerves."

Achilles ruffled his hair. "I used to be that way too."

Automedon shoved him off with a hint of a smile before leaving the changeroom. When one member of the team left, the rest usually followed, regardless of who it was.

"Hey Pelides," Odysseus called from around a block of lockers. "You know what these boxes are?"

The changeroom was suddenly quiet now, empty except for a few stragglers. Achilles' ears were ringing. As he rounded the corner, he saw Agamemnon at his locker while everyone else was crowded around one of the benches. He shoved his way in between Ajax 2 and Diomedes to see the stack of boxes.

"It looks like doughnuts to me," he said scornfully.

Odysseus rolled his eyes. "Thanks. But where are they from? Athena wouldn't... wait a sec."

He grabbed the receipt off the box on the top of the pile. "What the hell?" Odysseus muttered.

Ajax 1 looked curiously over his shoulder, but Achilles snatched it from Odysseus, causing the other boy to bark out a loud '*Hey.*' He ignored him. On the back of the receipt was a smudged note in cramped handwriting.

*To the Captain.*

*Don't underestimate the people you mess with.*

*Don't threaten people you don't understand.*

*Don't let your tongue run faster than your thoughts.*

*Someone you claim to care for is leaving.*

*She's being saved from a monster.*

*I think you know the monster quite well, actually.*

*Best regards,*

*A.P*

*Oh, and Captain? Never, ever, insult someone's daughter.*

Achilles rounded on Agamemnon, who slammed his locker shut.

"What. The *fuck*. Is this about," Achilles demanded flatly.

"Dunno what you're talking about Pelides," Agamemnon said. "C'mon Menelaus. We've got to win your honor back."

Odysseus and Ajax 1 looked at each other as Agamemnon left the changeroom. Menelaus followed reluctantly. Diomedes snatched the note from Achilles, who didn't even try to hold on.

"Oh *shit*," Diomedes whispered, looking up from the note with wide eyes. "Is this about that old guy who came here? The one Agamemnon..."

"Insulted to extreme lengths?" Odysseus offered, grabbing his bag from his locker. "Yeah. Probably."

Achilles pressed the heels of his hands into his eyes. "Why would he give us *doughnuts*? That's so weird."

Someone came skidding into the locker room, panting.

"What?" Ajax 1 called, reading the note again and shaking his head.

Patroclus practically slid into the row of lockers they were standing by. His eyes were wide, panicked.

Achilles didn't remember running over to him, but he ended up gripping Patroclus' arm. "What?"

"Your team is really fucking stupid," Patroclus said, breathing heavily. "Apparently the Trojan's *coach* gave them those. So no one knows what's going on. Athena's pretty mad. Best get out there. They're about to get on the bus."

# The (Actual) Iliad

Two minutes later:

I

T HE MUSES COULD SING of the rage mounting inside Achilles by the time he made it outside, with Patroclus, Odysseus, Diomedes and the Ajaces in tow. Things had escalated to a full on disaster. Menelaus was sitting on the steps of the school, pale faced and shaking. He was covered in... something.

"What the hell is *happening*?" Achilles demanded, skidding to a halt next to Agamemnon's brother.

Someone was yelling around the corner. More than one person. It barely masked the sounds of retching, which made Achilles start to feel nauseous.

Menelaus' eyes were wide as he pushed his hair back. "Everyone's sick."

Patroclus swallowed audibly before continuing on around the corner.

Achilles ground his teeth together. "Where's that fucking note?" he hissed, looking at Agamemnon's friends.

Diomedes handed it over without complaint. Odysseus was the only one who seemed remotely calm, with his calculating eyes trained on the corner of the school, where everyone would have been getting on the bus. Sirens started wailing in the distance. Achilles scrunched up the note in his fist, entirely by accident as he marched down the stairs.

"You should probably change," Ajax 1 said to Menelaus.

Achilles didn't wait to see if he would agree. His fury mounted with every step, gaining the speed of a tempest pulled by a thousand horses. When he rounded the corner, he stopped short. Nothing could have prepared him for what he saw. Thirty or so members of their team, doubled over on the ground. The people who hadn't eaten the fucking doughnuts were trying their best to help, rolling their teammates onto their sides so they didn't suffocate in the grass or choke the vomit. It was awful. *Beyond* awful. And it was all Agamemnon's fault. Achilles didn't understand why Athena wasn't ripping into their unworthy captain, but then he remembered that she had no idea whose fault it was.

"Agamemnon!" Achilles yelled, storming across the grass, hopping to avoid the chunky puddles. "*Agamemnon!*"

He distantly noticed Patroclus on the phone beside the bus, his school uniform stained. Athena was next to him. They were probably talking to the hospital. Agamemnon stood on the opposite side of the bus, like he was hiding from the mess he'd made. *What a fucking coward,* Achilles seethed, his feet crunching on the parking lot gravel. The team captain looked up from his phone, seemingly shocked that someone had found him. Achilles lunged forwards, grabbing the front of Agamemnon's warmup jersey. Agamemnon shoved him off, sending Achilles stumbling backwards.

"*Why,*" Achilles asked incredulously, "would you keep pushing even after her father offered you *money*?"

Agamemnon had the audacity to snort. Achilles could have punched him right then and there, but he wanted an answer. *Needed* an answer.

"Just because you and your girlfriend have a boring fucking relationship doesn't mean I have to," Agamemnon said.

Achilles almost asked '*What girlfriend?*' but then remembered his little thing with Briseis. He swallowed. Agamemnon stood in the shade of the bus, lurking like he was half made of shadows. Achilles was having a bit of a hard time seeing him as he stood in the glaring sun.

"Agamemnon," Achilles said through his teeth, taking a step forwards. "That's fucking *stupid.* The man didn't want you with his daughter. You don't fuck with old rich parents. They've got resources. And now we're going to have to *forfeit the next game* because of *you.* We're giving the Trojans a lead with no effort on their behalf, all because you stick your *fucking dick where it doesn't belong.* This is *your* Godsdamn war and you've lost it all before we've even got a chance to fight. You *let the entire team down,* and it's your fault they're all vomiting their fucking guts out, because of those *stupid* doughnuts from the Trojan's coach *himself.* Did you *know* that your preppy little plaything's father was friends with *Apollo Phoebus?* Because he Godsdamn is and now you've gotten us into this mess. This is *your fault!*"

The sirens were much closer now, so Achilles didn't hear what Agamemnon said next. The older boy caught onto that, and paused. Achilles wasn't sure how Agamemnon could even think up a response to his accusation so quickly. It made him want to start *screaming,* because then the team captain wouldn't be able to get a word in. Agamemnon stared at Achilles with murder in his eyes as the ambulances pulled up. There were probably fire trucks too. People were barking orders. It was almost louder than the changerooms, and Achilles could see students crowding to the windows, trying to see what the fuss was. Achilles ground his teeth together so hard his jaw popped. He took a step closer to the boy in the shadow of the bus.

"Achilles, you don't understand *any* of this," he growled, his eyes as hard as flint. "You still have a fucking girlfriend. Chryseis was the first one I've actually *liked.*"

In the corner of his vision, Athena and Patroclus came around the bus.

He tried not to laugh at Agamemnon. "So you're letting the entire team suffer for it? That's fucked up! Do you know how *selfish* that is?! You're such an ignorant dick. *Gods.* "

"And you're just a pretentious ass who's annoying as hell!" the older boy snarled. "You would do it for your girlfriend too!"

Achilles almost came out to Agamemnon by accident. He nearly yelled '*Boyfriend, you idiot!*' But he stopped himself with the little self restraint he still had. Unfortunately, it was *all* the self restraint he had. He found himself advancing on Agamemnon, very quickly closing the three feet between them and slamming him into the side of the bus. He was about to break that selfish asshole's nose when someone hauled him away.

"Let. Go of me," he demanded through clenched teeth, watching helplessly as Agamemnon stumbled away from the bus.

"Violence won't solve this," Athena whispered in his ear.

Immediately, Achilles stopped resisting. This was his coach he was talking to. Not someone to fight. Or injure. After a long moment, Athena let go of him. He took a deep breath. The air was full of dust. It was in his mouth too, cracking between his teeth. Agamemnon wiped his nose with the back of his hand, the anger in his eyes more resigned. But it was still burning bright.

"Hey Pat," Agamemnon said, looking away from Achilles.

Athena's grip on Achilles returned as his muscles tightened at the nickname. Why was she letting Agamemnon get *away* with this?

Patroclus raked a hand through his curls. "What?"

"Go find Achilles' girlfriend," Agamemnon said, his voice filled with danger. "I need to talk to her."

Diomedes, Odysseus, Menelaus, and the Ajaces came around the bus as Patroclus started away, looking over his shoulder to raise his eyebrow at Achilles. He wanted to go after him, but Athena's grip on the back of his shirt held him in place.

Agamemnon took a deep breath. "Did someone go with the team to make sure they're okay?"

"Assistant coaches," Odysseus said, wiping his hands on his shorts, seemingly unbothered.

"*You* don't get to ask if they're okay—" Achilles started, fury boiling through him again with renewed vigor.

Agamemnon stepped out of the shade. "One more word from you, Pelides, and you're suspended until *I* decide you're coming back."

Athena didn't even react. Achilles wasn't sure when she had let him go, but he *was* sure that she wouldn't hesitate to grab him again. He had to literally bite his tongue to stop himself from saying anything.

The captain smirked, like he enjoyed smushing Achilles under his heel. He turned away, looking towards his teammates like this was all a nice stroll in the park. "Good. Now, we're going to have to forfeit this game, because we don't even have a full lineup..."

Achilles stopped listening. He sat down on the ground, not caring that it was a gravel parking lot. The sun was hot on his back, making his shirt uncomfortably warm. What did Agamemnon want with Briseis? Fuck. He couldn't believe he had dragged her into this. (*This* being the mess that was the football team.) Achilles couldn't understand why Athena was letting Agamemnon get away with this. Did she *want* them to fail? A giant fly started buzzing around Achilles' head. He snatched it out of the air and threw it towards the cluster of senior football players. *Take* that, *you Oedipus',* he thought as the fly circled back to him. He growled under his breath. Should've just killed the stupid thing in the first place.

"... wants what?" Briseis' voice floated up from around the bus.

"No idea," Patroclus replied softly.

It was much quieter now. Achilles swallowed thickly, wishing Briseis hadn't come. The sick (poisoned) members of the team were gone now, as were all the trucks. For some reason, it seemed worse. The air was dry, making everything sound a bit muffled. Achilles hated loud places, but he also hated quiet places. The middle ground was where he was happiest. So. Not now.

Briseis and Patroclus came around the corner. They stopped when they saw the congregation of Agamemnon's men, with Athena and Achilles a little farther off. The whole thing was miserable. Briseis looked worried. And a little bit sick. She met Achilles' eyes, asking a question he couldn't answer. Patroclus watched Agamemnon warily, his brow furrowed.

"Ah!" Agamemnon said jovially. "Briseis, darling!"

Achilles, Patroclus, *and* Briseis cringed.

She tentatively stepped forwards. "What do you want?"

"Well, it's Achilles' fault that I have no girlfriend," Agamemnon started, hands clasped behind his back as he walked towards her. "So I think it's only fair that you become mine."

"No," Patroclus said abruptly, inserting himself between Agamemnon and Briseis. "That's... not okay."

Briseis was staring at Achilles in horror. He stared back at her in equal horror. This was *horrific.* Briseis opened her mouth to say something, but ended up just holding her breath.

"And what Achilles is doing isn't okay either," Agamemnon said with a shrug, as if he was discussing something mild, like the weather. "And if you say no... well. There will obviously be consequences. Achilles getting kicked off the team is one of them. And

I could get Patroclus replaced. I could also... end your exchange program early. Frame that girl you like hanging out with for selling illegal shit. Get her expelled. Make sure all your friends end up miserable. Y'know."

Achilles looked up at Athena, feeling as sick as his teammates must have, pleading silently for her to do something. She didn't even acknowledge him. The coach just stood there, arms crossed, expression stony.

"There's no way," Briseis whispered. But she looked afraid.

*Everyone* looked afraid, except for maybe Odysseus. Achilles wasn't sure how the fuck Agamemnon had gotten so much power, but his threats weren't empty. His little sister was in juvie now, because of the whole adderall ordeal. Patroclus was certain that she was innocent. Agamemnon was good at getting people to do what he wanted. Achilles hated him for that. (Among a multitude of other disgusting attributes. If Achilles ever got asked why he hated Agamemnon, the person who asked would be in for a *very* long conversation.) (Achilles' two passions were football and hating Agamemnon.) (That wasn't entirely true. He was passionate about other things too. But right now, he was extremely passionate about hating Agamemnon, even though it wouldn't get him anywhere. And he was also passionate about not getting kicked off the team. If things continued this way, he would take action himself.)

Agamemnon shrugged. "Okay. Fine. Who do we start with?" He turned to Odysseus. "What's that girl's name?"

"Iphis," Odysseus said. (Achilles was *also* passionate about hating the tiny spark of excitement in his former friend's voice.)

"Riiight," Agamemnon replied, walking towards the school. "Let's get her expelled."

Achilles was proud of Briseis for not responding as long as she did. She waited, a storm brewing in her dark eyes, until Agamemnon was almost around the bus.

She didn't turn around. "Fine," she said, just loud enough for him to hear.

He stopped, looking back at her. Achilles wanted to punch the predatory smile off his fucking face. Patroclus stared at the brownish blue sky, arms wrapped protectively around himself.

"I knew you'd get it," Agamemnon purred, smugly walking back over to her.

She stared him right in the eyes. "Darling, I'm not your girlfriend. I hate you. I'm just playing along for my friends," she said softly, leaning so close to Agamemnon that she might have been trying to kiss him. Achilles barely heard it. "I will make your life like hell."

With that, she spun on her heel, and marched back to the school.

Agamemnon turned to face everyone, his smile a hideous thing. "Feisty."

That did it. Achilles leapt to his feet, not caring what Athena did anymore. "Shut. The *fuck*. Up!" he yelled, shoving Diomedes out of his way. "That's not okay. You're..." he struggled, trying to find the right words to describe how *horrible* this boy was. There was nothing. "You're..." Achilles stopped.

The captain crossed his arms. "What're you gonna do, Pelides?" Agamemnon leaned closer. "I *won.*"

Athena walked past them, everyone pausing to watch her go. After all of this, she was leaving. She was supposed to make sure shit like this didn't happen. And now she was *leaving.* Patroclus looked after the football coach, his eyes wide. He met Achilles' gaze, his mouth falling open.

"I don't think you did," Achilles hissed as Athena's footsteps receded. "You've taken the thing that means the most to me in the whole world. And now..." Achilles stepped back, putting his hands up. The semi circle of senior players parted for him. "I quit. I'm done with this," he said, getting a kind of sick satisfaction from the surprise on everyone's faces. "Fuck you, Agamemnon."

"No way. You're not quitting," Diomedes said, his face pale. "You can't."

Achilles laughed coldly. "*I'm* not just quitting. I'm taking the offence line with me. Once they find out that you did this, *Captain,* I'll have no trouble at all. You've stolen my honor, stripped me of dignity, and now, you're going to suffer for it."

Before anyone could say anything, Achilles marched back through the center of the circle. Even Agamemnon moved out of his way. He didn't wait to see if Patroclus would follow. It might be better if he didn't, seeing as Achilles had just said some things that he already regretted. Achilles stormed across the lawn, walking past pools of vomit and discarded football bags. Janitors and teachers were trying to clean it up, but it seemed like they were struggling.

He made it around the school, collapsing onto the stairs in his and Patroclus' little alcove. He hid his head in his hands.

"So are you going to join drama club now, or what?" Patroclus' voice came from beside him.

Achilles laughed miserably into his hands. "I'm sorry," he whispered, feeling like he had recently been run over by a bus. "I got a bit carried away."

"Yeah, I figured," the other boy said. Achilles could hear the smile in his voice. "I won't take it personally." He paused. The mood darkened. Achilles pulled his head out of his hands. "It's not... fair, what he did to Bri. Or... remotely ethical," Patroclus said, glancing at the empty football field.

"Do you get why I hate him, now?" Achilles asked, knowing that he probably wouldn't play on that field again. He might never play again. It hurt to think that. But there was also some solace in the thought.

Patroclus snorted. "I always got why you hated him. I just thought it might be bad for you to broadcast it to everyone. Now... he's not your captain, so. Maybe don't make posters about why you hate him and put them all over the school, but it doesn't *really* matter. I guess it didn't ever matter."

He bumped Achilles' shoulder with his own. A single crow perched on the fence around the field, cawing at the world. Achilles thought it might be nice to scream.

"I should call my mom," he said softly, resting his head on Patroclus' shoulder. "Maybe she'll be able to help."

"And I'm going to go find Bri. Maybe we can talk to admin cause..." Patroclus said, running his hands over his face. "I hope Iphis hasn't actually murdered Agamemnon yet. That would be bad. Can I meet you in the library in half hour?"

Achilles sat up, nodding. He didn't want Patroclus to go, but he got it. "See you."

"Love you," Patroclus said quietly, slipping inside before Achilles could reply.

He sighed, grateful for the cool breeze that swept across the dry lawn. Dark clouds were gathering on the horizon. It would rain soon. And he wouldn't have to worry about practicing in the soaking weather. The single crow hopped off the fence, swooping down and landing a few feet away from Achilles. The bird watched him, head cocked.

"Hello, bird," Achilles said, without really meaning to.

The crow cawed once, then hopped away. Achilles pulled out his phone. He opened it and stared at his mother's number. Before he could psych himself out, he clicked the call button, putting it on speaker. Thetis answered after three rings.

"Hi, this is Thetis, what can I do for you?" his mother answered. She must not have checked the caller ID.

"Mom?" Achilles said, letting his voice waver. "I... need your help."

Thetis couldn't remember the last time Achilles had asked her for anything. As her son explained the problem, she was glad he had come to her.

"They *need* me," Achilles was saying, his voice half drowned out by the sound of wind. "And I need to make f—Agamemnon regret his choices. That's why I left the team."

"They *do* need you, darling," Thetis said, getting out of her office chair and walking over to the window. The city was so far below her. "You're one of the only capable players on their team. And they took your honor."

"Exactly!" Achilles exclaimed. Thetis had to pull the phone away from her ear. Her boy certainly was passionate. She laughed silently, pulling out her airpods.

Thetis shut her laptop, sitting back down. "Achilles, I have a solution."

There was an awfully loud noise as her son accidentally covered the microphone multiple times. Thetis winced. He was definitely on speaker.

"Sorry," Achilles said, his voice no longer competing with the wind. "Had to put in earbuds. It's starting to rain."

She frowned at the wall across from her. "And you're still outside?"

"Yeah."

What a strange boy.

"Alright." Thetis paused. "I have a solution."

"I *knew* you would."

"Remember Zeus?" Thetis asked, smiling as she spun in her chair.

Achilles laughed. "Oh boy. That man."

"Yes. *That* man," Thetis couldn't help laughing along with him. "Well, he owes me. So I'll ask him to sponsor Ilium's team, and they'll start winning."

"And then my team will have to come begging for me to come back...?" Achilles asked hopefully.

Smart. "Yes, that is the goal," Thetis replied.

"Agamemnon's too proud," Achilles said suddenly. "He won't... oh shoot. Sorry. One sec."

The line went dead, beeping three times. Thetis smiled, shaking her head. Achilles was always a bit odd. But he was sweet. She wasn't a fan of this Agamemnon. He seemed like the kind of person who used his faulty authority to the breaking point, and then pushed further. She sighed, waiting for Achilles to call back. His phone had probably died.

It took five minutes for her phone to ring again.

"Sorry mom," Achilles said. "Just had to run inside. Started raining really hard."

He didn't sound like he had been running. *Good,* Thetis thought. She had come to terms with her son's incredible athletic ability after trying to send him to Nantucket. She had been an olympic swimmer, and she didn't want her son(s) to go through the struggles of being a world class athlete. But if it was what he wanted, she would support him. Pyrrhus, her second son, was just as gifted, if not moreso. He already had scholarships. Then again, he was in a big city. Achilles was living in *Where's That, Nowheresville.*

"That's alright," Thetis said. "I won't keep you long. Besides, I have to message Zeus. We'll see if he actually remembers me."

"He'll remember," Achilles assured. "Okay. Have a good night. See you... eventually. We won't—oh. I won't be playing at all. Never mind. Bye."

He hung up again. Thetis shook her head, not bothering to remove her airpods as she messaged Zeus.

Thetis:

> Hello. This is Thetis. How are you doing?

*Sent 4:09 PM*

She put her phone face up on the desk, opening her laptop again. The advertising firm was about to close a big deal, which was always exciting. She had written maybe three words in the final proposal when her phone vibrated.

Zeus:

> Hi Thetis. It's been quite awhile, hasn't it. Funny how people drift apart. As for your question, I'm doing quite well.

> Your son played very well in the first game this season. He'll definitely get a scholarship if he so wishes. How are you?

*Sent 4:11 PM*

Thetis:

> I'm sure my son played well. I expect no less of him.

> Though I've recently received some disturbing news from Achilles himself. I was wondering if I could ask you a favor.

*Sent 4:13 PM*

Thetis strongly disliked how Zeus texted, although she supposed she texted the same. She could have just called him. Calling made Thetis anxious, because she couldn't see the person's face. Very few things upset her, but phone calls were among them. Of course, no one knew about that. She was a strong, independent woman. (She was also lonely. But that's what came from being at the top.) Her phone pinged again.

Zeus:

Is Achilles alright? And of course. I promised all those years ago, didn't I? What do you need?

*Sent 4:18 PM*

She sighed, not wanting to explain the whole thing. It would take a long time to type. But type it she did.

Thetis:

Achilles is fine, but his honor is damaged.  There was a large problem at Mycenae Academy when the captain, Agamemnon Atrides, decided he would not break up with the daughter of Chryses, from Ilium. Phoebus decided that the best way to help his friend, Chryses, was to poison ninety percent of the Stallions team, so they would be unable to play the first game.

It is therefore forfeit, in the Trojan's favor.

*Sent 4:15 PM*

Thetis:

> Achilles tried to open his team captain's eyes to how flawed this was, which was countered with threats of suspension from the team. Atrides then summoned Achilles' girlfriend, and threatened her into becoming his girlfriend instead of Achilles'. You see how flawed this is? There as no staff intervention, though Achilles said something about going to administration. Achilles, completely mistreated and dishonored, quit the team, because he was finished with the ungrateful disregard from his senior teammates.

*Sent 4:18 PM*

Thetis:

> Now, I hear you have perhaps agreed to sponsor the Stallions this season. I ask you to revoke your promise, and sponsor the Trojans instead.

> This will help them start winning the season, and as the games progress, the Stallions will grow more desperate, realizing their grievous error.

> They will then beg for my son back to come on the team.

*Sent 4:21 PM*

Thetis:

This will be their punishment for casting out my son as if he were worthless, when he is really the only thing holding them safely out of the Trojan's reach.

I apologize for the length of these messages, but I think you will see how the explanation was necessary.

*Sent 4:24 PM*

It took a long time for Zeus to reply. Obviously. That novel would take anyone days to read. As the minutes ticked by, Thetis found herself unable to concentrate on the proposal. Her heart was beating faster by the second, her hands growing sweaty. She flipped her phone over so it was face down. That didn't help either. Instead of writing, she opted to stare at the three dots showing that Zeus was typing. She almost dropped her phone when the message came through.

Zeus:

> By Jove, that sounds like quite the ordeal. I didn't realize that Agamemnon Atrides was such a snake of a boy. Well then, I cannot support such lies and disrespect. Of course, Thetis. I will sponsor the Trojans.

*Sent 4:38 PM*

Thetis let out a breath, a smile spreading across her face.

Thetis:

> Thank you very much.

*Sent 4:40 PM*

# II

Z EUS COULD HARDLY BELIEVE what Thetis had said. He was thoroughly disappointed in the Mycenae captain, for one, but also in his daughter, who was the coach. Athena. He usually chose to fund her school, because she was, in all honesty, his favourite child. Zeus was, in truth, confused how two of his children had ended up coaching at the two schools he constantly chose between. It created a larger divide in their family. Not like it mattered anymore. He had done that all by himself. Athena had called him, three or four days after the poisoning incident. No one on her team had died. That was a relief. They would be set to play again in a week and a half, he was informed after asking. Apollo, of course, denied any involvement with the Mycenae Stallions, but Zeus knew it had been him.

Botanical poisonings weren't common, and Athena had said it was apparently some plant called hyacinth had been the cause of the illness. When these incidents occurred, it was always his crafty son. (And they occurred more than once in the last fifteen years.)

Apollo was rich enough to pay his own bails. Zeus was pretty sure the authorities were afraid of his son now, so they didn't even pursue the case. Officially filed under *Food Poisoning*. Zeus had to respect Apollo, because he certainly was clever. Maybe not the state's best football coach, but also not the worst. He'd be glad for the money that was about to be donated to his team.

The drive to Mycenae Academy was short from Zeus and Hera's mansion on the outskirts of town. It was a humid Friday afternoon. The weather couldn't seem to make up its mind. Eventually, they'd move to the house closer to Illium, because of the changed sponsorship. Zeus' silver convertible didn't even stand out in the student parking lot where he pulled up. He thought about Thetis and her son as he walked into the school. Thetis, who, many years ago, was going to become his mistress. The third one that year. But a psychic said something about Thetis' son being greater than his father, and Zeus didn't want to risk that. So he offered her a favour and sent her on her way. He had also lead her to her a husband, but that hadn't ended very well. In fact, it had ended almost as soon as it had started. In an apology, he had offered her whatever her heart desired, yet again. And apparently, this was it.

Mycenae Academy was a bright school, with clean windows and a quiet lobby. Open, white, with couches by the door. He had fond memories of this place. His footsteps were almost the loudest sound in the room as he made his way over to the office. The woman at the front desk waved at him. He knew he had slept with her at some point, but couldn't remember her name, so he settled on waving back.

He walked at a luxurious pace, into the office. The secretary got to her feet like he was royalty. Zeus chuckled, assuring her it was alright to sit.

"What can I do for you today?" she asked, trying to discreetly organize her desk while looking up at him.

Zeus put his hands in his pockets. So much lint in there. Disturbing. He'd need a new cleaning staff. The current ones were slacking off, and he didn't know who did the laundry. They'd all have to go.

"Could you possibly page Athena and Agamemnon Atrides down here?" he asked, leaning sideways on the desk.

"Right away, sir," she said brightly, nodding. "Just one moment please."

He thought that was rather contradictory, to tell someone that their request would be carried out immediately, then ask them to wait a moment. Not that he was entitled. He understood people needed time to do things. But perhaps they shouldn't... go about opposing what they had just said.

The secretary picked up a phone on her desk. "Pardon the interruption. Could Pallas Athena and Agamemnon Atrides make their way to the main office please? Athena and Agamemnon Atrides to the office please. Thank you."

She sounded so much more professional over the PA system. Less of a blustering mess.

"Thank you," Zeus said, sitting down in a gray leather chair to the left of the door.

The chair creaked. *Good,* Zeus thought. *They're polishing the leather.*

It took five minutes for his daughter and the idiot boy to get to the office. Agamemnon Atrides had just lost his team the very thing that could have won them the season. Actually, he had managed to lose *two* things that could have won him the season. Achilles Pelides *and* the sponsorship. But Zeus wouldn't give him the disappointment easily. He would make sure it hurt.

Athena came in first, wearing jogging pants and a cardigan. *Not appropriate for a teacher at a private school, but he supposed that she wasn't really a teacher anyways. And the school had offered her a position as coach. She could, and would, do whatever she wanted. Headstrong, his daughter was.* Agamemnon followed, his school uniform strangely tidy. Zeus hadn't expected such a supposed heathen to take care of his uniform. Though, to get away with said supposed heathenism, he must be a good student.

"Father," Athena said as Zeus stood up, a smile on his face. "And what do I owe the pleasure?"

Father and daughter shook hands. He appreciated the professionality of their relationship. Athena was as serious as a spinal injury.

"Please," Zeus said, looking to the secretary. "Do you have a private room we could speak in?"

The woman bustled up and lead them down a hallway.

She knocked on a door near the end of the hall, then opened it. "Right in here."

Zeus thanked her again, stepping into the conference room. It, like the lobby, was pristine and minimalist, with a light wooden table surrounded by quality office chairs. The windows allowed the light to stream through sheer curtains, so none of the overheads were turned on.

"Have a seat," Zeus said, gesturing to the chairs.

Agamemnon stood at the door for a long moment, as if trying to decide whether he should take the seat at the head of the table. Zeus claimed it first, helping the boy make the choice.

Once Athena and Agamemnon had chosen spots, on opposite sides of the table, in the chairs next to Zeus, he smiled.

"Though the decision has yet to be formally consummated," Zeus said, clasping his hands in front of him on the table, "I have put forward my withdrawal notice to the bank, saying that I would like to donate to the Mycenae Stallions."

Agamemnon smirked, showing a crack in his schoolboy exterior. Zeus was here to teach this boy a lesson. He was glad Thetis hadn't been lying about the youth afterall. Just that look alone, with the glimmer of self–satisfaction and narcissism hiding in the depths of his gaze, was proof enough for Zeus.

"Thank you sir," the boy said after a long moment. "Will that be all? I have a very interesting physics lab that's taking place in a few minutes."

Zeus nodded. "You may go."

Agamemnon opened the door, and left, his pace quickening as he neared the end of the hall. Athena looked over at Zeus, her gaze impenetrable.

"You aren't sponsoring my team, father," she said softly. "Do you doubt me? Or my intelligence?"

Zeus laughed, leaning back in his chair. "Definitely not, Athena, dear. Though, I *do* question your decision to let that boy remain captain."

"This is because of Pelides, isn't it," Athena said. Lighting fast, as always. Her potential was wasted on coaching teenage boys to play football. But Zeus wasn't here to tell her what to do with her life. If she was happy, it didn't matter. "Look, Father," she said, leaning forwards. "Agamemnon is captain because the players follow him, no matter how mediocre or horrible he is. That boy has some kind of disturbing charisma that people are just *drawn* to. And Achilles, Father, is a brilliant player. But see? He's reactive. And a little self–centered."

Zeus looked out the window at the concrete compound, with blocky benches. It was out of sight from the front of the school. He had helped fund it. Actually, he *had* funded it. Donating to schools helped with reducing taxes.

"Athena, Apollo poisoned your team because of your captain's behavior," Zeus said, still staring outside.

Athena huffed. "It's not that simple. Yes, I agree. Agamemnon is quite the trouble child, but the players *follow* him. And Apollo is needlessly petty, so. He would have poisoned my team whether Agamemnon was on it or not. Do whatever you want, but if you think this will teach him a lesson, it probably won't. Apollo poisoned the whole team because of Agamemnon, and he's still swaggering around like he rules the place."

"You're contradicting yourself," Zeus said, looking at his daughter, who shrugged.

She raised her eyebrows. "Do I contradict myself? Very well I contradict myself. I am large. I contain multitudes."

"Whitman," Zeus said with a nod. (All her wasted potential drove him near the brink of insanity. But she was happy. It was fine.) "Very eloquent."

Athena stood up from her chair. "The team got poisoned on account of Agamemnon's actions, but that doesn't mean it wouldn't have happened anyways. That's what I meant."

"Ah," Zeus replied. "I'm donating to Apollo regardless."

"We're still going to win," Athena said, walking around the table the long way. "With your help or not."

And Zeus didn't doubt it.

❧ ☙

Hector's mother always insisted on a Sunday dinner. Anyone was invited, as long as they told Hecuba one day in advance. Tonight was special though. His dad was celebrating a triumphant result in a major case. He owned a successful law firm, Priam and Sons, it was called, though none of Priam's sons wanted to go into law. Hector might, just to make his parents happy. They *said* they didn't care what he did, but he knew his dad didn't want to sell the firm. It was his empire, built up from bank loans and blossomed into a rich city. The loans had been paid off decades ago.

Helen and Paris were sitting on the floor across from Hector and Andromache, who were on the couch. Aeneas was there too, along with some of his dad's work friends. Their other cousin, Deiphobus, chatted with Priam, who thought of him like a son. Hector sighed. His parents treated every man like he was a son, and every woman like she was a daughter. He and Paris' needs often came last. But it was fine. He loved his parents, no matter how hospitable they were. It was nice to have the house lit up late into the night, filled with laughter and the clinking of glasses.

"Hey," Aeneas said, sitting down on the arm of the couch. "Apparently the Mycenae team is okay now."

Paris groaned dramatically. Helen patted him on the shoulder like she was using a wooden spoon instead of her hand.

"I thought we would be able to win the entire season by forfeit," Paris whined.

Hector took a sip of the champagne his mother had provided, just to hide the sarcastic snort of laughter that tried to escape.

"Even *I* knew that wasn't going to happen," Andromache said, tucking her feet up onto the couch. "And besides, the only way that would happen is if half the team died and they somehow continued the season. Do you want that?"

Helen looked up at Aeneas, her eyes wide. "So everyone *is* alright?"

He nodded, clasping his hands on top of his knees. "Apparently they're all out of the hospital now. We're playing them next Friday or something."

Helen let out a breath that sounded like she had been holding for weeks. She had been worried about her people at Mycenae. Achilles, who she apparently still texted, had told her that Agamemnon refused to stop dating one of the Ilium cheerleaders, so Mr. Phoebus had *poisoned* their team. And apparently Illium's best players quit the team. Hector didn't *want* to believe that Mr. Phoebus would do that... but he seemed like the kind of man to get revenge in the stupidest ways.

"Did anyone find out which cheerleader this was over?" Paris asked out of nowhere, nearly knocking over his glass of Sprite as he sat up straight.

"She was a sophomore," Aeneas said. "Chryseis. Everyone called her Crissy. She moved to California or something because of Agamemnon." He paused. "Apparently."

"Apparently what?" Helen asked, shifting to sit cross legged.

"Apparently she left because of Agamemnon."

Helen laughed, one short harsh bark. Paris jumped, startled.

"I honestly wouldn't put it past Agamemnon to drive someone out of the state," Helen said, downing her drink in one gulp.

Hector wondered if she'd ever been drunk. No one knew much about Helen. Not even Paris, who hovered around her most of the time. Andromache probably talked to her the most, but she never said anything about the Mycenae girl. They were Helen's stories anyways. She'd tell them if she wanted to.

Hector's mom came into the living room, a plate of appetizers in hand, a giant smile on her face. Entertaining was what she loved to do best.

"How's everyone doing over here?" she asked, setting the plate down on the coffee table. "Are we okay? Needing anything?"

"I love your sweater," Helen said with a bob of her head.

The sweater in question was a white knit, with tiny pearls sewn in to the yarn.

Hecuba smiled. "Oh you're just the sweetest. If you want to borrow it, just let me know." She looked around at the group one more time. "You sure you're good?"

"Yeah," Hector said. "Thanks mom."

"Oh I get it," Hecuba said with a grin. "Not cool to have your mom around. Oh no. I'm not a cool mom at all, am I. Well. Dinner's in about twenty minutes."

"I think you're a very cool mom," Andromache called after her.

"Me too!" Helen said.

"Okay okay we get it," Paris complained, gently thunking his head on the table.

Helen actually laughed at Paris' theatrics. Hector had to smile. Paris could be annoying as hell, but he was also pretty funny. Sometimes.

The doorbell rang and Hecuba came out of the kitchen, shaking her head. "Who could it possibly be? Everyone who asked to come is here. Must be important," she said to Priam as she disappeared into the entrance hall.

"Do you think someone died?" Helen asked, her voice low. Hector almost laughed, but then he realized she was perfectly serious.

Aeneas frowned at the leap. "Who would have died—oh. No, Helen, all the Mycenae players were okay."

She warily stared at the place where Hecuba had left. No one else was paying much attention to the unexpected visitors.

"We have more guests!" Hecuba announced, two men following her into the house.

Andromache looked at Hector to see his reaction. Zeus and Mr. Phoebus were standing there, behind his mother, with broad smiles on both their faces. They were related. Hector could tell, in their jawlines. Of course, he knew that Mr. Phoebus was Zeus' son. It just wasn't a fact Hector frequently thought about. Everyone in the room fell silent. Zeus was the richest man in the state, except for maybe the Governor. Maybe richer than him too. He was a man greeted with praise to his face and followed by rumors behind his back.

"I've come here to make an announcement," he said, deliberately tugging on the cuffs of his tweed suit. It probably cost more than the sofa Hector was on. "This year," he said, pausing for dramatic effect. Hector's heart sped up, just a little. Could it be? Maybe...

"I have made the decision to sponsor the Ilium Trojans!"

Paris looked over at Hector with eyes the size of the inexplicably giant buttons on Mr. Phoebus' vest.

"Fucking finally," Andromache muttered under her breath, which made Aeneas laugh.

Hector didn't quite believe it. Ilium hardly *ever* got sponsored. Only when their team was obviously superior. This would mean... probably some new gear, guest coaches, maybe a week long camp. Hector laughed quietly, getting off the couch. Mr. Phoebus gave him a tiny smile and nod of acknowledgement.

"Can I get a glass?" Mr. Phoebus asked Hecuba, who nodded excitedly and ran into the kitchen again.

She reappeared momentarily, handing Mr. Phoebus a flute of champaign. He gave her his tiny smile, then raised his glass. Hecuba offered Zeus a drink as well. The gray haired man accepted it courteously.

"First," Mr. Phoebus said, "I'd like to give a toast to Priam, old friend. Congratulations on your victory."

A cheer rose among the gathered, glasses clinking, eyes full of pride. Hector couldn't believe this was happening to him. Andromache got to her feet. The rest of their group followed. Helen sheepishly tapped her empty glass against Hector's, shaking her head. His flute was nearly empty too. He shrugged, with a smile that he was sure made him look... unstable, at best.

"And now!" Mr. Phoebus called, his face that seemed to have been carved by a master stoneworker glowing with joy. "A toast to Hector, who makes everyone around him a better person. An exceptional player, the best Ilium football captain in years, and the man who makes me look bad as a coach! Thank you!"

The guests raised their glasses in Hector's direction before drinking. If Zeus' sponsorship hadn't left his head spinning, such high praise from his coach would have completely blindsided him.

"See?" Andromache whispered in his ear. "You're a perfectly fine person, even though you're always trying to be better." She paused. "You are kind of a jerk sometimes. Not to me, obviously. But if you weren't... that bad boy aesthetic wouldn't really fit. Stupid lip piercings."

Hector laughed, louder than he meant to, wrapping an arm around her and slapping Aeneas on the back.

"We might have a chance this year," he said, feeling giddy and slightly insane.

All the possibilities of the future yawned out in front of him, nearly endless. Helen sat back down, looking a little bit lost and a little bit guilty. *I hope I never feel like that*, Hector thought, as he spun Andromache around. She was so graceful, laughing as her long hair fanned out behind her. It seemed like it was in slow motion. It felt like being on top of the world. *And I hope that, before I die, I have this feeling again.*

# III

# Ant Men

Achilles:

We're done playing. Agamemnon's the reason y'all got sick so. I'm going in strike.

*ob.

*ob

*ON, GODSDAMMIT

*Sent Thursday*

Automedon:

> Isn't that a you thing? Should we all just… quit?

*Sent Thursday*

*Peisander has left the chat*

Achilles:

> Wow. He obv doesn't care about honor. so long wide receiver

*Sent Thursday*

Eudorus:

> I'm with you agamemnon can die in a fucking hole

*Sent Thursday*

Achilles:

> THANK YOU.

*Sent Thursday*

Pheonix:

I dunno Achilles is this a good idea will we get back on the team next year?

*Sent Thursday*

Automedon:

The point isn't to quit for good. I'm with Achilles right now. He just explained how we'd just quit for a bit and make them beg to get us back then save them later. It's about not tolerating being treated like this.

*Sent Thursday*

Menesthius:

K Sounds gooc

*Sent Thursday*

Alcimedon:

JUSTICE FOR ACHILLES

*Sent Thursday*

Patroclus snatched the phone from Achilles' hand, interrupting the tenth reading of the conversation since most of the team had been discharged from the hospital.

"Just because they didn't reply doesn't mean they're going to play," Patroclus said, stuffing Achilles' phone into his back pocket. "And besides. The team's missing more than half its starting offense line. That'll do enough damage anyways."

Achilles shrugged hopelessly. "I just. Agh. I'm so jittery."

"Yeah, that's why you play football," Patroclus said, bumping into Achilles to avoid smacking into someone else. "Also, why is that group chat called Ant Men?"

"Because ants can carry twenty times their weight and we carry the entire team on our backs because we're the only good players. Odysseus isn't on this chat, by the way."

"Very clever," Patroclus replied.

"Let's ditch," Achilles suggested, not knowing where the idea came from.

He expected Patroclus to strongly oppose, but he just frowned. "We don't generally do that."

"No, you're right," Achilles agreed. "Because we're *generally* good students. But I can't focus. I keep thinking about Bri..."

Patroclus had gone after her last week, when Agamemnon pulled his awful stunt. She was upset. And when she and Patroclus went to admin together, the principal just told them not to be dramatic. That the whole thing wasn't real. That they were making up problems where there were none.

So Briseis was *really* upset. Who wouldn't have been? Achilles felt like it was his fault. He kept nearly failing tests. That wasn't something he did. Briseis had been sitting at Agamemnon's table for lunch everyday. She was in an Instagram post on his account. Patroclus said she needed space, but she'd be fine. Iphis had nearly punched Achilles when she found out. She yelled at him, at least. It was good. No one else had dared to be mad at him to his face.

Achilles missed Briseis like a limb. It was funny how someone could become a part of your life so quickly. It felt like he had known Bri for his whole life, even though it had only been a few weeks. Iphis still sat with them, and chatted with Patroclus. They were a strange pair. Patroclus with his opposition to aggression, his soft voice, and curiosity. Then there was Iphis, with her Doc Martins, her loud laughter, and her... aggression. But somehow they worked. Achilles only hung out with her because Patroclus liked her. He didn't mind their friendship before Briseis came along. And then *he* had had someone to be with when Patroclus and Iphis were hanging out. But now Bri was gone and...ugh. He was kind of upset that Patroclus got along with both girls so well. But now Bri was (rightfully) angry. And Iphis was distant.

"C'mon," Patroclus said, grabbing Achilles' wrist. "Let's ditch."

It was cool outside for once. There was a breeze that lifted the stray hairs around Achilles' face and blew them into his eyes. Patroclus had let go of his arm once they got out.

"Never took you to be someone who'd agree with skipping class," Achilles said as they meandered into the small man–made forest by the school.

Patroclus laughed softly, barely audible over the rustling of the leaves. They were turning orange now. The mischievous wind lifted a couple off the branches, hypnotizing them through the sweet smelling air. Achilles felt a weight lift off his chest. Not a big one. And certainly not the entire weight that sat there. But some of it. They walked in a comfortable silence. It was the kind of silence that Achilles had learned to love. The kind that lived in the margins of excited conversation, but dominated the serious or the pondering ones. The only silence he could live in. That in–between silence, with the person he cared about most.

After a time, (because no one was counting) they reached the stream that ran through the school grounds. It was diverted into a culvert a few hundred meters later, because it would have crossed the main lawn. The stones crunched under their shoes. Achilles could feel their shapes. Patroclus sat down on the bank, his arms loosely draped over his knees.

"You okay to just sit here?" he asked, staring at the clear water. "I didn't ask. People usually go to the mall or something when they skip."

Achilles laughed, threading his fingers through Patroclus' curls. He had forgotten how nice it was to just... be.

"First of all," Achilles said, breathing deeply, "I hate malls. And I'll follow you anywhere. Except the mall. Maybe. Depending on the day, I'd follow you to the mall." He paused, shaking his head. "It's so peaceful. What if we studied out here? That would be cool."

"That was more than first of all," Patroclus said, looking up at Achilles. "Where did second of all start? How about third of all?"

Achilles shook his head in mock disappointment before sitting down. "How could I. Not specifying which statement was second and third of all? I should be arrested. By the word police."

Colourful leaves swirled along the stream, dancing to music he couldn't hear. But he could imagine it. A sort of singer–songwriter folk ballad.

"What're you thinking about?" Patroclus asked, linking their hands together.

Achilles stared at their fingers. "A ballad for the dancing river leaves."

"That... was not what I expected," Patroclus replied, a smile in his voice. "But very poetic."

"What's that bracelet?" Achilles asked, reaching over and pushing up Patroclus' sleeve. "I've wondered about it for years. You never take it off."

The other boy frowned for a second, holding up both of their hands so he didn't have to let go.

"Oh!" he exclaimed, apparently remembering. "It's a medical bracelet."

"For *what*?"

"Once I had an anaphylactic reaction to something. I don't even remember what it was. It's never happened again. I was... maybe six?"

With his empty hand, Achilles held the bracelet still as he turned his head to read it.

*Patroclus Menoetius*

*Unknown Allergy*

"My parents wanted to put Do Not Resuscitate on there, but I'm not terminally ill, so that didn't happen," Patroclus mused.

Achilles looked back up at the other boy, his face screwed up in confusion. "They obviously resuscitated you."

"No. Just used an Epipen. I didn't flatline."

"Why would it say do not resuscitate? Isn't that something old people want? Weren't you young when it happened?"

Patroclus swallowed. "I... yeah. I just. It was my parents who got the engravings. My dad, to be specific. If I um. Died, I guess. Well. They wanted that to be it. No more possibility of. Uh. Me."

Achilles was holding his breath. He exhaled, then let go of Patroclus' hand and wrapped his arms around him. He didn't quite know what to say. The words lodged in his throat. Patroclus leaned into him, as if asking for reassurance.

"It's not on there," he said quietly. "So it's okay."

"I think it's the exact opposite of okay," Achilles replied, his voice hardly more than a whisper.

Patroclus laughed humorlessly. Achilles sat up, and stared at his profile. This beautiful human carried so much pain. But beautiful humans usually do. That was just the way it went.

"Throw it in the river," Achilles blurted.

Patroclus looked at him like he was insane.

"What?" Achilles asked. "You don't need it anymore."

They got stuck in that moment for a long time, a brown haired boy who was realizing he didn't have to cling to all the things that hurt him, and a blonde haired one, who was learning that pain can be hidden well behind a placed laugh, a gentle smile. Patroclus looked down at the bracelet.

The words weren't on there, but they may as well have been. *Do not resuscitate.*

They were the words of his father. Not his. He *wanted* the chance to live. He held his wrist out to Achilles.

"Undo it for me?" he asked, feeling like the rocks on the bank of the stream had somehow gotten into his throat.

Achilles undid the clasp, letting the metal bracelet fall into his palm. Before Patroclus could change his mind, he snatched it up and threw it into the middle of the stream. The splash hardly made any noise. Patroclus stared at the spot where it had disappeared. He couldn't believe what he had just done. He could feel Achilles staring at him, waiting apprehensively for his reaction. It felt weird, not having the bracelet on his wrist. He felt lighter. Like maybe he could float away.

Patroclus laughed. At first, it was that kind of laughter that stayed hidden behind a smile. Achilles slumped against him, relieved. He was okay. Okay*er*. When Achilles started laughing, Patroclus' laugh burst free of the smile, drifting up to the dying leaves.

*We're going to be alright,* Achilles thought. *We'll be okay.*

⁂

Briseis was trying to figure out how Apollo poisoned the team. Because then she could poison Agamemnon. She had spent… far too much time around him. Patroclus had told her about the whole thing after she left. Achilles had been upset enough to quit and take the majority of the offense with him, so that was a slight consolation prize. But she was still stuck with Aga–fucking–memnon. It made her want to smash her head into a wall. She supposed she could have just marched away, but… part of her wanted to make good on her promise. She needed to make his life a disaster.

Currently, she was waiting in the main foyer. Briseis had stopped keeping track of what day it was, because it didn't matter anyways. She saw Iphis in art class, women's studies (ironically) and after curfew. Sometimes at lunch. That was enough to keep her alive. Iphis understood. Together, they would write strongly worded letters to Admin, who had basically tried to gaslight Briseis into thinking she had made up the whole problem. Iphis comforted Briseis, and then they would laugh at Agamemnon's expense. Iphis Iphis Iphis.

The team was better now, and they had been practicing for awhile. So it was time for a game. And Briseis was getting dragged along, on a bus full of people she hated. Achilles wouldn't even be there. Patroclus probably quit after Achilles did, so she'd be forced to sit with Agamemnon. Athena, the coach, was chatting with her assistant coaches as they waited for the team. She pretty much pretended Briseis didn't exist. That was fine. Briseis wanted to bash Athena's teeth in. It was her fault that this was happening. She just *left* when Agamemnon was ruining her life. Aren't teachers supposed to stop things like that? Athena definitely did *not.* (And *neither did the Admin.* They said, to Briseis' face, that Agamemnon would *never* do something like that.)

Briseis sat down on the floor, leaning against the door frame, her eyes closed. The concrete was cold against her legs, even through the skirt and shorts. It felt good. Kind of distracting, for a moment at least. She swallowed. The fact that she was missing art class to watch a football game made her want to scream. But one day, this would all pay off. She'd have *so* much blackmail. It just sucked that her time with Iphis was being cut short to watch Agamemnon. Hopefully he failed. Hopefully someone tackled him so hard that his head popped off.

Briseis opened her eyes, internally debating whether or not she should make a break for it. In the end, she pulled out her headphones, deciding to stay. This time, at least.

"Bri?" someone said, just as she was putting them on.

She looked up. No one in Agamemnon's gang called her that. She didn't respond to it if they did. But there was Patroclus, standing over her, a frown on his face.

"What're you doing here?" he asked, placing his giant bag on the floor and squatting down in front of her.

Briseis couldn't help but smile. "I'm... being dragged along," she said, feeling something alive and bitter squirm through her stomach. "But you didn't quit!"

"No," he said, almost succeeding at hiding the regret in his voice. "I didn't quit."

She could have hugged him. So she did. Got off her butt and nearly knocked him out of his precarious crouch. He let out an *oomph* of surprise, then laughed a little, hugging her back.

"Please sit with me on the bus," she nearly begged, her face in his sweater.

"Of course," he replied. "Not like I'd want to sit with anyone else."

Agamemnon didn't put up much of a fuss when Briseis sat with Patroclus. *Much* being the keyword there. He did glare at her, saying considered to be quite rude. He *also* put his hand hand in her hair. It made her want to throw up. Or. Poison him. Both would be good. Patroclus stood up, and Agamemnon put his hands in the air and walked away, muttering something else that was considered quite rude, but this time it was directed at Patroclus.

"Shit," he muttered, sitting back down.

Briseis watched warily as Agamemnon took his seat at the front of the bus with Odysseus.

"You're losing your girlfriend," Odysseus said, far louder than necessary.

Agamemnon snorted. "To *him*? No fucking way. He's already Achilles' pet."

Briseis stood up, marched to the front of the bus, and hit him over the head with her satchel. Several of the football players let out soft '*Ohhh's.*' There was even one '*Get wrecked.*' Athena wasn't on the bus yet. *How nice*, Briseis thought.

"What the hell, woman?!" Agamemnon demanded, looking up at Briseis, his eyes alight.

"Probably on her period," Odysseus said sagely, meeting Briseis' gaze with a smirk. That fucker thought he was untouchable.

"Oh don't you *dare*," Briseis said under her breath, feeling her face heating up. "That's  degrading and—just because you think it's okay to insult people doesn't *make* it okay. How can you stand being such a *horrible* person?"

She felt someone's hand on her wrist. Ignoring it, she pulled a tampon out of her satchel and chucked it at his face. It hit him square between the eyes. The satisfaction Briseis got from that action was far greater than anything she had ever done. Odysseus was staring at the tampon in his lap like it was actually a bomb. She smiled sweetly, then let herself be dragged back to their seat. Obviously it was Patroclus. He disagreed with violence, even when it was justified. (Iphis would have backed her up.) Athena entered the bus just as they sat down. Patroclus glared over at Briseis, but she could tell he was trying not to smile.

The rest of the ride went without incident. Patroclus kept telling her how awful Achilles felt. Briseis wasn't even mad at him, really. She just hadn't had the opportunity to *see* him. Patroclus actively sought her out during study hours, and Iphis lived in the same building as her, but Achilles was sort of hiding. Or avoiding her. Of course there had been a giant uproar about him quitting. Whenever she had glimpsed him in the hall, he was surrounded by concerned people demanding answers. He just looked tired.

She told Patroclus this, and he nodded sadly, staring out the dusty window at the golden fields. Briseis picked a hole in the seat, then covered it with her leg. The bus was so fancy, she'd probably get sued if they found out who had done it. Although, there was a crude dick drawn on the back of the seat in front of her, definitely in Sharpie. So maybe no one would care. She might start a riot if they got mad at her about the hole though. That would mean they stepped in when a bus was being destroyed, but just stood by when her *life* was being destroyed. (Maybe that was a tad dramatic. She felt like she had the right to be.)

⁂

The first thing Odysseus said when they got off the bus was: "Man, you have horrible taste in women."

The first thing Odysseus said when they walked into the changeroom was: "We'll be fine. Pelides isn't important. And our offense is fine. It's just made up of... tenth graders. "

The first thing Odysseus said when they walked onto the field after their warmup was: "I thought Zeus was sponsoring us?"

Agamemnon had ignored the first two statements. The third one made him look in the direction Odysseus was pointing. Zeus (and it definitely *was* him) sat on the Trojan's bench, chatting with Hector. Their coach, Apollo, stood smugly behind the bench, hands clasped behind his back as his as his haughty gaze met Agamemnon's. The lights were too bright, the grass too soft beneath his feet. There were people in the stands. All of them could see his complete and utter stupidity.

"That's interesting," Odysseus said, sounding mildly amused.

Interesting was one word for it. Zeus had *told* him that they were getting sponsored. He lied. Agamemnon's jersey and shoulder pads felt too tight. He could hardly breathe. After Briseis smashed his head in with her bag on the bus, he had been ready for a good first game. That was impossible now. Impossible.

"*Fuck*," Agamemnon said, spitting on the turf that seemed to be swallowing him.

He hoisted the team bag over his shoulder, and marched on autopilot to their bench. Odysseus followed, never taking his eyes off of the Trojans. The Stallions followed him. They always followed Agamemnon. Except for Achilles. And the offense line,*apparently*.

The freshmen and sophomore players were alright, but they were no match for the junior and senior players on Ilium's team. Zeus' sponsorship would have given them the opportunity for guest coaches and specialized workshops to accelerate those players, but now that was gone. Agamemnon threw the bag to the ground with more force than necessary. He wanted to punch the metal bench, but that was a horrible idea. Unless... they pulled out.

"Odysseus," Agamemnon growled under his breath.

The quarterback turned to look at him. "What's up?"

"We're leaving the league."

This made him raise an eyebrow, ever so slightly. "Um. Why?"

Greater Ajax sidled up beside him with Diomedes and Lesser Ajax in tow.

"Because," Agamemnon hissed through clenched teeth. "*Look.*" He gestured aggressively towards the other team's bench. "We've got an offensive line of literal children, we have no Achilles, and we don't have Zeus' money."

Ajax 1 had his arms crossed. "You're saying we don't have a chance?"

"I'm saying... yes. Exactly that. Do you want to be humiliated? For an entire season?"

"You're forgetting that we have decent defense," Odysseus said, looking over at Zeus.

The old man had the audacity to wave. Odysseus had the audacity to wave back.

"We're playing," the quarter back said, with absolute certainty.

Agamemnon felt like the air was turning his lungs to ice. "That's not your choice."

"Actually," Lesser Ajax said, "It's more of *Athena's* choice. So it's not yours either. And we all wanna play, right?"

Diomedes nodded. Both Ajaces did as well.

Odysseus shrugged, meeting Agamemnon's eyes. "We're not quitting. We'll play and lose like men."

Aphrodite was far too close to where Helen was sitting. She was right by the bench, where Helen and Andromache had sat the first game. Andromache wasn't feeling well, so Hector had told her to stay back. Now, Helen was sitting with Priam and Hecuba. In between them, actually. It felt odd, to be at a sporting event in the stands. The Mycenae cheerleaders were by the Stallions' bench, chatting amongst themselves. Their red uniforms stood out against the stands behind them. Helen wished she was over there when they burst out laughing. Someone must have made a joke about Agamemnon. She was trying to keep her eyes off Menelaus, who sat on the end of the bench, which was a lot emptier than normal. She spotted Patroclus with a dark haired girl sitting on the ground, a few feet away from the team. Achilles wasn't there. A *lot* of the players weren't there. The ones who apparently... quit. Because of Agamemnon.

"Look at them," Hecuba said fondly, not noticing the rabbit-hole Helen was going down. "Paris was always so much better around adults."

Helen looked down to see Paris and... Pandaras, standing beneath Aphrodite, who was leaning over the rail to talk to them. Hector was still with Zeus. Agamemnon had posted on his Instagram story about how Mycenae was getting sponsored, but that was not true. Zeus was with the Trojans. Helen wondered why, and then decided it was probably Agamemnon's fault.

"Helen, dear," Priam said, squinting at the field, "Would you mind telling me the Stallions' players names? I haven't paid much attention to them this year."

"Of course," Helen replied. "When the game starts."

Hector jogged onto the field for the coin toss. The stands were nearly full, and they erupted in thunderous cheers. This was ridiculous. It was high school football. Helen couldn't wait to get out of here. She was going to go to Los Angeles when she was finished school. They had come up with a plan, she and Menelaus. But she would go with or without him.

The Trojans won the coin toss, and Hector chose to start on the left side of the field.

"What a weirdo," Priam said affectionately, shaking his head. "Everyone knows to choose to receive the ball."

"Not our Hector," Hecuba replied with a grin. "Always the left side of the field."

Today, she was wearing a pair of ripped black jeans embroidered with roses, leather Blundstone boots, a beige sweatshirt, and a baseball cap with the Trojan's logo on it. Helen wished she had the ability to dress herself. Godsdamn school uniforms. The Ilium ones were very purple. It disturbed her. (At least the skirt was plain.)

The game started three minutes later, with the Stallions on offense.

"Um, okay," Helen said, leaning forward to try and identify the players for Priam. "Well there's Peisander, who's playing wide receiver over on the left of the field." She squinted. "It's super weird, because none of the other normal offense players are out there. Achilles usually plays running back, but it looks like... Idomeneus is playing that. *He* plays tight end most of the time, so it's a bit. Odd. That he's playing Achilles' position."

"Who's that?" Priam asked, pointing to the quarterback, who got tackled by a Trojan Helen didn't know.

"Odysseus. He's really smart, but it looks like his plays aren't going like he wants them to. The players aren't doing that well. Eudorus and Automedon generally play tackle, but they're not here either. Antilochus is there, though. Guard on the right side. Menesthius and Phoenix are *supposed* to be the left guard and the right wide receiver, but... actually I think Athena's playing her second offense line up. I don't know any of them."

Priam frowned, stroking his white beard. Around them, the crowd started screaming. Fumble. Helen sighed. The Stallions' offense had been their saving grace, but without them... the Stallions were pretty ordinary.

"I'll tell you the defense players when they get on," Helen said, shivering in her purple sweater.

She had forgotten that it was getting damper out now. It was almost the end of September. The summers were so hot and humid that it was like swimming through the air, and trying to breathe underwater. Anything below seventy degrees was chilly enough for more sweaters.

Helen looked up at the sky, which was a cold lilac colour. The air smelled like fall and popcorn. The brisk scent of wind and the warm one of butter. It never smelled like this back home. Because Helen was used to the constant presence of hay and dashed hopes. Everyone who wasn't filthy rich had a kind of drained air about them. She supposed it was the same here, but she had been hanging around... the filthy rich people.

Ten yards weren't reached by the end of the third down, which pissed Helen right off. If *she* had been playing for the Stallions, they would be doing better. She had wanted to try out, but the coach told her that she should go try out for cheer. Now that she looked, there were a couple girls on the Trojan's bench. In gear. Why had she never noticed that before?

"Helen, dear," Priam said, leaning forwards. "Who's the kicker?"

"Nestor," she replied, still shocked at the revelation. "He's a year older than everyone. There's a pot on why. Was it because he skipped preschool and got held back? Or was it because he spent a year in jail? Or did he run away for a year? The list goes on. It's ridiculous."

She might never find out what the answer was, if she wasn't back at Mycenae by the end of the year. He'd promised to do a reveal once he graduated. Helen liked the prison rumor, but that probably wasn't true.

Once the field goal was scored, there were maybe four minutes left in the quarter. Hector came off the field, sweaty, but grinning. Hecuba waved and he rolled his eyes, but waved back at her. She was the mom Helen always wished she had. Hector bumped into Paris, stopping him as he ran on. He nearly flopped to the ground, but his older brother held him up, muttering something in his ear.

Helen practically heard the indignance in the way Paris walked away. For some reason, Paris was always getting hit on. Yes, he was not bad looking, if you were into uncooked spaghetti sad boys, and he was sort of funny, but as Helen got to know him more, she realized how often he complained. Then she realized that almost everyone complained constantly. That was one of her pet peeves. She tried not to complain because she had been through worse. Not that she was saying her problems were worse than everyone else's. All she meant was that it didn't feel right to complain in her situation. Paris did a lot of that. But she didn't *hate* him.

The Mycenae defense line ran onto the field, yelling at each other. In a comradely way. She got stuck looking at Menelaus, who was one of the farthest players away from the fifty yard line.

"That's Menelaus," she said, remembering to say who they were out loud. "Cornerback on the right. Agamemnon's the middle linebacker."

"He's the... interesting one, right?" Hecuba asked as the play started. She didn't wait for an answer before screaming something to the players. To Helen, it sounded like: "Lats gaow rojaaaans!"

Helen waited for a moment to see if Hecuba would want an answer. She didn't. "Ajax 1 is playing left tackle—" She winced as a Trojan player got crushed. "Um. As you can see, he's probably the biggest player on the team. Ajax 2 is playing safety back there... well actually he's running up the left side of the field for... um never mind. Diomedes is the left outside linebacker, and. Yeah. Schedius is the right tackle, Abantes is the other safety, and I have *no* idea who the other cornerback is. Menestheus is the left end and Euryalus is right end. That's pretty much it, I think," Helen said, putting her hands under her legs in an attempt to keep them warm.

"Well then," Priam said with a nod. "Thank you. I appreciate the tour."

⁂

By halftime, the teams were tied. Menelaus couldn't find Helen in the stands, but he was sure she was there. She had been at the last game. Agamemnon sprayed him with a waterbottle, taking his attention away from the stands. His brother wanted something.

"Hey Menny," Agamemnon said, shoving Menelaus' head down. "Paris is over there. He stole your girl. Go challenge him to a fight."

"What the...?" Menelaus asked, feeling his face scrunch up. "Why? Haven't we already declared war over my so called honor?"

Agamemnon huffed, plopping down into the ridged metal bench. "Dude. We could *end* the war if you just won a little fight. Wouldn't that be nice? Menny, think about it. You've literally got twelve minutes, so think fast."

His brother wanted more drama. But Agamemnon was the conductor of everything. Iphigenia was gone because of him. Menelaus knew that, even if he wouldn't tell the truth. Their little sister would *never* sell drugs. At some points in his life, Menelaus wished he could just clobber Agamemnon, but he was bigger and sturdier, which would just lead to Menelaus ending up on the ground. And besides, his older brother was their parents' favourite.

The fake grass bristled under his cleat as he kicked the turf like it was the spine of a living creature. "Gods. Fine. If it means no more of this aggressive shit." *And if Helen comes back. I'd fight for her.* Helen would hate that.

Players from both teams were getting rough. The refs, true to their word, weren't calling any of the fouls. Agamemnon loved it. Menelaus was a little bit less enthusiastic.

Agamemnon smiled wolfishly. He always did that when he got what he wanted. "Go tell him," he said, pointing across the field.

Menelaus sighed, and jogged off around the sidelines. It felt wrong to go right across the fifty yard line when he was organizing a back alley brawl. Just thinking about it made him cringe. But Helen. But stupidity. But listening to Agamemnon. Helen wouldn't even come back to Mycenae. She would find this degrading to women. It probably was. No. It definitely was. This whole 'war' thing was flawed because Helen never agreed. But Agamemnon wouldn't be talked off this ledge now. Menelaus sighed, feeling like an outsider as he entered the group of Trojans; red in a sea of purple.

Paris was by the edge of the crowd, yelling up to someone. Menelaus stared momentarily at the Trojan helmet logo that was spray painted on the side of the stands before tapping the other boy on the shoulder. His helmet was off, and some of his fluffy hair was plastered to the sides of his head.

"What do you want?" he snapped upon first seeing Menelaus.

Menelaus sighed, hopping from one foot to the other. "Let's sort this out right now. You against me, for Helen."

He wished he could take it back the second it left his mouth. It was awful and ridiculous.

Paris' eyes went wide. "You... wanna like, fight me?"

Menelaus shrugged, leaving it open for interpretation. Maybe he could just convince Paris to give up. Doubtful, but possible.

"Um." Paris' heart pounded as he tried to discreetly wipe his palms on his the bottom of his jersey. "That's not a good idea."

Menelaus shrugged again. Paris didn't really want to fight for Helen. Their relationship was almost nonexistent. They spent a lot of time together, but it wasn't really *time together,* in a sense. Neither of them had feelings for each other. It was more of a begrudging friendship.

"Fine," he muttered under his breath. "Fine. I'll... fight you. I guess."

Aphrodite, who was near the conversation, picked up her purse and leaned over the rail. A group of football players had gathered there.

"Pandaras," she said, tapping one of the boys on the shoulder.

He looked up. "What's going on?"

Menelaus and Paris were heading across the field now, going by the perimeter. Aphrodite pointed one pink manicured finger after them.

"I need you to fight Menelaus when I get Paris," she said.

The boy furrowed his brow, then thought better of disregarding her wishes. It gave Aphrodite a rush of pleasure as he jogged after the two boys. She looked up into the stands, shading her eyes against the floodlights.

"Helen, darling!" she called shrilly, finding the girl she was looking for a few rows up.

When Helen heard her name, her neck jerked in the direction of the voice, almost against her will. Aphrodite was waving at her with her fingers, a smile on her face like she had just made out with a lemon.

"Come with meeee," Aphrodite sang, her voice traveling across the crowd like a dove over a battle. "You've got somewhere to be! A hot date with a lovely boy!"

Hecuba and Priam both frowned at Helen, but didn't ask as she got to her feet, grumbling under her breath. *Fucking Aphrodite.* Helen had finally been having a half decent night, and now she swooped in to ruin it.

❧❧❧❧❧ ❦❦❦❦❦

Menelaus and Paris slipped off the field, and into the hallways where the 'fans', if they could even be called that, weren't allowed. Neither of them knew how to go about starting a fight, but didn't want the other to see his ignorance. Paris led them out, into the growing evening. The sweat on his back made him chilly as a gust of wind cooled his body temperature. *Gods,* Paris thought. *Why did I* agree *to this?* He pulled off his helmet, placing it on the ground. Menelaus stood a couple feet away, arms crossed. He surveyed the area. It was just outside the stadium, with a chain link fence to Menelaus' left, and the wall to his right. They were sort of in a sparsely lit alleyway, because at his back, a few hundred meters down, was a road. Ilium confused Menelaus.

"So um," Paris said, crouching beside his helmet. "Do we just…"

Menelaus shrugged, swishing his cleat through an oily puddle. "Suppose so. You ready?"

Nerves were making Paris' hands shake. His mind raced as he tried to remember how to make a fist that didn't break his thumb. He didn't actually have time, because Menelaus smashed a (proper) fist into his jaw. It was kind of surreal. Paris hardly felt any pain, but his teeth clacked together and his mouth tasted like… that iron supplement his mom had made them take for years. So, blood. Not that the supplement had blood in it. Just that blood was the ironiest thing in the alleyway. His feet fumbled underneath him. When he opened his eyes the world was a bit fuzzy.

A burst of adrenaline flooded through Menelaus as he tackled Paris, throwing him to the ground. He hardly noticed the trickle of blood spilling from the corner of his mouth. The other boy groaned, curling onto his side. The rational part of Menelaus knew that this was enough. He had *won*. But Agamemnon's voice whispered in his mind, '*Teach him a lesson he won't forget.*'

And that's when the smoke bomb went off. The air was crowded with pink. Pink. All he could see. Everywhere. Menelaus had no idea what was happening. It made his eyes and throat burn.

Paris, on the other hand, was being rescued. Someone had lifted him up and was dragging him towards the end of the alley. He was *also* confused, his feet feeling heavy as cinder blocks as they scrabbled on the pockmarked concrete. Paris honestly thought he was being kidnapped until the weird pink smoke was gone. (So he *hadn't* hallucinated that.) He looked over his shoulder, trying to get a good look at whoever was dragging him. Everything was a little bit blurry, but he'd know that face anywhere. Aphrodite. That made a weird kind of sense.

When they made it to her convertible, which was waiting at the end of the alley, he croaked out a miserable, "Thank you," which just made her smile sweetly at him.

"Let's get you home," she said, hoisting him into the back of the car.

Paris was honestly shocked to find Helen sitting there as well. True, she did look like she wanted to set fire to Aphrodite's extravagant hairdo, but she was there. Probably against her will. Paris wasn't sure how Aphrodite had gotten him down that alley in her six inch heels, but he was still alive. Menelaus wasn't going to kill him today. (The more he thought about it, the more convinced he was that Menelaus was trying to murder him.) (That was not true.) (But Paris was Paris, so was now afraid of the red haired cornerback.)

# IV

As the smoke cleared, Menelaus rubbed his eyes, trying to get them to stop hurting. Pandarus, who had arrived just when the pink smoke exploded, stood on the fringes, waiting to see what would happened. Now, as Menelaus stumbled into the cleaner air, Pandarus leapt forwards and smashed his helmet into Menelaus' elbow. At the exact moment Menelaus stumbled into the fence, Agamemnon and Hector came running out of the stadium and into the alley.

"What the—?!" Agamemnon demanded, barreling towards his brother, who sunk to the ground, gripping his arm.

Menelaus felt like his arm was splintering. Pandarus stood in the middle of the alley. Hector stopped next to him, eyes wide.

"What is happening?" Hector demanded, yanking Pandarus' helmet from his grasp. "What the *fuck is happening?*"

Pandarus snatched his helmet back. "Aphrodite told me to, okay? She took Paris away."

Hector threw his hands in the air. "And why was *Paris* back here?"

"To end this," Menelaus muttered, from where he was sitting. "Can someone get me a medic? Please?"

Agamemnon, deciding that his brother was fine, stood up. "This is fucking ridiculous. I suggested that they fight for Helen, so we could end this now, but *apparently* someone doesn't understand the honor code, which means you don't *run away* during a fight, and you don't get someone else to smash a helmet into your opponent when they're stumbling around trying to get pink fucking smoke out of their eyes!"

"Go back inside, Pandarus," Hector said, shoving him towards the door. "That was low, man. Really low."

"Guys, can someone get me Patroclus?" Menelaus asked, trying hard to mask the pain in his voice.

Agamemnon ignored him, because there were more important matters at hand. "Hector, you know what this means, right?"

Hector ran a hand over his head, letting out an exasperated breath. "Yeah."

One of the lights popped. Agamemnon tapped his cleat on the ground, the clicking almost echoing. The football field felt so far away from this strange little alley, even though they were right beside each other. Out here, the real world was waiting. There were no refs on dark roads with flickering streetlights and puddles covered in rainbow film. Menelaus groaned, hitting his head against the chain link fence. *Agamemnon would be Agamemnon.*

He'd help Menelaus when he had gotten what he wanted from Hector.

"So you know this means we still have a war," Agamemnon said, crossing his arms.

Hector ground his teeth together. "I get it."

They stood there, locked in a stalemate. Captain against captain. Menelaus was surprised that his brother didn't murder Hector right then and there.

"Good," Agamemnon said, patronizing. "Well, should we get back to the game?"

"Be my guest," Hector replied, matching the other boy's venom.

He waited as Agamemnon turned and gestured for Menelaus to stand up. The younger boy's jersey was filthy, with remnants of pink dye clinging to the mud that caked his back. He hobbled over to the door, Agamemnon behind him. Hector followed them in.

It might have been the most tense moment of Hector's life, walking down the hall with these two guys. Agamemnon kept glaring over his shoulder, as if making sure Hector hadn't pulled a knife on them. The sounds of the crowd getting settled for the second half of the game were muted in the dark passageway. The sound exploded to almost deafening as the three of them snuck back onto the field. The clock on the scoreboard said there were two minutes and forty seven seconds left in half time.

Agamemnon gave Hector one more withering look before dragging Menelaus over to their bench. It wasn't *Hector's* fault that Menelaus and Paris decided to fight each other. He sighed, running his hands over his face again.

Why were people so idiotic? It was beyond Hector's mental capacity to contemplate at the moment. He jogged back over to his team, some of which were watching the cheerleaders do a routine on the field, and some of which who were crowded around Mr. Phoebus.

"Where were *you*?" Aeneas asked as Hector ran up beside him.

"Paris thought it was a good idea to fight Menelaus, and then that idiot over there," he said, gesturing towards Pandarus. "Decided to smash his helmet into Menelaus after Aphrodite set off a smoke bomb to rescue Paris."

Aeneas didn't even blink as he squirted water through the face mask of his helmet. "Well that's exciting. So I'm assuming this... war thing isn't done, then?"

"It's never done!" Euphorbus said, sidling up with Scarpedon in tow. "Agamemnon wants war? We're giving it to him! That kid over there with the red hair looks injured. One of their offense players can't play for the rest of the game! I mean, a couple of our guys are a bit screwed up, but still. It's the first real game. It's uphill from here."

"That red haired kid," Hector replied grimly, "Just beat up Paris in the alley."

Scarpedon snorted. "Serves him right. That kid needed a beating."

Hector glanced up at the clock just long enough to watch the seconds tick from three to zero. The buzzer went and the cheerleaders ran off the field, waving their purple and yellow pom poms in the air. He didn't disagree with Scarpedon. Hector actually wished Aphrodite hadn't swept Paris away before he could get some sense beaten into him.

It was the Trojans turn to receive first, so Hector sat down on the bench next to Zeus. Aeneas, Euphorbus, and Scarpedon sat down to Hector's right. Glaucus and Antenor were on the field. They both played guard.

"Teams are pretty evenly matched in defense, at least," Zeus said, not taking his eyes off the field.

Hector was surprised the man was even watching the game, but he nodded. "We're not quite sure what happened with their O–line. They used to have a lot of good players."

"Mistakes were made," Zeus said. "Many players quit in a stand against events that transpired. I support their decision, but I cannot sponsor such a fractured team."

"Right," Hector replied, leaning forwards, chin in his hand.

Mr. Phoebus was at the field as jogged past the bench, like his own running would make Idaeus go faster. Hector wasn't sure why he had the ball, but somehow, he managed to avoid all of the Stallions' defense. The purple clad members of the stands were cheering louder and louder as Idaeus burst forwards, barely avoiding Agamemnon's desperate leap. Hector stood up, adding his own voice into the building noise. Idaeus crossed into the end zone, throwing the ball to the ground. Excitement charged air with a kind of electricity. First touchdown of the game.

"Hit 'em high! Hit 'em low! Hit 'em where the Trojans go!" the cheer team sang, waving their pom poms around in the air.

Aeneas shook his head, and yelled over the noise, "That cheer needs to not exist."

Hector was laughing, but he nodded anyways.

A few minutes prior, on the other side of the field, Menelaus sat on the bench as Patroclus and Machaon inspected his arm.

"Um," Patroclus said, wincing as he looked at the bruising. "I think your radius is probably fractured. You said someone hit you with a helmet there?"

Menelaus nodded. That sounded so stupid. How had he not noticed that guy, full on jumping at him? The pink smoke had certainly been interesting. That was why he didn't realize. But it still *felt* like a failure. Agamemnon's war wasn't over, and now he was going on about Menelaus' honor even more than before. To the point of awkwardness. Like, you can only talk about one guy's honor so much before he starts to feel self conscious.

"That means I can't play anymore," Menelaus said glumly, watching the kid who had replaced him as corner-back fail to sack the player with the ball.

Machaon raised an eyebrow. "Yeah. That means you shouldn't play. We'll get the proper medic over here in a moment." He got to his feet and walked over to Athena.

They hardly noticed when the touchdown was scored. Menelaus sighed. It had been because the one corner-back hadn't been fast enough. Agamemnon had tried valiantly to stop him, but just ended up getting a faceful of dirt. Briseis had been sitting on the turf a few feet away from the bench, trying to make sense of the game, but Menelaus had heard her snort when Agamemnon bailed.

Now she was next to Patroclus, asking what she could do to help. He said there wasn't much. They just had to wait. And if she couldn't speed up time, nothing could be done. The defense line came off the field for, pissed as all hell. Menelaus didn't want to tell Agamemnon he couldn't play. That would give him another excuse to rant about his lost honor. Luckily, Machaon, on his way back, caught his arm and muttered something to the team captain.

"Gods, Menny!" Agamemnon yelled over at his brother. "I can't believe that! They're fucking savages!"

And that was that. The actual medic came over, complimented Patroclus, and then dug around in a giant bag, producing an arm brace.

"Best I've got for now," he said, gently sliding it over Menelaus' arm. "We'll have to get you to a clinic after the game. To see an X–ray."

Menelaus nodded, wincing as he did up the brace. Patroclus gave him a pitying look, pressing his lips together in a line.

"It's my fault." Menelaus shrugged.

"Never said it wasn't," Patroclus replied with a soft laugh. "But it still sucks. Let me know if you need anything. Ice, Gatorade, gummy worms... I've most likely got it. Unless you want a better offense. Sadly, Achilles won't cave."

The red haired boy shook his head, grimacing from pain and smiling at the same time. Patroclus sat back down beside Bri.

"I'm getting more and more convinced that this game was invented by someone who was heavily intoxicated," she said, furrowing her brow as Odysseus yelled something and threw the ball to a kid who was probably a hundred pounds max. "Or someone who was a strong believer in toxic masculinity."

Patroclus snorted, squinting against the lights. "It's a strange game. But Achilles loves it. So... I know about it. A little bit, at least."

"Achilles says you're good enough to play on the team," she said, looking over at him.

He made a *pfft* noise, waving his hand as if he could brush away a comment like he could a floating piece of lint. "He flatters me. And also, he doesn't know what he's talking about."

"Hey," someone said, putting a hand on Briseis' head.

She looked up to find Agamemnon standing behind her. "Don't touch my hair," she snapped, smacking his hand. "What do you want?"

"Gods," he muttered, crossing his arms. "You're such a piece of work."

Briseis turned around so she was sitting, looking up, and facing him. She smiled. "Didn't I tell you I would be? Also, you're losing, if you didn't notice."

The captain pulled off his helmet, crouching down so he was at her level. His long hair was under a red bandanna, a few strands hanging out on the sides of his face. She grabbed one of them and tugged. He wasn't expecting that, and lurched forwards, threatening to fall out of his squat. She smiled sweetly before kissing him.

He pulled away from her aggressively, wiping his mouth with the back of his hand. "What the fucking hell does your chapstick taste like?" he demanded.

"A pig," Briseis said, wiping her mouth off as well.

"Yeah, I can tell," Agamemnon replied, disgusted.

"Why? Do you like it? I got it specially for you." Briseis asked, batting her eyes sarcastically. "Because you probably kiss pigs in your spare time, when every single woman has rejected you and you're lonely."

Patroclus hadn't turned around, and Briseis could feel his shoulder quaking. He was either laughing or crying. Hopefully laughing. Agamemnon still hadn't stood up. She just wanted him to go away. He grabbed her chin, forcing her to meet him in the eye. Not that she hadn't been doing that already.

"I'll break you," he said quietly. "Just you wait."

"Not if I hit you over the head with actual textbooks next time," she replied vehemently. "And I *won't hesitate.*" She flicked his nose. He flinched and let go of her.

Cheers erupted around them again, reminding Briseis that she wasn't alone with this immature thug.

"*Fuck,*" Agamemnon muttered, standing up. Fumble. Again. The game was more important than Briseis. For now at least. He marched over to Athena, leaving Briseis staring at the sideboard, shaking with suppressed laughter.

"Are you okay?" Patroclus whispered. "Should I have stepped in?"

Briseis turned back around, swallowing as she shook her head. "No. I'll handle him. Do what Achilles couldn't. But no one will stop me if I *do* decide to hit him over the head with textbooks. Can I have a kleenex please?"

Patroclus rooted through his medical bag, producing a wipe. "Is this good enough?"

She took it from him without replying, smearing it across her mouth, trying to rid it of the lip balm and Agamemnon. Patroclus snatched the square out of her hand when she put it *in* her mouth.

"That's an alcohol wipe!" he scolded, putting it in a plastic bag.

Briseis shrugged, shivering. "Sorry. The chapstick is horrible."

"What *is* it?" Patroclus asked, frowning. "There can't actually be pig lip balm, is there?"

"No. But it's close. Bacon. Fun fact, Agamemnon made an offhanded comment about hating bacon, so Iphis and I ordered some," she said, watching Patroclus' face change from concerned to impressed. "Guess it works?"

Patroclus rubbed his eyes, shaking his head. "Whatever you've got to do, I guess."

# V

B Y THE FOURTH QUARTER, everyone on the Stallions' team was done. Agamemnon thought that they definitely should have quit. As he watched Hector absolutely destroy some sophomore who was standing in for one of the players who pulled out, he held in a growl. Even though they were close to tied, there was... Agamemnon glanced up at the clock. Fourteen minutes and 54 seconds left in the game. He had the urge to smash his head into his helmet. Another one lost to the Trojans and their annoyingly persistent cheerleading squad, who, at the moment, were waving around their hideous pompoms with surprising vigor. Crissy wasn't there. She was long gone, to California or Florida, if the rumors were right. Agamemnon was honestly surprised that Helen hadn't joined cheer at Ilium, but it was probably better for Menelaus if he didn't have to see her.

Someone tapped Agamemnon on the shoulder. He pulled himself out of his frustration at the cheer squad just in time to see Aeneas intercept the ball from Odysseus and take off down the field. The deafening support from the Trojan's side of the stands was ridiculous. *What do they think this is, the NFL?* Agamemnon thought bitterly, before remembering why he had looked up in the first place. Diomedes was standing beside him, watching the play with an expression of mild disgust on his face.

"What?" Agamemnon demanded, turning away from the field as the stands erupted, sending echoes of pride up into the bitterly cold sky.

The other boy shook his head as the player on the breakaway finally got tackled. By Odysseus. The quarterback. He should *not* have been the one to do that. The disappointed '*awwwu*' gave Agamemnon a jolt of satisfaction. This game wasn't over just yet.

"Well that was dumb," Diomedes said, blowing out an annoyed cloud of air. The night was getting brisk, so his breath was white, swirling across the darkness of the sky. "Well. Athena wanted me to run something by you."

Agamemnon waited. The Trojans called a time out, for whatever reason.

"And that is?" he asked after a long, irritating moment.

Diomedes shrugged. "I dunno. She wanted to talk to me, with you there."

"Lead the way," Agamemnon muttered, sarcastically gesturing towards their coach, who was standing with her arms crossed, away from the team.

Athena wasn't wearing a jacket. Just a scarf, wrapped proudly around her neck, like it was only there for show. She stood away from her team, surveying the stands with the air of someone who was above it all. The lights, the crowds, the excitement. She was above human emotions. As Diomedes and Agamemnon trotted over to her, she sighed, watching her breath dissipate into the night. The cold burned her nostrils and made her lungs wish for warmth. Technically, she could just leave. It didn't matter, because tonight they would lose. It was their first game with the shoddy offense line, and no matter how good Odysseus was, football couldn't be played by one person.

"You wanted us, Coach?" Diomedes asked as the two of them stopped.

He looked a little bit cold, with his shoulders hunched up by his ears. The boy was trying to play it off by crossing his arms, his helmet loosely gripped in one of his hands, but Athena still found it amusing. Her captain, on the other hand, stood there like the imposing brick wall he was. Agamemnon was riled up. She could see it gleaming in his eyes. Hungry to play. He would get another chance very soon.

"Yes," Athena replied, "I did. I have a strategy."

Agamemnon glanced back at the clock. The orange numbers cast a glow over the field that was more noticeable at night, reflecting across the players' helmets.

"Since Menelaus is unfortunately out for the game, and our replacement is... less than adequate," Athena said quietly, "I need you to try something. Specifically Diomedes." Agamemnon opened his mouth to interject, but Athena shook her head. "I need you to know about this so you can explain it to anyone on the team who questions him," she said, pointing at Diomedes with her thumb. "Got it?"

"Yes, Coach," the captain replied, slightly put off.

The clock was now down to twenty seconds. Athena pulled Diomedes over so he was standing beside her.

She pointed at one of the offensive players on the Trojans' team. "See how he's walking with that limp?" Diomedes nodded. "And that other guy. The one who keeps stretching his shoulder. Study the offense for the next ten seconds, find out who has injuries or sore spots, and then hit them in that exact place. I need them to not score again for the rest of the game. Take as many players out of the game as possible. Is that clear?"

Diomedes smirked and shoved his helmet back on his head as the buzzer went off. Athena didn't generally encourage more violence than necessary, but she had been watching the refs for the entire game. Whoever paid them off paid well, because they called offside, facemask, and downfield pass, but that was it. And players on both teams were doing far more than that. Agamemnon let out a bellowing yell that sounded like a war cry, which was quickly taken up by his teammates. The cheer squad started screaming as well, which led the entirety of the Stallions' fans to do the same.

Of course, the Trojans did the same, so the noise was almost comical, in a painful kind of way that sent blood pounding through everyone's bodies. How could people get so excited over this game? Athena saw the sports med trainer and his friend plugging their ears. They were the only smart ones here.

True to his word, or his... smirk, Diomedes was able to get three players out of the game and onto the bench to get medical attention within six minutes. At this point, everyone was watching the clock more than the game. The score was close, but with the Stallions' offense, there wasn't much hope. On the bench, Menelaus closed his eyes. He had really hoped they would win this game, but without Achilles... it was kind of hopeless. And now that Menelaus wasn't playing, there was a hole in the defense. Not that he made much of a difference. Diomedes was flying all over the field with renewed energy. Menelaus has seen him talking with Athena and Agamemnon, so that was probably their doing. He didn't want to be here anymore. The day had gone on too long and—

There was a collective gasp. Menelaus opened his eyes out of pure curiosity.

On the far side of the turf was a pile of three people. Patroclus was already running across the field with his awkwardly shaped first aid kit, Macahon, the older trainer who had been playing in the game, following closely behind.

"Did you see what happened?" Macahon asked, catching up to the Patroclus.

Patroclus nodded, slowing down as he reached the growing crowd. "Can I get through please?" he asked, gently moving people out of the way. Diomedes was standing awkwardly beside a Trojan player, who was on the ground, clutching a shoulder that was most definitely dislocated. Beside him was Aphrodite. *She* was in shock, her perfect hair coming loose, her designer clothes rumpled as she sat up. Patroclus and Macahon immediately darted forwards, no longer caring about politeness.

"What the *fuck,* man?!" a huge guy declared, shoving people out of the way.

He was storming towards Diomedes, anger warping his features.

Diomedes put up his hands. "Chill out dude, it was an accident."

"Ares, no..." Aphrodite chided quietly, at the massive man. It sounded like a question, but only Patroclus heard her, because he was trying to hold her wrist still. It was broken. He was glad she hadn't noticed yet. Hopefully the actual medic would get here before she had that realization.

"Stop," Machaon said with as much authority as one can muster towards a giant man and a tall boy who look like they're squaring up to have a fight.

"Get out of the way," someone demanded. "Medical attention coming through."

The crowd parted, letting the harassed–looking sports med doctor into the center of the circle just as Diomedes decided it was a good idea to punch the man, Ares, in the stomach. Aphrodite screamed, but not because of that. The adrenaline was wearing off and she... saw her wrist. The doctor shooed Patroclus out of the way, taking over. Machaon was now dragging Diomedes out of the circle, having a quietly heated argument with him.

"Aphrodite was an *accident.* I tackled that player out of bounds and she was walking there!" Diomedes said heatedly,

"But then you had to punch that man! He wasn't doing any-thing to you," Machaon replied with the same intensity.

"Yeah well. He was *going* to hit me. Did you see him? I'll bet he goes around killing people for fun! I had to defend myself!"

"By throwing the first punch?"

"Fuck yeah. I had to assert my dominance!"

"Oh my—"

"Yes, and before you say anything stupid..."

As they crossed the field, Zeus was just making his way over to the scene, curious about what was taking so long. What he found was a gong show. Aphrodite, crying with a brace around her wrist, the Trojan player literally screaming bloody murder as the doctor reset his shoulder, and Ares, doubled over on the ground.

*Godsdamn,* Zeus thought, taking in the scene. Aphrodite was married to one of Zeus' sons. His name was Hephastus, and Zeus had no idea how he had convinced Aphrodite to marry him. Ares was obviously having an affair with her, because she was unsatis-fied in her marriage. Aphrodite had had *several* affairs. (Zeus and Aphrodite were very alike, and it disturbed him.) And for reasons unknown to Zeus, Ares now treated *him* like a father.

"Zeus!" Ares called angrily. "That boy! He broke Aphrodite's wrist! And then he punched *me!*"

Zeus frowned, stroking his beard. "Well it seems like that was probably an accident," he replied.

"No!" Aphrodite shrieked. "It was on *purpose!*"

"Dear, I don't think anyone besides Helen has a personal vendetta against you," Zeus said empathetically, turning away from the chaos.

He had honestly expected something more exciting with that crowd.

When Aphrodite (and Ares, for no good reason) left in an ambulance twenty minutes later, everyone was freezing. Most people didn't actually know what was going on, and the refs were ready to just call the game, but both teams insisted on playing the last few minutes. Or, in Agamemnon's words: "We're men. We fight to the bitter end," which he declared to the ref with perfect sincerity. The ref looked to Athena, but she just shrugged. To the bitter end it was.

# VI

TWO MINUTES BEFORE THE buzzer went, both teams had pretty much given up. The score hadn't moved since the Aphrodite catastrophe, and the Trojans were still on the third down in the Stallions forty yard zone. Diomedes was done with the game. The only one who seemed to remotely care was Agamemnon, but even he was slowing down. Their defense had pretty much become a line, and the Trojans were just playing pass at this point. Everyone was just running out the clock. That was... until Glaucus, who didn't have the ball, bolted forwards. Agamemnon started to yell something, realized the quarterback still had the ball, and shut his mouth.

"Diomedes!" Glaucus bellowed, causing the other boy to blink.

He had been staring into space, but as the Trojan player barrelled towards him, Diomedes dropped into a ready position.

"I challenge you—" Glaucus was yelling as he rammed into him, head first.

Ajax 1 was standing next to Diomedes as this happened. He just watched, slightly baffled by the event unfolding in front of him. Football, as far as he knew, didn't generally involve tackling people without some kind of prompting. And he *definitely* knew that it didn't involve wrestling on the ground and screaming at each other. Ajax wondered briefly if he should pull them apart as Glaucus punched Diomedes in the stomach, but then his teammate grabbed the Trojan player's helmet and threw him onto the ground. Ajax snorted. This was ridiculous. The refs weren't stopping anything so while Diomedes and Glaucus fought... something out, both teams slowly made their way over to where Ajax was standing, all muttering in amusement and confusion.

"What is *happening*?" Agamemnon hissed from behind Ajax.

He shrugged, frowning at the captain through his helmet. "The Trojan guy just... ran at him for no reason," he said softly.

"This... is for... Aeneas' mom," Glaucus finally said, loud enough for Ajax to hear clearly as Diomedes rolled off his back and grabbed the cage of Glaucus' helmet.

It sounded like Diomedes was laughing. All anyone heard from what he said next was, "Milf," which just made Glaucus slam the other boy's head into the ground.

"I'm not wrong!" came Diomedes' muffled yell as he tried to hit Glaucus from his awkward position.

"Hey! Hey!" The ref was finally trying to get through the circle of players. "This is unsportsmanlike condu—"

The buzzer went, cutting the ref off, and eliciting a roaring cheer from the stands. The Trojans side of the stands. Agamemnon swore under his breath, pushing Ajax 1 out of his way. Or... *trying* to push Ajax out of the way. He didn't even have to take a step. *Agamemnon's so funny*, Ajax thought, hiding a smile.

"That's enough," Agamemnon said to the players on the ground. Like that was going to do anything.

They didn't hear him. Hector and Aeneas shoved into the center of the circle. Hector shook his head in disappointment as he and his teammate tried to haul the players apart. Ajax 1 looked to Agamemnon, who nodded. They grabbed their man, expecting a struggle. Instead, Glaucus rolled onto his back, practically giggling. Diomedes did the same.

"What the fuck...?" Hector glanced over at Agamemnon, who just shrugged.

"Not the milf jokes," Glaucus gasped in between gales of laugher. "Not the milf jokes."

Diomedes snickered, pulling off his helmet and sitting up. "*Always* the milf jokes."

Aeneas crossed his arms. "If this is about my mom, I will literally punch you."

Glaucus shook his head, still laying on the turf. The refs has given up at this point, leaving the players to do whatever the hell they were doing. The game was over, and so was their pay. Both teams were still on the field, watching in confusion and amusement as their players laughed on the ground.

"As lovely as this is," Hector started, sounding like a disappointed grandmother, "I think we should probably pack up and get off the field so the people who clean it don't have to stay up until three in the morning."

"Remember, Stallions, we have a long bus ride. Let's get cleaned up and on the road," Odysseus yelled from somewhere near the back of the crowd.

Hector nodded. "It's getting kinda cold too."

The Stallions started filing away, back towards their bench.

"Good game!" Aeneas called after the retreating team.

Agamemnon gave him a sarcastic salute. Menelaus, on the other hand, jogged over and shook Hector and Aeneas' hands, even though one arm was in a sling.

"I'm sorry about my brother," he said, glancing back over his shoulder like he might accidentally summon Agamemnon. "And about Paris too. Aphrodite took him, I think."

Hector snorted and shook his head. "No hard feelings about Paris. He'll be fine." He looked down at the brace on the younger boy's arm. "Are *you* okay? Pandarus..." Hector rubbed his eyes. "I don't even know what to say about that."

"Menny!" Agamemnon yelled from across the field. Briseis was standing a few feet away. She had her arms crossed as she tapped Agamemnon on the shoulder.

Aeneas glared over Menelaus' shoulder. The younger boy laughed sadly. "Yeah I'm good. See you later." As he walked away, he looked back. "Good game by the way!"

As Menelaus jogged over, Agamemnon turned to see Briseis. He smiled. She shuddered.

"What?" he asked aggressively, making her flinch.

"You're gonna leave me the fuck alone," she said under her breath. "Because if you touch me, try to talk to me, or even lay eyes on me, I'm going to complain to multiple police stations, and take this to the board of directors at our school. And then, I'll take it to the board of student exchanges, and then I'll take you to court. And there's nothing you can do to stop me. I don't want to pretend to tolerate you anymore." With that, she marched away, back to Patroclus, who had been a minor part in convincing her to do that. More like... encouraging her.

Agamemnon stood there, unable to comprehend as his team rushed around him. *Fuck.*

In the middle of the field, Diomedes finally got to his feet, meaning to follow Menelaus. He and Glaucus had played club football together last year. The stands were clearing out quickly because of the damp chill in the air, but Diomedes held out a hand to the other player.

"That was a good one," Glaucus admitted, letting himself be hoisted to his feet, then shaking Diomedes' hand. "Nice doing business with you."

Hector and Aeneas were watching with curiosity from a few meters away as Diomedes said something under his breath, making Glaucus snort. Aeneas raised an eyebrow, sharing a puzzled look with Hector as the two players started taking off their jerseys. Once they had handed them to each other, they shook hands again, and parted ways.

"What are you *doing*?" Hector asked, an odd smile on his face as Glaucus made his way over to them.

They were the last three on the field. It was strangely peaceful. The lights hid the stars behind their glow, but they couldn't stifle the darkness of the sky beyond it. The air was frosty, to the point where it hurt Hector's lungs to breathe in. Rare. Glaucus laughed, and didn't stop walking. Hector and Aeneas hastened after him, sharing another bewildered look.

Their friend waved the red jersey in the air. "It's just a game, guys. Sure, it's fun to play at being men, but we're not. This is our last hurrah, as some may say." He let the other two catch up. "I dunno. Diomedes and I played football over the summer. We did stuff like that all the time. Breaking rules is something we don't get to do very often without... someone screaming at us. So why not break the stupid ones? Who cares what colour jersey I wear? I'm still on y'alls team."

Glaucus pushed open the door into the underside of the stadium, gesturing for Hector to go in first.

"That was weirdly insightful, coming from you," he said as he walked inside.

Glaucus shoved Hector's head down from behind, snickering. "I can't believe you fell for that bullshit. I dunno. Diomedes just said it would be funny. And *man*, that guy's sense of humor is fantastic."

Aeneas sighed. "Because my mother is absolutely hilarious," he said under his breath.

The sounds of the Trojan's locker room filled the hallway. Hector had actually forgotten about their win.

He smiled, gently ramming into Aeneas' shoulder. "Are you seriously defending her right now?"

The other boy snorted. "I feel the need to protect her, but she just does all this crazy shit... yeah okay. Glaucus, my mother is a good source of humor."

Glaucus gave him two thumbs up before pushing open the door to the changeroom. The smell of sweat and energy drinks flooded out into the no longer quiet hall. Hector smirked and followed his teammate in. He was greeted with shouts of a victory that didn't quite feel earned, but was well deserved.

⁂

Hector pulled his phone out of his locker after he finally got there. The team had made it very difficult for him to move with their aggressive cheering and singing of their poorly written team chant. The first message made him pause, halfway through changing. His shirt gripped in one hand, he frowned.

Andromache <3:

> I'm here to pick you up. When you're ready.

*Sent 9:35 PM*

Aeneas looked over his shoulder.

"I thought she wasn't feeling good," he said, closing his locker door. Most of the team had left by now, gone to the team room. Mr. Phoebus probably went to the liquor store. He did that sometimes. Brought cheap alcohol after they won. Hector didn't particularly approve of this, but he was their captain, not their coach. It didn't really matter what he thought.

Scarpedon and Euphorbus were the only other two left in the change room.

On their way out, Scarpedon grabbed Hector's T-shirt and whipped him across the back. "Good game, captain!" he yelled as they passed.

"Can I have my shirt back?" Hector asked, holding out a hand without looking away from his phone.

"Tomorrow," Scarpedon called from behind a row of lockers.

Hector sighed. "How about now?"

"Fine." The shirt came flying over.

"Thanks," Hector replied, finally having to finish his scrutiny of Andromache's strange message to catch it. "Good job! Can't wait for next game!"

"We're gonna bust some Stallion *ass*!" Euphorbus called as the door closed behind them.

Aeneas closed his locker door and threw his bag over his shoulder. "Are you gonna go home?" he asked.

Hector shrugged. "I'll see what Andromache wants."

"Good plan," Aeneas said. "See you tomorrow."

"Yeah."

Aeneas bumped into Hector's shoulder on his way out. He put down his phone and pulled his shirt on before replying to her.

Hector:

> I thought you weren't feeling good.
> you okay?

*Sent 9:52 PM*

It took her a couple minutes to respond. He kept anxiously glancing at his phone while he grabbed everything he needed from his locker. The moment he yanked his sweater over his head, his phone buzzed. He struggled for a moment, semi–stuck in his hoodie. The message on his screen did nothing to help with the anxiety mounting in his stomach.

Andromache <3:

> Yeah I'm fine. You almost done?
> I need to talk to you.

*Sent 10:00 PM*

Hector:

Coming now

*Sent 10:00 PM*

He grabbed his bag from his locker and accidentally slammed it shut. She wouldn't come pick him up if she was going to break up with him, would she? *Fuck.* He pulled up his hood as he walked out of the changeroom, jogging down the hallway. His parents had gone home after the game, probably to interrogate Paris and Helen about their abrupt disappearance. Hector's footsteps were swallowed by the excited whoops still coming from the team room. His heart was beating faster than it had during the game. When he burst out into the cold, he saw that the parking lot was mostly empty. It was crazy how fast people cleared out when it was chilly. Andromache's little old BMW was parked underneath one of the lights, making it glimmer with dew.

Hector hadn't been in that car for a long time. They normally took his everywhere, or more often, they just walked. He shivered, jogging over to where she was parked. His legs were stiff, but that was just part of playing sports. When he got closer, he slowed down to a walk, breathing deeply. Nothing was necessarily going to happen. It would be fine. He stopped beside the driver's window and tapped gently on the glass. Andromache looked up quickly, her eyes wide. She had been crying. That made Hector even more nervous. Not that she didn't normally cry. It was just that she didn't normally stare into space like that. When she was alone, she was usually on her phone, talking to someone, checking her social media, writing poetry in her notes app or stuff like that.

She rolled down the window a crack. "Get in."

"Okay—" Hector started saying, but she rolled the window back up as he was talking.

As he walked around the car, all he could think was *what did I do?* And this led to a super speed replay of as many of their interactions as he could remember, trying to find something that had possibly... ruined them. He exhaled. They were supposed to get married after school. Obviously she didn't know that. He was planning to propose over the summer. So they weren't *supposed* to get married. Hector was *hoping* they would. His hands were damp as he pulled open the passenger door and swung into the seat. The old leather creaked with the impact, which made him close the door as gently as possible. Nothing to aggravate Andromache. Breaking her car would definitely be a red flag. He put his bag on the floor at his feet, turning to face her.

Andromache was breathing so evenly that it was scary.

"Hey—" he started.

"No," Andromache said, cutting him off again. She didn't take her eyes off the empty parking spaces in front of them, but she could feel the tears welling there. She swallowed, willing them to go away.

"Look," Hector started, leaning forwards. "Whatever I did—" He cut himself off on his own this time. The leather creaked again as Hector tentatively reached out and put a hand on her shoulder.

"What're you trying to tell me?" he asked, trying to sound calm, and failing.

Andromache pressed her fingers into her eyes. This wasn't how this was supposed to go. She didn't actually know how this was supposed to go. She let out a harsh breath.

"I... fuck," she whispered through her hands, "I can't... I don't know how to say this."

Hector stopped breathing. "No. No... I—Andromache, baby, you don't know what you're talking about—"

"No," Andromache said again. "Hector, I do. Can you just. Let me talk?",

He closed his mouth. There was a prickling climbing up the back of his throat. No. No he wasn't going to cry now. He took a breath. It would be fine.

Andromache finally looked over at him, tears still on the brim of falling. The bags under her eyes were like hollows in the low light. *How had he not noticed?* She slowly removed his hand from her shoulder. In truth, she was afraid. She could feel her pulse jolting through her body, the blood rushing in her ears. Right now, they were on a precipice. They could catch each other, or fall.

The words tumbled from her mouth before she could think again. "I'm pregnant."

Hector's mind went blank. "*What?*"

That was not what he had been expecting. The breakup talk he had been imagining in his mind seemed ridiculous now. Andromache stared at him, her eyes wide as he smiled. She wasn't sure how to react. She had been imagining him freaking out and leaving her. Maybe this was the start of him going insane. She swallowed, hiding her hands in the sleeves of her sweater.

"I thought you were gonna break up with me," he said, relief and disbelief battling for supremacy in his tone.

Andromache laughed, and quickly stifled it. "I thought you were gonna break up with *me*."

Hector held out a hand. She took it shyly, suddenly feeling like it was their first date again. He wrapped both of his hands around hers.

"Fuck," he said under his breath.

Andromache was suddenly certain that this would be the moment where the happiness ended. He would get out of the car, and that would be it. A tear fell from her eye, dripping down onto her light blue coat. It left a water stain as it tumbled, down down down. She inhaled, preparing herself for the worst.

Hector looked over at her, his eyes stormy and serious. "I am so sorry."

Again, she was... confused.

"Andromache, I can't believe... oh Gods. This is my fault. I thought we were okay. I thought we were safe... I'm... yeah I don't know what else to say. I feel like I'm sorry doesn't really... cut it." He pressed her hand to his forehead, closing his eyes. He had messed up her life. Either way... she would have to go through something awful and it was his fault. It hurt him to think about her hurting.

As she stared down at the most baffling boy she had ever met, Andromache was once again mystified. Hector presented himself as someone who didn't give a shit. And sometimes he didn't. But for some reason, when he was with her, he *did* care. So much. He looked up at her, guilt and pain blatantly written across his face. She didn't know how to respond.

"Okay," he said, letting out another breath. It was going to be okay. They were gonna be fine. Hopefully. "So, if you want me to be there, I will. No matter what. Obviously if you want me to. I... don't really know anything about...anything. But. I'll do whatever you need."

She laughed cautiously again, unsure how to take any of this. "You don't... care what I do with it?"

Hector raised an eyebrow, still looking up at her. "It's your body. I have zero say over what you do." He smiled sadly, without showing his teeth. "And I love you. So. I'll do whatever you need. Like I said. I'm not going anywhere." He paused. "Unless you tell me to. Go somewhere."

She sniffled, but she was smiling down at him. "I love you too," she said. "But still. I'm very disturbed by the... need some men have to control what women do with their bodies."

Hector nodded, swallowing again. He was a bit shell-shocked. But it was okay.

Andromache cleared her throat. "Um... Hector?"

"Yeah?"

"I have a weird request," she said softly, her voice trembling a little.

He nodded, letting go of her hand and awkwardly reaching an arm around her. Andromache didn't mention how uncomfortable it was. She was glad to have him here. The world was scary, and she knew she could handle it. It was just... so much better with someone who cared.

"I really... I don't want you to get hurt," she continued, leaning over the divider between the seats. It was cold in the car. Hector was warm. "And I think... it would be better if you stopped playing football."

Hector stopped breathing again.

"Hector?" Andromache asked tentatively, peering up at him. This couldn't be the last straw. It just *couldn't*. They could *not* go through everything they just went through, only to have him leave over football.

It started to rain outside, pattering gently across the windshield. Hector watched it falling in front of the light that cast a yellow glow across the now almost completely empty parking lot. Stop playing football.

"Look, Andy," he said, as gently as possible. "I think... if I could get Agamemnon to stop paying off the refs, then it would be way less dangerous."

She bit her lip, nodding.

"I think I can get them to stop," he said again. "And then. I think... well. Have you seen the Stallions offense? They're tiny. And there's no way I could possibly get hurt on the field."

"I just don't like the way that they're playing," she replied softly. "But I trust you."

He pressed his nose into the top of her head. She was wearing a knit hat that smelled like clean laundry.

"It's my last season," he said. "Then I'll be done for good. I swear."

"Okay."

"Do you want to stay at my place?" Hector's parents had been clear that when he and Andromache had turned eighteen, she could stay over, as long as they were *safe*. (Which. They were. But apparently not.)

"Yes."

"Do you want me to drive?"

She nodded again. "But can we sit here a moment?"

"Always."

⁕ ⁕ ⁕

That night, laying in bed with Andromache curled up against him, Hector tried to come up with a plan to end the 'war' for Helen. He wasn't quite sure how it had become a real thing. Staring up at the little light up stars that Andromache had on his ceiling in the shape of their initials in a heart, he ached. There was no way he could do this without... Agamemnon's approval. And that generally meant unnecessary violence. Pandarus and Aphrodite had ruined the chance to fight it out with Menelaus... but maybe... Hector internally smacked himself. There was no way that this was a good idea.

Andromache didn't want him to get hurt. There was no way that challenging someone to a fight would be what she wanted. But if no one else got hurt... and if he *won*, Helen could go back to

Mycenae academy, and the refs would start calling dangerous fouls. Hector ran a hand over his face. This was a horrible idea. A truly horrible idea.

But it was one that could work.

# VII

HECTOR LEFT AT SIX the following morning. Getting up that early on a Saturday was painful, but it had to be done. He slipped out of the room as quietly as possible so he didn't wake Andromache. She was almost completely hidden under the duvet, breathing softly. His door had a tendency to screech, so he closed it slowly, praying it would cooperate. With a pair of shorts and a T–shirt in hand, he tip–toed down the hall to the bathroom. After changing and brushing his teeth, he emerged again and tapped on Paris' door. It was the farthest room from the stairs, which annoyed Hector to no end because his younger brother was always thumping down in the middle of the night to do Gods know what.

"What?" Paris mumbled from inside his room.

Hector threw open the door, letting the dim morning light stream into the dark room. Paris groaned, rolling over in bed, blankets rustling as he hid from Hector.

"Rise and shine, bitch," Hector said, loudly enough for Paris to hear, but quiet enough not to alert their parents that they were up.

He marched into the room and flicked on the lights. "We're going on an adventure."

"Hector," came someone's groggy voice from the floor on the other side of the bed. "Kindly... of course, but what the fuck."

He hadn't realized that Helen was in here, but it made sense. Aphrodite had brought them home last night and probably locked them in Paris' room or something equally crazy. Helen usually went in the guest room. It did make him almost laugh that she was sleeping on the floor.

"Sorry," he whispered. "You can go back to sleep once I get this slug out of here."

"Whyyyyy?" Paris groaned again, but this time he sat up.

"Because you fucked up last night, buddy. We went over this when Aphrodite banned us from leaving this room," Helen said from the floor. "Hector... the man–killing man of all men... is probably gonna try and remedy your errors."

Helen knew she didn't make much sense when she was tired. Her filter disappeared completely. (Although, it was there less and less nowadays.) But she thought she deserved to speak her mind about Paris for a second. She was sleeping on his floor for Gods' sakes. Without a pillow too, because *apparently* he needed all three that were on his bed. What a weirdo. Paris theatrically flopped backwards, making the springs creak right in her ear.

"She ain't wrong," Hector said from by the door.

"Why do I need to *be* there though? You know me fighting someone won't turn out well and then Helen will have to leave..."

Helen thought that might be kind of nice, but she had enough common sense to keep her mouth shut. Now wasn't a good time to argue with Paris.

Hector sighed. Helen could picture him running a hand over his head. "Okay well," he said. "I'll just go tell Agamemnon that Helen's going back anyways."

Wouldn't that be nice? Helen didn't let herself dwell on that thought for too long. She just wanted to go home... but her home was sort of here now. The people in Ilium were less dramatic. And Paris wasn't a horrible friend. She only had one more year. It would be fine.

Paris let out a tortured sign. He honestly... didn't really if Helen left. He'd miss her sarcasm and company, but they were friends. Maybe they could still text. Paris huffed again. He felt like he was so deep into the hole Aphrodite had dug that there was pretty much no way out.

"I'm leaving in ten minutes," Hector said in response. "It's up to you what happens."

That was one thing Helen didn't miss. Her siblings and their constant aggression.

"Also, sorry again Helen. I didn't think you'd be in here."

"Yeah, I didn't either. I must've fallen asleep while lecturing your brother while Aphrodite thought we were doing more explicit things," she muttered, burying her face in the too small blanket that Paris has given her. "But it's fine. Have fun being a man."

Hector snorted, turned off the light, and gently closed the door.

At eight in the morning on Saturday, Agamemnon got a DM from Hector.

@hector235466532:

We should meet somewhere bring your best player(s) and I'll fight whoever you want me to.

To make up for Paris'... stupidity

In Case that wasn't obvious. We're in town now so. Lmk where to meet you

*Sent 8:09 AM*

Agamemnon never woke up this early on the weekend, but Menelaus had just called, telling him that his arm wasn't actually broken. Only bruised or fractured or something. Agamemnon was actually kind of impressed with Hector. He hadn't been expecting anything after Pandarus literally *shattered* the honor code. Just full out... violence.

The rest of his friends wouldn't be thrilled about getting up this early. Especially after the late bus ride home from the game. It was awful. Athena didn't really say anything, and everyone on the team was disappointed. On some level at least. Most of them seemed to think that they could still get better. This was a chance to show

Hector who was the better team, with or without Achilles. (Even if it wasn't entirely true.)

But Agamemnon saw the truth. If Zeus wasn't sponsoring them, and if Peleides wasn't on the team, then they were trash. Agamemnon hated losing. Quitting was better than losing.

One of the perks of being team captain was that Agamemnon had his own room, so after getting ready as fast as he could, he messaged the D–line group chat. Which wasn't the real defense line group chat. It only had his friends in it, but they were the players that... made the defense good. So Agamemnon figured it didn't matter.

## The stallions only hope

Agamemnon:

> Important meeting in the parking lot. ASAP>>>

*Sent 8:15 AM*

And as he walked briskly down the dorm hallway, not caring about his heavy footfalls, he replied to Hector.

@its_agamemnon_atrides_cowards:

> baseball diamond. Shouldn't be busy today. And there's a bunch of trees around.

*Sent 8:21 AM*

Hector replied almost immediately.

@hector235466532:
Sounds good

*Sent 8:22 PM*

It was a bit of a walk to the school from his dorm building, but Agamemnon took his time. He didn't particularly care that he was the one who had *called* the meeting. It was better when other people showed up before him, because then he didn't have to wait around. He was wearing a white collared school shirt with their uniform sweater over top. Agamemnon found that he preferred to look put together. People took him more seriously.

The chill after the rain was burning off now, but the air still clung to the inside of his nose, regardless of the bright sunlight. This time of year was his favorite, but only because the football season happened to coincide. He hated that it was his last year ay Mycenae. In the real world, he'd have a bigger chance of having to face the consequences of his actions. He clenched his jaw at the thought, but didn't have much more time to think about how frustrating reality was.

The majority of his defense players were standing around in a huddled clump beside the staff parking lot. Agamemnon shoved his hands in his pockets as he made his way across the last of the soaking grass and over around the black barricade that bordered the parking stalls.

Ajaces, both greater and lesser were sitting on the curb, while Diomedes and Odysseus stood across across from them with Menelaus. So technically, the group chat wasn't just defense, because Odysseus was on there. Whatever.

"What's up?" Diomedes asked as soon as Agamemnon joined their little circle.

He smiled, kicking a pebble across the scuffed concrete. "Hector thought of something to restore our honor."

Menelaus sighed passive aggressively, but everyone ignored him.

"See, other people actually *do* care, so it's not just me," Agamemnon said, eyeing his brother, who suddenly found the ground fascinating. "And he wants to fight with someone on our team for Helen." Menelaus looked up abruptly. "Yeah. So, you could actually get your girlfriend back."

Ajax 2 raised an eyebrow at Ajax 1 as Agamemnon kept talking. "Don't you think it's kind of ironic that he's causing this whole war over Menelaus' 'stolen' girlfriend when he literally tried to steal *Achilles'* girlfriend?"

Ajax 1 glanced up at their captain to make sure he hadn't heard the last comment, then shook his head with a small smile. "Fucking bastard," he muttered, which made Ajax 2 laugh.

"Do you think this is *funny*?" Agamemnon demanded, stopping mid-sentence to snarl at his friends. "Because it isn't. It's not funny, okay?" The two of them nodded solemnly. "Good. Now. Who's going to fight Hector?"

That question was met with Menelaus' enthusiastic volunteering. And *that* was met by Agamemnon's blatant disagreement.

"Menny, you have a... sort of broken arm," Agamemnon said, disappointment dripping from his voice. "There's a very low chance that you could beat Hector with *both* your arms. So that means there's exactly zero chance of getting Helen back."

"Gee, thanks for the vote of confidence," Menelaus muttered under his breath, his shoulders slumping.

Agamemnon crossed the circle and clapped him on the back. "No hard feelings. You're just smaller than him and he's a fucking beast." He turned to face his friends, clapping his hands together. "So. Who's gonna fight him?"

The second time the question was asked, it was met with dead silence.

Agamemnon looked around with the air of a displeased author-ity figure. "This is actually really depressing," he said, crossing his arms.

"Well why don't *you* do it?" Ajax 2 suggested boldly.

The captain scoffed, looking down on the Ajaces. "I can't get hurt. I'm invaluable to the team."

Odysseus ran his hands over his face. It was too early for this. "Why don't we do one of those online hat name picker things?"

A hot gust of wind swept across the parking lot, making every-one uncomfortable. Even Agamemnon.

He grunted. "Let's do it in my car."

This was met with general agreement, and the group all ran over to the student parking lot, vaulting over the barrier between the two concrete pads. Not many students brought in their vehicles, but Agamemnon liked leaving campus on the weekends. It took some smushing, but all six of them settled in to the convertible, crowding around Odysseus' phone.

"Ah, much better," Odysseus said sarcastically as Diomedes slammed the door shut. "Just what I wanted today. Chilling on top of the bros."

"Shut up or you're going back outside," Agamemnon replied from the driver's seat.

Diomedes snorted. "You know what? *You* could just fight Hector. No one would mind."

The AC roared to life as Agamemnon started the car. Ajax 1, who was in the front seat sighed in relief. Agamemnon leaned into the backseat to see Odysseus' phone.

"Okay so... I'm putting Diomedes' name into our online hat..." Odysseus said absently, distracted by his phone, "And Ajax 1, and Ajax 2, and um..."

"Yourself," Diomedes added helpfully. "Don't forget your own scrawny ass."

"Ahhh," Odysseus said, shaking his pointer finger with a sarcastic smile on his face. "That's what I was missing." He looked back down at his phone. "I'll type that in. My... Own... Scrawny... Ass. Perfect. Okay. And I'm pressing the button... now. Ooh, ooh, it's shaking the names... and now one of the little animated papers is coming out... it's floating in the air... and... and... dramatic reveal! It's Ajax 1! Our champion!"

Diomedes shook his head. "Damn. I was really hoping it would be—"

"Me," Odysseus finished his sentence with a guileless shrug. "Guess it wasn't meant to be."

"Hey Ajax," Menelaus said from where he was pressed into the door on the right. "You're okay with that, right?"

The giant boy laughed. Agamemnon pounded him on the back. "Of course I am. Hector won't know what hit him."

❧ ❦

Paris and Hector had been sitting on a picnic table at the community baseball diamond for a solid half hour. It was an out of the way little place, surrounded by poplar trees. Their leaves were starting to turn yellow, with the state on the cusp of fall. On the other side of the empty parking lot, a brown river meandered past, carrying debris from who knows where.

They had even gone to get breakfast at some place that thought it was a good idea to sell milkshakes first thing in the morning. So obviously that was what they got. Milkshakes at eight am. Breakfast of champions. Now, the empty drive thru cups sat beside them on the top of the table. Hector leaned on his knees, his feet resting on the seat. He was actually starting to hope they wouldn't show up, but that was just when a red convertible pulled into the empty gravel parking lot. Hector's SUV was the only other car there.

"Why did you bring me again?" Paris asked. He had calmed down somewhat since coming out of his bedroom, but he still wished he was at home. His mom would have made breakfast and then he had plans with some of the soccer guys. All of that was *not* happening now.

Hector pushed up his hoodie sleeves, picking the flaking paint on the table as he watched Agamemnon and his crew get out of the car.

"Have your phone open," Hector said. "Just in case you need to call 911. I wouldn't put it past them to all attack me and leave."

"Hector," Paris said, his eyes going wide. "If they did that, I don't think they'd just ignore me. They'll attack me too—"

"Yeah, well," Hector replied, getting to his feet and hopping off the table. "I don't *think* it'll come to that." He paused. "Hopefully."

His heart skittered around in his chest as he watched four guys tumble out of the backseat.

"Hector?" Paris asked anxiously as a giant guy stepped out of the passenger door. It was one of the Ajaces.

Agamemnon offered Hector a brief wave. "Hey!" he called as he started walking across the field, towards the picnic table. "Good to see you!"

Hector looked over his shoulder and rolled his eyes to Paris, who relaxed the slightest bit. His face was still paler than normal, but at least he wouldn't be an impediment to Hector's status. If anything, Paris being a little scared was good, because Hector wasn't. Not outwardly, at least. But it would be fine.

He waved back, without really waving. It was more of him holding his hand in the air for a brief moment. "What's up?"

He had never come up against Agamemnon on the football field. Hector had seen him up close during the coin toss, but always in football pads. The guy in front of him was no less intimidating than he was with his gear. Anyone else wearing their school uniform on a weekend was fair game to pick on, but Agamemnon just seemed like a business man who was part of the mafia. (It didn't really help that he was surrounded by giant guys.)

Hector smirked, raising an eyebrow. "So? We ready?"

The one guy who wasn't physically scary shook his head. "I was just messaging our sports med guy. In case…"

Agamemnon scowled. "Which one?"

"Machaon said he's asleep, which is impossible, seeing as he replied but… yeah he's not coming. And…" He glanced back at his phone. "Patroclus said he's not spending more time with us then he has to because we're awful people. And now he's apologizing, because apparently that was Achilles on his phone…"

"Great," Agamemnon said sarcastically. "Didn't need the play by play, but thanks."

"Damn," the Stallions QB muttered to the kid beside him. Agamemnon's brother, Menelaus. His arm was in a sling.

Hector pointed to the kid's arm. "Dude, is it broken?"

He shook his head. "Just out for a few weeks," he replied glumly.

Agamemnon clapped his hands twice, making sure everyone's attention didn't wander too far away from him. "Are we ready?"

Hector was wildly satisfied that he could look down on Agamemnon as he nodded nonchalantly. "All good. Who am I taking down today?"

"Oh, I highly doubt that," Agamemnon sneered, gesturing to the giant kid on his left.

Hector had a feeling it was going to be him. He kept the smirk on his face.

Covertly, Hector sized him up, offering the guy a hand. "Hector."

"Ajax," the other player said, accepting Hector's handshake.

He nodded, even though he already knew. "Nice to meet you."

"Are we ready?" Agamemnon asked, impatient. His blood was boiling for a win. A win at *anything.*

"Good to go," Hector said, pulling his hoodie off and throwing it on the ground beside one of the trees.

Ajax nodded. The sun was shining now, heating up the moisture in the air. Ajax walked over to the middle of the red dirt in the baseball diamond. Puffs of sand rose to the air around him as he walked. *Dramatic*, Hector thought, following him. He looked over his shoulder to see Paris still on the picnic table, with Menelaus sitting an awkward distance away. His brother was on his phone, but he was watching the red haired boy more than the screen.

Agamemnon was pretty much out of hearing range, so when Ajax leaned forwards slightly and said, "I actually have no idea how to start something like this," Hector genuinely laughed.

"Just hit me," Hector replied, cocky like all hell let loose as he dropped down into a ready position.

When Ajax shrugged and threw the first punch, Hector ducked. He had been super into boxing a few years back. Hitting his opponent in the stomach, he darted out of the way again. Ajax grunted. He whirled around. Agamemnon was depending on him.

As they traded blows, the red dust made the air thicker. It stuck to their clothes and got in their eyes. They lunged at each other, Hector taking a glancing blow to the head. He stumbled. Tripped on his own feet. Fell backwards. The dust clung to his white shirt. Ajax almost had him. Somehow, Hector got up faster than Ajax could lunge forwards. Hector landed another hit. Ajax nearly doubled over. *Fucking Hector,* he thought. He inhaled. Sweat and sand filled his nose. Ajax hadn't planned this very well. His ribs hurt. Hector started pummeling him again.

Paris hated watching the fight, but he couldn't make himself look away. Agamemnon was standing with his teammates, a couple meters to the right. Sometimes, he would yell at his guy, then turn to his friends and they would mutter amongst themselves. Nervous. Menelaus was now sitting next to Paris. Not an awkward distance away anymore.

"Hey," the red haired guy said, not taking his eyes off the fight.

Ajax finally landed a good hit, causing Hector to stumble again. Paris had never seen his brother in a full on brawl with someone, but he knew for a fact that it had happened before. Hector was blinking rapidly now as he backed up. Swiped a trickle of blood away from his nose. He laughed as he smeared the blood on his jeans, then leapt forwards, faster than Paris had ever seen him move, clobbering Ajax with unchecked aggression.

"Paris?" Menelaus asked again, making him jump.

It was hard to focus on the other boy's words as Ajax grunted. Agamemnon was yelling at him again, and Paris fought the urge to leave.

"What?" Paris asked, slightly frustrated.

Menelaus was staring at him now, his eyebrows raised. "I just think this is ridiculous. All this fighting. For no reason."

Paris plugged his ears, closing his eyes. The dust from the baseball diamond was in the air now, making it thick and dry. He could feel it in his throat.

"I know it is," he replied, his own voice amplified in his head. "Helen can't just leave. Aphrodite is being weird about it. That woman is all for this... war thing. In the car last night she was talking about how honorable it was to have people fight over you."

Menelaus pulled Paris' hand off his ear. "And why does this woman have control over Helen?"

Paris shrugged with a sigh. "I don't know. She should just leave, but I think Aphrodite is paying her tuition."

Now Ajax was bleeding too, but Paris couldn't tell from where. It might have been Hector's blood, because it was just on his hands. Menelaus shook his head. He put his feet up on the picnic table and laid down.

"Wake me up when they're done," he said, pulling his baseball cap down over his eyes.

Paris gave him an unenthusiastic thumbs up and pulled out his phone, trying to ignore the fight noises right in front of him. Until he realized he had earbuds. He put them in and turned up his music as loud as he could.

"Oh my Gods," Hector muttered, his hands protesting against their boxing position.

The sun was high overhead now, beating down on them. Sweat trickled down his back. His poor *filthy* white shirt.

Ajax didn't make a move. He just nodded. "Yeah."

They circled each other slowly, feet dragging.

"We should take a break," Ajax suggested, glancing over his shoulder to where Agamemnon and the gang had settled in. It looked like Odysseus and Diomedes were playing cards.

Hector was glad his opponent had suggested it. They were both worse for wear. It had been a stupid long time since they started fighting and Hector felt like he had been smashed into by a full battalion of soldiers.

"Good idea," he said raggedly.

Ajax let out a heavy breath and sat down right where he was. Hector followed in suit, crouching first, then laying down. Ajax laughed, but it turned into a hacking cough.

"You okay?" Hector asked, his eyes closed against the sun.

"Fine," Ajax replied, spitting in the dirt. His throat tasted like blood. And he had bitten his tongue, so the stale iron taste crowded his mouth too.

Hector nodded, feeling bruises blooming all over his body. He grinned. What a good way to spend a morning. The crunching of footsteps brought him out of his reverie, so he cracked open an eye.

Everyone, including Paris, had rushed over and were staring down at them.

"So?" Agamemnon demanded, not caring that Hector had blood dripping from his nose again or that Ajax was developing two black eyes. "Who won?"

"Shut up," Paris said, crouching beside Hector in a strange moment of bravery. "Are you guys okay?"

This of course, was met by indignation from Agamemnon. "Says you. This whole thing is *your* fault, dumbass."

Paris ignored him, looking Hector in the eye. "Do you need me to call 911?"

Ajax laughed again. He laid down when the coughing started, throwing an arm over his eyes to shield them from the light. "Nah. Don't even worry about it," he said, in between hacks.

Ajax 2 went over to him with a water bottle.

Agamemnon loomed over Hector, his arms crossed. Hector could finally open his eyes all the way now that the Stallions' captain blocked out the sun. He snorted, wishing he had thought to bring water. His throat was dry, caked with sand, and burning like nobody's business.

"Tie," he said smugly, watching with glee as Agamemnon's face broke into a horrible scowl.

Hector sat up, blood rushing to his head. He ignored it, even as the world shook a little. "Hey Ajax," he called. The other boy looked up. "Do you wanna keep going? Or should we get lunch?"

"I'm done with this shit," he replied, his head thunking against the ground as he lowered it again. "Let's go for drinks."

Paris got to his feet, annoyed. "I'm taking the car, Hector," he said. "I've got places to be."

To this, Hector just laughed. He was too tired to deal with Paris' antics. It didn't matter anyways. He'd find a way home eventually. As Paris stomped off, shuffling up a cloud of dust in his wake, Agamemnon looked at his teammates. If there was anything worse than spending the afternoon with *Hector* of all people, he couldn't think of it.

"I'm gonna go back to campus. Spread the bad news," Agamemnon said gruffly. "Anyone who wants a ride back has to come with me. Otherwise you're walking."

Ajax sat up, frowning at his captain. "Thanks for that," he said sarcastically. "Makes me fight and then ditches me at the fucking baseball diamond? Classy."

In the end, Menelaus and Ajax 2 stayed. Even though those Menelaus weren't legal yet, they went to a pub for lunch. It was dark, with stained glass windows, plenty of cheap food and beer. The main reason they went was because it was close by. Hector hadn't expected a meal after a ridiculously long fistfight. He did have shocking amount of fun watching the replay of the previous night's hockey game, talking football, and ignoring real life for awhile. The whole endeavor was slightly shadowed with guilt, because of Andromache. But he was doing this *for* her. Though... he supposed his plan hadn't actually worked. (That was a problem for later Hector.)

After, they walked back to Mycenae, which took a solid hour and a half at the pace they were going. Very slowly, because Ajax had acquired a limp, and Hector felt like he was turning into a tree. Hanging out with the opposing team wasn't something Hector had ever done before, but he learned that they weren't all horrible people like their captain. Ajax 1 even drove Hector home, which was a testament to how not horrible he was, seeing as it was an hour long drive at the very least.

# VIII

On Saturday, Zeus called his brother. He was sitting in his office, his feet on his antique wooden desk. Hera had started bothering him about the size of the bust in the front hall, and how she hadn't been included, so he practically ran up to his office. She wasn't allowed in there. Zeus thought the bust of himself was perfect. He honestly hadn't *thought* to include Hera.

When he finally picked up, Zeus greeted is brother with enthusiasm. "Poseidon! How've you been? It feels like forever since we last talked."

Poseidon, who had just gotten back from a three month trip to Australia and was trying to deal with jet lag was far less excited. "Who uses the phone anymore? Just text me when you need something."

Zeus laughed jovially. "You always were a funny one," he said, kicking off his desk and spinning around in his chair. He was now facing his bookshelf full of first editions and marble sculptures. "So. I was wondering if you would be able to—"

"It's football season, isn't it," Poseidon said, sounding extremely unimpressed. The background chatter coming from his brother's side of the phone made it difficult for Zeus to hear.

He sighed. "Poseidon, where are you? It's awfully loud and I can't make out what you're saying."

"I'm in the Dallas airport. Just got back from surfing in Australia, remember?" He paused. "Oh wait. You don't care about anyone but yourself." The chatter died down minutely. "Is that better, oh heavenly one?"

"Much. Thank you," Zeus replied. "Yes, you were correct. It is football season."

"So you *could* hear me," Poseidon grumbled. "And yeah, I know. That's the only time of year you call me."

Zeus exhaled, noticing something askew on the shelf. He held his phone between his shoulder and his ear as he pulled a little figure of a woman's body off the shelf. It was covered in a thin layer of dust. He'd have to get the cleaning staff to come in here again. He hated showing people how to do their job. (That reminded him: he had to *fire* his cleaning staff. So much to do, so little time.)

"Yes. I'd like you to go to Ilium Academy this year. You'll be staying at Hestia's bed and breakfast. I'll pay whatever you think is reasonable, but I need you to be there as soon as possible," Zeus said, already finished with this conversation. He didn't agree with his family. They just couldn't accept that he was better than them, and that irked some people.

By the way Poseidon huffed, Zeus could tell he was running a hand through his hair. His brother, for some odd reason, preferred to have his hair long. He had been a part of the NFL for a couple of years before he decided that surfing was a better use of time. He quit, moved to New Zealand, came back, and was now thinking about moving to Australia. Little did Poseidon know that Zeus actually did pay attention to his life. He made sure to keep track of his family members and their spouses and their exes, just in case they tried to be more successful than him.

"Fine," Poseidon replied, sounding pained. "I'll be down there in a few hours."

With that, his brother hung up. Zeus put down the statue and took his phone away from his ear with a smile, satisfied by the outcome. Poseidon would go help that team with their plays, and expose them to professional tactics. A few days prior, he had sent Ilium Academy a very large cheque to better their football program. That had been met with immense gratitude from the Phys–Ed department, which was always nice. Hera loved the giant bouquet they sent over.

Zeus now had everything in place. Thetis' request had been fulfilled. The Stallions, without the help of Achilles... and more than half of the offense players, had lost. They would *continue* losing until something changed. The last game didn't have an embarrassing difference in score, but it was enough to upset the team. Especially Agamemnon. Athena had kept her mouth shut ever since their argument over sponsorship, which was slightly upsetting, but his daughter would get over it. She always did.

When Athena got the Facetime call from her father, it piqued her interest enough to pick up. He always called over the phone, claiming to despise modern technology.

He had his wire frame glasses on, and was watching himself on the screen with concern. Athena raised an eyebrow.

"Did you need something?" she asked, curious.

Athena had been sifting through some paperwork at home, trying to figure out how she could teach full time at a notable university that had offered her a job. She would have to ask if their schedule was flexible, because she wanted to finish this football season, at the very least.

Zeus smiled, waving awkwardly at the screen. It was rare to see her father acting like he was old... but this was too much.

Athena shook her head. "Unfortunately, Facetime doesn't flatter you, Father dear," she said.

He laughed. She knew it was his forced laugh, because it was a little bit too loud. She just smiled and waited.

"Athena, darling, I'm using this stupid, modern technology because I have to have a serious talk with Apollo and Aphrodite, and it will look kind of suspicious if you're not here," Zeus said, his voice breaking up a little bit as the connection struggled. "I wanted to let you know that practically none of this applies to you. So I'll now be adding them to the call... and hopefully Aphrodite is with that Ares fellow. I'd like to talk to him too."

"Ah," Athena said, shuffling her paperwork into a pile and resting her phone against the vase in the middle of her dining room table, where she was sitting. "Very clever of you."

Zeus nodded, though she could tell he was distracted by the way his eyes were darting back and forth across the screen. Soon, two little boxes popped up, with Aphrodite's number and Apollo's contact in the middle. (Athena refused to put that woman's contact information into her phone.) It was a gamble as to who would pick up first, because both people in question, in Athena's opinion, were haughty and ridiculous. Athena watched for another moment before pulling her pen from behind her ear and continuing with the paperwork.

"Father!" Apollo's voice came through the system, falsely excited. Athena could recognize a customer service voice when she heard one. "To what do I owe this pleasure?"

Her half brother was always a suck–up, to a certain extent. Other times, he had no regard for what his parents thought of him. For example, when he went around poisoning football teams for no good reason. (She was still bitter about that, and would be for a long time.)

"Hello Apollo," Zeus said, switching from the tone he used with Athena, to one of stern control. "We're just waiting for Aphrodite, and then we'll get right down to business."

Aphrodite popped up, her makeup freshly done. *Speak of the devil,* Athena though with a smirk. Like Zeus had wanted, her hulking... man–friend was in the background. They were sitting on a couch that was so white it took a moment for the camera to adjust. Imagine having something that impractical. If there was one thing Athena hated, impracticality was it.

"Welcome, Aphrodite," Zeus greeted, just warmly enough to make the woman smile.

"Oh!" Aphrodite said, like she was shocked to see the person who had called her. "Hello!" She scootched over, putting a respectable distance between herself and Ares. "Say hi to Ares! My personal trainer!" She turned the camera around to face the hulking man covered in tattoos.

He didn't look very bright, but he waved with a grimacing smile. "What's up, y'all?" he drawled, his voice at least two octaves lower than Aphrodite's.

"I'm just calling with a little bit of... a request," Zeus said, leaning back in his office chair.

He seemed to have figured out Facetime now, because he looked as grand and stately as ever. He somehow managed to get that air of perpetual disappointment down. Athena was mystified by her father sometimes.

Aphrodite turned the camera back around with a chipper grin. "Anything for you!"

Apollo nodded, but Athena could tell he didn't want to be there. His slight brows were furrowed a bit, and he kept yawning. His camera was propped up against something, because he was braiding his hair at the moment, probably trying to distract himself.

"*Great*," Zeus said. "So I'm going to name names, but I think we all know that some of us here have... perhaps interfered a little bit too much with this so called war..."

Aphrodite put her hand up and Zeus motioned for her to speak.

"I just want to say, before you get too far," she started, suddenly sounding like a teenage girl in trouble, "That Hera keeps talking to Athena about the season. She secretly wants Mycenae to win."

Zeus raised his eyebrows. Athena sighed, resting her forehead between her pointer finger and thumb.

"Is this true, daughter?" her father asked. "There won't be any consequences for you. I just want to know what my meddlesome wife has been saying?"

Athena nodded, without lifting her head. "We did talk once or twice."

"One moment please, everyone," Zeus replied. "I just have to call my darling wife up here join the discussion."

With that, he got out of his chair and left the camera frame. Apollo muttered something under his breath and began undoing his braid.

"Well this is fun!" Aphrodite exclaimed. "Family meeting and all."

No one replied. Athena wanted to tell Aphrodite that she was hardly a part of the family, seeing as she was blatantly cheating on her husband with her 'personal trainer,' but she restrained herself. Barely. Apollo started doing his hair again, and Aphrodite began talking softly with Ares. It took Zeus five minutes or so to return to his camera. He had brought Hera in as well. Athena was surprised. She had been certain that Zeus' wife wasn't allowed in his office, but there she was. Apparently this situation called for a complete overhaul of protocol. Funny.

"Hello again, everyone," Zeus announced, though all the people on the call had already focused on him. "Now, I'll make this as efficient as possible from here on out."

Hera was obviously upset. She was twirled one of her dark curls around her finger, then went about rolling up the sleeves of her button–up shirt, all with a stormy expression on her face.

"It has come to my attention," Zeus continued, "That the five of us have been heavily influencing the little game that the schools are playing. The *war,* if you will." Aphrodite opened her mouth to say something, but Zeus held up a finger. "From now on, we are going to let it play out. With zero interference from us."

"Now that *you've* accomplished your meddling, it's time for the rest of us to just *stop?*" Hera asked, eyeing the back of Zeus' head with disgust. "Convenient timing."

Zeus closed his eyes, taking a supposedly calming breath. "It doesn't matter, my dear, because we're *all* going to stop. Alright?"

"Yessir," Aphrodite replied with a winning smile.

Apollo nodded with pursed lips.

"I'm glad we all agree," Zeus said. "I hope to see you all soon. Have a pleasant rest of your day."

With that, he hung up. Athena didn't bother moving her phone. It turned off on its own. And besides, her stepmother would be calling soon, to vent about the fight she and Zeus were probably having at this exact moment.

# IX

T HE DAY AFTER THE useless fight, Agamemnon was attempting to do homework and failing. Studying around friends was never actually studying. Odysseus and Diomedes were currently trying to write a ballad about Vin Diesel, which was taking on the air of a sea shanty. Agamemnon pulled out his phone and started scrolling through Instagram. They were sitting in the Ajaces' dorm room, which was on the second floor, overlooking the courtyard in the middle of the residences. The window was wide open, letting the hot air in, along with the occasional insect. Agamemnon flicked a little fly off his leg, flopping backwards onto the bed where he was sitting.

Crissy had posted a picture where she was sitting in the sun. The caption said: **salty and sweet.** She moved so far away. How annoying. He scrolled past it when he felt his face heat up. Next, there was an ad for a summer training program. He ignored that as well, because this was his last season, unless he got a scholarship, which was becoming more unlikely by the hour. Whatever. He'd just become a business tycoon. A post from the @THE_Ilium_Trojans showed up on his feed, and it made him want to gouge his eyes out. It was a video clip of fucking Hector slamming into some poor offense player. The *caption* was what made it worse: **Breaking. The. Stallions. More like ponies. What happened there?** Agamemnon literally snarled at his phone, throwing it onto the mattress.

"Dude, what?" Ajax 1 asked from where he was laying on the other bed.

He had two black eyes now and was covered in bruises. He was... a little bitter about the day before, especially because no one had warned him about Hector. But then again, Hector couldn't really be blamed for that, so it had to be Agamemnon's fault.

The captain looked out at the room, making sure he had everyone's attention before slamming his head back down.

Odysseus and Diomedes shared a curious look from where they were sitting in the middle of the floor. Ajax 2 and Phoenix both put down their textbooks. (Phoenix hung around sometimes. He had been pretty shocked the team believed the whole 'Achilles forced me to quit' excuse, and still tolerated him.) Menelaus had said he actually wanted to get work done, so he was absent.

"The Trojan's are bragging about their excellent playing skills," Agamemnon huffed. "How they *broke* us."

Odysseus hummed. "Well. That's not *technically* true, but we did lose to them so... "

"*Some*one can't stand that," Ajax 1 muttered with a sigh.

"Well I hate losing," Diomedes replied, frowning at the sheet of poorly written lyrics on the floor in front of him. "If Peliedes would just come back—"

"Aha!" Agamemnon exclaimed, sitting up. Everyone jumped a little. "Why didn't I think of that!"

"Think of what?" Ajax 2 asked, spinning around in the desk chair he was sitting in to face the captain.

Odysseus was nodding now, rubbing his chin like he had a real prospect of growing a beard. (He didn't. The best he could do was a sketchy peachfuzz.)

"That has merit actually..." He looked up at Agamemnon. "It has merit if you wouldn't have dishonored him, that is."

Agamemnon rolled his eyes, punching his thigh with the bottom of his fist. "There has to be a way..."

More skeptical looks were shared between the boys in the room. Phoenix tapped his pencil on the edge of the desk.

"Okay," Agamemnon said definitively, rubbing his hands together. "Odysseus, write this down." He waited until his friend pulled out a page of notebook paper and got a pen ready. "So. You, Ajax 1, and... Phoenix! You're in with Achilles, right?"

"Yeah, I guess we're friends," Phoenix said with a shrug, throwing his pencil onto a stack of paper.

Agamemnon clapped once, standing up. "Perfect, perfect. I highly doubt Achilles will listen to me, so that's why I'm sending you guys." In truth, Agamemnon was sending two people that were imposing. Ajax 1, with the evidence of the fight painted on his face, and Odysseus... who really didn't get along with Achilles.

If needed, Phoenix could act as a mediator. "Odysseus. Are you ready?"

"Ay ay cap'n" Odysseus said, smirking down at the paper.

"Great," Agamemnon said. "So here's what I want you to tell him. If he comes back, with the offense line, then I'll admit that what I did was wrong. I'll say it was all in a moment of senseless passion, and that all will be forgiven."

"Woah," Ajax 1 laughed. "*You*, admitting that you were wrong? That's a gift in itself."

Ajax 2 reached over and flicked his ankle. Ajax 1 looked up at him, offended, but then saw Agamemnon's unimpressed glare. "Sorry sir," he said, with no sincerity at all.

"If you're ungrateful, you can just leave," Agamemnon snapped, crossing his arms. "I'm doing this for the team, dumbass, so if you have nothing useful to say, keep your mouth shut."

Ajax 1 ignored him in favor of closing his eyes.

"Back to business," Agamemnon declared, pacing about the room. "Now, after that, offer him straight eighty percents in all his classes for the next two years, ten thousand dollars, and... three fucking horses, for all I care."

"That's... generous?" Odysseus said, glancing over at Diomedes, who's eyes bugged out of his head.

Agamemnon held up a finger. "I'm not done yet. Next, offer him the best fake ID money can buy, a new guitar... he likes that, right?" He turned to Phoenix, who nodded with pursed lips. "Also, once I graduate, I'll make him a part of my family, which will give him a good chunk of profitable land, if he so chooses. He can decide which one of my cousins he wants to marry, and he can be the godfather of my firstborn child. And *also*, he can have his Briseis back. Haven't slept with her once."

"There might be a reason for that," Ajax 2 mouthed to Phoenix, who turned away from the room, cough–laughing into his fist.

This was ignored.

Ajax 1 sat up, crossing his arms. "There's no way we're offering Briseis. She's not yours, buddy. Not to mention, she broke up with you. You literally haven't seen her in days. And she's her own fucking person. She can make her own choices. She's not property, okay?"

All the players in the room turned to stare. You weren't supposed to just... stand up to Agamemnon like that.

Ajax 1 shrugged. "It's fucking true."

"Alrighty," Agamemnon said, sticking his hands in his pockets, not willing to admit he was slightly terrified. "Oh! Wait." He pointed at Odysseus, who was scribbling out the Briseis line. "This is the most important thing. He can have all that only if he apologizes to me. He has to submit to my command. And if not... well it sucks to be him, right?"

"Riiight," Odysseus nodded, writing down that last piece. "So. Is that everything? For certain?"

The captain paused, mulling it over. "Yeah. I think we're good. You have exactly what I said written down?"

Diomedes glanced over at the paper. "Think so," he replied with a nod.

"Good," Agamemnon said, sitting back down on the bed. "Best of luck on your mission."

There was a moment of silence.

"Does anyone even know where Achilles is?" Ajax 1 asked from his bed.

Blank stares met his question.

"Go find him," Agamemnon said, like it was actually a helpful answer. "It can't be *that* hard."

⁂

Achilles was finally (almost) relaxing. Things were okay. Of course he missed football, but funnily enough, he was getting by alright. Iphis had started bringing Briseis around again, and they seemed like they didn't want to kill Achilles. They had good stories about planning pranks they pulled on Agamemnon, before Bri had... ended it. The two of them just left, claiming to need to do art homework. Patroclus had blatantly laughed at them, then covered his mouth when Iphis glared.

Now, it was just him and Patroclus. They were outside by the football field. Studying had sort of been a thing, until Achilles went to get his guitar about an hour ago. It was too nice out to focus on schoolwork. They could do that later. *Could* being the keyword there. They probably wouldn't. For now, Patroclus was laying on his back, his head propped up against Achilles' knee. He asked how that was possibly comfortable, but Patroclus had shrugged, not caring. Or maybe he was genuinely happy there.

It didn't matter. If he was happy, Achilles was happy. Achilles was playing a mashup of songs without singing the lyrics, fiddling around with the music. Guitar was what he loved. The singing came second. And it was harder to improvise when he was singing.

"Pelides!" someone yelled.

Patroclus sat up, trying to find the source of Achilles' last name.

Achilles ignored it and kept playing.

"Hey, Achilles!"

*That* he couldn't quite ignore. Achilles looked over his shoulder to find Odysseus, Ajax 1, and Phoenix walking briskly over to them. Patroclus sighed. Apparently they could only go without football drama for so long.

Achilles put down his guitar when they reached him. "What's up, y'all?" He *tried* to sound excited. He really really did.

Ajax was sporting two black eyes and a giant bruise on his jaw. Achilles knew it wasn't from football. What the hell had Agamemnon done this time?

"Wanna come to the caf? Get something for lunch?" Odysseus asked innocently.

Patroclus looked at Achilles, unimpressed.

"Caf isn't open weekends," Achilles said. "We've got snacks in our dorm though. We can go there." He paused. "Because you obviously want something. You wouldn't talk to me otherwise."

Phoenix sighed, rubbing a hand across his hairline. "Yeah, let's go there," he answered, trying to halt any extra animosity.

Patroclus stood and started picking up his textbooks. He really didn't want to go inside. Especially with these guys. Not that he would get hurt. Just that he spent enough time with them over the week. The weekend was supposed to be a break.

Achilles zipped his guitar into its case. There were very few things Achilles took proper care of, but the guitar, made of a pretty light wood, was one of them. After slinging it onto his back, he grabbed the last of the books. When Patroclus opened his mouth to protest, Achilles shook his head, bumping into the brown haired boy's shoulder as they started walking. Briseis had taken the blanket with her when she and Iphis left. Achilles had put up a fuss about the bugs, but she hadn't listened to reason, which was... fair.

"So," Odysseus said, messing with his curls. "How've you been?"

Achilles wanted to take back what he had said about going to their dorm. He was *not* in the mood to deal with Odysseus.

"It's been great, actually," Achilles replied with a sunny grin. "I didn't realize how much I could get done without having to deal with Agamemnon all the time."

Ajax 1 snorted. When Odysseus glared at him, he put his hands up. "Wasn't me."

Patroclus didn't understand the appeal of football boys. They were loud, obnoxious, and generally thought they were on top of the world. Minus Achilles of course. Though... he did tick off all those boxes at times. In an endearing way.

"You're an idiot," Odysseus said under his breath to Ajax, before turning to Achilles. "So is your dorm one of the ones with the kitchen space?"

Achilles nodded. "There's like, a dining room. Sort of. But yeah it is. There's no way I'm letting you into my actual room." He was thinking about the storage bed and the conclusions that would be drawn from that little hiccup. Not good ones.

"Why?" Odysseus demanded, wiggling his eyebrows. "Are you hiding something?"

"Yes," Patroclus deadpanned. "We're actually hiding a very long rope and a body."

Phoenix laughed. Achilles wasn't sure why his old friend was here, but he was glad it wasn't just Odysseus.

"Guess I'll have to report you," Odysseus replied with a shrug. "For the rope, that is. Dangerous stuff."

Ajax 1 was shaking his head like he couldn't believe he was here. Achilles agreed. He had just wanted to spend the day doing nothing. When they got to the dorm building, Achilles punched in the code on the door and led the way to the elevator. His mother had paid specifically for a nicer room on the top floor with all the fancy shit that Achilles had insisted he would never use. Now, he was grateful as he punched in the second code to get into the common space on their floor.

It was decorated like a dentist's office waiting room, but people had started putting up posters on the walls, so it was becoming a little less abysmal. There was a kitchen that no one ever used, except for the snacks that got stocked in the cupboards every week. Across from that were a few tables, a couch, a TV, and some comfy chairs. The room was bright and minimalist, with hallways leading away on either side to the rooms. It didn't look like teenage boys had *ever* set foot in there. That just showed how magical the cleaning staff were. As far as Achilles knew, Briseis and Iphis were the first girls to come in all year.

"Damn," Odysseus said, observing the space. He had been into the senior boys' lounge before, because Agamemnon lived on the top floor, but he had to play impressed. Maybe that would make Achilles cooperate. (Hopefully.) (Probably not.)

Achilles gestured for them to sit at the island, which had a couple of leather stools next to it. Ajax's stool creaked as he sat, but he wasn't bothered. It happened all the time. Phoenix sat beside Ajax, with one stool in between them.

Achilles set down the textbooks and his guitar, hopping up onto the counter across from them. Patroclus quickly scooped the discarded items up, disappearing into the hall to put them back in their room. No use carrying around textbooks if he didn't need to.

Odysseus sat himself between the other two football players and leaned forwards on the counter. A power position.

"So," he declared, looking at Achilles and resenting him. "We're here today because Agamemnon asked us to do him a favor. And we support our captain. Unlike someone here."

Achilles sighed, resting his elbows on his knees. "I never claimed to support our captain." He paused, considering. "Actually, I think I was blatantly vocal *against* our captain."

"How about you listen to me instead of being a smartass?" Odysseus retorted, eyes glimmering with excitement.

Patroclus emerged from the hall, frowning. "I've been gone for thirty seconds and we're already insulting each other? Oh boy. This is gonna be fun," he muttered, walking over to the kitchen and opening up a few of the cupboards.

"You don't have to stay if you don't want," Achilles offered gently. He really *hoped* Patroclus would stay. There would be less conflict if he was there, but Achilles knew how much Patroclus *strongly disliked* these guys. Patroclus shook his head, getting out a bowl and pouring a bag of Munchies into it.

He slid it across the island towards the three football players. "Pick out what you don't want."

Phoenix gave him a thumbs up.

Ajax muttered a quiet, "Thanks," as he grabbed the bowl.

"Alright," Odysseus said, steering the conversation back to where he wanted it to be. "So Agamemnon was hoping that you would hear him out."

Patroclus jumped up onto the counter beside Achilles, staring intently at Odysseus.

"What're you waiting for?" Achilles asked impatiently.

Not a good sign. He was already fed up.

Odysseus pulled a folded piece of notebook paper from his back pocket. "Okay." He cleared his throat. "Agamemnon is willing to say to you, and I quote him directly on this, so don't kill the messenger, 'If Achilles comes back with the offense line, then I'll admit what what I did was wrong. I'll say it was all in a moment of senseless passion, and that all will be forgiven."

Achilles scoffed. "No fucking way."

"We're just getting started," Ajax said, mournfully shoving a handful of snacks into his mouth. "I think I should have quit. Just so he'd give all this shit to me."

"But you're not Achilles," Odysseus reminded him. "Continuing on. Agamemnon will provide you with 'straight eighty percents in all of your classes, for the next two years, ten thousand dollars, and... three fucking horses, for all he cares.'"

Patroclus put his face in his palms. This was getting out of control. Achilles resisted the urge to put a hand on his thigh.

"Agamemnon's gonna give me horses?" Achilles asked, looking between the three guys in front of him. "Why?"

Phoenix shrugged, mystified.

"We're not done yet!" Odysseus interjected, waving the paper in the air. "He's said he's offering you the best fake ID money can buy, a new guitar... he likes that, right?' and *also,* Agamemnon literally said, 'Once I graduate, I'll make him a part of my family, which will give him a good chunk of profitable land, if he so chooses. He can decide which one of my cousins he wants to marry, and he can be the godfather of my firstborn child. And *also,* he can have his Briseis back. Haven't slept with her once.'" Odysseus frowned comically. "Maybe I shouldn't have read that last part. Whoops."

Patroclus glared up at the quarterback through his fingers. "Briseis isn't Agamemnon's. She's a human, not a goat. She broke up with him like. Last week. And Achilles can't *take her back* for that exact reason."

Ajax was trying to murder Odysseus with a death stare to the side of his head. "I *told* you to take that out. That's not okay," he hissed through gritted teeth.

Odysseus ignored him.

"Is this a joke?" Achilles asked, trying to wrap his head around everything that Agamemnon supposedly said. "Bri isn't mine. Guys, do you realize how *sexist* this is?"

"Sadly no. Agamemnon sees no problem with it and that's exactly why he should be in jail. And also sadly no, to this being a joke," Ajax replied, sounding like he was at the end of his patience. "And he'll give you all of that *other* shit if you come back with the offense line. He doesn't appreciate the members of his team that he has."

"Apparently we're desperate enough to offer you this," Odysseus said, folding the paper up again and slipping it into his pocket.

Achilles laughed harshly. "There's no way there isn't a catch to this," he said, shaking his head. "And I'm not freaking marrying one of his cousins. That's weird. Again, did no one teach this fucker that there's such thing as equality? Or... we're *trying* for equality, at least. It's men like *him* that pull everyone back! Last weekend, we went to a women's rights march! We learned a lot of very important things! And Briseis got so many compliments on her sign! It said *Fuck Agamemnon and all the men like him!*"

Patroclus still hadn't taken his face out of his hands.

"Welllll..." Phoenix said quietly. "There's kind of—"

"Oh!" Odysseus exclaimed, like he had just remembered some-thing. "I wouldn't really call it a *catch*. It's more of an... apology."

Ajax sighed again.

"And that means...?" Achilles asked, scratching the side of his face skeptically.

"You can have all that, minus his cousin, *if* you apologize to him for your reckless behavior, and submit to him as captain of the team."

Patroclus looked up just in time to see Achilles burst out into disbelieving laughter.

"He wants *me* to apologize to *him*?" Achilles scoffed, raising his eyebrows at Odysseus. "I don't think I've ever heard something *that* fucked up. I gave everything for this team. I fought and he did nothing. He stays on defense, by the bench, keeping everything for himself."

"Look, Achilles," Odysseus said, trying to be placating. "C'mon, man. We need you to play. We're already losing the season. We're backed into a corner here—"

"And who's fault is that?" Achilles demanded, leaning so far forwards that Patroclus was worried he'd fall off the counter. "*Agamemnon* is the only reason I had for leaving the fucking team, okay? Either he apologizes to *me*, or I don't play until he's gone. There's your choice. Go run back to your little captain and tell him *that*. What a chauvinistic *pig*. He won't even to talk to me face to face. He could offer me ten or *twenty* times as much as he has, and I wouldn't accept it."

Ajax made to get up, but Odysseus grabbed his arm. Patroclus grabbed the bag of munchies and threw it across the island to him. Ajax continued drowning his sorrows in the snack mix as Odysseus got to his feet.

"You know what, *Achilles*?" Odysseus said, menacingly soft. "It'll be your fault when we lose this season. Does that scare you?"

Achilles barked out another laugh. "Y'all are more scared than I am. And y'know how I can tell? Agamemnon literally sent you guys to *beg* for me to come back."

Patroclus closed his eyes, resting his head against the cupboard above him. He hated it when people got like this.

"Achilles," Phoenix cut in, trying to think of a way to resolve some of the tension. "Can you listen to me? As a voice of reason?"

Phoenix had been Achilles' mentor the first year he played football. That was before Agamemnon was captain. The team had been such a good place back then, with returning players there to teach the newbies, and make them feel included. Agamemnon abolished that. Achilles sighed. He actually did trust Phoenix's guidance, to some extent.

"There's no reason here, but I'll listen," Achilles muttered, looking down at his hands.

"Thanks man," Phoenix said, shocked that Achilles actually shut up. "I wrote down this story a little while ago. Actually, while we were walking over here. So not that long ago. I thought it would be interesting. It's based on a true story. I just... had to make a couple changes."

Achilles glanced at his older friend, his eyebrows raised. "You're telling me a story?"

"I thought it might be helpful," Phoenix said with a shrug. Achilles sighed, resting his chin on his hand. "In case we ran into this situation." Phoenix pulled out his phone, finding his legend. "So um... once, there was this warrior. He was kind of like you actually, Achilles. Just on crack. And he didn't play football. This is ancient. Like so long ago. So he wasn't on crack. Probably some ancient steroid thingy. But not important. Anyways..." Ajax smirked. Phoenix glanced up at Patroclus, whose face was unreadable, and then continued. "So this warrior, was called Meleager, but that's not *super* important. The only thing important about him was that he was his village's champion.

"Until one day, his commander made a simple mistake, and supposedly dishonored the warrior, who, in a rage, retreated to his castle to sulk. When his village was attacked and people were *begging* for his help, he said 'No fuck you all,' and locked his doors. His people were literally dying, Achilles. Literal death was happening because of this dude's arrogance. *People. Were dying.*"

"Move on," Odysseus grumbled, crossing his arms. He didn't appreciate that his methods hadn't worked.

Phoenix widened his eyes in exasperation. "Gods. Fine. Okay, so the death was happening. And Meleager turned them away, no matter how much gold and shit they offered him. Finally, this dude who was apparently some advisor came along and was like, 'Meleager's wife! Named Cleopatra! Please help us! When this jackass comes to sleep with you, cry at his feet and beg for him to save his people! Because you're his wife! Named Cleopatra! And he will listen to you!'" Phoenix glanced up at Patroclus again, but he was deliberately looking at the ceiling. "And then that happened. Cleopatra was like, 'Heyyyy babe you need to fight our besties are dying,' obviously while crying, and Meleager was like, 'Huh. Never thought of that before'.

"So he went to fight, and they won, but no one gave him any gifts *or* recognition, because they realized he was a dick who cared more about himself than his friends and family. The end," Phoenix finished, looking around the room to gauge reactions.

Ajax was pretending to snore, but Odysseus seemed to think it was at least *half* clever.

"Smart," Achilles said flatly, meeting Phoenix's eyes under a heavy lidded gaze. "You pretty much put my exact situation into 'ancient times' and thought I wouldn't notice? Except there's no Cleopatra. Who's that supposed to be? Like, how dumb do you think I am? Agamemnon offering me eighties was insulting enough. I may be close to failing *math,* but that's it. And now... wow." His eyes darted over to Patroclus, who was still looking up. Weird. "I appreciate the effort, Phoenix. I really do. You can stay if you want, but I'm not taking Agamemnon's offer. I'm not apologizing to him today, or ever so he can just butt out."

Ajax got to his feet, and this time, no one stopped him. "See ya, then," he said as he stomped out of the lounge.

Odysseus shot Achilles a last withering stare before following Ajax out. The room was dead silent for the next couple minutes, save for the dripping of the faucet and their breathing.

Phoenix broke the silence with, "I didn't really wanna do that." Achilles nodded.

"But I still think you should come back," he said after another long moment. "The team sucks without you. I don't think we have a chance at winning divisionals if you don't play."

The faucet let out a long dribble of water as Achilles shook his head. "I can't."

Phoenix sighed, then pushed away from the island. "Imma head out. Nice seeing you though."

Achilles half waved. "Yeah," he replied as his friend left the room.

The instant the elevator disappeared, Patroclus blurted, "If I was a girl, that's what my parents were gonna name me."

Hopping off the counter, Achilles turned to him, an eyebrow raised. Patroclus finally looked away from the ceiling, pressing his palms onto his eyes.

"And you know this how?" Achilles asked, resting his forearms on Patroclus' knees and staring up at him.

"They told me," he said, smiling faintly as he took his hands off his face. "Both names mean the same thing."

Achilles cocked his head. "And that is...?"

Patroclus snorted. "The one thing I'm not. My name and Cleopatra mean *the honor of the father.*"

"Wait, so was that on purpose?" Achilles asked, standing up abruptly. "Did Phoenix use that name on purpose?

The boy on the counter shrugged, opening a cupboard beside him and pulling out a package of Cheetos.

He tore it open as he replied, "That's a pretty wicked coincidence if he didn't."

"So he knows," Achilles said, his throat constricting.

Patroclus shrugged, offering Achilles one of the orange puffs. He ate it out of his hand, regardless of the sudden fear they'd been discovered.

"He could," Patroclus said, surprisingly calm. "Or he could have just thought the name was pretty. It might have been part of the original legend too. I don't know how much intellectual credit I want to give Phoenix... but. Well. If he doesn't tell anyone, it's fine."

Achilles' phone pinged. Patroclus reached down and pulled it out of his pocket. He opened his mouth, then closed it again.

Bri:

> so agamemnon said you had the opportunity to 'get me back'? what is he on? did you say yes? i thought we were over treating me like property. did you think this is funny? i'm a fucking person and i'll make my own choices.

> achilles?

> i will seriously clobber you if you think that this is alright

> sorry that was iphis. but i swear you have to have a good reason to do this or else i'm literally not talking to you ever again achilles pelides this is such a mess

*Sent 4:46 PM*

"What does it say?" Achilles asked, already going pale.

Patroclus swallowed, his face lit by the glow of the screen. "Um... what's your good reason for not adequately defending Briseis?"

"*Fuck*," Achilles muttered, pushing his hair out of his face. "I... um. Well..."

"I'm calling her," Patroclus said, shaking his head slightly.

He placed Achilles' phone on the counter, putting it on speaker.

When she picked up, Briseis was ready for a fight. "So? Answer? Now?"

"Bri—" Patroclus started, but she cut him off.

"No. Patroclus, I love you but don't try and make this better than it is. Achilles. I know you're there. What's your answer?"

Achilles could feel his stomach sinking through the floor. "Yeah," he replied weakly. "Agamemnon just... I didn't actually believe he'd give me anything he offered. What did he say to you?"

"Mhm," Briseis replied shortly. "He said that he offered me back to you and that you fucking turned him down because of your honor." She was fuming. "This is *ridiculous.* I can't. This fucking sucks, guys."

She sounded like she was going to cry.

"Bri," Patroclus said again. This time, she didn't bite his head off. "No. That's not what happened. Are you going to believe something *Agamemnon* of all people said? He's trying to get in your head. Ajax said he told Odysseus to erase that part. And Achilles wouldn't accept you back because you're not his to accept. Bri, you can make your own choices. It isn't up to idiots like us to mess up your life. We have our own lives to ruin, and you have every right to make your own choices."

Briseis didn't say anything.

Patroclus continued softly, "We'll figure this out. Or you'll figure this out. Whatever you like."

Achilles gnawed on his lip, trying to think of something comforting to say. He stood there, his back pressed up against the island as Patroclus picked up the phone. Briseis was breathing evenly on the other side.

"You don't have to talk to us," Achilles said anxiously. "We'll leave you alone if that's what you need."

"This fucking sucks," she finally whispered into the phone.

Patroclus grimaced at the screen, then at Achilles, who have him a tentative thumbs up. But then Briseis started laughing. It was a sad sound, full of broken promises and mistakes.

"But y'know what? I guess. It's not as bad as Agamemnon. If anything like this happens again... well. I'm done. If you guys are involved in... my destiny again, I... don't know what I'll do," she said, sounding lost. "If more members of the team come to you and offer me up, call me. So I can scream at them. They're all scared of me anyways."

"Of course," Achilles replied, nodding even though she couldn't see him.

"But there won't *be* a next time," Iphis said, aggressively chiming in to the conversation. "Because I will literally murder that man." She paused. "And ever since the unofficial breakup...

"Sorry," Briseis said sheepishly. "It's not quite ruining my life. I just. Being treated like property is. Gross."

"I'll go over there right now and tell Agamemnon that," Patroclus offered.

Achilles shook his head and mimed chopping cords, mouthing '*no*' repeatedly.

"Please don't," Bri said with another laugh. "That's a good way to get killed."

"Not if I go with him," Achilles suggested.

"It's fine. We don't want you guys dead," Iphis interjected, sounding like she was over this. "Yet. We don't want you dead *yet.*"

There was a noise that sounded a lot like someone being pushed onto a bed. "Shut up," Briseis said, laughing.

Patroclus' eyes went wide. "Okay, time to hang up. Do you want to go somewhere for dinner?"

There was a moment where Achilles thought they had lost the girls entirely, because all he could hear was giggling. He mouthed '*hang up,*' as he plugged his ears, frantically shaking his head. Dinner wasn't worth hearing this.

"At six thirty," Bri called.

"Great!" Achilles replied, and then lunged forwards, hanging up the phone.

After a moment, Patroclus sighed.

Achilles grabbed his hand and hauled him off the counter. "Wanna go back outside?"

"It's raining now."

"Exactly," Achilles said excitedly. "It'll be fun."

This was met by a fond eye roll. "Fine." And Patroclus let himself be dragged away.

# X

THE NEXT GAME WAS even worse. Diomedes and Glaucus wore each other's jerseys for the first quarter, because they thought it was hilarious. (No one else agreed with them. It gave nobody an advantage because it was equally as confusing.) Agamemnon made them switch back after fifteen minutes. Ridiculous. They weren't taking anything seriously. The loss that happened on the following Friday was almost an all time low for the Stallions. Seven to twenty–two for the Trojans. Agamemnon couldn't believe Achilles. The boy had the audacity to refuse his gifts, and continue to let them lose, all for his so called 'honor.' But the captain would *not* cave. Either Achilles came back and apologized, or Agamemnon died. Those were the options that would allow their *former* running back onto the field again.

As the championships crept closer, the Stallions were starting to worry. If Agamemnon didn't find a way to boost morale, they were as good as shit. When the defeated team started filing back onto the bus, Agamemnon pulled his coach aside.

"I have an idea," he said quietly as he watched his teammates sullenly walk past them.

Athena was impressed. Agamemnon hardly ever did anything for his team. He just expected them to sort themselves out. Though, this idea could be something vindictive. She withheld her praise, giving him a nod.

"I think," Agamemnon continued as Odysseus passed, offering him a weak salute, "That we should stay here this weekend. There's a waterpark just a couple miles outside of town and we can go there tomorrow."

The coach held back a smile. He was actually thinking about others. How strange. Her captain must have some other plan, but this was a clever enough idea.

"Agreed," Athena replied. She checked her watch. It was just after seven. "I'll book us into a hotel for the night."

Agamemnon's eyes were shocked, reflecting the yellow from the lights that flooded the parking lot. He had *not* expected her to agree so easily.

Athena gestured for him to get on the bus. "After you."

He clanged up the stairs, rushing to sit in the seat across from Odysseus and Diomedes. The former looked up, a question on his face.

Agamemnon threw down his gear bag and sat, leaning across the aisle. "We're staying here tonight," he muttered. "In some hotel. And going to the waterpark tomorrow."

The Ajaces sat behind him, and greater Ajax rested his elbows on Agamemnon's seat. "How'd you do that?"

"What?" Agamemnon almost snapped, looking over his shoulder at his teammate.

"Convince her to let us stay?" Ajax the lesser added, like it was obvious.

Agamemnon gave them a self–satisfied smirk. "As captain... I just used some of my magic, I guess."

"Coach and Agamemnon are hooking up," Diomedes whispered loudly across the bus.

Athena turned around in her seat, clouds of anger rolling across her normally passive face. "That is unacceptable," she declared, making everyone, even those who weren't involved in the conversation, shrink back.

Their coach generally let things slide, but when she got upset, it was terrifying.

"Sorry," Diomedes blurted, raising a hand briefly. "My bad." His apologies were almost never sincere, but anyone could hear the undertones of terror in his voice.

"I appreciate your regret," Athena said before standing. "We are going to be staying here tonight, at the Oikos Inn, as an exercise in team bonding and as a moral boost. I'm going to pretend that I set ground rules, but you can do whatever you like. Having said that, if you get into trouble, fully expect me to take no responsibility for your actions. Tomorrow, we will be taking a trip to Naiaid Falls Waterpark. Swimsuits will be provided, I suppose."

"Yes coach," came the reply of forty–five players, just before they burst into excited conversation.

Patroclus sunk lower into his seat. Briseis had decided not to come to the games anymore and he fully supported that, but now he was going to be stuck with these people for the entire weekend. And he hadn't brought extra stuff. He sighed, grimly resolving that he would just stay in his hotel room and study.

The exams were getting more frequent now, as they slowly approached midterms. He honestly hadn't given the big tests much thought. Too much other stuff to worry about. Patroclus glanced around the bus, surveying the players chatting excitedly, and scrolling through their phones. Machaon was here, he supposed, so he wasn't *completely* alone. But he could be spending time with Achilles and Iphis and Briseis, which sounded a lot better than going to a waterpark with football boys.

As the bus started crawling out of the parking lot, Patroclus pulled out his phone and called Achilles. He picked up on the first ring.

"Hey what's up?" Achilles asked, sounding sleepy.

Patroclus glanced around to make sure no one was watching. "Were you sleeping?" he asked in return, a tiny smile on his face.

Achilles laughed. "Sort of. Maybe. I was watching this Swedish thing on Netflix and then... yeah. I guess I was?"

The clouds outside the bus window were starting to stain orange with the slowly descending sun.

"That's funny," Patroclus replied, knowing *exactly* what he had been watching.

"Did you need something?" Achilles asked, a tiny bit anxious. "Are you okay?"

"Yep. Athena just decided that we were suddenly staying here tonight. And going to the waterpark tomorrow—"

Achilles clicked his tongue. "Darn. That would've been fun." He paused. "Wait, so you're not gonna be here tonight? Or tomorrow?"

Finally. He had gotten the point.

Patroclus nodded, still staring out the window. "Yeah. Unless you wanna come pick—"

"Yes yes yes," Achilles cut him off, jumping up and rooting around for his keys. Patroclus laughed softly at the commotion. "What hotel?"

"Oikos Inn" Patroclus replied, running a hand through his hair. "It's kind of a long drive..."

"I," Achilles stated boldly, still rummaging around, "would travel any distance if it meant I could see your bright smile. And also," he said, dropping the dramatic act, "It's fun driving with someone." A moment of silence followed. "Aha! Found them. Your chariot shall arrive in... probably an hour. Sorry to leave you with them for that long."

A piece of wadded up paper hit Patroclus on the head.

"Sorry!" a player yelped. One of his friends was giggling. "I was tryna hit..." he trailed off as Patroclus waved it away and tossed the paper back. "Thanks!"

"All good," Patroclus said to Achilles. "See you soon."

When they got to the hotel, which took about ten minutes, everyone got assigned a room, and chaos ensued. People were running around, trying to find their roommates, leaving to find dinner, crowding the lobby... the staff probably would have complained if they weren't bringing in such good business.

Agamemnon and his crew, minus the Ajaces, sat in front of a fake fireplace, waiting for the mess to die down. Athena walked past, taking with Achilles' trainer friend. Patroclus.

"I have a lot of homework and stuff to do," he was saying. "So I'm going to get picked up."

Their coach nodded. "If I'm around, which I probably will be, let me know when you leave."

He gave her a thumbs up and walked over to the sitting area on the other side of the lobby. Agamemnon watched him for a moment, wondering if he could use the boy to get to Achilles. It probably wouldn't work.

Antilochus, Nestor, and Idomeneus came walking over, distracting Agamemnon from his schemes.

"You all wanna come find dinner somewhere with us?" Antilochus asked, leaning on the back of Menelaus' chair.

Diomedes looked to Agamemnon, who shrugged, and then nodded.

"Epic," Antilochus said.

⁂

The Trojans were partying. Everyone on the team had gone over to one of their team members house. Rhesus. Played kicker. His parents were away for the weekend. Classic. Hector had told Andromache she didn't have to come, and he had, at her request, dropped her off at his house.

When they had broken the news to Hector's parents, the reaction was far less horrific than they had expected. Hecuba had asked Andromache what she wanted to do, very calmly. Priam was a little distant, but he had come around to the idea after awhile. In the end, they both trusted Hector, and they loved Andromache like she was already an official part of the family. When his mother had pulled Hector aside, and asked about marriage, he pulled out the ring he had bought the month before. '*For the summer,*' was all he had said. She had hugged him. And now Hecuba was doting on Andromache's every whim and need. It would be okay.

The music was loud, the bass pounding through Hector's skull. It was dark, inside and out, but he could make out Helen, dancing with some girls he didn't know. He also knew Paris was nursing a drink in the kitchen. That kid. He shouldn't drink too much, or else he would end up in a terrible mood. For days. Like, even after the hangover wore off. Hector was usually the one who had to deal with him too. Way more people were here than were on the team.

Scarpedon sidled up to Hector, a red plastic cup in his hand. He pounded Hector on the back. "That was a great game, man." He had to shout to be heard. "Where's Aeneas?"

"Good job," Hector yelled back, scanning the room again. "You guys played really well. Aeneas' probably upstairs or some shit."

Scarpedon whistled, hitting Hector again. "Where's your lady?"

"Home. Where's *yours*?"

The other boy laughed, pointing with his free hand. "Good one. You're a funny man." And then he wandered away, joining Euphorbus, who was laughing with some girls on the far side of the living room.

Hector sipped his own drink, bored out of his mind. That was when Dolon, a small kid with brown–nosing tendencies, ran up to him, waving his phone. It left giant streaks of light in Hector's vision.

"What's up?" Hector asked, squinting at the screen. He was slightly surprised to see that it was one thirty in the morning, but the Instagram post was more interesting than the time.

Agamemnon had posted a picture of him, Diomedes, Odysseus, Ajax 1 (who was asleep on with his head on his arms), Ajax 2, Menelaus, Idomeneus, Nestor, and Antilochus sitting around a conference table. The caption said **Couldn't sleep. Strategy meeting.** And the location... said that they were ten minutes away, at Oikos Inn. Hector took the phone from Dolon, holding it in the air.

"Hey!" he yelled over the music. People looked over in his direction, realized that it was *Hector* talking, and quieted down. Someone turned the music off. "This is gonna be so funny. Guys, the Stallions are still in town and they're having a *strategy meeting* in the conference room of the hotel on fifth. Who's gonna sneak over there and record it? I bet they're in there tryna remember how to play football, because they're fucking in*competent*."

This was met by laughter. Maybe Hector was a bit drunk. It didn't matter. This would be great.

"Who's gonna go?" he asked again. "Fifty bucks if you do."

"I will!" Dolon said eagerly.

Unfortunately, this was also met by laughter. Subtle laughter, but laughter nonetheless.

"No other takers?" Hector asked, looking around.

Scarpedon made eye contact with Hector and smirked.

Hector nodded, giving Dolon back his phone. "Okay, you're on buddy," he said.

"*Yes!*" The kid pumped his fists and ran out the door.

Helen was glaring at Hector, but he was doubled over, giggling as the room burst out into gales of merriment.

Dolon had to squeeze past a few people making out in the hall to get outside. The night was humid, but somehow kind of chilly. All he wanted to do was make Hector see him as an actual person. He was tired of being the waterboy. He ran down Rhesus' street, past two expensive motorcycles that the defenseman had proudly displayed. The start of his collection, he had explained earlier.

The sounds of the party faded, until Dolon could just barely hear the bass. He popped out of the neighborhood, onto fifth street. The streetlights were a lot brighter here, and cars whipped past. Fifth turned into the highway eventually. The neon sign for the hotel where the Stallions were staying lit up the parking lot with a green glow.

When a break in traffic came, Dolon darted across the street. He was fast. Everyone underestimated him. He would be a great player one day, if only they would let him *play*. Dolon went around the side of the hotel, searching for the meeting rooms. He found them, at the end of a row of big windows. One had a light on, spilling bright splash of yellow onto the dark grass. Dolon settled down, crouching below that window, and opened the voice memo app.

Ajax 1 woke with a start when he heard rustling. He frowned, rubbing his eyes. How long had he been asleep? Didn't matter.

"Did anyone hear that?" Odysseus asked, his voice a whisper.

Ajax 1 half raised a hand. "Yep," he replied. "Imma go look."

He didn't wait to see what Agamemnon would say, pushing out his chair and walking over to the open window. He put his hands on his hips, squinting into the night. A few meters away, he could see... something. He cranked the window shut.

Turning back to the room, he shrugged. "I think there's someone spying on us."

"Those *bastards*," Agamemnon snarled, getting to his feet.

Antilochus looked to Idomeneus. "Did you not post something with our exact location, captain?"

Agamemnon put his hands on the back of his grey chair, leaning forwards. "See, and that's where I got them," he whispered. Menelaus sighed audibly. "No, Menny, don't sigh like that. Now we know that their team is together. And they sent someone, because they think we're too dumb to notice. So who's gonna go get the spy?"

Odysseus raised his hand, wiggling his fingers in the air. Agamemnon pointed at him. "Yes. A worthy candidate. Who will you take with you?"

The quarterback pointed at Diomedes with his thumb and the captain nodded. "Perfect. Two strong fighters."

Both boys stood up, sharing a look of excitement.

"And if you catch him," Agamemnon said as they made their way to the door, already tiptoeing, "Maybe... go infiltrate the Trojans party. Just to show them who's in charge here."

Nestor sighed, stacking his fists and resting his head on top of them. "You know this isn't going to win this war," he said as Odysseus and Diomedes snuck out.

The two of them shuffled out of the conference room, past the tired receptionist. Athena had paid the hotel extra so they didn't get mad at her team for breaking the rules. The receptionist watched the two boys sneak out, but she couldn't make herself care. The meeting rooms were supposed to be closed right now, and so was the pool, but neither of those things had happened tonight. Life goes on.

Dolon, on the other hand, had not taken the closed window as a sign to leave. He had just snuck closer to the window, holding his phone dangerously close to the sill. Though he could barely hear what was being said, he needed proof that he had been there at least.

"Hey," someone said, standing very close to his right.

He jumped to his feet, heart rocketing away from his body. Someone on his *left* shone a flashlight in his face.

"Guys—" he started frantically, knowing that this was *bad*. It got even worse when he was slammed up against the wall. He inhaled sharply, feeling the wall shudder a bit. His ribs groaned in protest.

A face came into his vision, which had been mostly taken by the flashlight. "Who're you?" the boy demanded, spit flying onto Dolon's face. He flinched away, his breath struggling like it was being squeezed through a narrow rubber tube.

Slammed into the wall again. This time his head hit the rough stucco. It bit into his scalp. The world was ringing.

"D–dolon," he managed. He sounded like he was choking. It *felt* like he was choking.

He was lifted by the front of his shirt by the guy without the flashlight. He struggled against the grip, trying, with shaking hands, to tear the other boy's hands away.

"Do you go to Illium?" the flashlight guy demanded.

Dolon nodded, shaking all over. The guy dropped him. Dolon fell to his knees. It was over—he got kicked in the stomach.

"Spying son–of–a–bitch," one of the two muttered.

He was retching on the ground as they kicked him. Pain. Everywhere.

"S—" Kick. Eruption. "Stop—" Kick. Explosion.

Dolon curled further in on himself, waiting for more to come. The skin on his face. Felt far too tight. And the saltwater was dripping into. The grass. They stopped. He opened his eyes. Both boys had crouched down. Towering over him.

"If we stop, what's in it for us?" one of them asked.

The grass was rough against his cheek. When he spoke, he almost threw up. "The party," Dolon managed to wheeze.

"Where is it?"

Dolon choked out the address, and then rolled onto his back, panting. It felt like they had kicked holes in him.

"Anything else? What if that's not enough?"

Panicking, Dolon racked his memory. What would keep them from hurting him again? "Motorcycles," he said, when everything else came up blank.

Odysseus looked at Diomedes, who flashed him a grin, then picked up Dolon, hoisting the smaller boy over his shoulder. The spy was tiny. No one was out at this time, so there was no one to question how Diomedes was carrying a body over his shoulder as they meandered through the neighborhood that Dolon had given them. As soon as they were within a three block radius of the house, the sounds of the party filled the air. They quickened their pace, adrenaline and anticipation pumping through their veins like a drug.

By the time they got to the house, it was just about two in the morning. The house was one of those faux mansions, built to make the owners seem richer than they were. It had opulent but clearly off–brand touches, like the ornate wire balconies starting to rust or the string lights where three of the bulbs were out. Dolon groaned in pain.

Ignoring him, Odysseus looked to Diomedes. "Do we just go inside? Or would we get jumped?"

Diomedes had spotted the motorcycles on the driveway.

"Dude," Odysseus said, poking his friend who hadn't heard a thing.

"Sorry what?" Diomedes asked, looking at his teammate.

Odysseus shook his head. "What do we do?"

"I thought *you* were the strategist," Diomedes grumbled.

The music blasting inside the house got louder as someone opened up a window in the living room and climbed out. She stumbled as she landed, dropping to her butt in the flowerbed. Odysseus sighed.

"Okay, plan," he said, staring at the house. "I'm going in to get the motorcycle keys, and when I get back, we're gonna ring the doorbell, drop... Dolon and then ride, okay?"

Diomedes grunted in affirmation as Odysseus ran up the steps and slipped inside. No one even noticed him come in. The entrance way was packed with people and littered with garbage. He knelt down beside the little table that had an array of dried flowers displayed on it and grabbed the bowl of keys. It a was horrible idea to leave valuables out at a party, he thought as he picked out one of the motorcycle keys, then the other. He glanced around but still, no one had noticed him. Odysseus smiled to himself and slid the bowl back onto the table. It was sticky. Probably from the upturned solo cup hanging from a dead peony.

He snuck back outside, apologizing when he bumped into some guy who had his hands halfway up a girl's shirt. The guy was distracted, so he didn't seem to care. About the bump *or* the apology. Odysseus snorted as he stepped out. It was an incredibly similar temperature outside and inside. Muggy and hot. Diomedes gave a questioning thumbs up, to which Odysseus responded with a nod. Part one of their plan was complete with zero complications.

Odysseus pulled out the keys, glancing at the flowerbed girl. She looked like she was asleep. He wasn't too worried about her anyways. Diomedes walked up to the door and then waited as Odyssseus ran over and got on one of the motorcycles. This was the sketchy part. Diomedes took a deep breath, placed Dolon on the doorstep, rang the doorbell, and bolted away. Odysseus was holding out the key, but they fumbled for a moment, nearly dropping it onto the driveway. Diomedes somehow caught it and jammed it into the ignition just as the door opened. Both bikes roared to life. Odysseus whooped with laughter as they peeled away. (They had both gotten their motorcycle licenses when they first turned sixteen.)

At the door, people were crowding around Dolon, who rolled onto his side, moaning. Rhesus shoved through the crowd just in time to see his prized bikes round the corner. His mouth fell open and he pointed after them.

"What the fuck—" he asked, too drunk to comprehend what was actually happening.

Hector crouched over Dolon as he looked down the street. *Fucking Stallions,* he thought as he hoisted the kid up and brought him into the house.

✦✦✦✦✦ ✦✦✦✦✦

At the hotel, Diomedes and Odysseus drove the bikes into the parking lot, still laughing.

"Oh my *Gods*," Odysseus said, nearly wheezing. "That was whack."

Diomedes pushed down the kickstand of his bike, nodding as he caught his breath. He pulled out his phone flashlight and started inspecting the motorcycles. "Bruh," he whispered, astonished. "This is a fucking Triumph Bonneville."

"No shit," Odysseus balked, rushing around to see. "You're not kidding. Holy fuck."

"This bike is dope," Diomedes whispered reverently.

Agamemnon and the rest of the 'strategy meeting' crew filed out of the hotel, their leader looking around the parking lot.

When he saw his players crouched by the bikes, he pointed a triumphant finger. "I *knew* it was you guys with the motorcycles."

Everyone walked over to inspect the machines. Even Ajax 1 was impressed. The one Odysseus had ridden turned out to be a Panigale V4, which elicited much excitement. After a bunch of swarming around the bikes, they agreed that they should put them in the hotel garage and come back for them on Sunday. They would have the keys, and hopefully most of the Trojan's would be too drunk to remember what even happened.

# XI

Briseis was glad Agamemnon was all talk. She had broken up with him and no one had gotten expelled, or framed for drug dealing. No one was dead in a ditch or from a freak accident on the field. And no one was hurt. Because of him, that was. She was sitting in AP English, Patroclus in the desk next to her. His chin rested on his folded arms, and he stared blankly ahead. He wasn't paying attention. Briseis started taking notes more diligently because her friend would never ask for them, but would be grateful when she offered. She was worried about him. Briseis glanced up at the empty desk near the front of the class where Achilles had been moved to, but he was in a Guidance Meeting at the moment. It was so much quieter in here without him.

It was a grey day outside, the rain spitting weakly at the windows. Not falling hard enough to be considered a shower, but just heavy enough to make it miserable. The wind buffeted the building, roaring dully in the background of the lecture. Patroclus shifted to stare out the window. Briseis watched him for a moment before going back to the notes on how to write an analytical essay. It would have been interesting if she weren't so distracted. There was another football game tonight. The team had gotten back on Saturday evening, ready to play again like they hadn't lost miserably. That mood had gotten less certain as the week went on. Patroclus seemed to grow more distant as the season went on. He was spending so much time with the football guys.

The problem was, he never complained. Iphis had gone home for a family emergency on Monday, leaving Briseis alone for... not more than a couple of hours. It was Wednesday now. Iphis must have texted Patroclus, because he came and walked her to all her classes. Patroclus would make a offhand remark about how much *Achilles* wanted to be playing and was failing to hide it. But he never said anything about how unhappy *he* was.

"Mr. Menoetius?" Mr. Coeus, their English teacher, finally asked. Briseis had known it was coming. "Are you alright?"

Patroclus sat up, eyes wide. "Sorry, sir," he said, scrubbing a hand through his hair. "I'm fine."

The teacher gave him a skeptical look, but continued with his powerpoint. Patroclus dragged his hands over his face, opening his notebook for the first time all period. Achilles, bless his chaotic little soul, had been up almost all night, every night since the weekend. (He *tried* to be quiet and let Patroclus sleep, but he just. Couldn't stop talking sometimes. Without football, Achilles had almost no outlet for his energy.) And on top of that, midterms and state championships were in two weeks, and now he was also trying to make sure Briseis didn't get kidnapped or something… it was not going well. Three teachers had already asked him if he was okay.

Ten minutes later, he gave up on taking notes. Hopefully today's lesson wouldn't be too important. When the bell rang, Briseis poked him. He had his head down on his desk again, breathing softly, until she jabbed his arm.

Patroclus took a sudden deep inhale before sitting up. "Sorry," he muttered, blinking hard as he quickly gathered up his untouched school supplies. "You ready?" he asked, getting to his feet. He was hoping to avoid another member of the staff questioning his wellbeing.

Briseis nodded, but didn't move to stand. "Maybe you should… sleep in my room tonight or something," she offered quietly, purely out of concern.

"Do you know how that would look?" Patroclus asked, raising his eyebrows with a ghost of a smile. "It would be great. Achilles would feel like I was annoyed with him, and everyone would think I was sleeping with you." Briseis shrugged, and he shook his head. "Achilles has to sleep eventually. C'mon. One more class til lunch."

Finally, Briseis slung her bag over her shoulder and got to her feet. As they walked out of the classroom, almost the last ones, she said, "I don't think Achilles is human."

The hall was crowded, and darker than usual with the clouds outside.

It felt sleepy, almost, as Partroclus frowned at her, a glimmer of humor in his eyes. "And by that you mean?"

She leaned over and stage–whispered in his ear, "I don't think he actually has to sleep."

Her friend snorted, nodding. "Yeah, me neither. He's beyond such mortal necessities."

"Who's beyond mortal necessities?" Achilles asked from behind the two of them.

"Speak of the devil," Briseis said to Partroclus, who shook his head. "Look! We can even summon him!" she added, gesturing to Achilles with sarcastic amazement.

Achilles pushed his way between them, throwing an arm around each of their shoulders. "Wait, so I'm the devil?"

They took up about half the hallway like this, but once people recognized Achilles, their annoyance faded away. It was surprising that he was still so popular, after the whole debacle with the football team.

"Yes, Achilles, you're the devil," Briseis said, nodding at him with complete sincerity.

He looked uncharacteristically thoughtful for a moment before apparently deciding that this could be accepted as a fact. "Good to know."

Patroclus laughed softly, shaking his head.

"Okay here's my class," Briseis said, pointing to the art room with her thumb. "Release me, you heathen."

"Aren't heathens people who follow the devil?" Achilles asked, letting her go. "And if I *am* the devil—"

Briseis cut him off with a wave and a, "See you at lunch."

"No, Achilles, heathens aren't devil worshippers," Patroclus said, slipping out from under Achilles' arm now that Bri was gone. "It just means you're not a part of Christianity, Judaism, or Islam."

Achilles raised his eyebrows as they picked up the pace, rushing to their next class. "*Technically,* a heathen *could* be a devil wor-shiper then."

They pounded up a set of mostly empty stairs to the second floor.

"Why are we even talking about this?" Patroclus asked, giving Achilles a heavy lidded glance and smile as they walked into their classroom as the second bell rang.

"Just on time," their teacher, Ms. Cleo, said with a grin as they both sat down in their desks.

She wouldn't mark them as late either way, but she liked to make it seem as though she didn't have blatant favorites.

Their desks were at the back of the class, which had been a compromise, because Achilles preferred the seats by the wall, and Patroclus always sat near the front or middle. About halfway through the lesson, Achilles kicked Patroclus' foot. He glanced over without turning his head. Patroclus still felt bad about the last class, hating to be singled out for anything, good or bad. Achilles leaned on his desk so he could see Patroclus' face. Of course he had been paying attention to him, but today... Patroclus looked run down.

"You should say you're sick for the football—" he whispered, only to stop when the curly haired boy glared at him.

Right. Achilles tore a piece of paper out of his notebook and then tore a smaller piece off of that. He wrote, *You should just not go to the football game. I'll leave the room so you can sleep or whatever you want. I know your kinda pissed at me. Just say your sick.*

He handed it to Patroclus, who reluctantly accepted it and read it in his lap. Absentmindedly, he pressed his pencil to his lips. Patroclus' shoulders slumped a little as he glanced over at Achilles. The other boy was watching him with this annoying concern in his green eyes. Agh. Patroclus had thought he was doing a good job of hiding his minor irritation, but sleep deprivation... apparently wasn't his friend. He flipped over the note, tapping his pencil on the tip of his nose. When he handed it back to Achilles, the blonde boy met his eyes, staring at him for a second before looking down at the scrap of paper. Patroclus smiled weakly, then turned back to his notes.

Achilles swallowed, reading the note. *Love, you spelled you're wrong.* He glared over at Patroclus, who smiled down at his paper without glancing up. Achilles rolled his eyes, holding back a grin. *And fine,* the note continued. *Normally I'd say no. BUT. I feel really bad and I don't actually... yeah I'm feeling a bit sick. And also I'm sorry. I know you're annoyed about not playing, but you're okay with it. I'm just tired. I'm sorry.*

"Achilles?" Ms. Cleo asked, making him look up.

"Yes?" he replied, quickly trying to read the slide up on the projector.

She smiled at him expectantly. "What're your thoughts on the collective versus individual identity of Americans?"

Patroclus gave Achilles a knowing side eye as he pretended to think about the question.

He had no idea what the answer was, so when he opened his mouth, it was purely meant to be a joke. "Well. I think there's a projection of how the individual is supposed to behave, based of the supposed collective identity of the country. For example, people all over the world are said to believe in the *American Dream,* but what is that, really? The American Dream was created in an era where America was supremely messy, with a golden facade and a dark underbelly. So individual Americans are expected to follow this ideal, but what is it? We're supposed to be a country of free thinkers, where liberty, equality, and hard work are praised. But equality is... just not happening. Between anyone. So the collective identity is dissolving into individual choices, because there are definitely people who perpetuate the stereotype of the rude, uninformed American. And... yeah."

A girl in the front of the class actually turned to stare.

"Wow," Ms. Cleo said, nodding like she was impressed. "Thank you for that. I appreciate your thoughtful answer."

Patroclus had a hand over his mouth, looking up at the ceiling with his eyes, trying not to laugh. *Good,* Achilles thought, folding up the note and slipping it in his pocket. He honestly had no idea what just came out of his mouth, or if it even answered the question. He was pretty sure he had just avoided it and talked in circles. Whatever worked.

By the time Iphis marched into their Women's Studies class, ten minutes before the final bell rang, Briseis was just... not working anymore. Their teacher, Ms. Melpomene, gave them a free period to research something, and then she left. Half the class was gone. Briseis was texting Achilles, who had convinced Patroclus to stay back from the football game. They were going to meet in the library and figure out what to do next. *This* was when Iphis came in. Her hair was wild, her sweater drenched. The few people still in the classroom glanced up, then went back to their work. Briseis felt her face break into a giant smile.

Iphis' boots left puddles on the floor as she stomped over to Bri. She sat on her empty desk, uncrossing Briseis' legs and resting the tips of her feet on the chair.

"Hey babe," she said under her breath, ruffling a hand through her soaked hair and spraying droplets of rain onto Briseis.

Briseis couldn't stop smiling as she looked around, seeing if anyone was paying attention. The three other girls in the classroom were wearing earbuds. She leaned forwards, resting her arms on Iphis' legs. The relief she felt was immense. Like releasing a breath held for far too long. It had been so lonely without her. (Achilles and Patroclus were great, but they weren't *Iphis*.)

"Why're you back?" Briseis asked, staring up at her.

Iphis smirked. "What, did you miss me?"

Briseis buried her face in her arms, nodding as her face heated.

Iphis put a hand on the top of her head. "Aw. Well. I'm back."

She wasn't *supposed* to be back until Friday. Briseis sat back up, eyeing Iphis skeptically as she dried off her own forehead.

"Why are you soaked?" she asked, putting her hands on Iphis' knees.

The short haired girl glanced at the door and then leaned closer. "I had to take a fucking Greyhound bus here, but then I walked from the station."

Briseis raised her eyebrows, unsure of how to reply to that. "What *happened?*" It was definitely something Iphis would do, but... still.

She laughed sharply, sitting back and ignoring the fact that Ms. Melpomene had just come back into the room. To be fair, their teacher was used to Iphis, so she didn't say anything.

"How was your trip?" Ms. Melpomene asked, gathering a pile of papers off her desk.

Iphis looked over her shoulder. "Well. I had a great time. My grandma's dying, but then I pretty much got disowned, so I told them I didn't *want* to be in that family anyways, and that I'd figure shit out from there. So I took the Greyhound back."

Their teacher made panicked eye contact with Briseis, who was still trying to comprehend Iphis' words.

"Good thing I'm here on scholarship, huh?" Iphis said, with a thumbs up and a smile that couldn't be real.

"Iphis..." Ms. Melpomene started, her eyebrows betraying her worry. "I'm so sorry. I'm here to talk if you need. This is... oh gods."

Briseis took Iphis' hand, and the other girl looked down at her. Briseis whispered, "I'm not gonna offer you help cause I know you won't want it. Come to me if you need it. I just... fuck, Iphis, that sucks. I wish I could make it all go away."

"You do," Iphis smiled, with one side of her mouth. Her eyes were empty. "It'll be okay," she said, looking back at their teacher as the bell rang. "I'll figure it out."

Ms. Melpomene scrutinized Iphis for a long moment before nodding. "Please. This door is always open."

Iphis hopped off Briseis' desk, still holding her hand. She saluted to their teacher with her free hand as Briseis grabbed her bag off the back of the chair. They left the classroom, which was plastered with posters of famous women. All of them looked so serious. Briseis wasn't sure what to think about them. (She did know that none of them would be pleased with the way the world was going.)

"Where're we going?" Iphis asked as they joined the stream of students lazily making their way through the hall. It was a funny thing to ask, since she was the one dragging Briseis.

After the last class, no one rushed, making it almost impossible to get anywhere with any efficiency. And today, no one wanted to go outside, making it claustrophobic. Iphis didn't let that slow her down.

"Library," Briseis said after apologizing to someone that Iphis had body–checked. "Unless you want to… go somewhere else."

Iphis glared over her shoulder. "Don't."

"What?"

"Don't pity me, okay? It was my choice. It's been fucking awful every time I've gone home. I haven't lost anything."

"Sorry," Briseis said, biting her lower lip. Iphis was nothing if not blunt. At least Briseis knew she liked her. There's no way Iphis could pretend to have feelings for someone.

Iphis' gaze softened as they turned out of the main hall. "No," she said, stopping beside a row of lockers. It was empty, dark, and dramatic in this passage because of the giant windows. Iphis pulled Briseis forwards. She stumbled, not expecting it. Iphis was leaned against the wall, still holding her hand. "*I'm* sorry. I'm tired and I just spent an hour walking in the rain."

Briseis nodded, her eye–line perfectly on Iphis' mouth. The corner quirked.

"Careful babe," Iphis whispered. "We're in the middle of Republican nowhere. You're not in Cali anymore."

"Just quickly," she whispered back, glancing up to meet her gaze.

Iphis sighed sarcastically. "Fine. If you insist."

Briseis leaned forwards, pressing her lips briefly to Iphis'. She didn't want to pull away, but she did. Too soon.

"Hey platonic bestie," Iphis said under her breath, which made Briseis laugh, resting her head on the other girl's collarbone. "Let's go to the library." She paused as Briseis stepped back. They started down the hall. "Hey... can we not tell them about this? My family, that is?"

"I guess so," Briseis replied with a sad smile. "If that's what you want."

Iphis grinned, hugging Briseis to her side as they went. "Thanks."

When the two of them finally found Achilles and Patroclus in the library, it was pouring outside. The guys were all the way in the back of the giant room, at a table that Briseis had never seen before.

It was a perfect place to be on a rainy day. Patroclus was laying on the floor, surrounded by textbooks, an arm thrown over his eyes to block out the light. Achilles actually seemed to be studying, but upon closer inspection, he was reading a large book that was completely irrelevant to any of his classes. The page Achilles was reading had a picture of some *extremely* disturbing birds.

"Where did you *find* that?" Briseis asked, pulling away from Iphis to glance over his shoulder. "And what the hell is it supposed to be?"

Achilles glanced up and beamed. "Oh... the library was getting rid of a bunch of stuff and they said Patroclus could take whatever he wanted. And this gem... well. I had to read it." He showed her the cover. It was called *Codex Seraphinianus, by Luigi Serafini.* "It's written in an undistinguishable language. And the art is *terrifying.*"

"Patroclus, why did the library even have this?" Iphis asked, pulling out a chair next to where he was laying.

He shrugged hopelessly, without taking his arm off his face. "Don't ask me."

Achilles and Briseis were giggling now, so Patroclus sat up. "Wait," he said, looking at Iphis. "Aren't you supposed to be away 'til like. Friday or something?"

She swallowed, busying herself with pulling a notebook out of her bag. "Yeah. But plans changed. It's all good."

Patroclus opened his mouth to say something else, but Briseis shook her head at him. He frowned, but laid back down with a sigh. Briseis grabbed a chair and started looking through Achilles' mystery book with him. It was quiet, save for the sound of Iphis' pencil and the rain outside. Occasionally, Achilles found a particular image he thought he should share.

After about twenty minutes, Achilles said, "I feel like my brain is getting murdered."

This made everyone laugh. Patroclus' phone buzzed from somewhere among his textbooks. He sat up again, patting the ground. Iphis bent down and handed him the phone. He gave her a tired smile and a muttered, "Thank you," as he checked his messages.

Machaon:



*Sent 4:01 PM*

Machaon:



*Sent 4:15 PM*

Machaon:

Patroclus where are you

*Sent 4:22 PM*

That was the last message.

"Oh *fuck*," Patroclus muttered under his breath, pressing a hand to his forehead. He had told the sports med teacher that he wasn't going to the game, but he hadn't told Machaon.

"What's wrong?" Achilles asked, all humor dropping from his face.

Patroclus held up a finger and replied quickly.

Patroclus:

I'm so sorry. I'm feeling super sick rn. I told Mr. Asclepius.

*Sent 4:27 PM*

He let out a pained breath, looking up at his friends. "So funny story. I told my teacher I wasn't going to the game, but I didn't tell the team, so now Machaon's mad at me."

"Whoops," Iphis said with a shrug. "Mistakes happen. And who cares about their opinions? Football boys are gross." She looked at Achilles. "Yes. All the time. You're gross too."

Achilles shook his head, scandalized.

Patroclus' phone buzzed again.

Machaon:

> This game is so bad. I need you here.
> Argh. How do you tape an ankle?

*Sent 4:28 PM*

Machaon:

> Memnon's out for the first
> half at least.

*Sent 4:30 PM*

Machaon:

> And Idomeneus just got hurt too.
> The trojans aren't winning rn but at
> this rate we're gonna have to play
> the jrs. Not good.

*Sent 4:34 PM*

Patroclus sighed. "Achilles, can I tape your ankle? To remind Machaon?"

❧❧❧ ❧❧❧

When the game finished, half of the actually good players were injured. Apparently including Hector, at the hands of some random freshman who was on for Idomeneus. Patroclus felt slightly better, but he was just as stressed as he would have been if he went to the game. Machaon had gotten hurt in the literal five minutes he played, which had caused a mild panic that was resolved somewhat well when the other boy knew how to wrap a knee. In the end, the injured players were Agamemnon, Idomeneus, Antilochus, Odysseus, Diomedes, Machaon, and Nestor, which made Achilles think that the Trojans were actually *trying* to seriously hurt the senior players.

"Give me your phone," Achilles said as Patroclus glanced down at the device again.

Patroclus sighed.

"This was supposed to be a *break*," Achilles persisted, holding out his hand.

Iphis, who had long since given up studying and had gotten some food an hour ago menacingly put down her fork. "I won't hesitate to attack you," she said, wiping her hands on her skirt.

"Maybe we shouldn't attack him..." Briseis replied, now half focused on a math worksheet.

"One sec," Patroclus said, his eyebrows scrunching together. "Nestor just texted."

Nestor:

> I really need to talk to you when we get back. It shouldn't be too long now this is important. Where can we meet?

*Sent 7:09 PM*

Patroclus:

Wherever's fine. Do you need me to bring the first aid stuff?

*Sent 7:09 PM*

Nestor:

No it's about the season and Achilles

*Sent 7:10 PM*

Patroclus:

I thought we'd already talked about this. He's not coming back unless Agamemnon apologizes.

*Sent 7:10 PM*

Nestor:

Just meet me in the foyer yk those couches off the main hall? The school building closes at like 9 right and we'll be back soon. I'll text you when we get there.

*Sent 7:10 PM*

Patroclus was still on the floor, sitting cross legged in his textbook graveyard. Achilles leaned over to try and see what he was typing, but he was too far away. He yanked on his french braid, trying to ease some of the pressure on his scalp. It had been a long day.

"Cellular device, please?" Achilles said when Patroclus put it face down on his History textbook.

"I won't touch it until Nestor texts again," Patroclus promised, looking up at Achilles with a grin that innocent, but unsure.

Iphis scoffed. "What does *that* delinquent want?"

"Nice word," Briseis mumbled without looking up.

"He wants to talk about the absent football star," Patroclus said.

Achilles dramatically melted to the floor, landing with his head in Patroclus' lap.

"Impressive," Iphis said, her mouth full of mashed potato. (She had acquired that, among other random foods earlier, which included mac and cheese, a package of granola, baby carrots, and chicken nuggets. )

Patroclus started undoing Achilles' hair.

"I thought I *told* them," Achilles whined, his eyes closed. "And why don't they talk to *me*?"

"Well, honey," Patroclus said softly, "You weren't the most *cooperative* person to negotiate with."

Iphis pretended to retch. "Too much PDA."

Briseis actually looked up. "Let them have their moment. Like you said, we're not in California."

The blonde girl muttered something under her breath, but had no more complaints. Achilles huffed, wrinkling his delicate nose.

"Fine," he said. "But that isn't very relaxing. And Nestor... he's not the greatest person, Patroclus." He opened his eyes. "I think Iphis wasn't too far off when she said delinquent..."

"Agamemnon is worse," Briseis stated bluntly.

No one could argue with that.

Patroclus' phone buzzed.

"Don't die," Achilles said as he sat up, letting Patroclus go. His hair fell in loose waves around his face. He looked so young.

Briseis frowned at Patroclus, who smiled as he got to his feet. It was forced, but he placed a hand on Achilles' head and some of the pain in his eyes lessened.

"Damn," Briseis said as she looked at Achilles and his hair. "You've got a kind of... merman vibe."

Achilles tossed his head, making a face like an over–the–top model. "Please," he said, his voice husky, "Come explore the wonders of the deep with me."

"Shut up, you *weirdo*" Iphis muttered, curling a disgusted lip at Achilles.

Patroclus had a hand over his eyes, laughing. "You're ridiculous."

He flipped his hair again to smolder over his shoulder. "Why thank you, handsome sailor—"

"Aaand I was leaving," Patroclus said, practically bolting down the library aisle.

Achilles shook his head before tying his hair back into a bun. "He couldn't handle it."

"Neither could I," both Iphis and Briseis said at the same time, with the same ironic tone.

Their conversation faded into the stacks of books, getting lost in the vast, dusty space as Patroclus made his way towards the doors. He passed a couple people who were studying, but it was pretty much empty. Waving to the librarian who was working tonight, he slipped out into the hallway. The lights were still on, making it much brighter than the library with its desk lamps and occasional strip of LEDs. He didn't see anyone until he got to the foyer, where some of the football players were still loitering. Antilochus waved to Patroclus and he waved back. Antilochus was an exception to the general rule of football idiocy. He and Automedon. And Achilles, most of the time.

Patroclus found Nestor and Machaon in a little furnished alcove just off the left side of the entrance hall. The older boy was scrolling through his phone, and only looked up when Patroclus sat down on the couch across from him.

"Hey," Nestor said, setting his phone on the glass coffee table between them. "What's up?"

"Not much," Patroclus replied, putting his hands under his thighs. "You?"

"Nah," Nestor said, leaning back against the couch. "We tied the game, so that's better than losing, I guess. But that was just cause Hector was out."

"Hey, can you tape my knee?" Machaon asked, getting stiffly to his feet and offering Patroclus a roll of athletic tape.

Patroclus nodded, taking it and kneeling down in front of him.

"So," Nestor said. "I had this idea." He paused, looking over at Patroclus, who ripped a strand of tape off the roll. "I know I don't know you very well, but listen. I know you tried out for the team sophomore year. Because you're really good. But when you got accepted, you quit."

"Right," Patroclus said, half focused on the tape and not sure where this was going. "Isn't this about Achilles though?"

Nestor nodded, a small smile spreading across his face. "You're about the same height as him. Same build, give or take." Dread began to settle in Patroclus' stomach. "So what if... you put on his gear."

"No." Patroclus said, tearing another strip of tape. He finished off the job and stood.

"Thanks," Machaon said quietly, stepping out of the alcove. His footsteps receded down the hall.

Nestor watched him go, then turned and held up his hands as if to pacify Patroclus. "Hear me out," he said, like a politician might. "You put on Achilles' gear and come play with us, no one knows the difference. And then we win. And go to State championships. And then to Nationals. And everyone thinks you're Achilles. *Achilles* won't have to risk his honor, because you'll be there for him."

"I'm not *nearly* as good as him—" Patroclus said, feeling blood pulsing through the tips of his fingers.

The older boy cut him off. "Dude. Chill. It's just an idea, but if Achilles learns that he has that much power over a team even when he's not *actually* playing, he might come back. It wouldn't be you for long. 'Cause he cares about you, right? And I think you're as good as him. Almost, at least. And just in case you didn't realize," Nestor said as he made to stand. "This is all so people stop getting hurt. Like, with Achilles back on the field, we win, and then get the hell outta this messy league. And when I offered this idea to Agamemnon... he said he'd stop paying off the refs."

If people stopped getting so hurt, it would make things better. But was it worth it? Patroclus held up a hesitant finger as the older player took a step towards the hall. "Wait..."

Nestor looked over, hope flickering skeptically across his face.

"Okay," Patroclus said, dragging his hands over his head. "Fine."

"Fine what?"

"Fine, I'll ask Achilles about it," Patroclus replied, annoyed. When Nestor opened his mouth, he kept talking. "And no, I don't know when, or if it'll even work. He'll most likely continue being stubborn, and refuse to give me his stuff, but I'll try."

Nestor nodded, trying to keep a smile off his face. "Thanks man. I appreciate it." He walked out of the alcove, only to poke his head back around the corner. "Hope to see you on the field soon."

Patroclus gave him an unenthusiastic thumbs up, and then let his head fall into his hands. This was shaping up to be a disaster.

# XII

H ECTOR COULDN'T BELIEVE THEIR... luck. Two games 'til district championships, and the Trojans had won more than the Stallions. He *was* concussed, but that didn't really matter. It was minor. He could deal with it. Especially with the next game more than a week away. It would take place, unfortunately, at the Stallions' home field. Even though they had been part of the decision to play at Ilium, they claimed the Trojans were winning due to home field advantage. But it was okay.

The mood at Ilium Academy was crazy. Any member of the football team walking down the hall would be followed by cheers and shouts of excitement. There were even banners up in the cafeteria now, congratulating the team and wishing them luck. That's where Hector was sitting. Andromache was next to him, and Aeneas was sitting on his other side. Helen sat on the across table, alone now that Paris had just left. He had seen some of the soccer guys and bolted. Helen liked hanging around Hector and his friends. They were less... confusing than Paris, who had been quiet lately. And Helen didn't necessarily *mind* that, but he had almost become her ally. Almost.

"Don't you think the banners are a little much?" Helen asked, watching some people from the Spirit Club put up a giant photo of Hector. He observed the process, a disturbed expression on his face.

"I didn't..." Hector started, then stopped, looking at Aeneas. "When did we *take* those photos?"

The other boy frowned, staring up as the banner unfolded. "Um. I honestly have no idea."

"Last year," Andromache said, focusing on an essay she was editing. "Like, in the first week of summer after the senior tryouts. When they decided you'd be captain."

Aeneas and Hector looked at each other, frowning.

"I still don't remember that," Hector finally said.

No one got to reply to that, because a whole group of junior players came into the cafeteria. They were met by an uproar that drowned any possibility of conversation for at least three minutes. It sent Hector's head pounding. He should probably have stayed home, but how could he?

Andromache was at school. Hector had no right to complain, in his own humble opinion. When the noise died down, someone tapped Hector on the shoulder. An icky feeling settled into his stomach as he saw who it was. Dolon.

"Hey man," Hector said, turning around on the bench so he could face the kid. "What's up?"

Dolon had ended up in the hospital for a few days after the...
disaster of the party a week ago. This was the first time Hector had
seen him back at school.

Aeneas stood up. "Dolon!" he said, offering the tenth grader a
fist bump. "Glad to see you back! How're you feeling?"

He had a purple bruise running along the side of his neck, disappearing under the collar of his school uniform. Hector cringed.
When Aeneas had stumbled downstairs on the night of the party,
*he* had been the one to call the ambulance. When Dolon got picked
up, Aeneas went with him until his parents had arrived. And when
Aeneas got back, he pretty much screamed at Hector. It hadn't
been a good night.

"I'm alright actually," Dolon said with a smile that looked more
like a wince. "Won't be back this season though."

Aeneas sat back down, nodding. "Well, I'm glad you're okay."

"Just thought I'd come let you know about...practicing with you
guys, I guess, since I never played," he said, glancing at Hector.
"And also... sorry about this whole thing. It's totally my fault."
This he said to the floor.

Hector could see Andromache glaring at him out of the corner
of his eye.

"No," Hector said, guilt for what had happened to this kid rag-
ing in his throat. "No, Dolon, it's my bad. Completely my fault."

Dolon looked up, eyebrows raised. "Uh... no I'm the one who
failed the mission."

"And I'm the one who *created* the mission, where I *wanted*
someone to fail." That wasn't what Hector had meant to say, and

it earned glares from everyone at the table. Dolon's mouth fell open. Hector sighed. "What I'm trying to say, is that none of this should have happened. And I'm sorry about your ribs and shit. That fucking sucks."

The younger kid was staring at Hector like he didn't quite know what to say.

"You should definitely try out next year," Hector offered. "You could be a great player."

Dolon shrugged ruefully. "I think football isn't really for me. But good luck with the rest of the season!" He hiked his bag further up on his shoulder and walked over towards the vending machine.

"That's the kid who got beat to a pulp, right?" Helen asked, watching Dolon with pity.

Hector shamefully scrubbed a hand over his head. "Yeah maybe. But he looks like he's okay now."

"I hate football," Andromache said bitterly, putting her pencil down. "The whole... culture of it is so *violent*, and for what?"

"Is this needless aggression still about what school I go to?" Helen asked, leaning on one hand.

Aeneas laughed. "I honestly have no idea. Menelaus hasn't been playing. But I think he's coming back next week. I think it's more about seeing what we can get away with now."

"Says you," Andromache snapped. "Who was it who suggested that we try to hurt their key players a few games ago?"

The boys looked guiltily at each other again.

"*What*?" Helen asked, incredulous. "That was a thing?"

Hector swallowed slowly, breathing to calm himself. "That was our *coach*, so you can't really blame us for following his leadership. And the Stallions did it first!"

"This is a fucking cult," Helen muttered under her breath.

Aeneas raised his eyebrows and nodded. "Well. As lovely as this has been," he said, gathering up his mostly empty tray, "I must take my leave, because I'm potentially failing chemistry."

Andromache grabbed her stuff, shoving it haphazardly in her bag. "I'm coming with you."

"Do you want me to—" Hector stared, but they were already leaving.

Helen looked after them the same way she had watched Dolon.

Hector sighed, pressing his fingers into his eyes. "This is my last year with this game," he said to Helen. "There's literally three games left. It shouldn't be such a big deal."

Helen's pity stayed as she turned her soft gaze to him. "Y'know, she's just worried about you. And she's tired and in pain, and she just wants you to be okay. That's why she's so snappy."

"Yeah," Hector said, drumming his fingers on the purple plastic tabletop.

Someone pounded him on the back as they walked by, shouting, "Go Trojans!"

He didn't even see who it was. It wasn't likely that he would have known them anyways.

"Well," Helen said, getting up from the table "Best of luck in your scholastic endeavors. See you later."

The rest of the week was a bit chaotic. Hector's concussion left him unable to do a lot of concentrating, so his classes were spent staring out the window until the light got to be too much. Paris 'accidentally' flipped a breaker switch on Thursday, which just made Hector question his brother. Then, it turned out that *Helen* had 'accidentally' flipped the breaker switch, which made for an interesting story. Paris muttered something about Helen being mad about a Chemistry test, and one of the electrical rooms had been unlocked, so they went in there and… flipped switches for fun? All the power went out for about two hours. When someone had asked what happened, Helen had jokingly blamed it on Paris, been cut off, and was then unable to remedy the joke. Paris was a shockingly good sport about it, apologizing to the principal and moving on like nothing happened. Which made Hector question his brother even more.

At the practices, Poseidon, Zeus' brother who used to be in the NFL, worked them hard but it was worth it. Hector wasn't supposed to be doing anything football related for at *least* a week, but he had to try some of the drills. When the next week rolled around, their guest coach was spewing strategies like a fountain, to the point where Mr. Phoebus had to step in and ask for him to stop overwhelming the team. Hector loved it. His players were thriving. He never would have guessed that the Trojans football team could be so coachable.

On the Friday of the game, the team left their classes early to get on the bus. The air was crackled with excitement. Andromache and Helen came with them, along with some of the other players' friends, making the team bus more crowded than usual. Not that they had the chance to use it this season. It was always fun driving to a game, the players getting louder and louder the closer they got. Hector could feel his pulse thrumming in his ears.

"We're gonna *crush* them," Scarpedon announced from his seat across the aisle from Hector, as they pulled into the Mycenae parking lot,

This was met by enthusiastic cheering so intense that the windows shook.

Agamemnon watched the Trojan bus pull into the parking lot from the field. The Stallions had been training their asses off every possible moment they could get, and he still wasn't sure that they could win. The Trojans were just too strong, especially now that they had been working with Zeus' guest coach. Normally, at this time of year, the excitement of a guaranteed spot at State Championships would be like a drug to the whole student population. They hadn't even made posters this year. Whenever people saw Agamemnon, they saw him as a failure. And it *was* his fault. He couldn't get their star player back, and the whole team was suffering for it. The whole *school* was suffering for it.

The Stallions players filtered out of the back doors, making their way over to the field in groups of red jerseys. They looked like they had already lost. Agamemnon ground his teeth together and slammed his helmet down onto the metal bench. The trainer, who was sitting a little ways down, jumped, glancing over at him with eyes wide. Achilles' friend. Agamemnon scowled at him.

Menelaus walked up to his brother, who was glaring over at Patroclus. This would be his first game back playing after his stupid injury, but after talking with some of the team, it seemed hopeless already.

"What's up?" Menelaus asked, curious about his brother's sudden aggression towards the trainer.

Agamemnon grimaced, looking over at Menelaus. "The team's gonna fail."

"Now now," Athena chastised, walking over to the two brothers. "You don't know that."

Agamemnon tipped his head towards the dusty blue sky, letting out an exasperated breath. "Have you *seen* the looks on their faces?"

Menelaus turned away from his brother, watching the Ajaces make their way across the field, followed closely by a group of freshmen. Behind them, Diomedes, Nestor, and Odysseus came out of the school, heads together, discussing something that probably wasn't as important as they were making it out to be. In the parking lot, players were now filing out of the Trojans' bus and into the school. Menelaus sighed. This was so far beyond his honor now. At this point, all the aggression were about Agamemnon's pride, and Achilles' hubris. No one had even mentioned Helen in like, a week. Though, that was actually good Menelaus supposed, because the whole thing had been convoluted since the very beginning. Helen would get to choose what happened after the season was over.

As the Stallions made their way to their coach, people started settling down in the stands. More cars were pulling into the parking lot, probably having followed the Trojans' bus. They'd have a shit–ton of fans following them. But the Stallions had their fair share of devoted parents and donors too. Menelaus recognized a few of them. His own parents were unfolding lawn chairs on the other side of the field. *Ugh*. He wasn't in the mood for that.

Athena called a team huddle, instructing them to begin their warmup. They weren't going to talk. They weren't going to laugh. They were going to listen to their captain, and they were going to play one hell of a dirty game. This was the maker or breaker of the season. Odysseus took the offense line with him to one half of the field, and the defense followed Agamemnon to the other. As they ran a lap, Menelaus saw Briseis and that blonde girl sitting by Patroclus, as well as one of the former offense players, Automedon. He waved to Menelaus sadly as he passed.

"*Fuck*," Ajax 1 muttered as they ran. "If only *half our good players* came back."

"You got that one right," Menelaus replied, scowling at the stands over his shoulder.

The Stallions' warmup was lower intensity than usual, due to the general lack of motivation. When they got sequestered into half the field so the Trojans could warm up, they left the field altogether in favor of sitting on the sidelines, doing 'dynamic' stretching. Athena wasn't impressed by this decision, and walked around ordering people to run laps.

Within the initial three minutes of the game, Paris scored the first touchdown. The Stallions' defense line had been broken already.

# XIII

I N THE STANDS, HELEN sat with Priam. It was really weird to be back here. She used to spend hours on these bleachers, watching the team practice. Menelaus ran off the field, his number 81 jersey pulling her attention away from the game. The Trojans had just scored. Paris, surprisingly. Helen was pretty sure he was just trying to prove himself to Hector, because what he did... hadn't been one of the plays they had been working on. He just took the ball and ran. That was the one thing Paris had going for him; he was fast. And the other thing going for him was the Stallions' weird lack of energy. Sure, Agamemnon was screaming at them, but it seemed like they didn't care. Helen didn't know if she'd even seen them so... unremarkable.

"This game doesn't seem... to be as high energy as the others," Priam observed, stroking his wiry beard.

Helen nodded, barely resisting the urge to yell at Antilochus as he nearly fumbled the ball. What was *happening*? Idomeneus came sprinting across the field, breaking their formation and apparently the play, because the shouts of indignation from the bench followed him as he smacked into the player tailing Antilochus, throwing the Trojan player to the ground. The crowd gasped at the tackle as both players jumped to their feet. Helen found herself on the edge of her seat as Antilochus gained five... seven... eight yards.

Another player was running at him now, and no one was there to stop him—no there was Idomeneus again. How had Helen never noticed him? This man was fast. And strong too. The rest of the offense line finally caught on, sprinting around the fallen players after Antilochus, dropping into formation just in case he needed to offload. Idomeneus got to his feet again, stumbling a little as he shot off down the field. The player he had tackled this time didn't get up so quickly.

Helen frowned. Where was Hector? This seemed like a moment where the captain would step in... especially now that Antilochus was past the fifty yard line now, dashing forwards into their zone. And it was only the first down. Maybe it had just been the defense line that was out of it. Which was still weird. The Stallions fans, who made up a much larger section of the bleachers and the camping chairs around the perimeter of the field were going crazy.

Hector's head was aching. He felt like his eyes were being drilled into. But that didn't matter, because the Stallions' player who had the ball was now running uncontested towards their endzone, because of that dude who kept tackling everyone. What the *hell* was that? Hector pushed his legs out of the slow jog he had been in, towards a full on sprint. When he caught up to the ball carrier, he threw himself at the guy, bringing him to the ground. It was a sloppy tackle, done at full speed, so the Stallion had a chance to offload the ball to someone right behind him. *Fuck.*

Luckily, Scarpedon bowled that guy over. First down done. Only three to go.

Odysseus was calling a play they did a lot. *Thoroughbred.* A simple passing play. Hector had figured out the code–names for at least half of the Stallion maneuvers. They were all named after kinds of horses. (Who had decided that? It was weird.) The Trojans just numbered their plays. It was more confusing. He called for a Cross–Rushing Stunt. The defensive line quickly fell into position, rushing the offensive line as the ball was snapped. They didn't make it five yards. In the third down, they tried a play Hector hadn't seen before, and it screwed with his players, who *should* have been fine with their zone defense, but apparently two weeks hadn't been enough to drill it into their heads.

Hector rolled his eyes as he took off down the field, tackling the kid who had been destroying the defense earlier. Unfortunately, he had made it into the twenty yard zone. The Stallions went for the field goal, but they missed. The ball ended up in Hector's hands. *Huh,* he thought, *I don't think I've ever caught a field goal attempt before.* And now the panicked Stallions players were charging towards him. Hector sighed and raced down the field. He could outrun almost anyone, except maybe that guy who was randomly fast today. Their runningback. Who wasn't Achilles. Helen had said his name was Idomeneus or something.

But no one was on his tail as he broke away from the majority of the players. Scarpedon and Euphorbus were behind him. He heard one of them hit the ground, but didn't look back. Odysseus came out of nowhere, trying to push him out of the lines, but Hector just sped up, tripping the quarterback on the way.

He was inside the twenty yard line now, and the ten... aand *touchdown.* Hector threw the ball onto the ground as three of his teammates slammed into him, yelling. The crowd, both Stallions and Trojans fans were cheering. It was impossible not to get excited when things didn't go as planned. After the excitement had died down a little bit, the ref signaled for a kick–off to the Stallions. No one on the Trojan's team scored another Pick Six, but the Stallions were struggling. Their quarterback was yelling, and it was something much harsher than horse breeds coming from his mouth. Their plays depended on a different kind of defense than Posiedon had taught, so nothing was working. In the fourth down, they scored the field goal they missed last time, eliciting some pity cheers from the crowd.

Paris was waiting to get back on the field when Hector came jogging off, with a swarm of players thumping him on the back. Hector broke away from the defensemen and made his way over to Paris. He wasn't expecting his older brother to grab the grill of his helmet and pull him over to the bench.

"Don't pull any fucking *showy plays,*" Hector growled, not letting go of Paris' helmet.

Paris nodded as best he could, trying to control his breath. He wasn't about to point out that Hector had just pulled one of the showiest plays of the season. His brother terrified him when he was like this.

"You don't get what that does, you *idiot*," he continued, finally releasing Paris. "It makes the whole team think they can leave their training in the dust and try to be a showpony."

"Paris!" Mr. Phoebus yelled from the sideline. "Get on the field! Now!"

Caught between his coach and his brother, Paris felt stuck to the ground. Hector spread his arms, exasperated.

"*Go,*" he said, like it was the obvious thing to do.

Paris darted away.

"Remember!" Hector yelled after him, sitting down on the bench. "This isn't fucking soccer!"

# XIV

B Y THE MIDDLE OF the second quarter, the Stallions were losing miserably. After the offense fumbled the ball again, Agamemnon got Athena to call a time out. The Trojans ran off the field, shouting and slamming into each other. Agamemnon cursed under his breath when he saw Idomeneus leaning on Antilochus as he limped towards the rest of the team as they gathered on the sideline. Odysseus ripped his helmet from his head, his face filled with unbridled anger. Agamemnon understood that feeling on another level. This fucking team was *inadequate.* Hector was even off the field, apparently injured or something, and they were *still* struggling.

"Okay everyone," Athena called, beckoning for the team to come in closer.

The players, sweat soaked and red faced, joined in a tight huddle.

"I know this isn't going how we wanted it to," Athena continued, calm as ever. She was calculating. If they picked up their game... it *was* possible for them to win. It would just take divine intervention. "Achilles and the offense line aren't coming back. And they aren't here to fix your mistakes."

Agamemnon looked over his shoulder to see the Trojan team laughing in their huddle, spraying each other with Gatorade bottles. He growled under his breath.

"What?" Odysseus hissed from beside him.

"We should pull out of the fucking league," Agamemnon answered, digging his cleat into the grass.

The quarterback scoffed, earning an icy stare from their coach before she continued with her stark motivational speech.

"Fuck you," Odysseus said under his breath.

Diomedes peered around him. Agamemnon couldn't see his face through his helmet, but he knew that he had his eyebrows raised.

"What are you *on*?" Diomedes demanded softly. "That's a stupid idea and you *know it.*"

"Guys!" Ajax 1 announced as Athena pulled out of the circle. "We're the fucking Stallions! We don't go down without a fight, because the fight is what we're *made of*!"

"And we don't *quit*," Odysseus spat onto the grass, making eye contact with Agamemnon as he did so.

Ajax 2 raised an arm. "We're drinking to that tonight!" he roared.

"Stallions on three!" Agamemnon matched his players intensity. "One–two–STALLIONS!"

The whole team, (or what was left of the whole team) bellowed their name, hyping themselves up for whatever was to come. The buzzer went off, signaling a start of the whole new game. Agamemnon ran onto the field, followed by his team. They might lose. This might be the most humiliating game of his life. But at least he wouldn't go down alone.

Patroclus had been watching the team huddle with trepidation. Nestor, when coming off the field, had given him a meaningful stare: '*you could do something about this mess.*' Patroclus was clenching his jaw so hard that the muscles behind his eyes were started to ache. What if... no. They needed him here. Idomeneus came limping over, supported by Antilochus.

"Dude," he said, sitting down next to Patroclus with a wince. "Can you just tape my ankle? I hafta get back out there."

Briseis was staring, horrified at Idomeneus' ankle as he rolled down his tall sock. Even Patroclus felt a little nauseous.

"I... think that's really broken," he said hesitantly.

Antilochus nodded vigorously. "That's what *I* was saying! He can't even put weight on it—"

The sports med doctor came running over, took one look at the ankle in question, then reassured them that he would take Idomeneus to the hospital. This was met with much annoyance from the player, but relief from the others. Patroclus turned his attention back to the game, feeling the anxiety mounting in his stomach. As soon as the sports med guy left with Idomeneus, Ajax 1, who had been sort of carrying the defense, went down and didn't get up. Machaon ran around the bench and grabbed the first aid bag, sprinting to Ajax before Patroclus could do anything.

They were up and hobbling off the field within moments, Ajax cursing under his breath. There was blood all over his white pants.

Automedon leaned forwards from one bleacher back and muttered in his ear. "This is a disaster."

Patroclus leapt to his feet. "How the hell did that happen?" he demanded as he slipped under Ajax's other arm, panic thick in his throat. There wasn't supposed to be blood in this game. Usually.

Briseis jumped out of the way as they sat Ajax down.

"Fucking *hell*," he growled, pressing on his thigh. "Some son-of-a-bitch fucking stepped on me when I was down. Full on jumped on me and *apparently* they're wearing like—" he paused, wincing as Machaon rolled up his pant leg. "They're wearing fucking track spikes. How did they—" Ajax stopped talking entirely when they got to the injury.

There were puncture marks in the perfect shape of a cleat on his thigh, oozing blood. Nothing too serious. Patroclus pulled out alcohol wipes and gauze, slipping on a pair of gloves. Ajax hissed through his teeth when Patroclus started cleaning the punctures. A new player ran onto the field to fill in for Ajax, and the game continued. (They were running out of backup players.)

A few rows back, Zeus sat with Hera and Poseidon. He was glad to see his promise to Thetis being fulfilled.

"No Achilles," Zeus said to his wife, "No winnies."

"Disrespectfully," she replied, her posture far too straight to be sitting on high school football bleachers, "That was a disturbingly awful joke, if humor was even what you were going for. That was enough to make Poseidon cry. See?" She gestured to Zeus' brother, who had his face in his hands. "Your attempt at a so called joke—"

Zeus let out a frustrated huff. "That is *quite* enough."

Hera made a face like she was imitating him inside her head. So childish.

Poseidon, contrary to popular belief, hadn't been crying about Zeus' painful humor. He hadn't actually been crying at all. The thing he was upset about was his former team. Poseidon was a Mycenae Alumni, graduating with honors and a contract into the NFL. He *hated* it when Zeus made him coach the Trojans. His brother leaned forwards, watching the game with a false intensity that Poseidon could smell a mile away. Zeus didn't care about football. He didn't care about anything but himself.

Poseidon sat up and leaned back, so Zeus couldn't see him. "Hera," he whispered.

Zeus' wife didn't move, but the eyebrow that Poseidon could see quirked.

"My team is losing," he continued, speaking as urgently as one can in the stands of a football game. "And I need to help them, but I'm not supposed to interfere. I *need* you to distract Zeus at halftime. Just for ten minutes. That's all I need, I swear."

Hera was smirking now, still watching the game with glossy eyes. At least she didn't pretend like Zeus did.

"And it'll help Mycenae win. I know you prefer them to Illium," he added, just for the extra credit.

Zeus' wife gave him the slightest of nods. Hopefully there would be enough time to explain the Trojans' defensive strategy.

"I'll be right back," Hera said cordially, with five minutes left before the second quarter ended.

Her husband didn't even reply. Just kept his beady little eyes on the football. Hera didn't pretend to understand this game, but she certainly *did* prefer the Stallions' school. They offered better scholarships and education. Hera picked her way through the metal bleachers, her high heels clanging against the benches as she awkwardly hopped over. Her skirt suit made it difficult to walk comfortably, let alone... get through a crowd of over–excited teenagers, and adults who acted like those teenagers.

The blonde woman near the top of the bleachers was sitting with her giant hulking sidepiece when Hera approached. Aphrodite's perfectly painted mouth parted momentarily in shock before she regained composure. What was her... mother–in–law doing here?

"Darling," Hera said, her voice like honey. "Be so kind and tell me how I can briefly seduce my husband to get back at him for something."

This surprised Aphrodite even more. She opened her mouth only to close it again, her brow furrowed.

"Well..." she started, getting an idea and digging through her purse. "*I* like this perfume!" she squeaked, whipping out a pink tinted bottle.

Hera resisted curling her lip as Aphrodite practically showered her in the stuff. It smelled strongly of vanilla.

"It's scientifically proven that men find this smell very... exciting," she whispered loudly.

Ares nodded empathetically. "It's true."

Aphrodite shoved a hand into Hera's hair. "Gotta mess it up. Can't be so professional. Let out your inner sex goddess," she whispered provocatively.

Hera wiped her palms off on her skirt, trying to look like she was at least some sort of grateful. This was something she *wanted* to do, after all.

"And talk low," Aphrodite said, leaning forward like she was sharing an important secret with Hera. "Get close, but not *too* close. Oh! Aaaand undo the top two buttons of your shirt." Hera looked down, about to protest, before she remembered she had *asked* for this advice.

"Right," she muttered, carrying out Aphrodite's advice.

"Ay–ay–ayayay," Aphrodite announced in a falsely seductive tone. "How have you not aged a day over thirty?"

Hera was remembering why she didn't particularly like this woman, but it was alright. Hopefully this would work. It had been years since Hera went anywhere *near* seducing Zeus.

"Thank you, my dear," Hera said, hopping off the side of the bleachers, not thinking about how she could have broken her ankle. "I'll see you around."

Aphrodite growled, then burst out laughing. "Have fun!"

Hera's heels sank into the grass as she walked, trying to strut like she had seen the blonde woman do. Into family dinner parties. Who *did* that? Hera didn't pretend to understand. She actually preferred to call it out and ridicule. When she made it back over to

Zeus and Poesidon, she stood in front of her husband, looking up at him.

It took him about twenty seconds to notice his wife, and when he did, he was... confused. Her hair was tumbling around her shoulders, flipped over the top of her head. And then she *winked*. Hera. *Winking.*

"What in Jove's *name* are you doing?" he called down to her as she smirked at him, beckoning with one finger.

The kids in front of Zeus were trying to understand what was happening. They kept dissolving into giggles, whispering to each other. It was very distracting, but so was Hera.

"Come with me," she said, her voice lower than normal.

Zeus laughed, trying to play it off as a joke. He couldn't. She didn't move. Getting to his feet, he apologized to the people he had to squeeze past.

When he got close enough to Hera to grab her arm, he paused, inhaling. "What's that smell?"

"You like it?" Hera purred, dragging Zeus by the wrist. "It's new."

They made it half way around the field before he thought to ask where they were going.

"The backseat of our car," she whispered, pressing her mouth to his ear.

He shivered. He wasn't sure where this new Hera had come from, but he wasn't complaining.

Poseidon had been waiting on the edge of his seat, watching closely as Hera led Zeus away. As soon as they were out of sight, he jumped down the bleachers, walking briskly towards the Stallions. They weren't even watching the game at this point. Most of the players off the field were sitting down, or milling around by their coach. Poseidon looked over at the clock. The buzzer went off, signaling the beginning of half time. He had about twenty minutes, if Hera could keep Zeus occupied for that long. As the Stallions trudged miserably off, Poseidon jogged the rest of the way, joining their half–formed circle.

He clapped a couple of times, turning the heads of several players. "Listen up!" he called. "Gather 'round guys, we don't have much time!"

The team shared confused looks, but they were too tired to argue. Poseidon crouched down, hiding behind the row of players that gathered at his back, just in case anyone saw him and thought to tell Zeus.

"Okay," he said, looking around the huddle. "Quick introduction; I'm Poesidon, Zeus' brother. Coached the Trojan team. Enough of that. I'm here to help you. They're playing zone defense, which means they're not going to go running after you if you run laterally. They'll just pass you off to another player."

"Question!" someone said on his right. "If they're doing that stunt thing, is there a way to counter it?"

"You guys know the underneath pass?" He looked around, seeing a few nods. "It stretches out the defense 'cause their receiver can try to run or look for a space in the latter. Try that. And the veer. Y'all are running the scenario where the QB keeps the ball, but try the version where the Dive Back fakes, and then you can decide what to do from there. Just try to confuse them a little."

When he moved onto defensive strategies, Poseidon stood up to demonstrate a proper ready position. This gave an opportunity for Iris, Zeus' assistant, to see him. Iris had better things she could have been doing, but Zeus had asked her to come to the game and watch for infractions of his No Interference Policy. When she saw Poseidon pop up from the middle of the Stallions' huddle, she frowned, sitting up taller to make sure it was actually him. It was.

Iris sighed. Poor man. Zeus would have his head. She gathered her pastel rainbow purse from her lap, picking her way off of the crowded bleachers. It was so humid today that she wanted to take off her sweater, but Zeus had ridiculous restrictions about her '*work attire*'.

For Poseidon's sake, Iris hoped that he would get out of that huddle before Zeus came back. She walked hastily across the empty football field, past a clump of referees who started at her as she went. Iris had seen Zeus and Hera walk to the parking lot. All she could do was... hope that they hadn't left. But she did find the other option slightly worrisome. Her heels clicked against the concrete as she walked across the parking lot, looking for Zeus' car. He had taken the white BMW X8 today, which ironically didn't stand out among the vehicles represented. All clearly wealthy, clean, and polished. Vehicles that screamed, '*I'm better than you.*' Iris had parked on the street at to Zeus' request. Didn't want to sully the beauty of the parking lot with her secondhand SmartCar.

When she *did* locate his BMW, Iris' nostrils flared. The car was... shaking. Zeus paid her *a lot* of money to do what she did, but this was almost too much. Almost. She took a short breath, hiking her bag higher on her shoulder as she moved towards the car. The windows were tinted, thank Gods. Iris tentatively knocked on the back passenger window. Unfortunately, she had done this before, though... the woman in the back with him had never actually been his wife. What a disturbing thought.

"What?" Zeus called from inside the car. Frustrated.

Iris swallowed. "Um... sir, there's been an infraction of your policy," she answered tentatively.

The window she was standing at rolled down. Iris fought the urge to close her eyes. Instead, she pursed her lips at the scene before her. The back seats were folded down, covered in a duvet or something. Hera was laying back, shamelessly topless, and Zeus' shirt was thrown over one of the front seats. His neatly styled hair was now a mess. Hera glared at Iris as Zeus leaned towards the window. There was lipstick smudged all over his face.

"You said there was infraction of my policy?" Zeus repeated.

Iris blinked, looking away from Hera. "Yes. Um. Poseidon. Was coaching the Stallions."

Her boss' gaze turned stormy as he looked back at his wife. "Is *this* why you were suddenly exciting?"

Hera shrugged, unimpressed.

"You seduced me so the school you wish to win would have an *advantage*?" he practically roared.

Iris flinched.

"You can't get your way all the time," Hera said calmly. She was used to this.

Zeus' breaths were far too even to be natural. Iris hated it when he got into one of these moods.

"I can't *believe* you, woman," Zeus growled, raking a hand through his hair. "Iris!" he yelled, looking over his shoulder.

"Yessir?" she blurted, clutching her bag tightly in her sweating hands.

"Go tell my hellhound of a brother that he needs to leave immediately," he ordered. "And that he will no longer be paid for his so-called *services*."

Iris waited for further instructions, but Zeus waved her away, exasperated. She didn't wait for anything else to happen. Iris ran as fast as she could in her heels, away from the car. (Maybe Zeus *didn't* pay her enough.) When she reached the Stallions' huddle, she could feel sweat dripping down her back. How did these boys play *football* in this weather? It was beyond her scope of reference. She waited until he slipped out of the circle, glancing furtively around. (Iris hated her job.)

"Poseidon?" she asked meekly.

He looked at her, and his face fell. "Shit," he muttered. "Lemme guess. He wants me to leave and he will no longer be paying me for my services."

"*So-called* services," Iris corrected, giving him an apologetic smile. "I'm sorry."

Poseidon ran a hand over his head. "You're just doing your job." He paused. "Is Hera okay?"

"She… knows how to deal with him," Iris managed. "I think."

"I have no idea how that eel tricked her into marrying him," Poseidon said. "Well. Hopefully she's okay. Well. My brother will cool down eventually. It'll be fine."

Iris nodded, somewhat aggressively. Zeus' brother started away.

"Hey," Poseidon turned around. "Do me a favor and tell me how the game turns out, alright?"

"Okay," Iris said eagerly. "I'll send you the score and everything!"

"Great," he said with a smile.

Iris hated that she was a people pleaser. It was exhausting. But at least Poseidon was nicer than Zeus. She glanced over at the score-board. She didn't know much about football, but she could tell it wasn't going very well for the Stallions, who were now crowding around their actual coach. As she made her way back to her seat, she passed a player in red crouching in front of a boy with curly hair.

Iris didn't overhear much, but what she did hear was this: "…could change the whole outcome of the game. We just need *you…*"

# XV

Hector's headache was horrible. He knew he shouldn't be playing. Andromache had gotten mad at him the night before, because she said she had been researching the side effects of prolonged concussion. He had told her it was fine. That *he* would be fine. Mr. Phoebus had pulled him out of the game about ten minutes before halftime, because apparently he was stumbling. The very same coach who had pulled him off was now giving him the maximum amount of Ibuprofen underneath the bleachers so he could play the rest of the game. *This* was not a good idea. But Hector did it anyways. He wanted to win this game, and he wanted to be a part of it.

On the other side of the field, Nestor was crouched in front of Patroclus, practically begging. Nestor had convinced himself that the only way to win this game was for Patroclus to come onto the field with Achilles' gear.

"Please. We just learned from Athena that if we lose this game, the Trojans are moving on to a better league. No divisionals, no states, no nationals. You *can't* let this happen to us," he implored, gripping their sports med trainer's knees. "You *know* it'll work. And Phoenix, Achilles' old mentor? He told me that you're the only one who could convince him. Achilles *loves* this game."

Patroclus blanched. Not Phoenix. He had told Achilles that stupid Meleager legend. With Cleopatra. That kid... shit.

"There's like." Nestor looked over his shoulder. "Ten minutes left in half time. And you *know* Agamemnon agreed to this plan!"

"Why is it always about *Agamemnon*," Patroclus hissed, shoving the grovelling player's hands off his legs. This was a losing battle.

Automedon had been listening the whole time, and the younger guy was excited. "You mean I could maybe play again?"

"This is a bad idea," Briseis cut in, grabbing Patroclus' arm. "You don't realize how dangerous it is."

Patroclus laughed anxiously. "I think I know how dangerous it is better than anyone."

"Dude," Nestor said sternly. "The team *needs* you."

Patroclus let out a frustrated breath. He hated being cornered like this. Then, he got to his feet. "Oh *fine*," he muttered. "C'mon Automedon. Let's see if we can get you guys back on the field."

Nestor whooped, jumping up from the ground. "I *knew* you'd see it my way!"

Briseis watched them jog off across the field, gnawing on her thumbnail. Iphis hopped down from where she had been sitting beside Automedon. Not by choice. That had just been the only place with a spot.

"Hey," she said, looking at Briseis with concern. "It's gonna be fine. Pat plays well. He just thinks it's a bit too much."

"He's so stressed out already," Briseis replied as the two boys disappeared from view.

Iphis didn't reply to that,

⁂

"Do you really think this will work?" Automedon asked anxiously as they rode up the elevator to Achilles' and Patroclus' dorm floor.

Patroclus drummed against the metal wall with his knuckle. "No clue."

When the doors opened, most... if not all of Achilles' offense players were sitting around the lounge. Eudorus, the most loyal to Achilles' cause, looked up.

"Hey!" he said, "What're you doing here?"

"Where's Achilles?" Patroclus asked instead of replying. His palms were sweating.

Menesthius pointed down the hall to where their room was. "Moping around in there like he does during games. He wishes Agamemnon would apologize."

"Great, thanks," Patroclus said quickly, taking off down the hall. He didn't have much time.

Automedon sat down on the faux leather couch next to Eudorus. "We might get to play again," he said excitedly. "Patroclus' gonna try and convince Achilles."

Phoenix, who had reluctantly agreed to Achilles' need for justice, scoffed. Somehow, he was still at good odds with the team.

"Fucking finally," he muttered, not looking up from his phone. "But still. Too late."

"You don't know that," Automedon blurted.

Patroclus heard the whole exchange. He was standing outside their dorm room, his head resting against the door. He was wasting time and he knew it. This was a horrible idea that he had let himself get pressured into. Achilles wouldn't even agree. What he *wasn't* expecting was when Achilles opened the door, sending Patroclus stumbling into him.

"What're *you* doing here?" Achilles asked, surprised by the general nature of the situation.

Patroclus pulled himself out of Achilles' startled grip, took a deep breath, and closed the door behind him. He walked over to the neatly made bed and sat down.

Achilles could feel the anxiety flooding off of Patroclus. He crouched down in front of him. "What's wrong?" he asked, taking the other boy's hands.

When Patroclus met his eyes, his gaze was full of turmoil. "If we lose this game, there's no divisionals. The season ends here."

Achilles swallowed, his eyebrows furrowing. "That... doesn't matter, love."

"Everyone will hate you," Patroclus whispered, looking down.

There was a long moment of silence.

Achilles tightened his grip. "If this is about what Phoenix said—"

"I'm not trying to convince you," Patroclus cut him off gently. "I just... I think if the offense players go back... less people will get hurt."

"But the league will keep going," Achilles pointed out.

"Achilles," Patroclus said with a pathetic smile. "They'll stop paying off the refs."

Achilles let go of Patroclus' hands and stood up. He paced along the carpet, his face troubled.

"But that'll be breaking my promise," he argued, though he was unsure.

*This is so hopeless,* Patroclus thought, hiding his face in his hands.

"What if you let me play in your gear?" he mumbled, praying that Achilles wouldn't hear him.

There was a roaring cheer from the football field. It was muffled by the distance and the damp heat, but it sent Patrocus' pulse skittering. The game had started again. He didn't have much time.

Achilles' pacing stopped. "What?"

Patroclus looked up from behind his parted fingers. Reluctantly, he repeated himself. "What if. You let me play. In your gear?"

The pause was so still, and so quiet, that it felt like someone had turned up the air pressure.

"I'm an alright player," Patroclus blurted, hating that silence. "And then it'll be like... breaking the rules. 'Cause if your phantom can help them win the game, that'll show Agamemnon how important you actually are to the team—"

"Patroclus—" Achilles tried to interrupt, but he kept pushing.

He got to his feet. "I know it seems stupid, but I think it could actually work and then they would stop ignoring the fouls and no one else would get hurt..." he trailed off when he saw Achilles expression. Soft, concerned... thoughtful.

Achilles closed the gap between them, wrapping his arms around Patroclus, who swallowed thickly. He closed his eyes, hiding his face in the blonde boy's neck.

"I'm just scared," Achilles whispered into his hair. "Because what if, in your grand quest for no one getting hurt, *you* get hurt?"

Patroclus took a shaky breath, inhaling the fresh scent of the Dove antiperspirant Achilles used.

"I *know* you're capable," Achilles continued, "But I don't... think I could live with myself if you got hurt in my place."

Pulling slightly away, Patroclus smiled, trying to look reassuring. "Hey. I won't get hurt. I promise. I'm fast and the other guys will have my back."

They rested their foreheads together for a long moment, breathing in the bittersweet silence.

Achilles broke it. "Fine."

Another cheer from outside. Patroclus' stomach dropped as Achilles let him go.

"I'm gonna tell the guys to get ready," he said, making for the door. "My shit's on your desk. I'll be back in a moment."

Patroclus nodded. When Achilles left, he hauled the giant bag off the desk. It fell to the floor with a dull thud. He could hear Achilles urging the other guys to get ready, which was followed by a ruckus of their own, loud enough to rival the cheering from outside. It had been a long time since Patroclus had put on football gear. The whole bag smelled like laundry detergent. His football uniform was another thing Achilles took immaculate care of. Patroclus smiled faintly as he pulled his shirt over his head, replacing it with one of Achilles' baselayers.

When the blonde boy came back to their room, he stood, leaning against the doorframe, watching Patroclus for a moment as he focused on adjusting the shoulder pads.

"I don't like this," Achilles whispered, walking up to him.

Patroclus didn't look up. "But it's the right thing to do."

Achilles studied him for another long moment before going over to his closet. He rummaged around, trying to find his helmet under piles of clean, yet rumpled clothes. It was at the bottom of the mess. That had been on purpose. Achilles hated seeing the red glaring out at him. Yes, he loved football. But he also hated his team. And what Agamemnon did... well, it was best not to think about it too much. He pulled the helmet out, inspecting it.

His mother had gotten some important artist to paint it for him. Instead of the basic red helmet with their logo on the side, it was painted in lifelike detail. There were three white horses running and rearing along the right side. Achilles could almost hear the pounding of their hooves against the dust painted beneath them. He felt one side of his mouth pull upwards. He had forgotten how *cool* the thing was. It was also how they would know that 'Achilles' was back. The hemet was his signature. So you could pick him out. (Yes, he knew it was kind of self–centered.) (No, he didn't care.)

Turning around, he saw Patroclus pull the red jersey over his pads. The last thing in place. Other than the helmet. Patroclus was grinning a little when he looked up at Achilles.

"So," he joked. "Do I look like you?" He spun in a slow circle, nodding as he went, with this goofy look on his face.

Achilles watched him, trying not to laugh. "Ninety nine percent," he answered, walking over to where Patroclus was standing.

He offered the curly haired boy the helmet. Patroclus took it, tracing a finger along the racing horses.

"This is insane," he whispered. "Bri would *love* those."

Achilles nodded, swallowing. "You should probably go."

Patroclus looked up. "I will."

He pulled Achilles forwards by his loose school tie, and kissed him. Because he could. Achilles inhaled sharply against his mouth, then relaxed, kissing him gently, one hand softly twining through his hair. When they broke apart, Patroclus laughed through his nose. Achilles didn't let go of him.

"I love you," Patroclus offered quietly. "And you look like a cyclops from this angle," he said in the same tone, making Achilles snort.

"Yeah," Achilles replied as he let go. "Well. Having one eye in the middle of your head is... sexy. *I* could pull it off."

Patroclus shoved him playfully as they walked out of the room. "That's disturbing, Achilles."

Achilles was a little lost as they entered the lounge room. He felt untethered. Sort of like he was a balloon, and someone had cut the string. But everything was going to be okay. It was fine. Their entrance elicited a cheer from the seven players standing by the elevator door. They were all in their red Stallions jerseys, helmets in hand.

"Okay okay okay," Achilles said, motioning for them to calm down. For a moment, he imagined going out with them. He shouldn't be sending someone in his place. This was ridiculous.

Then they started chanting Patroclus' name, making him blush. The feeling intensified, making Achilles feel like a balloon in a full–on gale. But he laughed it off. He pretended it was gone.

"Okay that's enough," Patroclus said, glancing over at Achilles, who took his helmet from Patroclus' hand.

Achilles gestured for Patroclus to face him.

Slowly, dramatically, excitingly, he lowered the helmet onto his boyfriend's head. "I now dub thee Achilles Pelides!" he announced, like he was having the time of his life. Everyone laughed. "But guys," he said seriously, turning to look at the players standing in front of him, "if he gets hurt, I will literally murder you myself."

This was met by earnest nods. Automedon said, "You got it, Captain."

Achilles smiled at this. Patroclus put a hand on his shoulder as someone pressed the elevator button. "Okay," he whispered. "See you later, cyclops."

"Takes one to know one," Achilles muttered back with a forced smirk.

"Well, I'm glad I found the only other cyclops in the world," Patroclus replied stoically.

Achilles shook his head. *I love you more than my own life,* he thought forcefully, hoping Patroclus had magically gotten mind–reading powers.

Adrenaline pumped through both of their veins. Patroclus hadn't seriously played a game of football since the beginning of tenth grade. He was rapidly trying to remember plays and maneuvers, while thinking about how Achilles played. Fearless. Strong. And fucking *fast.* Achilles was handing his control over to Patroclus, which shouldn't have made him this anxious. It was just the fact that he didn't... have control anymore. He sighed as Patroclus crammed into the elevator with the other players. *It'll be okay,* they both thought, taking deep breaths as the elevator door closed.

Achilles stood there for what felt like a hundred heartbeats. This was stupid. He laughed out loud, covering his eyes with a hand. *Stupid.*

# XVI

Briseis was starting to feel better about Patroclus. If he was gone much longer, there wouldn't be time for him to play. There were seven minutes left in the third quarter. No one else had scored, but the Stallions were pushing closer to the Trojans endzone. The score was still 28 to 6 in the Trojans' favor, but their momentum had slowed. There was... some hope. The second down ended, leaving their team at the 30 yard line on the Trojans' side of the field.

And that was the exact moment when eight Stallion players ran through the open gate at the far side of the field. Iphis felt Briseis tense and put a hand on her knee.

"It's fine," she whispered as confused mutters broke out among the crowd.

Somewhere, over those murmurs, the name, "Achilles!" was yelled. Apparently, it was the rallying cry.

The benched Stallions players roared in approval.

They started chanting the name, growing louder as fans joined in. "A–CHILL–ES, A–CHILL–ES, A–CHILL–ES!"

The cheer was adopted by the Mycenae cheerleaders, who started skipping along the bleachers, waving their pompoms around. The sound vibrations traveled through the air, infecting everyone with excitement. It resounded through the bleachers, through the crowds, through Briseis' very bones. She knew it was a lie. The player being swarmed by the Stallions wasn't Achilles.

Athena immediately subbed out the majority of her exhausted starting offense line. She hadn't played the younger kids, because the roughness would leave her short a team next year. Before Achilles ran out onto the field, she placed a hand on his shoulder. The boy turned sharply, looking up at her through his helmet. It was too bright to see, but he was wearing his signature red bandanna tied across his forehead. Athena smiled.

"I'm very glad you've become bigger than whatever struggles were inhibiting you from playing," she said.

Achilles nodded, clearing his throat. "Thanks coach," he said, sounding... not quite like himself.

Athena wondered if the boy was feeling emotional about playing again. She gave him a hard pat on the shoulder. "Get out there and give them hell."

He took off running, his number 37 jersey causing another ground–shaking cheer. It was good to have him back. Athena had let him go, only because lessons need to be learned. Achilles needed to find his individuality before realizing that he was truly a part of this team.

Sure enough, within twenty seconds of Achilles being on the field, a touchdown was scored. He blew past a giant player, somehow flipping him onto his back. This was the kind of thing Athena had missed in her offensive line. The willingness to be aggressive without breaking too many of the rules. The score went up. And up. And up. When the third quarter finished, Athena believed that they had been given the miracle that was needed. Achilles. *Back.*

When they came off the field, the offense line was met by calamitous cheers. The energy, of course, made the defense line play far better, locking the Trojans out for good. In final quarter of the game, the score was rapidly climbing, until... Achilles scored once again, leaving the score at 26 to 28. They got the extra two points. Tie.

Athena held her breath for as long as she could. There were still twelve minutes left in the quarter, so anything could happen. She couldn't help but hope... six seconds into the next play, the Stallions intercepted the ball and took off running. Athena had to let out her breath to laugh. *This* was the team she had thought they were. When Menelaus scored the touchdown, the crowd went wild, just like they had when Hector scored in the same way.

Paris glanced over at his brother, trying to gauge his reaction to this. He was too far away, and when the ball was kicked, then passed to him, Paris was blown backwards by the center player. His head slammed against the ground, knocking the breath out of his lungs. Hector would *hate* this.

And Paris was right. Hector's blood was boiling. This *Achilles* guy had no right to run onto the field after a month of being absent on his *own accord,* and turn the whole game around. It was just... very frustrating. Scarpedon was sitting on the bench, wincing as a harassed looking sports med doctor set his shoulder back in place. Achilles had dislocated it.

Apollo stood behind Hector, his arms crossed. He wasn't... sold, on the whole Achilles thing. Yes, it was silly. But his team was better than this. Eight new players shouldn't change their luck. (It clearly had.) (Apollo hated failing.) Hector put his head in his hands, shielding them from the sun as Euphorbus wandered over.

"Mr. Phoebus," the huge player said, distracting Apollo from the game. "Should we... do something about this Achilles guy?"

Apollo turned to look at his linebacker, an eyebrow raised. "And make a martyr out of him?"

"No," Hector cut in, rotating so his back faced the game. "It would make the team worried. About their best player, who was *no longer on the field.*"

"Hmm," Apollo mused, walking around the bench and peering over at the Stallions team. He could pick out the player that was Achilles. Or claimed to be. The boy hadn't taken off his helmet, which was odd in this heat. He wandered back over to his two players, who were looking expectantly at him. "Here's a secret," Apollo whispered. Both boys leaned in closer. "That, is not Achilles Pelides."

Euphorbus snorted. "He's just as good. So... does it even matter?"

Hector ran a hand over his head. "Yeah. It does. Whoever that is... well they're just as good as Achilles, but they're pretending to be someone they're not. But it *could* be Achilles. I dunno. "

"In the long run, this all means nothing," Apollo said comically. "But I thought that was interesting. And if you look at the bleachers," he continued, leaning over one of his own player's heads, "You can't see their sports med guy. The one with the brown curly hair. *He* is the one in Achilles' uniform."

"No way," Euphorus practically spat, leaning over Hector, who looked out as well. "*That* guy? The one who was always running around like his ass was on fire?"

Apollo nodded, tormented. "And you're letting him beat you."

Hector barely restrained a glare at his coach. "That's... not it. I think it's definitely Achilles."

Apollo shrugged. "Prove me wrong."

"He's the only reason we're losing," Euphorbus offered, crossing his arms. "If we can hurt him bad enough that he has to take off his helmet, then we're golden. They'll know it's not their star player, and then they can't martyr Achilles."

"Don't talk so loud," Apollo warned. "You have to make it seem like an accident."

The Trojans' field goal was scored, which was good, because every point counted. Especially nearing the end of the game. Hector and Euphorbus shared a meaningful look before shoving their helmets on their heads. The kickoff was a good one, high, far, making the players run for it. Hector had gotten someone else to play his position, and he subbed in next to Euphorbus.

When the quarterback got the ball and passed it to so-called-Achilles, they both ran forwards.

Patroclus caught the ball from Odysseus, planning to offload to Automedon when he got close to the defense. He was covered in sweat, but it felt so *good* to run like this. It was exhilarating. He could feel the wind through his helmet, streaming onto his face... he passed the ball off, only to run into a brick wall. And then the air was on his whole face. His head. No. That shouldn't happen—he was thrown up, legs suddenly gone from beneath him. Someone slammed into him. From behind. In the air. His arms were out beside him. Where was he? What the—

Before he could form a cohesive thought of panic, he crashed, headfirst into the grass. Something snapped. And the world exploded.

Helen was watching the ball when it happened. So when Achilles *passed* the ball backwards, the referee blasted on his whistle as the helmet went flying. One of the Trojan players collided with Achilles, and it almost looked like he... grabbed the rim of his helmet and twisted. Helen stood up, heart pounding as Hector... Hector came running up from behind. The ref blew the whistle again. He needed to stop—

But he didn't. And that player... wasn't Achilles. Patroclus. In Achilles' uniform. Helen saw it in slow motion. Hector pretty much threw him, snapping Patroclus' head back from the change in momentum. And then somehow they were both flying away from each other. The impact.

Patroclus landed on his head. There was a collective gasp of horror. Helen felt sick. Priam was standing now. People were running onto the field. Panicking.

Hector got to his feet as parents rushed past him, his heart thundering in his chest. He wasn't sure what happened, but he was sure it wasn't what he had been hoping for. Achilles' helmet lay a few feet away from him. *Shit,* Hector thought. *That thing really flew.* He picked it up, examining it. There were detailed horses painted on it in glittering paint. They were gorgeous.

"Hector!" Paris yelled, running over to him through the gathering crowd.

He looked up at him, unimpressed. "What?"

"*Fuck,*" Paris breathed, his eyes wide. "Didn't you hear the Godsdamn whistle?!"

"What whistle?" Hector asked, his heart still pounding from the sudden cut in exertion. It started sinking now too. "Did the ref blow the whistle?"

Briseis ran past Hector as he said this, trying to see over the crowd. She was crying. Iphis caught up to her.

"Bri," she whispered, "It's gonna be okay." It sounded like she didn't quite believe it herself.

"If you don't have first aid training," someone yelled, "Please leave the area. We need to give the paramedics easy access when they get here."

Briseis stopped breathing. This wasn't supposed to happen. This had never happened in any game *Briseis* had seen. This kind of thing wasn't supposed to *happen.* Iphis took her hand, swallowing thickly.

Athena stood near the center of the gathering, having been one of the first people to sprint over. She had been praying, '*not Achilles not Achilles not Achilles,*' and she had been right. This player was not Achilles. But he was almost as good as Achilles. Automedon, who had been the closest person to Patroclus when he fell was now bracing his neck.

The sports med doctor was there, asking Patroclus questions. He wasn't responding well. He kept drifting off, which caused a minor panic from all the people with first air training. This was not good. The boy started shivering. He said weakly that he couldn't feel his hands.

Machaon ran over with a space blanket, his face pale as the puffy clouds overhead. "Did someone call 911?" he asked, his voice quiet.

Athena nodded. "They said they're on their way."

Before Briseis could make it any closer to the middle, someone asked her if she had any first aid training. When she said no, they kindly asked her to go. Iphis had to drag her away, back to the Stallions, who sat silently in a circle. Agamemnon, Diomedes, and Odysseus were standing by the bleachers, which were emptying quickly. The game wouldn't be continued.

"Is he okay?" Antilochus asked when Briseis and Iphis had reached them.

Briseis sat down heavily on the bench. "No," she whispered. "And it wasn't Achilles."

This caused a wave of subdued confusion to ripple through the team, but no one found the energy to care.

"This was my idea," Nestor said quietly, staring down at his hands. "I told Patroclus he should play in Achilles' gear."

A couple of the offense players were anxiously pulling grass out of the ground.

"Achilles is gonna kill us," someone muttered.

Briseis hid her face in her hands. Why had Patroclus *listened* to these idiots? She should have stopped him. The wait for the ambulance was awful. The minutes ticked by slower than grains of sand dripping through an hourglass, one at a time. It started to get a little colder. No one on either team left. Hector and Aeneas sat on the bleachers, not talking. This was Hector's fault. It had even been on purpose. All to please his coach, in the spirit of 'it's my last year and all.' He should have listened to Andromache. Then none of this would have happened. And apparently it *hadn't* been Achilles. It had been their sports med guy. Achilles' friend.

When the sirens finally started wailing in the distance, Priam and Helen, who had been sitting a few rows behind Hector got up to leave.

"Wait," Hector said as his father passed.

Priam looked up. "You can have the car. Hecuba was going to see if she could catch the end of the game, but now she's just coming to pick us up."

"Thank you," Hector said, watching them go.

"You're gonna go to the hospital?" Aeneas asked.

Hector nodded, staring at the thinning crowd of people on the field. Parents had started leaving, making gaps in the circle. He could see the sports med trainer on his back, someone else supporting his neck. The doctor crouched next to him.

"I'll come with you," Aeneas said, taking a deep breath. "Paris probably will too, unless he wants to walk home."

The ambulance finally pulled through the giant gate that Athena had opened, and drove towards the center of the field. Athena had tried calling Patroclus' emergency contact ten minutes earlier. A woman had answered the phone. When Athena had told her the situation, the woman had screamed. Then hung up. His father hadn't answered the phone. His final emergency contact was Achilles' father. Athena left a message there. The paramedics took over from the harried sports med doctor, guiding Automedon through the process of removing his hands. They secured Patroclus' head and neck before transporting him to a gurney that they lifted into the back of the ambulance.

Athena elected herself to ride with him, seeing as none of his contacts seemed to really... care. What was she supposed to do in this situation? The inside of the ambulance was freezing cold, the walls covered with storage and devices. She sat down and buckled herself in as they peeled away from the field. From what she picked up, the injury was serious. One woman asked what happened, while the other outfitted Patroclus with a breathing apparatus. He wasn't really replying. Or breathing.

As soon as the ambulance left the school, Briseis and ninety percent of the football team ran after it. Antilochus offered to give the two girls a ride. Hector, Aeneas, Paris, Euphorbus, and Glaucus all piled into Priam's car. They were followed by the Stallions, and a few concerned parents of those players. The sun was starting to set, staining the sky with a myriad of pinkish hues. It was horrible. Briseis wanted Antilochus to step on the gas. Automedon, Ajax 1, and Ajax 2 had all squeezed into the back of Antilochus' car. The speed limits felt so slow when Briseis' heart was pounding so fast.

She kept swallowing, fighting the urge to cry. *Not yet*, she thought. One day, she and Patroclus might laugh about this. It could still be okay, couldn't it?

# XVII

Patroclus wasn't quite sure what was happening. People were talking to him. Talking *at* him. It was hard to hear over the roaring in his ears. There was pressure on his neck. Pain was traveling through his body like lightning. And he couldn't feel his hands. Or his feet. He did know he was going to the hospital. The lady standing over him had told him that several times. She was telling him to keep his eyes open now. She had told him *that* before too. He was just so tired. And everything felt like it was on fire. He couldn't remember why he was here. What had *happened*?

The memories were more like... a feeling. An inkling of running. Playing football. A hint of talking with Achilles. A whisper of laying in the middle of the field, surrounded by terrified players. But none of it was certain. He swallowed, his eyes too big for their sockets. It distracted him for a moment. From everything. Everything was just so *tiring.*

Hector was starting to panic now as he followed the ambulance in his car as closely as possible. *What if he died?* Hector was thinking as he almost ran a red light. Stomping on the breaks, he threw everyone forward. Achilles' helmet slammed against something in the trunk. (Hector hadn't known what to do with it.) He felt sick.

"Hector?" Aeneas asked when the light turned green and Hector stomped on the gas.

The streets were practically empty. Everyone in a car at this time would be a tourist on the main strip or someone returning late from work. Hector clenched his jaw and ignored the speed limits.

"Hector," Aeneas repeated, more sternly this time. "It'll be okay."

Somehow, Hector seriously doubted that. His stomach rolled sluggishly. *What if he had killed someone?* And deep down, Hector knew it hadn't been an accident. He and Euphorbus had *planned* that hit. Euphorbus sat silently in the backseat. He didn't look like he was breathing.

When the ambulance turned off the main street, into the emergency loading dock, Hector pulled over and got out of the car.

Paris stuck his head out a back window. "What're you doing?"

Hector was rooting through his trunk, already pulling off his football gear. "I can't... fuck. I can't find him and make sure he's okay if I'm running around in tight white pants and shoulder-pads."

Paris retreated back into the car. Aeneas got out moments later.

"You can't follow him in there," he said softly, leaning against the trunk's rim, facing away from Hector. "They won't let you. The doors probably have passcodes."

Hector ignored him, pulling a pair of jeans over his football pants.

"Hector," Aeneas stated, almost urgently.

He looked up, meeting his cousin's eyes. "I'm going in. Go into the lobby with the guys."

Without waiting for a reply Hector jogged away from the car and his teammates, guilt driving him forward.

Inside, Patroclus was in a room. They had kept him on the wheely table thing. And they were hooking him up to beeping machines. There was so much *beeping*. It was drilling into his head. Athena was here, standing quietly in the corner of the room as doctors whispered grim things. Patroclus hated hospitals. Athena tapped on one of the nurses shoulders. She said something too quiet for him to hear. And then she slipped out of the room. The white room. Bright.

"Where... is she going?" he asked, his voice cracking painfully.

A doctor looked down at him then glanced to the nurse, who came and knelt beside Patroclus' bed.

"She's just going to make sure the team knows where to wait," the nurse said softly. "They all came to see if you were okay." The nurse was... trying to be comforting.

He knew the answer to the team's supposed question. He wasn't okay. And probably... wouldn't be again. Nodding with the neck brace on didn't work, so he thanked her. Her pitying smile made his struggling insides squirm.

"...we're going to try and get him into surgery right away..." Patroclus heard a doctor mutter as he and the nurse left the room.

He was alone. With the beeping machines. *Erratically* beeping machines. He tried to breathe, panic beginning to crawl up his throat. It felt like tiny hands, digging sharpened nails into his trachea. And swallowing...

Someone walked past his room. It looked like... Hector. Yeah. He was on the Trojans' team...

"Hector," Patroclus called, his voice barely a whisper. That was cruel. "Hector," he tried, again failing to make any kind of noise. Couldn't even make a dent in the air. It was swallowing him whole.

Hector heard his name, but he was sure he had imagined it. Afterall, it had barely been a whisper—but there it was again. He doubled back, his heart shuddering with too many emotions to even begin to unravel.

"Hector?" There it was again. Coming from the room on the right side of the light blue hallway.

He tried to breathe. It didn't work. So he walked. Left foot. Right foot. Left foot. Right foot... all the way to the door. And inside that door... was the sports med guy. Patroclus.

Patroclus smiled. He tried to. (He really tried.) But it hurt too much. So he swallowed. Hector was standing in the doorframe, pale as the snow. Patroclus had never seen snow in person before. Regret sparked weakly inside his chest.

"Hector," he said again, relishing the pain instead of ignoring it. Someone would hear him. And that would be enough. "I... need you to listen."

The boy glanced down the hallway before darting into the room. He knelt on the floor beside the bed. Patroclus couldn't see him there. (That was okay.)

"You need to tell Achilles that... this was an accident," he whispered, staring up at the white ceiling. "And... then you need to avoid him. He's so volatile—" Here, Patroclus had to stop and laugh. It felt like hot wire in his throat, and it sounded like choking. Hector inhaled sharply, shakily. Patroclus could hear him breathing. And he knew there were more things he had to say. "Achilles... might try to... hurt you. And you *have* to tell him that I was okay."

Hector got to his feet abruptly, heart racing. "No." He shook his head frantically. "No you tell him that yourself."

"Shh," Patroclus whispered, staring up at Hector, begging him to understand. "*Please.*"

Hector's hands were trembling as he reached out to Patroclus, then pulled his arms back. He wasn't sure what he was going to do. He had to help...

"Hector," Patroclus said, his voice even quieter than before. "Achilles will come for you."

The boy in the bed closed his eyes and took a deep, shuddering breath. Hector waited fearfully, straining to hear another. Instead, he heard the sound of three machines. Screaming at him. *No.* He tried to breathe. It didn't work. A doctor... came running into the room. He was followed by another. And another, carrying a defibrillator.

"Please step out of the room," a nurse ordered calmly.

Hector felt as though he were rooted to the spot. His brain sent too much information for him to understand.

"Step out of the room," came again.

His feet fumbled to find the ground, even though it was right below him. (As always.) He had killed someone. And that was what knocked the whole thing down. The tower of Hector. He tripped into the hallway, the door to the little room closing behind him. *No.* This wasn't how it was supposed to happen. Hector slid down the wall, pressing his shaking hands into his eyes. *He can't be dead.*

And: *They'll bring him back.*

And: *This can't be my fault.*

Inside the room, ten minutes later, a nurse peels a defibrillator pad from a boy's chest. She removes the neck brace. They'll need it for another patient. And she removes the needles from his arms. He was dead before they tried to bring him back, and he is dead now. The nurse closes the boy's eyes. A doctor had opened them to check for signs of life. And had forgotten to let him rest.

She swallows. He's so young. So full of potential. So full of beginnings. There aren't supposed to be endings for those like him. But people like him go everyday. The nurse pities the parents and friends of this boy. She leaves the lights on, stepping out of the room. Now she will go tell those waiting restlessly for good news. It will not be good news. And it will hurt.

*But life will go on*, she thinks. *It always does.*

"Are you a friend of his?" someone asked sympathetically.

Hector looked up to see the nurse who ordered him out. He almost threw up. He shook his head, then nodded. The nurse gave him a sad smile. He knew what she was going to say before the words left her lips.

"He didn't make it," she said softly. "I'm going to go find the people waiting in the lobby."

Hector nodded, clenching his weak fists in the hem of his white shirt. '*Achilles will come for you,*' Patroclus had said. That thought was terrifying. And on top of that... Hector was a murderer. But he was also the last one to speak with this guy. Patroclus' last words had been to the person who killed him. Hector couldn't see himself as a man in that moment. He was a boy. A scared, confused, little boy, with nothing to cling to except a dead spark of hope. And he was lost. Why hadn't he listened to Andromache? What would *happen* to Andromache now? She was going to leave him. He was going to lose her and get charged with murder and end up stuck in prison. It crushed him, the weight of all these unknowns.

A nurse walked past him, offering him another sad smile. *Fuck.* None of them would be smiling if they knew what he had done. He got unsteadily to his feet. Paris, Aeneas, and Glaucus came bursting through the doors at the end of the hall. Hector couldn't bear to see them, but the people who came through after were worse.

Odysseus, Antilochus, Ajax 1, and Agamemnon, all storming down the hall. Hector darted into Patroclus' room, his breath coming in short bursts. His teammates came in seconds before the Stallions players. The body stopped all of them short. No longer a living human. Just a... broken shell, with a white sheet pulled up to its neck. The neck that Hector had broken.

"You *killed* him?" Odysseus demanded under his breath, stepping into the room.

Aeneas shook his head rapidly. Hector felt like the world was shrinking, closing him in.

"It was an *accident*," Aeneas bit back. "Those happen all the time."

"You don't know how much he meant to us," Agamemnon muttered, shaking his head, a bitter scowl painted on his face. "He kept our team together. Literally. And he came in when we needed help the most. And *you*," Agamemon looked up at Hector, hatred burning in his eyes. "You made him pay with his life."

"This isn't a *game*," Automedon called from the hallway, his voice hoarse. "Someone is dead because of this... stupid war."

"And that was *your* idea!" Menelaus yelled from the back of the crowd that was forming around the door. "Agamemnon, this is *your* fault!"

"No," Aeneas said, trying to stay calm. "No it's *no*body's fault. We shouldn't be arguing—"

Agamemnon picked up a chair and threw it against the wall. "I want *justice* for what has been done!" he roared.

"This isn't a time for justice!" Hector replied, matching the other captain's intensity. "Someone *died*! Do you get that? He's *dead!* No one is going to hear his voice again. He's not going to class. He's not taping anymore injuries. He's not carrying your fucking team, because he's *dead!*"

The silence after that rung like a fire alarm.

"And who's fault is *that*?!" Odysseus broke the silence with a sledgehammer that nearly knocked Hector to his knees.

"Everyone!" someone was yelling from the hallway, pleading for quiet. "Please—"

"We can't blame each other for what happened!" Euphorbus yelled, pushing through the Stallions, joining the fight. "We have to work this—"

"Work this *out?*" Agamemnon scoffed, gesturing aggressively to the body. "We fucking *can't*, because a key member in *working this out* is gone because of something you planned with your coach!"

The sounds of the fight resounded through the emergency ward. Briseis and Iphis sat in the waiting room. The whole team had disappeared into the back after claiming they were going to the bathroom, and now... the yelling was definitely them. It was making Briseis' chin wobble. She couldn't keep the tears from falling anymore, so she stared up at the ceiling, letting them leak from the corners of her eyes. When her teeth started chattering, Iphis stood up.

"I'm going back there," she declared, her voice shaking.

Briseis didn't reply, but also didn't move to stop her. Iphis marched to the doors, pressed the red button, and disappeared inside. Sure enough, she saw the entirety of the football team, gathered around a single room. So many people were yelling. It wasn't necessary. Patroclus would hate this. He *would have* hated this. There's no way the hospital would allow this if he were still alive. Iphis hated herself as she walked down the hallway. She wasn't even sure why.

She stopped about ten meters away from the chaos. Nurses were trying to calm everyone down, practically begging for them to stop. *People were trying to sleep, to relax, and they were making the hospital an unsafe environment.* Iphis stood there, staring. *This is what he gets.* The one time her friend could truly rest, and he's been surrounded by screaming football players.

Antilochus slipped out of the mess. He passed Iphis, standing in the hallway like she was stuck there. The hospital was giving him a headache. As were the tears he was trying to hold back. *Fucking hell.* None of this made any kind of sense. He hated how everyone was yelling at each other. It was disgusting. Someone had died. Not just someone. *Patroclus* had died. He was a person they all knew. He was quiet and sweet and kind and... gone. Antilochus paused, pressing a fist to the wall. His nose was prickling again. He wouldn't cry. Not yet. He took a deep breath and stepped out into the waiting room.

He was going to go tell Achilles. He had the right to know. *It must be awful*, Antilochus thought as he forced himself forwards.

*He's just sitting in his dorm... and he doesn't know. So it isn't awful. Yet.*

"Antilochus?" someone asked.

He looked over, just as he was about to go through the automatic door. Briseis was standing there, her hands covered by her school sweater sleeves. She tried to smile at him, but her tears fought against it. She shrugged helplessly, trying to breathe quietly.

"Come outside," he said, swallowing hard.

She followed him into the humid dusk, wrapping her arms around herself. The air prickled against her legs. Antilochus sat on the curb, looking out at the cul-de-sac meant for dropping off visitors and patients. Briseis stood behind him for a long moment, not quite ready to ask the question. Of course, she already knew the answer. It was just... nice to live in a world where she didn't know that answer for sure.

"Wanna sit?" Antilochus asked, looking back at her. She nodded, wiping her nose with the cuff of her sweater.

Antilochus was stalling, and she knew it. But if it was to comfort Briseis... so be it. He didn't really know her, but she was around. And she had been through some shit with Agamemnon. Antilochus knew she and Patroclus were tight. Briseis walked over and sat down next to him, huddling in on herself, despite the warmth of the night.

"So?" she asked, her voice smaller than the single star trying to shine through the city lights. "He's gone?"

"Yeah," Antilochus replied, feeling the weight of the sky on his shoulders. "He's gone."

Briseis laughed softly. It didn't feel worse, somehow, hearing that answer out loud. It just made it real. For a moment, Briseis looked up at the indigo night. She smiled, before the wave of pain crashed over her. There was a blissful second as she let go of her oblivion.

Patroclus had been... her rock. Rocks weren't supposed to disappear, just like the ground was supposed to stay under you. Her quiet laughter turned to even quieter sobs, the two mingling together in a song of broken hearts. Antilochus looked over at her, and let himself break. Just for a moment. It was overwhelming. And it was a reminder. A brutal one. They were mortal. One second could mean the difference between carrying on or... an ending.

"I'm sorry, Bri," Antilochus whispered, wiping his eyes. "I wish..." He trailed off, not quite sure what he was going to say.

"I wish a lot of things," she said, picking up his sentence where he left it. "And..." Briseis' voice broke. She inhaled, determined to finish. "I wish—he hadn't done what Achilles wanted."

Antilochus took a deep breath. He held it in for awhile, feeling his lungs. Grateful that he was alive. He got another chance. Another minute, at least. Antilochus let out the air he had held captive. And now it was time to tell Achilles. He glanced at Briseis, who had her hands tangled in the coily hair on the sides of her head.

Tentatively, he placed a palm on her shoulder. "Text me if you need anything," he whispered. "I'm gonna go tell Achilles."

"You shouldn't have to be the one to do that," she blurted, staring over at him with wide eyes.

He shrugged, getting to his feet and wiping his nose. "But I think I should. I know how I'd want someone to tell me that the person I was closest to had died. And I think... no one else understands how to be kind to him."

"Okay." Briseis gave in easily. She didn't have the energy to fight him. And she didn't want to face Achilles, even though she was scared to admit it.

Antilochus kicked a pebble across the road. "Okay," he repeated, and walked off into the night.

Briseis watched him go, her vision clouding with salt water. The world blurred like an impressionist painting. It wasn't supposed to go like this. Patroclus wasn't supposed to... die. A sob escaped her lips, and she quickly covered her mouth, trying to shove it back in. Patroclus was an island. He was supposed to be untouchable. Through everything with Agamemnon and Achilles, he had listened to her. Calmed her down. Talked her off ledges over the phone in the bathroom at three in the morning. And she knew that he was that to Iphis. And to Achilles. But who had held onto him?

Patroclus, with his soft laugh and generous eyes. He believed in people. Supported them in a quiet way. And those he loved... had exploited that. Briseis choked on her tears. Of *course* she had asked him if he was okay. She had offered help. She had done the minimal amount of work to keep their friendship a mutually beneficial thing. The horrible part about it was that Patroclus never *complained.* The closest he had come was one afternoon, when Achilles was off doing something for a class.

They had been sitting in the grass, sincerely trying to study for a math final. (The math finals. He'd never get to write them. After all that studying.) Patroclus had flopped down backwards to stare up at the clouds. Briseis gave up on studying then, because it was harder to concentrate when your partner gave up.

"Y'know what?" Patroclus had said, almost wistfully, "I think I'm bad at setting boundaries."

Briseis was sort of shocked at the strange remark.

"I just. Don't tell people when it gets to be too much.." There had been something bitter in his voice. "And of course, people don't realize what's going on." He paused. Then laughed. "Sorry. I'm not making sense."

Briseis had swallowed, staring over at her friend. He had saved her from Agamemnon on the first day of school. He was constantly helping her with homework. He always made sure she was doing okay, at the very least. (He'd never ask that again.)

Briseis shook her head, even though he couldn't see her. "No. I think that's... well. I get it. Sort of."

Patroclus looked at her, tilting his head away from the clouds.

"I'm just... so tired," he said, a regret stained smile parting his lips. "I wish I knew how to just make it *stop.*"

The birds had been twittering merrily that day. Patroclus shrugged awkwardly, laying his head back down. Briseis didn't know how to answer. She swallowed, trying to come up with something to say. Anything, that could be interpreted as somewhat useful.

Patroclus sighed. "But it's okay," he finished his sentence, long after the pause should have ended. "I've lived like this my whole life. I'll figure it out someday." (He wouldn't. He'd never figure it out.)

At the time, Briseis had thought about it for ten more minutes, and dismissed it as something she couldn't help with. They had made daisy chains, taking pictures on the lawn. *Not the pictures,* she thought, remembering all the stupid selfies and group photos she had on her phone. Patroclus, smiling and alive alive alive...

"*Fuck,*" she whispered into her hands, pressing her palms into her flooding eyes. *Why him?* She thought, over and over. It played in her head until the words echoed. They bounced off the inside of her skull, and crawled up the back of throat. They ravaged her body with shivers, breaking chips off her heart. That question. It hurt. So badly. She briefly wondered why. And like an impossible math problem, the cause of her pain is simple.

This question. It hurts because she can't, for the life of her, find an answer.

# XVIII

Antilochus drove. He wasn't paying attention to the road. Not really. Just the feeling that the world seemed a little bleaker. A little emptier. He stopped at a red light, no one else in the intersection. He rested his head against the steering wheel, trying to breathe. It hurt his lungs. He didn't want to tell Achilles. Antilochus didn't know Patroclus all that well, but he knew Achilles. Stubborn and dramatic as fuck for sure, but... he cared about Patroclus more than anything. For a moment, he wondered. Were they friends? Or more? But then he realized it didn't matter. The light was green.

He kept going. The houses bled into each other like they had forgotten how to stand apart. Streetlights left streaks in his vision, but he hardly noticed. Too soon, he pulled into the student parking lot by the dorms. It was so dark out now. How late was it? The air was less muggy. It almost had a crispness to it. Antilochus forgot to lock his car, and only remembered when he was almost at Achilles' building. He paused. And kept going forward. It didn't matter, really. The grass was soft beneath his shoes. Light from the dorm spilled across the ground as Antilochus opened the door.

The common area on the bottom floor was empty. It was probably past curfew, or close to it. The space echoed around him as he walked across the wooden floor. The elevator took a long time to come. Those few seconds were an empty, endless time, stretching out in front of Antilochus in an eternal runway, disappearing into the darkness. He waited, watching a little clump of dust blow across the floor, carried by some mysterious air current. That was when he realized he hadn't pressed the button. Shaking his head with a hint of self–deprecating amusement, he jammed his finger onto the little *up* square. The elevator dinged merrily, opening its doors. He stepped inside, punching in the extra code Achilles had shared with him when they had been closer. His dorm was on the top floor, so it was nicer. And more expensive.

Before the elevator door slid open, Achilles had been sitting on the kitchen counter. He hadn't gone down to the cafeteria for dinner, instead making himself a sandwich from the food in the fridge. The remnants of the tomatoes and cheese sat on the cutting board on the other side of the sink, the knife resting haphazardly beside them, sort of propped against his unwashed plate. He had been thinking how weird it was, for the team to be out so late. Maybe they had gone out for dinner. Hopefully they won. But... wouldn't Patroclus text him about it? Achilles was scrolling through Instagram, looking for any celebratory posts when he heard the elevator. He let himself smile a little, putting his phone down, then picking it up again. He didn't want to seem creepy or anything. Or like he had been waiting in the kitchen for... five hours.

When the elevator dinged, and the doors glided open, Antilochus saw Achilles, sitting cross legged on the kitchen counter.

He looked up, beaming. "Hey—" The smile slid sideways a little as Achilles cocked his head. "Hey Antilochus," he said, composing himself.

Antilochus was backlit by the elevator, his hands stuffed into hoodie pockets. He was still wearing his football stuff, minus the shoulder pads. Not who Achilles had been expecting. He swallowed, putting his phone face down on the counter again.

"What's up?" Achilles asked, his brows furrowed as he hopped off the ledge.

The elevator door shut again, leaving the two young men in a cool half darkness. Antilochus dragged a hand across his eyes. They were stung. Tonight wasn't supposed to happen like this.

Achilles took a step forwards, his heart climbing up his throat. "What is it?" he asked again, more sharply now.

"Achilles..." Antilochus started, only for his voice to shatter on the last syllable.

His friend was standing in front of him, trying to breathe. Achilles wasn't sure what was going on. He tightened his hands into fists.

"It's Patroclus," Antilochus whispered, barely holding himself together. He crossed his arms, gripping his biceps tightly. Watching. Waiting. What would Achilles do?

Surprisingly, the blonde boy let out a small, nervous laugh. "What about him?"

When Antilochus would look back on this moment, that silence... that pause, would be the worst moment of his life. He couldn't make himself spit the words out. Achilles' eyes were so full of doubt, warring with hope and disbelief. Antilochus could see the wheels turning in his head, all the possibilities that he dismissed and the ones he chose to believe. Even in the grey dimness, he could see as Achilles fought with the demons in his head. And the exact moment where his green eyes became hard.

"What. *About* him?" Achilles repeated, trying to ignore the pulling on his stomach. The flutter in his hands as they tried to shake. *No.*

Antilochus looked up at the ceiling. Achilles watched him swallow. Found himself holding his breath.

"He's gone," Antilochus whispered, hoping that Achilles would and wouldn't hear him at the same time.

Achilles laughed. It was so... hollow. More of a dry sob, disguised as something more disturbing. Antilochus looked at him, his burning eyes wide.

Achilles was shaking his head, a hint of a smile on his face.

"That's a lie," he said softly. He could feel acid coming up his throat.

"I'm sorry," Antilochus whispered, his voice ragged.

There was fire, roaring through Achilles' veins as he slammed Antilochus up against the elevator door. The crash... barely registered in his mind. He was burning and he was shivering and none of it made sense…

Antilochus' breath had been knocked out of his body. Achilles was holding him up against the door, something unhinged about the way he stood.

"Say it again," he said, his voice finally trembling. "*Say it again.*"

For a long second, Antilochus couldn't reply. Winded. Retching for air inside his mouth. Finally, with tears obscuring his breath, he managed to choke out, "He's dead, Achilles."

Achilles let go of him. Antilochus inhaled, his lungs struggling for a moment. The impact had crushed them a little, leaving a residue of pain. He put his hands on his knees, leaning over and staring at Achilles' socks.

"No," Achilles whispered. Ringing in his ears. Nothing. The sheer weight…it should have brought him to the floor.

Achilles felt it crawling up his throat as he shook his head. *How can I…?*

*"You'll… be okay, right?" Patroclus asks, holding both of Achilles' hands. "Because no matter what, I'm here. I hate seeing you like this."*

*Achilles laughs softly, pressing his mouth to the other boy's knuckles. "I don't know what I'd do without you."*

*"You'd be…"*

*"A fucking lonely insomniac," Achilles finishes. He glances at the clock. Two am.*

*Patroclus guides Achilles' face back, so he's looking at him. "Can you do something for me?" he asks, his brown eyes innocent and sincere.*

*Achilles nods. "Anything."*

*"Don't leave me," Patroclus says quietly, a sad smile teasing his lips.*

*"We'll run away to a vineyard in France," Achilles promises, taking Patroclus' one hand in both of his. "And then we'll live there until the end of our lives."*

*Patroclus looks up at the ceiling, then back at the boy in front of him. "You're my everything, even when you can't sleep."*

*They laugh.*

*"Y'know what? I actually hung the stars for you," Achilles jokes as Patroclus lays down, resting his head on Achilles' thigh. "The world was a bleak, starless place until I discovered my undying love for you."*

*Patroclus smiles, his eyes closed. "I feel so honored. Thank you."*

And then Achilles launched himself towards the kitchen. *I can't live without him.* Antilochus startled up, saw the knife on the cutting board, and threw himself at Achilles. They fell to the floor together, rattling the knife against the ceramic plate in a savage crash.

*I can't live without you,* Achilles thought. *I can't I can't I can't...*

Antilochus pinned Achilles' wrists to the floor, heart thundering as the boy beside him started trembling. The cry that ripped through Achilles sent Antilochus spiraling into a void. A sound, untethered, but soft. The blonde boy shook uncontrollably. Antilochus could hear his teeth clattering together. He was powerless. Aching. He hated this moment.

"Patroclus," Achilles whispered.

His face was wet, tears streaming down onto the kitchen floor. They clung to his jaw, as if trying to comfort him. All he wanted to do was die. He wanted to die. Achilles struggled weakly against his friend's grip. Patroclus' name ripped through him, over, and over. He pleaded. *Come back. Come back. I can't live without you.* There was no answer. Achilles pressed his face into the floor, letting the dull pain spread through his skull.

"Let me die," he whispered, his voice worn and ragged and broken. "Please."

They stopped fighting and his muscles throbbed. Antilochus shook his head, even though Achilles couldn't see. He just couldn't make himself say anything.

"I'm sorry," he finally said, feeling his throat constrict. "I can't."

Eventually, Antilochus let go of Achilles, moving to sit with his back against the cupboard. Achilles didn't move. He couldn't. He couldn't make himself get up. There was a bruise forming on his face from when Antilochus tackled him. It pulsed. He felt wrong. His throat was raw, and his eyes wanted to burst from their sockets. His stomach wanted to empty itself and his head... was stuck, repeating *he's dead he's dead he's dead* until Achilles wanted to plug his ears, and scream. But he couldn't scream. All that was left inside him was a dull, thudding pain. He wanted to be numb, but he could barely breathe. It felt like the world had collapsed in on him, burying him beneath layers rocks and rubble, six feet under.

Like he was supposed to be dead, but somehow he wasn't. He felt like a corpse. That somehow survived. It should have been him.

Achilles wanted to be dead.

"Do you... wanna go see him?" Antilochus asked after a long silence.

Achilles tried to open his eyes, but they stuck together. The salt water. He inhaled, sounding like he had a cold. His body kept shaking as he tried to open his eyes again. The seal broke slowly, ripping at his eyelashes. See him. Patroclus. Dead. The view of the floor blurred again. His throat tried to strangle him, but he forced himself to roll onto his back.

"Yeah," he said, his voice sounding like it had been attacked by a feral dog.

Antilochus took a shaky breath. "You have to promise not—"

"I'm not making any promises," Achilles interrupted, sitting up and running his hands over his head. "I'm getting shoes and we're leaving."

Antilochus stood, subtly pushing the knife behind him. Just in case. But Achilles ignored him, getting slowly to his feet and walking down the hall.

Someone peered out of their dorm as he passed. "Everything okay?" he asked, spotting Antilochus. "There were... noises."

"Yeah," Antilochus nodded, trying to sound... okay. "We're fine. Rough night is all."

The boy gave a sleepy thumbs up before disappearing again. Antilochus pressed his fingers into his eyes until he saw patterns.

One of his wrists was sore from when he fell with Achilles. Fuck. This was a dumpster fire.

"Are you coming or not," Achilles demanded from somewhere by the elevator.

Antilochus looked up. He was tired. It had been such a long day. "Yeah," he said, walking into the open elevator. Achilles must've called it.

He kept glancing over at the blonde boy as they walked out of the dorm, and to Antilochus' car. Achilles had a headache, pounding behind his eyes. When they got into the car, he took a deep shuddering breath, slammed his door shut, and stared up through the windshield. A wave of darkness threatened to sweep Achilles under, pulling him away with the tide. He clenched his jaw tightly as Antilochus backed out of the parking lot.

"Is he really dead?" Achilles asked as they rode through a stop sign. The words were soft. Almost gentle, in a childlike way.

Antilochus looked over at him. "Yeah. Tackled illegally by Hector and some other kid."

*Hector.* He had taken Patroclus. Patroclus had been killed. Achilles' breath clawed up his throat, shredding it to strips. Hector. Hector Hector Hector... Achilles inhaled and tried to count fire hydrants all the way to the hospital. Trying to avoid the brutal truth. Trying to avoid reality. Trying to hide, and run, and disappear.

Achilles' shoes were untied. He noticed that as he got out of An-tilochus' car. His dirty shoelaces slapped against the concrete as he walked towards the hospital doors.

"I'm... gonna talk to Briseis," Antilochus said. Achilles barely heard it. Briseis. Was sitting on the curb. Her face was in her hands, but she glanced up as Achilles passed. She didn't try to talk to him, or to stop him.

He was glad. The air felt gross as he walked across the concrete. It was warm and biting at the same time. He ignored it. The doors opened automatically, leaving Achilles momentarily blinded by the the lights. It was bright. Smelled like antiseptic. Everything was so... white. He blinked, blissfully numb. Because none of this could possibly be true.

"Achilles!" someone called.

His eyes stung as he looked around the waiting room. Menelaus was running over. His hair was damp, and his face gaunt. Achilles saw Athena, talking to... his mother. *What?*

"Achilles," Menelaus said again, pity twisting the name that came from his lips. The red haired boy stopped in front of him. "He's... back there."

"Take me," Achilles stated in a raspy monotone.

Menelaus swallowed, glancing over at their coach.

"Please?" Achilles asked, his momentary numbness cracking at the seams like the indifference in his tone.

"Okay," Menelaus said, taking a deep breath. "I'm not really..." He looked over at the nurses' station. "I'm not supposed to go back there because there was... never mind. I'll just–c'mon."

Achilles followed Menelaus through a pair of heavy white doors, his jaw set. It would be okay. That feeling briefly disappeared when he saw *Hector* of all people, sitting outside a room. He had no right. No right—

The guy with the shaved head glanced up as Achilles came down the hall. He opened his mouth to say something, but Achilles blasted through the door he was sitting by, motivated by pure spite and disgust. He didn't have time to prepare himself for what came next. Not that he could've anyways. It might have been nice to at least try. (But he didn't.)

Any kind of sense Achilles thought he had disappeared. A flash of the greatest agony lanced through him like a spear. It burned, leaving a searing hole where he was supposed to be. (Achilles was no more.) Patroclus, laying there. Silent. Still. Achilles lurched forwards, grabbing one of his cold, cold hands. Pressing it to his face. Limp. No. He was crying again, tears trickling from his eyes. Patroclus wasn't asleep. He wasn't breathing.

"Please," he whispered, gripping his hand harder. "Please come back."

Another flash. He was on the bed now, Patroclus' head in his lap. He combed his hands through those thick curls, his fingers catching as they shook.

"You can't..." Achilles pleaded, his tears dripping down Patroclus' still face. "You're supposed to *stay* with me. *I can't–live...without you.*"

Patroclus didn't reply. Achilles pressed his nose into that hair, feeling himself come undone. Ripped apart. Patroclus talked in his sleep. And now he was silent. Now, he smelled like his shampoo. He was so *still*. Patroclus. Patroclus...

"I love you," Achilles sobbed, his breath coming in rapid, hiccuping rasps as he gripped the white sheet with hands that had never shaken so hard. "I love you I love you I love you." Over and over. Like it could bring him back. No matter what he said, it *wouldn't* bring him back. Nothing could.

"Achilles," someone said, her voice stern and soft.

He took his face out of Patroclus' hair, but didn't look up. He wouldn't. Not even for his mother, who was standing at the door. He put his convulsing hands on either side of Patroclus' face, smoothing curls behind his ears. Achilles rested his forehead on Patroclus'. *This wasn't supposed to happen*. He was so, *so* cold. They were supposed to be together. No matter what.

The bed dipped towards his mother as she sat down. "Achilles," she said again, reaching towards her son, but pulling back. Thetis didn't know how to deal with this. "You're making a scene."

When Achilles finally looked up at her, it cracked her heart. His eyes were bloodshot, but it was the emptiness in his gaze that shook her.

"I hate it here," he said, his voice cracking painfully. There was a terrible smile playing at his lips that didn't reach his eyes.

Thetis took a deep breath, forcing herself to look down at the boy in her son's lap. "They need this room for someone else." She tried to be gentle. "They're going to move him to the... morgue. So we need to leave."

Achilles bit his bottom lip, looking back down at Patroclus. He felt like his chest was going to implode.

"I don't... wanna leave him," he said quietly.

Thetis watched a tear fall from her son's eyes, and down the dead boy's face. They sat there, Achilles quietly trying to hold back sobs as Thetis struggled to find something to say. This was their relationship, in essence. They both tried, but it was never enough.

"Peleus called me," Thetis said, just to break that almost quiet. "He said your coach called him, because he was Patroclus' third emergency contact." Achilles didn't move. "And he said he wasn't in town because of business. So I drove down here, as soon as he called me."

Achilles took a stuttering breath, tenderly wiping his tears off Patroclus' face. It hurt. His throat ached as he gently pulled himself out from under the other boy. Achilles was dizzy the moment he got to his feet. Thetis watched him, her eyebrows bunched together in pity. He glanced at her, still shaking, and then bent over Patroclus, pressing his lips to his forehead.

"I'm sorry," he whispered, almost inaudibly. *I should have been better.*

When he pulled away, he ran a knuckle down the cold cheek of the boy he loved. He wasn't coming back. He wasn't here. He was gone. Achilles forced himself to walk out of the room past his mother, without giving her a single glance. She didn't understand. And she wouldn't. Not ever.

Achilles felt a knot in his throat, screaming at him to turn around. To go back. So Patroclus wouldn't have to face whatever happened next alone. But he had to leave. If he tried to stay, he would just get hurt. No one paid him any attention until he walked into the waiting room.

Moments before Achilles came out of the white doors, Agamemnon had been trying to talk to Briseis. She and Antilochus had stumbled inside a good five minutes ago. Iphis, Briseis' bodyguard, had brushed past them, going outside. Briseis hadn't seemed to mind. So Agamemnon walked up to her.

"I think it's best we just break it off here," he had been saying, when she violently cut him off.

"I broke it off *weeks* ago, you insensitive *creep*!" she whisper yelled, her eyes red and puffy. "Leave me alone—"

Achilles had come out then. Briseis abruptly stood and rushed over to him, leaving Agamemnon to simmer over his frustrations alone.

When Briseis collided with Achilles, he tripped back a few steps at the force of her embrace. Patroclus had hugged him like that once. After he had been gone for a week at football camp.

"I am *so* sorry," Briseis said, her face pressed into his shoulder.

They were both trembling. Achilles felt sick as he slowly wrapped his arms around her. He hid his face in her hair to disguise the fresh wave of pain spilling from his eyes.

"It's my fault," he whispered, praying she would hate him.

Briseis made a choking sound. "I know," she said, the words tearing through Achilles like the furies themselves. "But I can't make myself blame you. As much as I want to."

"I wish you would," he replied, a muscle in his jaw spasming.

Thetis stood awkwardly behind Achilles as he pulled away from Briseis.

"You can have her back!" Agamemnon yelled from across the room.

Briseis turned and flipped him off. Achilles managed a heavy–lidded glare.

"I'm gonna go, Bri," Achilles said, exhausted, and feeling like he had been emptied of his will to live. "I'll see you soon, okay?"

She looked up at him, her face bleeding sorrow as she put a hand on his arm. "Text me please. Or call. I..." She covered her eyes with the hand she had used to comfort him. "I miss him already."

Achilles could barely go a couple hours without missing Patroclus. He hardly lasted a whole class. And now... he'd have to last a lifetime. That was ugly. It was messy and true and *ugly*. He tried to give Briseis a comforting smile, but it didn't work. He couldn't even fake it.

"Me too."

The football team had stopped talking now, staring over at Achilles with trepidation.

"Winning wasn't worth his life," Achilles said to them. His eyes were dry, but grief roiled in his stomach. "Fuck you, Agamemnon. This whole mess is your fault."

He turned away and walked out into the night. Briseis watched him go, her hands covering her mouth. Thetis followed her son, giving a nod of acknowledgement to the coach, Athena, on their way out.

"Where's your car?" Achilles asked, stopping beside the road. He wrapped his arms around himself like he used to do when he was small. He looked small. Achilles usually seemed larger than life, bursting at the seams with enthusiasm and energy from somewhere Thetis didn't know.

She pointed to a loading zone. Her car had been parked there longer than twenty minutes, but she didn't find a ticket in her windshield wipers. It probably happened here all the time. People coming and parking, only to stay longer than anticipated. Achilles walked listlessly as they went to the car, the sound of his shoes scraping the concrete as he dragged his feet.

"Do you need anything?" Thetis asked as she climbed into the front seat.

Achilles got in next to her. He sat there for a long time, staring unseeingly out the windshield. Then he turned to look at her, his eyes puffy and red. "Him."

And Thetis didn't know how to reply to that. So she put the car into drive, and started to pull away from the hospital. Someone ran out the door, waving his hands in the air. It looked like he was holding a... football helmet. Achilles turned to look out the back, frowning slightly. It was Hector. And he was holding Achilles' helmet.

"What the...?" Achilles found himself saying, and glancing at his mother.

Thetis raised an eyebrow. "Is that Hector?" she asked.

Athena had told her all about the boys who had 'accidentally' tackled Patroclus without his helmet on. It had been a freak occurrence, but Athena had apparently received a message from a family member. A former student apparently said it looked like the first boy had purposefully ripped the helmet from Patroclus' head. Achilles' jaw was clenched as tight as a fist as he watched the boy wave the helmet in the air.

"He... yeah. That's my helmet," Achilles rasped. *He killed Patroclus,* was all he could think. *He took my everything from me.*

"Do you want to play again?" Thetis asked, finally pulling away from the hospital. She could see how tense Achilles was. *Poor Hector,* she thought, watching her son. "Because if you do, I'll call Hephaestus and get a new one painted."

Achilles inhaled, holding his breath in as he turned to face forwards again. It took a long time for him to answer.

"I'll play again," he said.

Alright. Something she could give Achilles, at the very least. Thetis assumed she'd have to deal with the funeral, since Achilles' friend had very absent parents. But she would sort that out in the morning.

Thetis' phone rang. Achilles picked it up out of the cup holder.

"It's Dad," he said, looking over at her, his face lit by the screen. It reflected off his glassy eyes, making him ghostly and inhuman.

"Do you want to speak with him?" Thetis asked, pausing at a stop sign. She wasn't sure where they were going, and she knew she wasn't leaving Achilles alone in his dorm. Not tonight, at least.

Her son nodded faintly, then picked up the phone.

"Achilles?" Peleus asked, from wherever the hell he was.

Achilles swallowed. "Hey Dad."

"I'm so sorry about your friend," he said, his voice full of sympathy. "That's an awful thing, if I ever heard one."

"Yeah," Achilles whispered.

"I'll be back tomorrow," Peleus said. "Tell your mother. There're keys to my house under the front doormat, if you need a place to stay."

"Thanks," Achilles replied, aching all over. "See you soon."

"You too, champ. You too."

# XIX

HECTOR STOOD BY THE hospital doors, holding Achilles' helmet in one hand. He hadn't meant to take it. Not really. And now the Stallions' player was gone. Hector stared at the place where the car had been moments ago. He had no idea what he was supposed to do now. In the end, he whined softly, running a hand over his head and turning to face the building. It felt like he was coming apart on the inside. *I killed someone,* was all his traitorous brain could think. *I killed someone.*

His phone rang. Hector jumped in shock, fumbling around to answer the call. His phone was in his back pocket, and had stopped ringing by the time he got it out. Three missed calls. Two from his mother, one from his father. It started ringing again. Dad. Hector swallowed, picking up.

"Hey Dad," he said, feeling like he wasn't the one actually talking.

Priam let out a relieved breath. "I'm glad you picked up." He paused. "Paris didn't know where you were and your mother and I have been worried since they called us…"

Hector swallowed, staring towards the dark sky. "Who called you?"

"No one," his father reassured, though he sounded… worried. A bit beyond that.

"Dad…" Hector started, feeling a wall crumbling in his chest. "Dad… I—" He pressed his eyes with the space between his pointer finger and thumb, trying to restore the numbness.

"I know," Priam said softly. "But your mother and I still love you. We know it was an accident."

This made Hector laugh humorlessly. "Dad, I killed someone," he whispered, for fear of anyone hearing.

"We know, son," Priam answered, his voice steady. "And we've dealt with it. No one's going to blame you. We pulled a couple of strings and they already believe it was a freak accident."

Surprisingly, Hector found little comfort in that statement. Because it hadn't been a complete accident, and he *felt* like he should be blamed for it. But he couldn't say that to his father. He couldn't say that to *anyone.* So he just nodded, breathing in the muggy air. It was what guilt felt like. His eyes were prickling, threatening to overflow. *No,* he thought, the voice in his head as hard as a bar of iron. *I will* not *cry about this. I've got no right.*

"Thanks," he said, not really knowing what else to say.

In the background, Hector heard his mother say "Is that Hector?" and his father, in the same muffled tone told her that it was.

"Do you mind talking to your mother?" Priam asked, his voice clearer now.

"Sure," Hector said, sitting down on the curb. He picked up a pebble and threw it across the street, watching it skitter away.

There was a shuffling as Priam handed the phone off to his wife. Hector pressed his hand into his eyes again. His ears rung dully.

"Honey?" his mother asked, sounding almost hysterical. "Honey, are you alright? Andromache's here and she's so worried about you. Do you know when you're going to be home?"

"Slow down," came Priam's distant, yet calm voice.

Hecuba let out a pinched exhale. "Sorry, Hector," she said, her vocal chords wound tightly around the words. "I'm sorry, honey… this is all…"

"A lot," Hector finished, feeling one corner of his mouth pull upwards. "I know."

The unshed tears finally retreated as his mother asked him question after question. They were all… nice questions though, like, '*How was your school day,*' or, '*Does the car have gas.*' No more of the, '*How're you feeling ones,*' which… just made Hector miserable. He felt miserable.

"You should come home tonight," his mother finally said. "I know it's a bit of a drive, but I want you here."

Hector found himself relieved. His parents still cared about him. For now, that was enough. Andromache burst into the kitchen.

"Is that Hector on the phone?!" she demanded. Hector could hear her as clear as if she were standing right next to him. He winced.

Priam's indistinctive soothing cut into Andromache's protest.

"Give me, the Godsdamn, *phone*!" she shrieked.

This couldn't turn out well.

"I'm... passing it over to Andromache now," his mother whispered. He could tell that she was cupping the microphone with her hand, so Hector could hear her more clearly. "But please go find Paris and whoever stayed, and bring them home. It's been a long day for everyone."

Hector swallowed. "Thanks Mom," he replied, his heart pounding. He wished she was *here*. Not an hour long drive away. Why couldn't this have happened at Ilium? It would have been so much... easier. Though he knew he couldn't complain. He didn't have the privilege of feeling inconvenienced in this situation.

"Here's Andromache," Hecuba said reluctantly. (She didn't want to let her son go.)

"Hector," Andromache demanded, saying his name like an order. "You need to come home. Now."

He nodded, agreeing with her rapidly. She didn't even seem to hear him.

"Why would you *do* that?" she continued, her voice full of fire. "Sorry. I know it was an accident. But why didn't you *listen to me?* Hector, I knew something like this would happen. You have to stop playing now. You've heard about Achilles, right?"

Hector put his head between his knees, watching an ant crawl across the pavement.

"Achilles literally stopped playing because Agamemnon refused to apologize to him. And then he sent a friend in his uniform?

That's messed *up*! Helen told me. She says Achilles is a good guy, but I don't believe her, because apparently Achilles was close to the guy who died, and I'm really scared that he's going to try and hurt you—"

"Andromache—" Hector tried to interject as panic crawled up his throat, but she kept going, gaining momentum as her voice climbed up an octave.

"There's so much on the line now, Hector. I don't think you understand that if anything fucking happens to you, you're going to have a son who won't have a father, and I'll have to deal with the whole rest of my life *without you* and I haven't had to do that for so many years I can't even remember how I did that, Hector. I know this sounds selfish, and that it *has* the whole time but I can't keep watching these horrible things happen and know that 'freak accidents' aren't just stories and I *know* you're not okay, because no matter how tough you seem, you're actually a kind, sensitive person who gets a little carried away sometimes, but I still *love you* and I *need you to be here*—" She cut herself off, inhaling deeply.

Hector stopped trying to suppress his tears now. They fell straight from his eyes, onto the street, making little puddles of misery. Windows into a darker world.

"I fucked up," he whispered, listening to her start to sob quietly.

She hiccuped, unable to control her breath. "And I… still… need you."

He swallowed thickly. "I'm coming home now."

There was a pause. They were both holding their breath.

"I love you," Hector whispered, wishing he could take back everything else he had done that day, except for those words.

"Drive safe," Andromache replied, sounding drained of all the fight that had been in her moments ago. "You're my world," she said softly after another pause. And then she hung up.

Helen had been standing in the entryway to the kitchen the whole time they had talked to Hector. Andromache now sat at the little round table, sobbing into the crook of her arm. Helen didn't know what to think. She couldn't get the image of Patroclus crashing into the earth out of her head. And now he was dead. Kind, sweet, gentle Patroclus. The only thing that had kept Achilles sane. He had told her that once. They had been painting each other's nails in the back of a grade ten History class. (It had been so boring. They couldn't help it.) His exact words had been *'I think I'd be insane without him. He keeps me being who I want to be.'* Helen wanted to text Achilles, but she wasn't sure what to say. They hadn't talked in at least three weeks. She missed her friends at Mycenae more than ever, in that moment, watching as Priam and Hecuba comforted Andromache.

Helen didn't belong here.

When they pulled up to Peleus' house, Thetis cut the ignition, then stared out the front window. Achilles did the same. She wasn't even sure he knew that they had stopped. Mother and son drifted through the ether of murky time, both lost in their own heads. Dark places, they were.

"Achilles," Thetis finally said, looking expectantly over at the boy next to her.

The streetlight cast eerie shadows across her son's face, exaggerating the hollows beneath his eyes. His eyes. They were exhausted as he turned to meet her gaze.

"Let's go inside," she suggested. "Your father will be back in the morning, and you can figure out what you want to do then. I'll have to go home, but I'll organize the funeral, and see you again when I do that."

It was too much for Achilles to fully comprehend, but he nodded anyways before getting out of the car. He hadn't done up his seatbelt. (There was no need for safety anymore.)

The night had gotten cooler. Achilles dimly noticed the hairs rising on the back of his neck from the chill. His eyes felt swollen. He should probably drink some water. Thetis locked the car behind her, and followed Achilles up the neatly landscaped yard. It was hard to see clearly in the dark, but apparently her former husband had changed the yard after she moved away. *Good for him,* she thought as Achilles lifted up the front doormat. It was shaped like a rainbow, but had different colors of brown instead of a full spectrum. How odd. Achilles inserted the key into the door, pushed it open, and walked inside. He left his shoes strewn haphazardly across the entry.

"Do you need—" Thetis started to ask, but didn't bother continuing as her son jumped lithely up the carpeted stairs.

She sighed, listening to the gentle thudding of his footsteps as he wandered around upstairs. She had forgotten how much this house creaked. Flicking on the lights in the living room, Thetis stared at the house that had once been hers. The furniture was different now too. Less angular than what she had chosen. Peleus always did prefer a more homey sort of feel. Thetis walked into the kitchen, rooting through the cabinets until she found a vintage red wine. So he still kept her favorites. She laughed softly, pulling out a glass, considering it, then leaving it on the counter. The bottle came with her as she walked to the couch, for once appreciating that it enveloped her instead of staying firm.

Thetis exhaled, placing the bottle on the wooden coffee table in front of her. The house still smelled the same. Faintly of lavender and clean laundry. She closed her eyes. It had been a long day, but she wasn't sleeping here. She would wait until Peleus got back, then leave her son in his care. He knew Achilles better anyways.

As it happened, Thetis did drift off, around three in the morning. The show she had been watching on her phone hadn't been loud enough, or maybe it just wasn't exciting. But she was woken by the sound of an electric razor, buzzing invasively through the house. It startled her at first, as she rubbed her eyes, trying to locate the sound. When she regained her senses a moment later, she discovered that it was coming from upstairs.

*Achilles.* Panic coursed through her as she pushed her heels off, letting them fall into the white carpet as she darted for the stairs, slightly dizzy from standing so fast. She had done this when he was young. Sprinted around, trying to make sure he was never in trouble. Always the concerned mother. That had worn off with time, but she felt the exact same as she reached the landing where the noise was coming from. Her heart pounded as she rattled on the bathroom doorknob.

"Achilles?" she asked, her voice louder and higher than usual. "*Achilles?*"

The buzzing didn't stop.

"I will *break down this door—*"

"It isn't locked," he said flatly from inside the bathroom.

Thetis stopped what she was doing immediately, embarrassment flushing through her face. She took a deep breath, twisted the knob, and pulled. The door was a stupid design. Pull instead of push. She hated it when she had lived here, but had forgotten in her time away. Wonderful. She opened the door.

"What are you *doing?*" Thetis demanded, immediately horrified at the mess her son had made.

Achilles stared at her through the mirror, devoid of emotion. The skin around his eyes was an angry red. He lowered the razor from his newly shaved head. There were piles of his wavy golden hair, strewn across the sink and the floor.

She stared back, trying to keep the disapproval out of her gaze. "You're shaving your head at three in the morning?"

"I feel like I'm drowning," Achilles whispered, absently pushing a clump of hair onto the floor.

Thetis should have hugged him, but she wasn't sure how. It had been so long since she had been... his mother.

"Leave me alone," her son said, the green of his eyes a shocking contrast to the bloodshot whites. "I'll clean it up."

❧❧❧❧ ❦❦❦❦

Achilles didn't know how much time passed. He had shaved his head and then cleaned up. His mother had left the next day. Everything was hazy. Shrouded in pain. Nothing even mattered anymore. His dad tried to get him out of bed, but he refused to eat. It was too hard, with the stabbing in his throat. The discordant hum in his head. The feeling of unraveling. Unravel*ed*. Every once in awhile, Achilles reached for his phone. To call Patroclus.

But his phone was still at the dorm. And Patroclus was gone.

❧❧❧❧ ❦❦❦❦

Briseis hadn't heard anything from Achilles in three days. He had fallen off the world. And she had too, just a little bit. Iphis was distant. Everywhere they went, they were followed by apologies. They were followed by whispers and rumors and false sympathy. Except for the people who had actually *known* Patroclus. The day after he died, the school's principal had made an announcement. There would be a memorial for him, after school on Friday, available to anyone who wanted to attend. And there was grief counseling, for those who needed it.

Neither of them wanted to talk to the counselors. Iphis and Briseis stuck together, coping in silent ways. Until Achilles came back on Friday.

The cafeteria noise seemed diluted lately. Less exciting. Less hopeful. Less lively. There was just less *life.* Briseis and Iphis had been sitting at a different table than usual. Patroclus' chair was empty now, as Briseis glanced across at their old spot. No one had taken up sitting there yet. And no one would, until some new freshmen who didn't know came next year. Iphis was trying to do a math assignment, and Briseis was attempting to help her when Achilles walked in. The noise had quieted even further. Iphis glanced up, her eyes going wide. Briseis turned to see what had caught her attention, and there he was, a red football helmet in hand.

Achilles Pelides.

Except he didn't look like himself. This wasn't Achilles. Not really. His hair was gone. He was wearing his sweater and blazer, both neatly pressed. His tie was done perfectly. Almost choking him. And when he looked across the cafeteria, Briseis could see how red his eyes were. He was bigger and smaller all at once. Scarier, definitely. Iphis glanced at Briseis, their gazes meeting anxiously. They had wondered, how Achilles would cope. Apparently, this was it. Without grace, but with intensity.

Achilles saw Iphis and Briseis staring at him. Like the rest of the student body. He kept walking, towards Agamemnon's table. The football players all looked up when he stopped in front of them.

Ajax 1 whispered something to Odysseus, who didn't take his eyes off Achilles.

"I'll play," Achilles said, his voice hoarse and rough. "If you'll have me."

Agamemnon hadn't been expecting that, and from the looks he got from his teammates, none of them had expected it either. He cleared his throat, staring at Achilles. The boy held himself differently. Less cocky, but more upright. Like someone who needed orders to follow.

Agamemnon smiled, leaning back in his chair as he spread his hands; a king forgiving an unruly subject. "Welcome back, Pelides. We'll go to Calypso's tonight to celebrate your triumphant return."

Menelaus stared between his brother and his... friend. Achilles nodded, almost mechanically. His return was the anything *but* a triumph. Menelaus rubbed the back of his neck, swallowing nervously.

"Thank you," Achilles rasped, turning from the table and walking away.

He sounded like someone completely different. Menelaus found himself unable to look away. Everyone at the table had bags under their eyes, a drag in their step. They were all tired, even though no one was willing to admit it. They were shaken, too. What had happened... was wrong, and they all knew it. Even Agamemnon, to a certain degree. But Achilles? He looked beyond tired. He hadn't replied to anyone's messages. Antilochus was still away, but he had been chatting with Menelaus and Automedon on the phone. Achilles had just gone silent.

Automedon got to his feet, shared a glance with Phoenix, then followed Achilles over to where he had just sat down. Briseis had gone to Menelaus yesterday, asking him about Achilles. Half the team had texted, more than once. He hadn't answered any of them. But now he was here. He looked like he had been though hell.

As Achilles sat down at Briseis' table, he didn't really acknowledge either of them. He could still hear echoes in his head, guilt and fear and shame and worst of all, anger. Hector had done this. And he would pay.

"Achilles?" Briseis asked softly, tentatively laying a hand on his shoulder.

He turned to her, as though he was surprised she was there. "Hi," he said, the word grating his throat. He shouldn't be here. Patroclus was gone from their lives because of Achilles' mistake.

"So you're gonna play for Agamemnon again?" Iphis asked, regarding the helmet Achilles had placed on the table. It was new. There were a lot of painted horses on it, different from the one Patroclus had worn.

Briseis shook her head at Iphis, though she was already too late.

But Achilles didn't respond with the hate he would have four days ago.

Instead, he just nodded. "I will. I have to..." he trailed off as Automedon came to a halt beside Iphis' chair.

"Hey," the younger boy said, stuffing his hands sympathetically into his pockets. "I just wanted to say that... I'm sorry."

Briseis felt something try to escape her throat. She swallowed it down, hard.

"I know you guys were close," Automedon said softly, his eyebrows bunched together. "And this sucks. So. If you need anything, most of us are here for you."

Iphis snorted darkly at that last part as she doodled on the corner of her math.

"Yeah," Achilles said, every outward part of him subdued. "I don't think you could ever understand," he whispered, locking his gaze into the other player's.

"Thank you," Briseis cut in, smiling sadly at Automedon.

He gave her an awkward thumbs up before inching away from the table and Achilles' jagged stare.

"They announced they're continuing the football league this morning," Briseis said to Achilles.

She couldn't get over his lack of hair. His face seemed so much harder now, all sharp jawline and jutting cheekbones. It drew attention to his piercing eyes... and their redness. He didn't reply to her, instead resting his head on his arms like he was trying to hide from the world.

"How long has it been since you slept?" she asked, trying to share a glance with Iphis, who kept her eyes on her drawing.

Achilles' shoulders quivered, ever so slightly. He muttered something that Briseis didn't hear.

She leaned down. "I'm sorry, I can't hear you."

He turned his head to face her, staring up with a haunted expression. "Since..." He trailed off and the rest of the sentence was implied. "I can't... sleep without..."

Iphis looked up now, her lips parted in concern. "Achilles," she chastised quietly. "That's almost a week."

Briseis swallowed as Achilles put his face back in his arms.

"I'm going with the team to some dinner tonight," he said, just loud enough for the two of them to hear.

His stomach growled.

"Tell me you've been eating," Briseis whispered, feeling her heart sink.

Achilles shook his head without looking up. "I... sort of. I tried."

"When?" Iphis demanded, standing up and leaning over so she would be face to face with Achilles if he looked up.

It took him a second to reply. "Wednesday night," he mumbled, sounding deflated.

"You're not going with the team unless you promise to eat with us after," Briseis said, leaning on one elbow to face Achilles. "And actually *eat* something."

He sighed, turning to peer over at her. "I..." Achilles stopped and gave her a self–pitying smile. "Okay." He paused, sobering quickly. "Can I stay with you guys? Or one of you?"

Iphis frowned, contemplating. "I can get my roommate to go to Bri's room and share with *her* roommate."

"Why didn't you do that before?" Briseis demanded, a half smile on her face.

The short haired girl smirked briefly. "I had to have *some* time to—" she broke off as Achilles sat up. "Sorry," she said softly.

"No," Achilles reassured her, shaking his head too aggressively for it to be nonchalant. "No it's okay. The bell's about to ring. I'll see you later."

❧❧❧❧ ❧❧❧❧

Menelaus drove Achilles to dinner. Agamemnon had offered, but Menelaus thought it would be better if Achilles didn't have to deal with his brother and Odysseus for ten minutes alone. Or maybe it would've been fine, because Achilles just stared out the window the whole time, sitting almost perfectly still. He thanked Menelaus when they pulled up at the restaurant, and walked towards the door without waiting.

He was so out of it that Menelaus wondered if it was even a good idea for him to play. Agamemnon had texted Athena as soon as Achilles left their table at lunch, and she enthusiastically accepted him back, regardless of his mental state. Of course, Agamemnon hadn't *mentioned* Achilles' mental state, but... whatever Athena said went.

The inside of the restaurant was dark and loud, full of guys watching the hockey game. Menelaus found it funny how exciting sports were to people. Helen would've agreed with him. He sighed, sitting down at the giant booth where half the senior and junior players were sitting. Agamemnon hadn't invited the younger members of the team. Just the ones who 'knew Achilles well.'

Achilles had slid into the booth next to Nestor, giving the older player a frighteningly intense side eye. Agamemnon, Odysseus, and Diomedes walked in, with the Ajaces in tow. That completed the members of the team attending. It was a little weird without Antilochus, but he had gone home for a week or two after dealing with... Achilles.

Menelaus was about to sit next to Achilles when Agamemnon shoved him out of the way. He plopped down next to their star player and threw an arm around his shoulders. Achilles didn't really move, but he also didn't shove Agamemnon off.

He was so mad at himself. *Why didn't I just... deal with Agamemnon and move on? Everything would have been fine, if I hadn't been so fucking caught up in my stupid games—*

"Tonight," Agamemnon announced, distracting Achilles from his internal struggle, "We celebrate the joyous return of our best player!" This was met with quiet applause. Menelaus stared up at the ceiling. "Achilles has finally agreed, at the expense of his fragile honor, to join us once again!" Ajax 1 cringed at this, but Odysseus stomped on his foot under the table. "To Achilles!"

There was nothing to toast with, but the team cheered anyways.

"I'm only here to give Hector what he deserves," Achilles said, an unmistakable air of superiority in his words. "Because he took something from me that means more than my honor."

The team stopped laughing slowly, each giving Achilles confused, if not concerned glances. Until Agamemnon burst out laughing, thumping Achilles on the back.

"If that isn't the truth!" he exclaimed boisterously, leading everyone else into stunted laughter.

Achilles barely realized what had come out of his mouth, but he pretended to find it as funny as the rest of his team did. And it hurt. Because he hadn't been joking. Hector had torn a piece of Achilles out and thrown it into the storm. Achilles had run in after it, only to lose himself searching for the most precious fragment.

When waitress interrupted the loud conversation to take everyone's orders, Achilles didn't partake. When he had tried to eat, he had thrown it all up. He knew he should try, but if felt wrong, to enjoy things, when Patroclu—*he* was gone. How *could* he enjoy it anyways? Who would he tell?

But he did knew one thing. Hector had to get what was coming for him. And then maybe Achilles could find a kind of peace.

Maybe.

# XX

T HEY HAD MISSED THE memorial service for Patroclus. Briseis felt a little guilty about it, but Achilles said, after getting back from the team dinner, that it wasn't enough. There would be a couple flowers and speeches from teachers and students who didn't really know him. That would be all. Achilles didn't want to go anyways. As the week rolled into the weekend, Achilles finally slept, if only for a couple hours. He drifted through his days without living them, staring at Patroclus' empty desk, usually next to his. Sometimes, there would be notes on them, or a live bouquet. It hurt. It hurt it hurt it hurt.

Football practice was the only reprieve. If it could even be called that. It was two and a half hours in his life, everyday, where he could become just another person. The team sort of avoided him, but at least he could *run*. Sometimes he felt a scream bubbling up in his throat, and was barely able to shove it down. Agamemnon kept rubbing the fact that he had come back in his face. Achilles didn't even care. He couldn't make himself *care*.

The next game happened on a Tuesday. Athena pulled Achilles aside as they made their way to the bus. He yanked his arm out of her grip, staring up at her defiantly.

"Achilles," she said as gently as she could. "I know you want to play—"

He scoffed, hollow and disbelieving. "I *need* to play."

Athena glanced after the rest of the team as they started boarding the bus, laughing and chatting like nothing was wrong with the world. She sighed.

"I just think it would be better for you to rest." Achilles opened his mouth to protest, but she held up a hand. "Can you honestly tell me that playing in this game would be a good thing for you? I heard you almost failed your LA final."

Achilles stared at his coach, feeling those acid tears climbing up his throat. They came so easily now, ready to spill from his aching eyes.

"I *need* to play," he whispered, just to hide the fact that his voice broke.

Athena sighed, crossing her arms. *This isn't a good idea. He's so volatile.* But she couldn't prevent him. Not when he was staring at her, his face a stark image of disaster. He *was* a disaster. A complete and utter disaster of a boy.

"Fine." She caved in.

The boy in front of her let out a sigh of relief that trembled like a dying leaf. "Thank you," he said, his voice stronger now.

He turned away, and walked towards the bus. Athena pressed a hand to her forehead. Hopefully no one else died.

Helen and Paris were laying on his bed, staring up at the ceiling. They were a solid three feet apart, not touching. That was how they liked it. Ever since he had gotten back from the hospital, Helen found his presence somewhat comforting. He was quieter now, unsure of himself. The blinds were open, letting the afternoon light stream through the window. It cast a long rectangle across the bottom half of the bed that spilled onto the floor in a flood of something that felt like a dream.

They had just come back from school. Even though they lived in the dorms, Hecuba and Priam's house was so close. Besides, Andromache had been staying here ever since she found out about the baby.

Downstairs, Andromache and Hector were fighting. It had started the moment the four of them had walked through the door. Everything had been fine on the walk back. Hector had even had a decent day, which was more than they could say for the last *five* days. He kept spiraling. But now, as demonstrated by the yelling in the living room, he still didn't want to abandon the team.

"You need to *listen* to me!" Andromache was almost screaming.

Helen sighed.

Paris let his head fall in her direction. "You okay?"

"It's been a long... while," she said, trying to find faces in the stucco ceiling.

Paris laughed softly, looking back up. They had come to a kind of wordless agreement. Helen and Paris weren't a couple, but they could be an odd kind of friends. She wasn't quite sure when it had happened, but she liked it better this way.

"I don't belong here," Helen whispered. The duvet rustled as she readjusted herself. "These last few months have been..."

"Fucking weird," Paris finished.

Neither of them said anything for a long moment after that.

"Andromache." Hector's voice cut through the levels of the house. "You just don't *understand*—"

"Oh I *understand* just *fine,* thank you very much. It's just you who won't let go of something that—"

"No I'm literally their *leader,* babe—"

"Don't *babe* me—"

"I'm just trying to help—"

"That's a complete *lie!*"

Helen groaned and pulled the pillow around her ears, trying to block out the noise.

"They've never fought like this," Paris said, throwing an arm over his eyes. It was scary. Hector and Andromache never fought, period.

Helen swallowed. "They sound like my parents," she replied, still able to hear almost perfectly. She had learned a long time ago that the pillow trick didn't actually work.

"What is *going on?*" Priam demanded, apparently just getting home.

Everyone's voices quieted down after that. Helen let go of the pillow and looked over at Paris. He was already watching her, concerned.

She ignored it. Her past was her issue, and she wasn't saying anything about it. Not yet. Maybe not ever. "Are you going to play tonight?" she asked.

Paris grimaced, taking his time to answer. "I think I will. Especially if Andromache can't talk Hector out of it."

"Do you even like football?" Helen asked, watching the boy she used to absolutely despise.

He propped himself up on his elbows, looking out the window. Avoiding the question.

"Paris?" Helen asked again, raising her eyebrows.

Downstairs, the door opened and Hecuba's voice joined the indistinct conversation. Paris huffed, though it almost sounded like a laugh.

"No. I hate football," he said with a self–deprecating smile. "It's just that Hector plays, and my parents seem to think Hector's a freaking god or something, so... yeah. I play 'cause Hector said I should join and then my dad thought I should too."

Helen nodded. "Too bad we can't trade spots."

Paris looked down at her, a puzzled grin on his face. "And by that you mean...?"

"I always *wanted* to play, but Mycenae didn't let girls try–out, so I did cheer instead," she said with an exaggerated frown. "I did rugby last year though. That was fun."

Paris' eyes went wide. "*Really?*" he asked with a shocked laugh.

Helen grinned. "Yeah."

"Too bad you weren't here for tryouts," Paris said, laying back down. "There's a couple girls who practice with us. They don't play, but Mr. Phoebus had a whole thing about sexism in sports."

"It's *still* sexism in sports, because where's the *girl's* football team?" Helen pointed out.

Paris nodded. "Yeah, I guess so." He paused. "Man. That *is* rough. Why is the world so..."

"Dominated by men?" Helen suggested. "I dunno."

Paris paused again, looking over at her with a smirk. "I think I'd be a fine cheerleader. You'd definitely play *football* better than me."

⚜

The game that night was brutal. Hector ended up playing, much to the chagrin of Andromache. He brought Achilles' helmet with him, meaning to give it back. Apollo said it was a good reminder of who they were up against. Most of the team thought it was badass to have. He didn't end up returning it. Achilles was practically unstoppable that night, especially after he saw his old helmet on the Trojan's bench. Somehow, his loss had made him faster, more terrifying. Harder. Zeus watched the boy in some sort of awe. Thetis' son. What a miracle of genetics.

"That Hector's still on the field," Zeus noted as he watched the game.

Aphrodite and Ares were sitting with Zeus, Hera, Poseidon, who had, after Zeus' abrupt dismissal, refused to leave.

"He's the one who helped kill that other boy, right?" Hera asked primly, not taking her eyes off the field.

Zeus rolled his eyes. "Kids get away with *anything* these days," he muttered, not entirely pleased that the team he supported literally murdered someone.

He knew it hadn't been an accident. At least, not entirely. Apollo was their coach. No one would die by accident on the field with his meddling son as their leader. Poseidon jumped to his feet as shouting broke out on the field. Zeus looked down to see Achilles and Aeneas brawling, just out of the sidelines. (Achilles had started it when Aeneas tried to push him out. Aeneas was on edge, so he engaged, even though he knew he shouldn't.)

Posiedon vaulted out of the stands, onto the field, separating the two boys with an uncharacteristic sense of urgency.

"See?" Zeus said, looking around at the others. "Poseidon was the one to break that up! The refs are just coming over now! They get away with *anything*."

# XXI

"We're ditching tomorrow," Euphorbus said, pulling Hector aside in the changeroom after the game.

They had lost. The Trojans were no match for the Stallions with Achilles and his offense players. Hector, Euphorbus, and Glaucus couldn't carry the defense alone. Especially since Scarpedon tore his rotator cuff in the game where... yeah. Hector was up to his eyes in shit with Andromache already, so he sat down on one of the benches with a halfhearted shrug.

"Party at my place at like, seven, too," the other player added with a waggle of his eyebrows. "Celebrating the fact that you and me aren't locked up. Seniors only."

This made Hector monumentally uncomfortable, but he didn't have the energy to say no. It might be good to let go. Relax for a little while and ignore the world.

"Sounds good, man," he replied, holding up his fist.

Euphorbus smirked, nodding as he pounded their knuckles to-gether. "Epic."

The changeroom was quieter than usual. The team had gotten used to winning.

"See ya later," Antenor said, saluting to Hector on his way out.

"Have a good night," Hector replied.

Paris wandered over to his brother once the room had emptied. Hector was changed, staring down at his phone. He was mindlessly scrolling back and forth between the two pages of apps he had. Paris sighed to let Hector know he was there, dropped his bag on the floor, then sat down next to him. He didn't say anything when Hector ignored him. It had been like that since they were young, so he was used to it. (But it still stung.)

"Hey," Paris said after a solid minute.

The motion–censored changeroom lights went out, leaving the exit sign the only source of light besides Hector's phone.

Hector finally looked up. "What?" he asked, already frustrated. The red glow reflected in his eyes.

"I..." Paris wasn't sure what he had come over to say. "I think you should just stop," he decided on, which definitely wasn't the *right* thing to say. But when had Hector ever held back talking to *Paris*? Never. He was always ripping into his younger brother with brutal honesty.

"Not you too," Hector groaned, getting to his feet. "I'm not having this fucking argument again."

Paris thunked his head back against the locker behind him. "I just don't *understand*," he said as Hector aggressively grabbed his stuff. "You and Andromache have a future! You have someone who *really cares about you,* and you're throwing it all away for a stupid sport! We're losing now, so there's no point in holding on to the end. And... Hector, you could have ended up in fucking prison. Because of this. What matters more? The rest of your life, or a literal *game*?"

Hector had stopped moving. Paris wasn't sure when, but he just sighed, getting to his feet. It triggered the lights again, pulling them out of the red–stained darkness.

"Are you coming?" he asked, grabbing his bag from the floor.

Hector turned, his face frozen, looking like he'd just been slapped. He scratched the back of his neck. "Yeah."

As he followed Paris out, Hector tried to convince himself that his brother was wrong. Everything he said wasn't supposed to make sense. He was *Paris* of all people. He was *supposed* to be an idiot who could never amount to anything. But what he had just stated... was honestly what Hector had been debating. Why should he sacrifice his entire future for a game he didn't want to keep playing? For a game that had ended someone's life?

Outside, it was still muggy. The parking lot had mostly cleared, leaving Priam's car idling by the stadium doors. Helen, Andromache, and their mom had stayed home for obvious reasons. When they got in the car, Priam looked over his shoulder. He furrowed his brow when both sons got into the backseat. Paris frowned as well. Hector always got shotgun. (That was the rule. Unspoken, but still very real.)

"Are you alright?" Priam asked his oldest son.

Hector nodded slowly, staring off into the distance. "Yeah, fine," he said, not really paying attention.

"Oookay," Priam replied skeptically, turning back to the steering wheel.

As they drove away, Hector swallowed a lump in his throat. He would stop playing. He *wanted* to stop playing. But he'd go to that party first, and *then* tell people. He'd let them down later.

"Hey, Hector," his father said, looking at him through the rearview mirror. "I heard some rumours about a party tomorrow night?"

This got his attention. "Yeah?" Hector asked. His parents hadn't asked about anything he did for at least two years. They generally let him live his life, as long as he didn't get in *too* much trouble.

"I'd... really prefer if you didn't go," he said, like it pained him.

Paris looked over at his brother, eyes almost glowing in the darkness.

Hector laughed, frustrated. "I'm gonna go," he replied.

Priam sighed, but didn't press the issue any farther. He had just realized that he and his wife may have made a mistake. They had encouraged the stubborn streak in their son. It was causing him and those who loved him so much grief. He pushed up his shirt sleeves, and stared down the road. It would be fine. Hector would do what was right in the end. He always did.

Achilles trudged into the main hall of the school with the team. It was late now, around nine o'clock. Agamemnon had an arm thrown across Achilles' shoulders as the team celebrated. They had screamed, pretty much all the way back to school. Achilles' head was pounding. Finally, all he wanted to do was sleep.

"Good fight tonight, men!" Agamemnon yelled as the team started going their separate ways.

Odysseus started up one last rallying cry that echoed through the empty building as the Stallions football team split into groups, laughing into the night. Agamemnon finally let Achilles free, clapping him on the shoulder.

"Glad you're back," he said heartily.

Achilles didn't respond, instead drifting away towards the door they had just come in. As he left, he saw Briseis standing just outside, her arms crossed.

"What's up?" he asked, coming to a stop next to her.

She tried to smile at him, but it stopped short of her eyes. All the smiles did that around Achilles now.

"We have to go back to your dorm," she said quietly.

Achilles found himself doing something close to giggling. For some reason, a part of his brain found it funny to be going back to that room alone. Having to sort through all the stuff. All the memories and stories and moments that weren't coming back.

"One of the girls in our building reported you. Iphis and I will get expelled if they catch you again." Briseis added. She didn't know why she felt the need to say it, other than that she was bitter. Someone had sent an anonymous complaint to the dean of housing, apparently, that Briseis was smuggling her boyfriend into the girls' dorm every night. She had gotten a warning email, threatening that further action would be taken against her if any more suspicious activity was reported.

Briseis waited until Achilles had finished his wheezing giggling mess. His laughter ripped her slowly apart, and when he stopped, those holes stayed. It reminded her that she wouldn't find Patroclus in the dorm, or anywhere, ready to crack a joke or to pester her about a quiz.

Briseis swallowed, hooking her arm through Achilles' when he started walking. "We'll go together."

He stopped, his haunted eyes clouded with confusion.

"I'll come with you," she said, trying to sound brave. "And we can do it *together*."

And that they did. The two of them walked across the empty, darkening lawn, arm in arm. When they got to the dorm building, Achilles stopped. Briseis had to pull him to the elevator. If he wasn't ready now, he'd never be.

"I... don't think I can do this," Achilles whispered as they ground to a stop on the top floor. His voice was full of gravel and exhaustion. "I just want to sleep."

"I have a fucking bio exam tomorrow," Briseis replied, dragging Achilles after her. "And we need to. Iphis and I will get expelled if you stay with us anymore," she repeated. Achilles probably hadn't heard her the first time.

Achilles let himself be led. He didn't have the energy to resist. And part of him *wanted* to go in there. It would give him another reason to let the weights settle on his shoulders. The anger and the pain. All that he was made of, now.

Walking into his room was easy at first. Briseis was gripping his arm, anchoring him to the earth with a single thread. But then he took a breath.

It smelled like dust. Dust and Patroclus' shampoo.

And then he stopped breathing. Briseis flicked on a light, shedding a yellow glow across the mess that had been Achilles and Patroclus. Except for the folded clothes, some in boxes. The things on the bed had started getting sorted two weeks ago.

"Patroclus was..." Achilles whispered, only to break off. "He was trying to organize everything."

Briseis felt her throat constrict.

Grief was so funny. It came in debilitating waves, crashing over their heads in a tempest. But sometimes, Briseis forgot. She would laugh, and actually send Patroclus a text message. Four times, she had gotten the *account discontinued* message. And sometimes, grief hummed in the back of her mind, singing along with her every move.

And for Achilles, the storm didn't end. It lived in the corners of his vision, making a home in his stomach, coming to life whenever he tried to close his eyes. It poured gasoline on the fire, until it was roaring, screaming, bursting from his body. His mind played the same words, over and over and over and it wouldn't stop. *He's gone. Hector's fault. He's gone. Hector's fault. He's gone.* Achilles wanted to tear out his hair. Except he had shaved it off. There was constant itching in his fingers, an urge to break things. But there was also the need to collapse. To lay on the ground until he felt no more.

Somehow, they made their way over to the bed. The one without the half cleaned mess. Achilles laid down, his hands shaking again. They did that all the time now. He was unsteady. Briseis awkwardly eased herself down so she was facing him. Achilles had his eyes closed, the worn plaid blanket pressed to his face as water streamed down into it.

Briseis folded an elbow under her head, eyes prickling. In this room, Achilles and Patroclus' souls seemed to have made a symphony together. It felt so... wrong, to be here with one of them, when the other was gone.

"I wish I could... bring–him–back," Achilles found himself saying. "I...need him."

Achilles hadn't let himself cry in days. But it was there, hiding barely under the surface. His emotions wreaked havoc on his brain and his body. Briseis hated it when people cried. She didn't know how to help, or what to say, and she always cried too. Instead of talking, she shuffled down, wrapping her arms around Achilles' waist, pressing her face into his shirt. He tensed, then almost relaxed. But he couldn't. Not completely. His brain thrummed with dreams, plans, adventures that would never be had.

Needless to say, he didn't sleep.

At four in the morning, Achilles untangled himself from Briseis. She was asleep, breathing fitfully as he climbed out of the bed. He couldn't stay here. Not tonight. Not with someone else, even if she was just a friend trying to help.

He didn't fully know where he was going until he ended up beside the river. The stream. Whatever it was. They had sat here on the bank, about a month ago, and Achilles remembered. He had been safe. A home was never something Achilles was guaranteed. Between his mother, his father, and their constant agonies, he bounced around, not letting himself get too close to anyone. Until... Patroclus. Quiet, shy, detached, just like Achilles. He couldn't explain it. *Alone, together.* Those words seemed to fit well enough. That's how it had been in the beginning, at the very least.

The sun painted the sky with rose colored clouds, pulling the darkness towards the morning. It was quiet, except for the birds and the stream, eager to go somewhere. Achilles wanted to go somewhere. Anywhere that wasn't here. Because now... there was just alone. Again.

"But I wrote a song for you," Achilles found himself saying, hopelessly begging for some kind of answer.

Patroclus never got to hear it.

The forest answered Achilles with the twittering of birds and a ballad for the dancing river leaves. It answered him with echoes of a prettier past as the trees dropped their crimson garments. It answered him with memories that made his chest cave in, until he could barely breathe. Patroclus' medical bracelet was in the river. A piece of him, missing, lost, hidden in the water. Achilles wanted it back. He ached for it, even though it was horrible. It was everything wrong with the world. And then... Achilles was up to his knees in the frigid water before he had a chance to think.

He stopped in the middle of the stream, watching the current fight against him, trying to drag him under. For a moment, he thought about it. Just laying down and letting go. It would, in his imagination, have been very poetic. But he couldn't, even if it was all he wanted. Because Hector was still out there, living.

Achilles kicked the water, sending a small wave upstream. He wanted to scream. Everything trapped in him needed to get out. It scrambled to be first, tearing his throat to shreds. Without consciously deciding, he ran through the water, throwing it everywhere. He was still wearing his school uniform, but it didn't matter anymore. His life was... falling. Achilles opened his mouth and screamed until his throat tasted like iron. The river tried to take his pain. But there was too much. His hands were numb as he rooted through the rocky bottom of the stream, shaking and drenched. He fell to his knees, trying to find that *fucking* bracelet. It was probably gone. If it was gone, Achilles would just stay here.

But something glinted up at him from the rocky streambed. He laughed silently, pulling the little metal chain out of the water. Laughing made Achilles cough. And that hurt. But he didn't stop. At some point, he started sobbing. A mix of the highest of highs, and the lowest of lows. His mind wanted to give up, but his body kept going. Achilles punched the water with as much force as he could muster, wracked with guilt and hope and burning fury.

*Patroclus Menoitaides*

*Unknown Allergy,* the bracelet told him.

Achilles crawled half out of the river, and collapsed onto the bank, shuddering violently. He held the bracelet tight in one unfeeling fist, gasping for air. Hector was still out there. Achilles wasn't sure what he was going to do. But he couldn't let it go. The only way out of this miserable place was if he...

If Patroclus was still there, none of this would have happened. And Hector... well. He had killed the best, kindest, brightest person in the world. Achilles opened his eyes, staring up at the ever lightening sky. He never claimed to be good. He had no standard to uphold, besides ruthlessness. Achilles' head pounded. He needed to eat something. And to sleep.

He would rest when *Patroclus* had been laid to rest.

And that would be Hector had been dealt with.

# XXII

AT LUNCH, DIOMEDES SAT next to Odysseus and Agamemnon. They talked about football, because what else was there to think about? Their team was on the way to winning divisionals, and then they'd go to Austin, and hopefully nationals after that. Things were looking up, barring the fact that someone had... died. But Agamemnon didn't care about that. He put on a show for Achilles, purely because they needed him.

"Diomedes!" someone called from halfway across the cafeteria.

Every one of the football guys looked up. (Because they all operated on the same two brain cells.) Achilles had come running into the cafeteria, his pants dripping water. Briseis stood up abruptly from her table by the vending machine. She hadn't seen Achilles since the night before. He had just... disappeared, leaving her to panic all morning. And here he was, running in sopping wet at lunch after missing all of his morning classes. Achilles didn't even see her.

"What, Achilles?" Diomedes asked as the erratic boy slid to a stop in front of him.

"I need your bike," he rasped, eyes darting around frantically.

Diomedes looked up at him skeptically. What did Achilles want with his stolen motorcycle? And could he even *drive* it? "Do you even—"

Agamemnon stomped on his foot under the table. Diomedes inhaled sharply, then bit his tongue.

"Okay," Agamemnon said. "What do you need it for?"

Achilles kicked the leg of Diomedes' chair absentmindedly. "Do you know what Hector's doing today?"

The leap in topics threw Agamemnon for a second.

Odysseus leaned back so he could see Achilles. "Yeah, they're skipping and then there's a party at like. Seven."

Menelaus swallowed, watching Achilles with trepidation. "Why do you want Hector?" he asked, leaning over and trying to see what Achilles was fiddling with in his right hand.

Achilles looked up like he had been struck. "I... wanna talk to him."

"You know, you could just wait til' school's done," Ajax 2 offered. "I'll drive you."

"No," Achilles said, holding out his empty hand. It was shaking. "Keys?"

"Fine." Diomedes grumbled, glancing at Agamemnon resentfully as he rooted through his pocket.

Menelaus leaned forwards, peering over the edge of the table to see the silver bracelet hanging from Achilles' wrist. He could see the red medical symbol on it, but couldn't see the back. He wanted to ask why Achilles was carrying around an alert bracelet, but he didn't.

"If you see Helen," he said as Diomedes slammed the keys into Achilles' waiting palm. "Let her know I say hi."

Achilles' gaze flicked up for a moment, like he didn't realize anyone was even there. He gave a curt nod, then walked briskly out of the cafeteria. Menelaus took a deep breath, trying to assure himself that everything would be fine. He bit his bottom lip, picking at a soggy fry.

"Was that a good idea?" Ajax 1 asked, still staring after Achilles, who seemed to be having an argument with Briseis in the doorway.

Agamemnon shrugged, taking a giant bite of his sandwich.

"Does he even have his license?" Menelaus asked nervously.

Odysseus shook his head casually, like what he was implying *wasn't* extremely illegal. "But he know how to drive one. So it'll be fine. Whatever."

"I hope he clobbers that son–of–a–bitch," Agamemnon said, spitting a chunk of lettuce onto the table. "Hector fucking deserves a good beating."

"He said he was going to *talk* to him," Menelaus cut in as his brother picked up the lettuce and put it back in his mouth.

Odysseus and Diomedes snorted.

Agamemnon hit his head against the table, muttering, "You idiot."

Ajax 1 gave Menelaus a pitying smile. "Have you played football with that kid lately?" When Menelaus didn't reply, Ajax shook his head, sucking in air through his teeth. "Talking will probably turn into fighting." He paused, his brow furrowing. "Wait, doesn't Achilles have a car?"

Diomedes frowned, leaning away from the table to see if Achilles was still there. He was gone.

"He *does,*" Diomedes said, incredulous. "Why did he...?"

"How mysterious," Agamemnon replied sarcastically. "I don't care. Just give him what he wants 'til we win Divs."

Briseis followed Achilles back to... Agamemnon's dorm, worrying as he shoved the motorcycle keys in his pocket.

"Achilles," she tried for the third time. "You should let me come with you at least."

He didn't reply again. He didn't have the energy. There was one thing on his mind, and there was no way anyone could take it from him. This was his one chance to make sure Hector... paid. A tiny part of Achilles felt horrible for even thinking like that, but that part was dying. It had been pretty much dead, ever since Hector had... murdered his other half.

"No," Achilles almost snarled, turning around as they walked into the dorm building. "No, Bri, I have to do this on my own and I can't... I can't have you with me. You're not helping. "

She stopped, trying not to flinch. The look on her face almost made Achilles stop. The hurt spreading across her gentle features mimicked the pain inside him; a disgusted, writhing thing with a mind of its own.

"Just *go*," he whispered, his voice a horrible, savage thing.

Briseis' nostrils flared as she set her jaw. "Fine."

He didn't even watch her go. Without waiting, he spun on his heel and marched to the elevator. On Diomedes' keys was a strip of paper with the code to Agamemnon's building. Achilles didn't even think about what he had said to Briseis. He had one purpose now, but he needed something to numb himself. Agamemnon kept a stash of cans and bottles under his floor. Apparently, he and Diomedes had ripped up the floorboards themselves. Achilles' dorm didn't even have wooden floors. And he didn't usually drink.

In Agamemnon's room, he found what he was looking for, then downed more alcohol than he intended. It scalded his throat, coming back up like acid. He coughed, swallowing thickly. His stomach churned as he shoved the bottle back into its place and put the carpet down again.

Diomedes' stolen bike was parked a of couple blocks away. Achilles eventually made it, dully thinking about how he'd probably die if he drove. He honestly didn't care. It had been months since he had driven a motorcycle. Maybe even a year. Odysseus went through a phase when they were friends. They were going to get their licenses together, but Thetis had found out. That was the end of Achilles' motorcycle career.

Once he figured out how to start the thing, the memories came back. Slowly. Like nectar. He shoved the black helmet on his head.

It felt like a football helmet, just... with a glass grill. As he took off, the bike rumbled beneath him like a chariot. It was a strange feeling, the hot damp air bending around him as he flew down the city streets, onto the highway. In his ears, he could hear a ringing as his stomach flipped. He hadn't eaten anything. After about forty–five minutes, he had to stop and throw up on the side of the road. He lay there, in the dirty grass next to the bike, shaking. Everything hurt.

*They're wrong,* he thought as he tried to will the acrid burn from his throat, *when they say rock bottom is the lowest you can go.*

❧❧❧❧❧ ❦❦❦❦❦

Hector had snuck out of his house early, if only to avoid everyone's anger. Hell, even Paris was mad at him now. He sat on a picnic table in some park, with a box of cereal and a bottle of cheap whiskey. He was going to stop playing football. Today would be his last day as the captain of the Trojans. Hector wasn't quite sure if he was ready to accept that yet. By the early afternoon, he was halfway to being drunk, and three quarters of the way to being ready to tell Andromache. To start the rest of his life.

But one quarter of him was scared. He didn't want to stop. He *knew* that he was spiralling off the deep end, and if he kept going down this path, it would end in heartbreak. He took another sip from the bottle, savoring the way it burned his throat. The clouds slid sluggishly by, the warm wind carrying the red and yellow leaves to wherever they would end up. It was hot, the air pressing up against Hector like it couldn't get close enough. He swallowed thickly, his eyes aching. *Fucking concussion.*

His phone buzzed, falling from the edge of the table, where he had mindlessly placed it. When he picked it up, the screen was cracked. He swore under his breath, running his thumb along the fracture. And then he laughed roughly. The phone was breaking like Hector. That was what he was doing, sitting here, hiding from reality. But just for one day.

The message on his screen was from Euphorbus.

Euphorbus:

Just got up you feel like coming over?

*Sent 2:43 PM*

Hector laid down on the table. He didn't want to deal with the team, but he would tell them after the party. He squinted at his phone the sun, holding his phone over his head.

Hector:

Sure you need anything? for later?

*Sent 2:45 PM*

Euphorbus:

Nah were all good

*Sent 2:45 PM*

It took Hector several minutes to make himself get up. The sun beat down on him. He rolled onto his side, pushing himself to his feet as he collected his bottle and his cereal. The whiskey was about a third gone. The cereal box was empty. He walked through the park, passing through meek shade from a sparse tree. When he got into his car, the air pressed his shirt to his body, everything damp. He pressed his hands into his eyes. *I shouldn't drive*, he thought. And then he put the keys into the ignition.

It wasn't far.

That night, Euphorbus' house was full. Of course it wasn't just seniors. It was the senior players, plus everyone they wanted to invite.

"Where's Andromache?" Antenor yelled over the noise. "I haven't seen her much!"

Hector was so drunk he could barely stand. He just laughed at the other player's question. Andromache would hate this. She *hated* it when Hector was drunk. She said something about unbridled aggression and cruelty.

Euphorbus hopped awkwardly over to them, spilling his drink all over the floor. The three of them giggled, holding each other up as Euphorbus stumbled into them.

"Hey hey hey," Euphorbus slurred, a lazy smile on his face as he righted himself. "I wanna... make an announcement. With you," he said, jabbing a finger into Hector's chest.

Hector nodded, letting his head spring back up violently. "Kay. Cool."

Euphobus gave him a thumbs up, spilling more from his cup. He turned around, and smashed the lightswitch for the living room on and off a few times. The noise quieted as people were distracted from their dancing and... other preoccupations. Euphorbus grabbed Hector's arm and pulled him in.

"Hey!" he yelled. "Attention, *please*!"

Someone whistled as Euphorbus dragged Hector onto the wooden coffee table. It was littered with plastic cups, some of which fell off the table spilling their contents onto the floor. Hector laughed at that too. They had rolled up the carpets that afternoon.

"We're here!" Euphorbus announced, gesturing broadly, nearly hitting Hector in the face.

This was met with a chaotic cheer that bled into the pounding music.

"But!" he cried, stumbling a little. Someone in front of him moved to catch him. Euphorbus gave them a winning smile as he stopped himself from falling. "We're here because we aren't in *jail*!"

People laughed at this, whooping.

Euphorbus joined in, almost manic. "We *killed someone* and—"

"We're above the law!" Hector bellowed, a grin on his face.

That was taken up as raucous chant. Someone turned up the music just as the beat dropped. The lights flashed blue, purple, red. In that moment, Hector felt profoundly powerful. There wasn't rhyme or reason to it. Just a slow motion moment that seemed to last an hour. On top of the world. Someone pulled Hector off the table and he was absorbed into the moving crowd as it chanted his name.

Outside, Achilles sat on the curb, the visor his helmet flipped up. It was nine thirty. He had fallen asleep beside the road, but he had finally made it. Diomedes' bike was propped up next to him as he listened to the cheering inside. Hector's name. He could hear it, almost as if he were in the crowd. It echoed through his head. *Hector.* He ground his teeth together. *Hector.* His eyes were pounding in time with the music. *Hector.*

Achilles abruptly stood. Before he could think, he walked across the dark street, stopping on the driveway of the house. A couple of people on the lawn looked over at him, their faces hidden in the night. Achilles didn't even notice them. *Hector.*

"HECTOR," Achilles screamed, his voice tearing pieces out of his throat. "*HECTOR!*"

His mouth tasted of iron and acid. He felt nothing.

The door opened, vomiting three people out onto the patio. They were laughing, stumbling as a crowd gathered behind them.

The people on the lawn had all disappeared. Scared. Achilles wasn't there to fuck around.

"Who's there?" Hector asked, leaning sloppily against the porch rail.

Achilles walked across the lawn, standing just beyond the circle of light from inside. His feet made no sound.

"I think you know," he said softly. He couldn't talk any louder.

Hector didn't know. He was too far gone to think about Patroclus' last words. He was too far gone to realize this wasn't a joke. He was too far gone to understand. Instead, he looked over his shoulder at Euphorbus, who just laughed.

Antenor leaned over, next to Hector. "We're just celebrating how Hector tamed the fucking Stallions," he said with a wicked grin. "Killed one too."

Hector whooped, body checking Euphorbus. They both stumbled, unaware of how Achilles' shoulders knotted. How he sucked in his breath and didn't exhale.

"C'mon," Achilles said, fighting against the knife in his throat. "Get on a bike."

The three boys paused. Hector scoffed.

"You wanna race?" he asked, smirking as he put his drink down roughly on the rail.

Achilles shrugged. "Or play chicken."

That sent the three of them howling again, pounding each other on the back. Achilles wished he could just strangle Hector right there. He could barely stand. He felt like he was on fire.

When Hector calmed down, he looked over at the kid with the motorcycle helmet. He was standing still as a statue.

"I'll go with you," someone new said in Hector's ear.

He glanced over his shoulder, eyebrow raised. His other cousin, Deiphobus, was standing there, a reassuring smile on his severe face.

Hector smiled back. "Let's go kick some ass," he whispered, then turned back. "Fucking fine," he declared. "C'mon kid."

He vaulted off the porch, falling farther than he expected. His knees buckled, but he caught himself before he went face first into the grass.

Achilles didn't react. He just walked over to his bike and started it up.

"Euphorbus!" Hector called. "Keys!"

The other boy saluted and ran haphazardly inside. Achilles flipped down his helmet's visor and revved his engine, one, two, three times.

Hector flipped him off. "Be patient, asshole!"

"Gotchyou!" Euphorbus yelled, throwing the keys to his bike at Hector.

Hector almost caught them, but they slipped through his fingers at the last moment. He swore and picked them up, grabbing a few strands of grass along with them. He looked over his shoulder to see Deiphobus give him a thumbs up. Hector wondered for a moment when his cousin had gotten there, but quickly moved on when Achilles pumped the engine again.

"Coming," Hector grumbled, jogging over to the bike on the driveway.

Achilles peeled away, down the residential street. Getting ready to face off. Hector laughed, getting onto the motorcycle and twisting the key in the ignition. It roared to life beneath him, rumbling. He waited for Deiphobus to get on behind him, but he didn't. When he looked around, his cousin was nowhere to be found.

"What the...?" he muttered under his breath, frowning.

Achilles' bike lights flashed a long way down the road. Euphorbus' house was on the outskirts of town, so only one side of the street had houses. There was a field to Hector's left, bordered with an old barbed wire fence. Most of it had fallen, and people liked to go there to make out. The grass was waist high. It seemed to whisper to him as he pulled away from the driveway.

"Hey!" Hector yelled. "You ready?"

The bike across from him revved in response. Hector's heart pounded in his ears and throat, muffled. He could feel his blood in his veins. But the part of his brain that had good judgment was... gone. For the night, at least. He smiled and replied to the mystery rider's call, roaring his engine in answer.

Looking over his shoulder, he saw that no one was outside anymore. Probably distracted by some excitement inside. No one would even see this. Hector sighed, turning back and starting to inch down the road, towards the other rider. The bike tires rolled against the pavement, popping over the gravel.

As soon as Hector started forwards, Achilles mirrored him. He could feel his blood singing as he pulled ahead. The wind whistled past him as his bike jolted, lurching towards Hector. The Trojan captain did the same. They were about three hundred meters apart, head on as they went faster faster faster faster faster—

And faster. Closer.

The bikes were so close—

The engines roared in Hector's ears—

He could see his own reflection in the other rider's helmet—

His face was distorted—

Wind.

Fear—

He jerked, veering away, moments before the collision.

His bike flew off the side of the road.

*Oh shit*—

His body tensed as gravity fell away.

And then... nothing.

Achilles didn't see it happen. He barely even heard the crash over his roaring engine. But when he did hear it, Achilles skidded to a stop. He had expected them to collide. But Hector... where was he? This was supposed to make everything okay. They were *both* supposed to be gone... but Hector. Achilles jumped off his bike, not caring whether it fell. It crunched as Achilles ran back. Hector's motorcycle was still running. It screamed into the night, tires spinning in empty air. But Hector wasn't there. Achilles wasn't breathing. His head pounded as he scrambled down the short incline, towards the field. The motorcycle lights barely illuminated the body lying crumpled over the fence. Achilles ripped his helmet from his head, retching again.

Fuck.

Hector… wasn't moving. His limbs were at the wrong angles. And… he caught in the barbed wire. Achilles' stomach clenched, but there was nothing there. He was shaking again, his body fighting against him. Hector was obviously dead. Achilles had killed him. No no no no no no no no… Achilles tried to swallow. He couldn't. He wanted to lay down and die. But he couldn't. He had killed Hector. And Achilles was still alive.

Before he really understood what he was doing, Achilles was dragging Hector up the grass. It took a bit of effort to pull him off the wire. He tried to ignore the dark trail the body left on the pavement. His ears were filled with white noise. It drowned out any proper thoughts. Just panic. And pain. Patroclus would hate this. He would have… nope. But he *couldn't*. He wasn't here.

Achilles found a rope in the back of Diomedes' bike, and heaved it onto its tires. He mechanically tied Hector's feet together. And then tied the rope under the fender. He walked back over to where Hector's bike was running. He picked up his helmet, and found Hector's phone laying in the grass. He looked in the case. He found Hector's address on his drivers license. He shoved his helmet back on his head. He walked back to the bike. He accidentally looked at Hector's face, bloody, bruised, a complete disaster. He almost had to take the helmet off again, because of the acid that burst into his mouth. He swallowed. He convinced himself to get onto the bike.

He nearly tipped over. He didn't want to drive. But he did.

At eleven thirty, Helen, Paris, Andromache, Priam, and Hecuba were finishing Monopoly. Helen won. Everyone was laughing, smiling, not thinking about Hector. Priam's oldest son had caused so much pain in the family as of late, but he wasn't there. They could have fun without him. Hector was stubborn, but he always came around. He knew what was best for everyone in the end.

"Does anyone need anything?" Hecuba asked, handing Priam her pile of hundreds. "Priam and I are going to stay and watch something, if you want."

Andromache got up with a smile and a shake of her head. "I'm just going to the bathroom."

She walked over to the front of the house, disappearing into the kitchen.

Helen slumped dramatically against Paris' shoulder. "You don't happen to have Oreos, do you?"

"Of *course* we have Oreos!" Hecuba said, like not having oreos was the worst thing in the world. "When Andromache told me they were your comfort food, I bought a whole stash."

"How did I not know about that?" Helen demanded, scandalized as she got to her feet.

Priam smiled over at his wife. A motorcycle roared outside.

Hecuba rolled her eyes. "Small dick energy—"

Andromache screamed.

Everyone's faces blanched collectively. Hecuba jumped to her feet, rushing towards the bathroom only to almost be bowled over as Andromache burst out of the kitchen. She stumbled to the front door, throwing it open. The motorcycle came back. Priam felt his heart in his throat as he got up and ran to where Andromache was standing. Helen and Paris followed, sharing wild–eyed looks.

Andromache started sobbing. She couldn't breathe. There wasn't enough oxygen. The motorcycle out on their street, driving in circles, was dragging someone behind it. The streetlights illuminated the face. A bloody mess. Andromache found herself trying to scream. Nothing came out. Someone grabbed her and bundled her against their chest. Paris caught one glimpse of what was happening outside and ran upstairs. Helen almost threw up. She followed him.

Hecuba stood, white faced and unmoving, watching as the body of her oldest son was dragged along the road behind a motorcycle. Priam held Andromache, trying to calm her. He could feel tears burning through his shirt. The person on the motorcycle pulled onto their lawn, dragging Hector behind him. No one moved as he untied the rope, leaving the body on the front lawn. Hector. Priam stared not at his son, but at the person getting back onto the motorcycle. His shoulders were rigid, but Priam could see his hands shaking. Priam's throat constricted as Andromache let out another audible cry, muffled by his shirt.

As the rider peeled away, Hecuba ran down the steps, collapsing by her son's body. Her boy. Her son. Her Hector. He was so stubborn. So serious. Always the voice of reason. Priam watched his wife beg with whatever power higher than herself, to please, please bring back her son. That parents aren't supposed to outlive their children.

Neighbors stepped out of their houses, sticking their heads out windows. All the noise must have woken them.

"How could he?" Andromache whispered, so softly that Priam could barely hear her. "How *could* he?"

Hecuba let out a soft cry that turned to heaving sobs. Someone called the police. They showed up and took Hector's body. Andromache eventually went to the couch, where she buried her face in the cushions and refused to talk to anyone. Paris came downstairs, said Helen was sick, and went back up. His face had aged years already, but neither of his parents noticed. Hecuba wouldn't even acknowledge her youngest son. Hector was gone. Dead. He was supposed to live. Priam patted Paris on the back when he briefly appeared, but otherwise... he didn't matter. His older brother was dead, and he was still the second favorite.

Priam answered the questions the police asked. He managed to hold it together until midnight, long after Hecuba had sobbed herself to sleep. And when he was so tired that his eyes started sticking, he finally let it in. His son was dead. Hector. Dragged around on the road, behind a motorcycle. Priam wondered who the rider was. It didn't matter, really. Because there was no future where he would have a complete family. All he had was a past.

Hector wouldn't ever meet his son, or get to propose. He wouldn't go to university or buy a house or move away. He was relegated to memory. And the last memory of Hector would be the horrible, searing image of his broken body being dragged across the pavement.

# XXIII

ACHILLES DIDN'T REMEMBER GETTING back to the dorm. His memory kicked back in when he pulled into the parking lot, drenched in cold sweat, his hands sticky. The buzzing of his phone was what jolted him into his body again. The motorcycle was parked, and he had apparently just removed his helmet, because it was in his hands. He was still shaking. Hector was dead. And Achilles was here. The thought made him... ache. On a level he had never hurt before.

He inhaled, his lungs wishing they could stop. He put Diomedes' helmet on the seat of the bike, and checked his phone. It was his mother. Achilles swallowed, and then answered. He never ignored her calls.

"Achilles?" Thetis asked tightly.

He looked up at the sky, the air making his throat hot. "Hey. Did you need something?"

"I'm just calling you to let you know we're going to have your... friend's funeral on Thursday. In two days. Well." She paused, computer keys clacking on her end of the call. "Less than that."

Achilles squeezed his eyes shut.

"Achilles?" Thetis asked again, her tone a half–step softer.

He rubbed a hand over his face. "Yep."

"It will be at the funeral home in your area, called Gates to Elysium. He will be buried there too, after he's cremated."

Achilles kicked a pile of gravel that had gathered on the concrete. There was no anger in him now. Just... a ringing. It was agony.

"But I need you to do something for me," Thetis was saying. "I need you to order flowers from the funeral home website, okay?"

"I..." he started, stopping to clear his throat. "Yeah. I can do that."

"For Thursday afternoon," Thetis all but repeated.

Achilles nodded. "Okay. I can. Do that."

There was a long, stretching silence, as wide as a canyon. Achilles could hear his own breath trembling through the phone.

"Thanks," he whispered.

This was what Thetis had been waiting for. "You're welcome," she replied, the smile obvious in her voice as she hung up.

Achilles stood there, in the darkness, holding his phone to his ear and listening to the nothingness. He had no purpose. He was a failed pottery project. He was so *alone*.

"Patroclus?" he said hoarsely, finding the single star that twinkled in the sky.

There was no answer. He hadn't expected one. Achilles let out a breath as he stumbled over to the dorm. Memories of Hector bubbled up like tar, trying to coat every surface. How his body had dragged along the pavement. The way someone in his house had screamed. How Hector's mother had run out onto the lawn with no regard for what anyone thought. And the feeling of blood, staining Achilles' hands.

He ran the rest of the way, across the grass, into the lobby, trying trying trying to pretend everything was okay. At the very least, okay. But it wasn't. Patroclus was dead. Achilles had just dragged someone's literal corpse behind a motorcycle. He was falling apart at the seams, and the horrible thing was... he couldn't make himself *care.* None of it mattered. Achilles was sure, so sure that he was just going to die. Someday soon, he would drop dead, and no one would cry over him. But it wouldn't matter. Because he'd be with Patroclus again.

Achilles skipped the elevator, instead bounding shakily up the emergency exit stairwell. The alarms had stopped working before he had even come to Mycenae Academy. He used to like running up and down the stairs in the morning. But now... he just wanted to get back to his room. He burst into his hallway with a vengeance, sprinting as hard as he could. Stopping himself would have taken a bit of time, but he grabbed the handle on his dorm, swinging into the room.

The door slammed shut behind him as he catapulted onto the floor. Achilles landed on his side, his ribs bursting into a pulsing ache. It helped him breathe. But the room still smelled like Patroclus. And it was covered in Patroclus' things. Achilles started shaking again as he tried to push himself up, off the floor. He needed to get the blood off his hands.

Achilles' body was giving up on him, pleading with him, *'sleep sleep please you need to stop,'* as he stumbled into the bathroom and ran his hands under the scalding water. His hands turned red, itchy, irritated, but he didn't stop. Even when the last of the blood flaked off, spiraling down the drain in a horrible dance. He felt sick. Again. But there was nothing in him, so he swallowed the acid in his throat, his eyes sticking on a note that had been taped to the mirror, so long ago.

Patroclus' neat handwriting.

*Today, I will release things that are out of my control*

He had loved that stupid saying. Achilles finally turned off the water, his hands dripping all over the tile floor as he left the bathroom. His eyes felt three sizes too big for his head as he picked his way over the... things he had thrown on the floor yesterday. in a fit of that now faraway anger. He should order those flowers for the funeral. But even thinking about it made him want to curl up in a ball and lock himself in the bathroom.

In a flurry of desperation and everything he couldn't name, Achilles started rooting through the mess bed. Once his arms were full, he wrenched open the door, *things* spilling from his arms. Onto the carpeted hall of the dorm. He stumbled into the main room and threw everything down on the couch. Back and fourth and back and fourth, body shaking, mind blurred. He ripped a piece of paper out of a binder. Scrawled *please, take this shit fight over it i don't care i'm done seeing it.* Left the note on top of the pile.

The room was a mess. Achilles went to kick a little stuffed bear that he had won at some carnival years ago, but he stopped. Bent down. Picked it up. Swallowed. Sat down on the mess bed. The springs creaked. Achilles *did* curl up in a ball, mostly to avoid some of the half packed boxes, but partially for comfort. This was how he slept as a kid. He needed to escape as he clamped his eyes shut, pulling the stuffed bear to his chest.

Sleep washed over him faster then he knew what to do with. The only option was to give in.

"Hey," someone whispered, their breath tickling Achilles' ear. "Achilles."

He stirred, confused. That voice... was more familiar than his own. His heart lurched into his throat as his eyes opened slowly. Achilles blinked against the light. For some reason, it didn't burn. A face leaned over, blocking the light. Brown curly hair, almost black. Kind eyes, crinkled at the corners. Soft smile, so gentle it hurt.

Achilles felt his mouth fall open. His vision blurred with tears.

"But you—"

"Shh," Patroclus said, his face drenched with tenderness. "I know."

Achilles rolled onto his side, his forehead resting against Patroclus' knees. Half his face was pressed into soft grass. He couldn't breathe. Patroclus. Was here.

"You shaved your head," Patroclus laughed fondly, running a hand over the short, blonde hair. "You said you'd never do that."

Achilles felt his shoulders shaking in gentle sobs. "I'm–sorry," he rasped, digging his nails into his palms.

The other boy laughed softly again. It dragged ropes of yearning around Achilles' throat. He felt like he was being buried alive.

"I miss... you," Achilles whispered into the grass, feeling a line of saltwater fall from the tip of his nose. "I love you. I *need* you."

"Achilles," Patroclus answered, no longer laughing. "I love you."

"But...?" Achilles asked miserably.

Patroclus reached down and put a hand on Achilles' face. He looked up, hating the sad smile on the brown haired boy's face.

"I need you to let me go," he replied, his voice almost inaudible.

It felt like the ground had been yanked out from beneath them. Achilles opened his mouth to say something else, but Patroclus pressed a finger to his lips.

"We'll be together again," Patroclus said, trying to reassure. "Just not quite yet."

Achilles laughed bitterly, surprising himself. "Not yet," he repeated. "I'm not whole without you."

"And I'm not whole without you," Patroclus answered sadly, his brow furrowing a little. "But we'll just have to be broken for awhile."

Achilles found he couldn't say anything. Patroclus pressed their foreheads together for a long moment that Achilles wished could last for eternity. But then he stood, and walked away, leaving Achilles laying in the grass...

He bolted upright, back in his room again, heart trying to tear itself out of his chest.

"Patroclus—" he found himself saying, only to stop.

The room was empty. Achilles was sleeping with a ghost. Or maybe his mind was just in so much distress. No. Oh Gods. Achilles ran his feeble hands over his head, digging his nails into his skull. He was shaking and shaking and shaking. Patroclus was gone. Hector was dead. Achilles had fallen off the deep end.

❧ ☙

No one left Priam and Hecuba's house on Wednesday. Andromache wouldn't stop crying. Hecuba sat with her in the basement, trying to calm her down. Helen could hear Andromache screaming even though she and Paris were locked in the bathroom on the top floor. Neither of them said much. They had been up all night. Hecuba and Priam had tried to go to bed, but Andromache started throwing up at two in the morning. Helen's stopped throwing up at around one. She had Paris with her anyways. He was sitting on the lip of the tub, his chin resting on his hands.

"Do you need anything?" Helen asked, her voice hoarse.

Paris exhaled, threading his fingers restlessly through his hair. "I... don't know."

He couldn't believe that *body* on the lawn had been Hector. Their dad had *told* Hector to stay home from that fucking party, but of course he went and now he was dead.

"Secretly, I always thought it would be easier if he died," Paris whispered, guilt sewn deeply into his words. "And now... I know I was really wrong."

Helen nodded from where she was sitting on the bathmat, across from the toilet. Paris brought in blankets the night before, and they were all piled in front of the door, in a weak attempt to block out the noise. Andromache was still sobbing.

"I'm an idiot," Paris muttered, shaking his head.

Helen couldn't wholeheartedly disagree, so she shrugged. "I think we all are, sometimes."

Paris grabbed a towel and threw it around his shoulders. "Hector loved to point out my specific idiotic qualities."

"That doesn't mean you have to be glad he's dead," Helen replied, looking over at him.

Paris laughed. It was a fake laugh that crumbled to tears on the edges. He was hurting. And his parents hadn't even checked in on him. That was why Helen was there, on some level. She rested her head against his knee.

"I'm sorry," she said with a shaky sigh. "I wish things could be okay."

He snorted. "That's the goal, isn't it."

Someone knocked on the door.

"Come in," Helen said quietly, sitting up.

The door shoved the pile of blankets out of the way, letting some of the stylish black tile peer through.

Priam poked his head in. "Just making sure everyone's alright," he said in a fatherly way.

Paris hated that tone. Especially when he had never, ever been on the receiving end of it. Until Hector went and fucking died. He exhaled.

"Anything else?" Helen asked, wiping rapidly at her eyes as they tried to spill tears again.

Priam ran a hand over his abundant grey hair, staring down at the floor as he leaned on the doorframe.

"*What*, Dad?" Paris snapped, leaning on his elbows.

"Drunk driving accident," Priam managed, his voice snapping like kindling on a fire. "They couldn't find anything about... the motorcyclist."

Helen clapped a hand over her mouth.

"Apparently he... went off the side of the road, into a barbed wire fence. Our Hector was a brave kid—"

"Shut up. Shut up, shut *up!*" Paris interrupted, jumping to his feet, his face curdled with rage. "You never loved me like you loved him so *quit* talking about his horrible death like he died saving the entire Godsdamn *country*! He was a teenager! A stupid teenager, who wasn't better than anyone else! Your *beloved, brave* son was *average!*"

The bathroom rung with the weight of Paris' words. Helen had both hands over her mouth now, tears streaming down her face. Priam gaped at his second son, frozen in place.

"And you weren't the only ones who loved him!" Paris continued, getting louder and louder as he spoke. "I know you think I'm *so* subpar, because I'm not a hulking beast, but Hector and I were *brothers!* We used to talk when we were younger! We grew *up* together, and just because I'm not *him* and just because we didn't always get along doesn't mean I don't *miss him!*"

Priam had never heard his son speak this much, with so much emotion. Paris' hands were clenched into fists, tears spilling from his eyes.

"Sometimes," Paris said, softly now. "Hector was all I had. And now I'm alone." He sat down heavily, the tub rattling.

Helen hid her face in her hands. She hated it when people she cared about were in pain. She hated it when she got trapped in the middle of things. She hated the whole world, for what it had done to this poor, poor family.

The door closed. There was a long beat of silence. Until Paris started laughing. Softly at first, bitterly, under his breath. Helen looked up at him as he threw his head back, laughing at the ceiling. It was the kind of laugh that dragged rusty nails through her insides. But Helen couldn't help it. She started giggling into her fist. Paris looked at her, his face alight with fury and helplessness and irrational joy. They howled together until their stomachs hurt. Until they could barely breathe. Until they started crying.

Grief was funny that way. It deranged them, picking them apart at the seams, and sewing them back together in the way that was best for survival.

On the morning of Patroclus' funeral, Thetis, who was organizing the chapel, got a surprise. Not necessarily an unpleasant one. Just... one. The flowers started showing up at nine thirty. She assumed that they would stop, but they just kept coming. Soon, the stage was covered, and they had to put the abundant blossoms by the seats and in the lobby. Harried and strung-out, Thetis directed the people who brought them. She accepted full responsibility for the disaster. She had asked her son to get them, knowing full well that he wasn't back to any kind of normal stability yet.

When the flower catastrophe had been dealt with, it was past one in the afternoon. Thetis collapsed into one of the pews, her nose running. She must have been allergic to one of the many varieties of flowers her son had ordered. *How much did that all cost?* Thetis wondered sullenly as she rubbed her eyes.

"Mom?" someone who was obviously Achilles called from the back of the chapel. "Do you need anything?"

He sounded tired. Thetis honestly didn't care. She looked over her shoulder, across the rows of wooden pews. Achilles was indeed standing in the entrance, which was half blocked by the cascading white arrangements that had been placed there. He looked like a painting, frozen there in between the flowers he had bought.

"How much did those flowers cost?" Thetis asked instead of answering his question.

She could see her son's blush from where she sat, right by the stage.

He scratched the back of his neck. "I thought flowers would be better than sacrificing people…"

Thetis sighed, turning back to the stage. (Disturbingly enough, she wouldn't doubt if that was sincerely her son's thought process.) People would probably start arriving at two so they could mingle in their sadness. Achilles was apparently skipping school. Again. She had gotten several calls notifying her of his absence. But it didn't matter. He was a lost cause. The school had said he barely interacted with his peers anymore, didn't participate in class when he was there, and that his grades were quickly declining towards miserable. It was fine. Thetis had another son. Achilles was Peleus' only descendant, but she didn't care about that. Her ex–husband had no idea how to deal with a stable son, let alone one who… even *thought* of sacrificing people for his friend.

Thetis looked back again, only to find the doorway empty of everything but flowers. Achilles wandered aimlessly into the small lobby. The roses and hydrangeas made him smile a little as he dragged his feet across the short, patterned carpet. Patroclus' body was here somewhere. Waiting to be burned. Achilles wanted to let go. He *wanted* Patroclus to be happy and free, but how could he let go of the boy who kept his feet on the ground? Achilles sat down on the floor in front of a couch. He hadn't talked to anyone since… Hector. He was too afraid. Briseis would hate him. Iphis didn't even really like him to begin with. They had only stuck around out of loyalty to the dead. Slowly, they would drift apart until Patroclus' memory was the only thing that tied them together.

*No,* Achilles thought, resting his chin on his folded arms. *I will not cry. I can be okay.*

The cynical voice in his head laughed. (It was honestly right.) Achilles knew he could pretend, but there was this deep–seated agony bubbling in the pit of his stomach. He still couldn't make himself eat. He was losing weight and his voice permanently sounding like sandpaper. That was another thing Briseis would chide him about. He didn't want to be cared for like a child.

Eventually, people started making their way into the funeral chapel. Achilles watched, his face expressionless, as Patroclus' mother walked in, her hands clenched tight around her clutch purse. She hadn't protected him when he needed it. She had let him go. She had no right to be at his funeral. But there she was, standing awkwardly by the door. Achilles' father stepped in behind her, laying a gentle hand on her shoulder. She flinched. Patroclus used to do that. Achilles bit his bottom lip. Peleus whispered something in her ear before spotting Achilles. He left her to her timid wall-flowering.

Achilles felt the couch sink with his father's weight against his back.

"Hey champ," Peleus said sympathetically, ruffling Achilles' nonexistent hair. "How're you holding up?"

"Fine," Achilles lied.

Briseis and Iphis walked through the door then, followed by Automedon, Antilochus, Menelaus and the Ajaces. Achilles fought the urge to hide. Instead, he offered a weak wave. Briseis' face lit up momentarily, as if she forgot the seriousness of the occasion, running over awkwardly in her lacy black dress.

She dropped down next to Achilles and pulled him to her. "I haven't seen you in *days*," she said angrily into his ear. "Stop disappearing on me like that."

He nodded, noticing she smelled like flowers. Briseis let go of him, then waved over her shoulder at Peleus, who smiled.

"I'm glad you all could make it," Peleus said, dusting off his pants as he got to his feet. "Patroclus was a lovely boy."

"Hear hear," Iphis agreed with a tight smile as Peleus walked off into the gathering crowd.

The service started at three thirty. Odysseus, Agamemnon, and Diomedes all made it, sitting in the pew behind the rest of the students. Achilles hadn't wanted to go to the front. He tried to tune the whole thing out. The service. Briseis clutched his hand tightly until it fell asleep and then long after. A few people got up to speak. Teachers. One of the librarians. Peleus. They all talked about Patroclus' ambition and goals. About his drive and dedication and kindness and gentle spirit. No one talked about how he died. Achilles couldn't stop thinking about him, alone in the hospital. He clenched his jaw. He didn't cry.

The room smelled of flowers. Almost sickly sweet. Just like the stupid background music in the slideshow of pictures. Nine out of ten photos had Achilles in them, smiling broadly, one arm thrown carelessly across Patroclus' shoulders. People would say Patroclus' smile was soft. Gentle. But Achilles knew it was secretive. He thought of all the secrets Patroclus carried to the grave. Now,

Achilles would carry them too. They'd never hold hands in public. They'd never get married. They'd never find somewhere they could just be themselves. They had been stuck here all their lives, hiding. And now they would never escape.

Peleus was on stage again. People turned over their shoulders, looking at Achilles. He straightened, afraid he'd missed something.

"Achilles?" his father asked. "Do you want to say a few words to end us off?"

No. He didn't. But... he owed it to Patroclus. For someone to say something deeper than surface level. Briseis released Achilles' hand, giving him a nod of encouragement. Her eyes were red, her face streaked with tears. Iphis gave him a thumbs up. Achilles' gaze strayed for a moment, down to their joined hands. He tore himself away from the things he'd never have, walking slowly up the aisle.

The carpeted stairs creaked as he jumped up, skipping the middle step. He turned to face the audience, standing next to his father. These people... all cared about Patroclus. And they were here to mourn him. But they didn't know him like Achilles did. He pressed his palms into his eyes until he saw colors. Peleus put a paternal hand on his shoulder. All it did was push Achilles farther away from reality. He exhaled, stuffing his hands in his pockets.

"Hey guys," he said, doubting anyone could hear his rasping voice. It didn't matter anyways. "Patroclus... well." Achilles laughed bitterly. "He was my best friend. More than that." Briseis made eye contact with Achilles, holding it calmly. He breathed. "I'd burn this place to the ground for him," he said with a sly smile that felt like a ruse. "And the funny thing is... I think we were meant to meet. We just sort of. Completed each other. Now I feel a bit lost without him telling me that the voices in my head are just that. Voices. Or to give me a reason to get up in the morning. Or to tell him the jokes that only he'd get. Or to let me copy his science worksheets." This drew a laugh from the crowd.

"I just..." Achilles broke off to hide the crack in his voice. "I miss him," he finished. Then, as an extra thought added, "When I die, I want our ashes together. In the same urn." Peleus frowned, but didn't say anything. Achilles stared out at the sea of people. "And that's all," he finished softly.

After Achilles left the stage, the service ended. There was time to... go view the body before it got cremated. Thetis had insisted, so Patroclus' parents, if they chose to come, could say goodbye. The single file line into the tiny room was short. Achilles made sure he stood at the end. Briseis went before him. She didn't know what she expected, but she *had* thought it would be less... awful. Patroclus' skin was pale, his eyes shut. She didn't go any closer than she had to.

"Rest well," she whispered, three feet back from the coffin. Her eyes prickled uncomfortably, tears blurring her vision. "You deserve it."

Achilles caught the last bit as Briseis walked briskly from the room, into Iphis' arms. His hands started convulsing when he saw Patroclus, his body almost as if it were wax. Unlike Briseis, he crossed the room, until he was standing with his hip bones against the wooden side of the coffin. He stacked his fists on the edge, resting his forehead on them.

"I'm sorry," he whispered, bile rising in his throat. "Patroclus I... killed Hector. It's my fault he's dead and it's my fault you're dead and I can't keep living like this." He paused, letting his shoulders heave once. "I can't keep living like this."

Again, no answer. Just dead silence. The *silence* of the dead. It was how Achilles' mind sounded. He was dead, on the inside at least.

Briseis and Iphis smothered him with their arms when he walked out. Bri cried into his black suit jacket. Automedon and Antilochus softly muttered their condolences from a little ways back.

"We'll be heading to the crematorium in five minutes," a lady in a black shirt and pants informed the lobby before retreating into the room with the coffin.

Five minutes passed in a whirlwind. People apologizing, putting their hands on Achilles, wishing him well... they all blurred together, overwhelming his fragile mind. He hadn't stopped trembling by the time the procession made it to the basement, where the coffin went into the metal door of the incinerator.

"Young man," the same woman who had announced their departure said, pointing to Achilles. "Would you like to start the cremation?"

Briseis and Iphis shared a teary side eye that made Achilles' mouth turn up in a ghost of a smile. He shrugged, sliding through the crowd.

"Just press this red button," she said, pointing.

He pressed it. And felt nothing. How could he? What was he *supposed* to feel?

"Now, this will be finished in about four hours," she announced. "You may go back upstairs, where a light snack will be served."

Achilles stood next to the machine, watching as people filed out. He didn't move, even when Antilochus walked up to him. The rest of the crew waited by the door.

"So are you coming up?" his friend asked, trying to be gentle *and* to be heard over the sound of the cremation.

Achilles shook his head. "I'm going to wait," he said, turning and making his way over to the grey stone wall across from the machine. "See you all later," he said with a sad wave as he sild down the wall, onto the cold yellow floor.

Briseis frowned at him, but then rubbed her arms. It was freezing down here. She opened her mouth to say something, but Iphis whispered in her ear. The two of them stood in the doorway for a long moment.

Achilles closed his eyes, listening to the sound of their footsteps, echoing away through the cavity that once held his heart.

❦

The next four days passed in a haze. Achilles couldn't think. People whispered after him wherever he went. He was chilled. Everything seemed to be tinged with grey. But he did sleep, curled on the floor in the blankets he and Patroclus had shared. Nothing mattered anymore.

On the weekend, he locked himself in his room, swearing he wouldn't come out. He swore it to himself, because no one came looking for him for a long time. Briseis eventually found him and sat outside his door for three days straight. She even skipped school on Monday. Achilles told her he was sick of feeling like he was pointless. He was tired of the darkness, but he *was* the darkness. And it was better this way.

It hurt less when he was alone, without the pity and the rumors. Especially now that word of Hector had gotten to Mycenae. Agamemnon congratulated Achilles, and he had started crying. He hated crying in front of people.

Until he was certain he wouldn't randomly burst into tears, or say something he'd regret, Achilles was staying right where he was, behind his locked door.

# XXIV

PRIAM SAT ALONE ON the front porch. He wasn't sure how long it had been. Since… Hector had. Died. Hecuba was asleep, even though it was one in the afternoon. She had been planning the funeral with some family members over the phone. It would happen soon. Eventually. On a Sunday. And Andromache had finally calmed down. A little bit. She was still obsessively looking through her photos. But Helen was with her.

"Dad," his youngest son called from the doorway.

Priam's chair creaked as he looked over his shoulder. The shadows under Paris' eyes could have been hollows through his skull. Like his father, Paris hadn't slept.

"Can I… sit?" the boy asked tentatively, gesturing to the chair next to Priam.

He nodded, and Paris strode over with purpose. So Priam *wouldn't* have the chance to apologize for all his errors. He sighed as Paris sat. His son looked uncomfortable as he tried to perch on the edge of the rocking chair. They were seats meant for… better times,

Priam supposed. They were made for relaxing, enjoying the view. Priam followed his son's gaze to the spot on the lawn. The view was no longer something that could be savored. There was a patch of dirt, where Priam had ripped up the bloody grass. Hector's body had been there, leaching awful images and memories into the ground.

"Dad," Paris started, still staring forwards. "I... don't think Hector dying was an accident."

Priam let out a huff of laughter, rocking back and forth in his chair. Paris finally glared over at him.

"I *know* what the police said," Paris all but snarled, scootching precariously closer to the edge of his seat. "But why would someone fuc—" He stopped, closing his eyes and taking a deep breath. "Why would someone drag him around on a motorcycle if it was an accident? Why wouldn't they just call the ambulance?"

*I should have paid more attention to raising this one,* Priam thought, eyeing his anxious son out of the corner of his vision. He sighed, turning his gaze to a spiderweb clinging to one of the wooden porch beams.

"Can you get Helen?" he asked.

Paris, who would have argued in the past, got to his feet and disappeared inside the house. Priam had a sneaking suspicion that he knew who the motorcyclist was, but he wanted to clarify first. He figured Helen would know the relationships of people at Mycenae Academy. Of course, he knew he might be wrong, but he had asked her, on the night the first boy died at that game, if his friends were... reactive people. Helen had just laughed nervously.

"You needed me, Priam?" Helen asked, stepping out onto the porch, followed by Paris.

Neither of them sat. They just stood protectively close to each other. Never touching, but kind of... hovering. Helen was wearing sweat pants and a hoodie, with the strings tied in a bow under her chin. She looked a little more rested than Paris, but she was carrying herself differently. Like she was cowering from something. Priam pushed himself to his feet, feeling the joints in his knees pop. When he turned to face the two teenagers, he tried to put a gentle smile on his face. (That was harder now.)

"Yes, dear," Priam said warmly, clasping his hands together in front of him. "I was wondering if you could tell me a bit about the Stallions' star player."

Helen's eyes stretched. "Achilles?"

Priam gave her an encouraging nod.

"Um..." Helen knotted her fingers together, twisting them around nervously. "He wouldn't kill someone, Priam. I know him. But..."

"But?" Paris asked, leaning around Helen to see her face.

"But... Hector did... kill Patroclus," she whispered. "I... think it was Achilles. On the bike."

Paris could feel heat rushing into his face. He didn't understand how his father stayed so infuriatingly calm. Achilles was a contributing factor to his brother's death, and his father fucking *smiled*.

"Thank you, dear," Priam said softly. "I just... want to hear it from him."

"*What?*" Paris demanded, stepping around Helen to face his father. "I—what?"

Priam gave his son a pat on the shoulder. "I'll be back in a couple of hours."

With that, he turned and walked down the porch steps, pulling his car keys from his pocket. Paris didn't even have time to yell after him. He stuck one of his thumbnails in his mouth as Priam got into his truck and pulled down the quiet lane. Helen glanced at Paris. His face was flushed a deep red colour.

"Let's...go inside," Helen said, weakly.

Paris didn't reply.

"Please? I...let's just sit in our fort, okay?"

They had made a fort last night, on the floor beside Paris's bed. It was quiet in there, and warm, and it felt safer than the outside world.

Paris exhaled, clenching his fists, and releasing them. "Okay."

Inside the truck, Priam dialed one of his old friends. Hermes, a jack—of—all—trades adventurer that Priam had known for awhile in university, somehow managed to end up working as a custodian at Mycenae Academy. He picked up on the fifth ring.

"Hel*lo*," Hermes announced in a singsong voice. "This is Hermes, what can I do for you today?"

"Hermes!" Priam replied jovially, momentarily forgetting his woes. It had been years since they spoke. "It's Priam! How've you been?"

The man on the other end of the line laughed in shock. "*Priam*! It's been a minute! I've been pretty good actually, floating between work, traveling, you know how it is. What about you? Did you need something?"

The rumbling of the tires over the highway filled in Priam's silence for a long moment.

He sighed, once again plagued by the weight of the world. "Unfortunately, my oldest son recently passed away—"

"Hector?" Hermes cut in. "That's *horrible*. I'm so sorry for your loss."

"Thank you," Priam replied solemnly. "I'm actually...on my way to Mycenae Academy right now. I need to talk to a certain Achilles Pelides about an incident involving a drunk driving accident."

Hermes inhaled sharply. Priam could hear him scratching the back of his neck.

"I know it's a big favor to ask," Priam assured, tapping his fingers against the leather steering wheel cover. "And I swear, nothing will happen to the boy. I just need to have a conversation with him."

The man on the other end of the phone made a noncommittal noise. "Well. Guess it couldn't hurt. As long as you don't... hurt him. Promise me you won't hurt him."

"Hermes," Priam chastised. "You know me. I'd never hurt a student."

"Just had to make sure you hadn't changed, pal," he said, a smile in his voice. "I'll meet you in the parking lot at... three."

"Thank you so much," Priam said.

"Anything for an old friend," Hermes reassured. "And I'm sorry about Hector. He was a good kid."

Priam nodded, letting out a slow, even breath. Hermes hung up the phone, leaving Priam alone with his thoughts and the empty stretch of road before him.

When he pulled up to the curb in front of the grand school's lawn, Priam cut the engine and stared at the brick building. The dorms were to the right, a small cluster of state-of-the-art student living spaces. He sighed, getting out into the humid day. Priam locked his truck and walked across the lawn, hands in his pockets.

Finding Hermes wasn't too difficult. The man stood, leaning against a concrete barrier in a parking lot that looked like it was for the students.

Priam raised a hand in greeting as he crossed the well-maintained grass. "Hermes!" he called.

His friend looked up from his phone, a small smile breaking across his face. "Priam!"

They hugged briefly, exchanged a few words, then made their way over to one of the newer looking dorms. Hermes pulled a giant ring of keys off his belt and unlocked a side door.

"This stairwell goes up to the top floor," he said as Priam stepped inside the industrial concrete passage. "And Achilles' room is number eight."

"Thanks again," Priam said with a wave as he turned and jogged up the dimly lit steps.

"Anytime!" Hermes called after him, his voice spiraling up the thin stairwell with Priam's footsteps.

When Priam emerged on the top floor, he was blasted with a jet of cold air. *Air conditioning,* he thought with approval. That was nice. The room numbers were screwed to the wall beside each door, lit by a completely unnecessary lamp. What a waste of electricity. Priam made sure to keep his footsteps soft as he walked down the carpeted hall, reminiscent of a hotel. When he found room number eight, he stopped, straightened his shirt, and stared at the door. There was no guarantee Achilles would even be in here. It was a school day, afterall.

Priam raised a hand to knock on the door, but pulled it back. Hector was dead. His first son. Gone. And it might be because of this boy. He swallowed a lump in his throat and rapped his knuckles against the wood.

Inside the room, Achilles jumped to his feet. He had *told* Briseis that she needed to go to class.

"Achilles?" a man's muffled voice came from outside.

Apparently it wasn't Briseis. Was it a teacher? Achilles could feel his heart pumping in his chest. Could he go out the window? Would that even be safe? Where was that chunk of rope?

"Achilles, are you in there?" the man said.

"No," Achilles replied, before he could think. He wanted to smash his head through a wall.

There was a pause. Maybe the man had... gone away?

"I'm Hector's father," the man said, even softer than before.

This made Achilles want to throw up.

"I just want to talk to you."

No. Achilles could *not* talk to this man. He couldn't.

"Please go away," Achilles said, trying to sound like he wasn't on the verge of tears, backed up against the door to hold it closed, just in case this man tried to break it down. "I... can't talk right now."

Another pause.

"Achilles," the voice came again. "I just... I promise nothing will come of this. I just want to know what happened to my son."

Achilles stopped breathing. Maybe... if he pretended he wasn't there...

"Please," the man begged, his voice breaking.

And it was the grief, filling the man's weak voice that made Achilles stop. He had sounded like that. What would *his* father do if Achilles died? Would he be weak, like this man, begging to hear the story of what happened? No. Achilles' father would be the one smiling gently at the funeral, pretending his son's death didn't hurt.

Before Achilles knew what he was doing, he unlocked the door and pulled it open. The man on the other side looked like an older, less menacing version of Hector. Same eyes, same square jaw, same wide shoulders. Just... not like Hector. Hector had been a murderer. This man's expression softened when he saw Achilles, body tensed, face pinched to keep the tears from falling. Achilles and Priam stared at each other for a long moment, the silence whispering things in both of their susceptible ears.

Priam was the first to move. He stepped into the dorm room, taking in the mess without a second thought. The photographs, strewn across the floor. The pile of blankets. The clothes. The urn, sitting in the middle of the clean bed. It was a picture of a boy undone. Priam picked his way over to the empty bed, perching himself on the edge so not to disturb the urn. Achilles stayed by the door, staring out into the empty hall for another long second. He closed it softly, still not turning to face Hector's father.

Watching the boy's back, Priam thought of agony. The way his breaths seemed so even. The way the whites of his eyes were red. The way he was holding his fists, to keep his hands from shaking. A youth; a memory; a disaster. Achilles turned to face him, ledges of impossible ice ready to become water and fall from his eyes.

"Did you kill my son?" Priam asked, meeting the boy's impossibly green gaze.

Achilles stared back intently. "No."

"Did you. Kill. My son?" Priam repeated, watching the tears get thicker and thicker.

"Hector... fell off the road. We were supposed to collide. He swerved to avoid the hit. And he went into the ditch...so I brought him home."

Tears finally slipped from Achilles' eyes, racing each other down his jawline, along the curve of his gaunt face.

Priam watched him. *What a haunted, lonely boy.*

"Because no one did that." Achilles looked down at his feet. "No one did that for Patroclus. And Hector *did* kill him. Hector took from me the one person who made me smile." Outside, a bird started to sing. He glanced up and met Priam's gaze, his jaw clenched. "I did better than Hector," he whispered, venom dripping from his words. "And Hector is *lucky*. You should be grateful. This world is so fucked *up*. It breaks us and it tears us apart and then it expects us to keep going when there's nothing left to *live for*." A floodgate burst at that sentence, tears cascading down Achilles' face and leaping to the floor. "Is that the answer you wanted?" he rasped, not giving Priam the chance to look away.

But all Priam did was smile. A gentle smile that made Achilles want to scream. Priam got to his feet as Achilles slid down the door, trying to keep his breath under control.

"I'm sorry," Priam whispered, crouching down in front of the boy on the floor.

He sat next to Achilles as he hid his face in his hands.

"I'm sorry my son took someone important from you."

"He was my everything," Achilles said, his voice muffled by his hands.

Priam had tears in his eyes as he put an arm around Achilles. The boy stiffened, taking a rapid, scratchy breath. Priam rested his head against the door, staring up at the ceiling. *I'm sorry, Hector,* he thought. *I know. I can't believe I'm comforting the boy who killed my son. But do you see how lost he is?* Priam sat there for about half an hour, wondering what had happened to Achilles' parents. What happened to *Achilles.* Why weren't they here with him? Why was he alone right now? The boy eventually moved, pressing his face into Priam's shoulder. Priam had done this with his own sons, but they had never looked like Achilles, with the redness of his eyes, or the roughness of his voice. Achilles was volatile and agonized, sobbing into a stranger's shirt, looking for comfort anywhere he could. It hurt Priam to know that there were kids like this.

"Thank you," he said softly, untangling himself from Achilles. "Thank you for your honesty."

Achilles didn't reply. He only moved so Priam could get out the door. Priam wasn't sure he should leave, but Hecuba had called him ten minutes ago. He was about to offer Achilles his phone number when he thought better of it, getting to his feet and squeezing out into the hall. Achilles wasn't sure what had just happened. The man, who was Hector's father, left. Achilles was on the floor, feeling empty, lost, and alone, as the door slammed shut. He was so tired of feeling this way, but he didn't know how to escape it. A truck roared to life on the street, cutting through the thick air.

Priam didn't think much on the drive home. When he pulled into his driveway, Hecuba was waiting for him. He swept her into a hug.

"It was an accident," he whispered into her brown hair. "And the boy on the bike just wanted to bring him home."

He could feel the heat of Hecuba's tears as they soaked through his shirt.

"That doesn't make it easier," she whispered. They stayed there a minute, swaying gently to a song they both knew but couldn't sing out loud. "We should go inside," Hecuba said, pulling back from Priam, but not letting him go. "I need your opinion on food and flowers."

Priam let himself be dragged inside after his wife. Andromache stopped Hecuba in the entrance, her hair tied in a disastrous knot on top of her head, carrying suitcases instead of bags beneath her eyes. She held up her phone. Both Hecuba and Priam leaned forwards to see the picture.

"I think this is a good one," Andromache whispered painfully.

Hecuba smiled fondly. The photo had been taken earlier that year, during the beginning of the football season. Andromache, leaned over the edge of the stands, smiling as she kissed Hector, who was in his football uniform, standing on his tip toes to reach her.

"It's perfect," Hecuba said with a misty eyed nod.

And so, they busied themselves with planning the funeral for Hector, tamer of Stallions.

After:

I

After Hector's opulent funeral, the football season resumed, much to the chagrin of the Trojans. The Stallions took the lead, with five games to three. Hector was replaced by Euphorbus, who, for all his merit, wasn't meant to lead. Besides, the whole team was in mourning. Boosting morale is difficult when the captain was dead. Everything felt subdued. The cheers were quieter. The crowds were smaller. The fields were safer. Agamemnon stopped paying off the refs. He later told Menelaus that he was 'sick and tired of all the violence.' The team knew that was a lie, but it held, because Athena supported Agamemnon for reasons unknown.

Achilles came out of his room after his talk with Priam. No one knew why he suddenly started participating in class again. He didn't tell anyone about Hector, or about the dead boy's father. The only place Achilles truly seemed alive was running down the football field, but only Briseis noticed. Achilles was her problem, it seemed. No one really cared about him, except for when he was boosting them to victory. Without Patroclus, he had lost that spark of humor, which made it hard to talk to him sometimes. But Briseis didn't mind. Achilles was smart. They studied together in quiet corners, Iphis usually sitting with them, copying their work. It was a balance. A careful, precarious balance with some resemblance of normalcy.

Helen came to all the football games. She'd started going to school again too. Andromache hadn't left the house since Hector's funeral, and there were questions about her even graduating. Hecuba and Priam met with admin and probably paid them a giant sum so she could get her diploma. Paris had stopped talking altogether. Priam even made an effort to engage his younger son in conversation, but Paris didn't want anything to do with it. He wouldn't even talk to Helen. They would sit together in silence, Paris resting a head on her shoulder.

Paris' mind was a dark place. Achilles had murdered his brother, and no one was doing anything about it. He couldn't *believe* that he was part of a world where someone as promising as Hector could die, and everyone else would keep living. It hurt to think about, but he couldn't stop. He spiraled down, down, down, and no one noticed a thing, except for Helen. No one really listened to her, and Paris couldn't bring himself to say anything.

Aphrodite had texted Paris. He didn't even know she had his number.

(Maybe) Aphrodite:

Achilles isn't anything special. He's just like you. Just a boy who killed your brother.

*Sent 1:45 AM*

And she wouldn't reply to any of his messages after that. What did she want from him? Hadn't she messed things up enough? Paris sent a screenshot to Aeneas, but he didn't know what it was about. Paris left it at that.

One night, he overheard Helen begging with his father as he snuck into Priam's office. The study. No one was supposed to go in there, except for Hector and Hecuba. So... essentially, Paris was the only one who wasn't allowed.

"I need to go back," Helen was saying, her voice soft and desperate. "My friends are in so much pain and I miss them."

Priam sighed. Paris could imagine him, rubbing a hand over his forehead. "I wish I could send you back, dear, but Aphrodite is paying for you here."

"Then *convince* her," Helen implored. "You don't understand what it's like to know people you love are suffering and not be able to help them!"

Paris hated it when she was upset. He almost broke his silence and abandoned his mission, just to go in there and defend her. (He didn't want her to go home, but he wanted her to be happy. She wasn't really happy here, even when things weren't a mess.)

"I do know, Helen," Priam replied quietly, the kitchen floorboard creaking as he stepped towards the living room.

Paris didn't go in and defend her. He slipped into the study, closing the door behind him. Achilles had killed Hector. Paris couldn't stop thinking about it. Hector had been Paris' role model. The person he looked up to, ever since they were tiny kids. Hector had taught Paris so many things, about how to act and live and be a human. Even if Hector was always annoyed at Paris, he had *shaped* him. Hector wouldn't agree with what Paris was doing now, but when did he ever? Now that he was gone, everything seemed less offensive. If only he would come back and insult Paris again. Tell him to do better. No matter what Paris did, his older brother would laugh, or correct him. Hector wasn't here to do that now. He never would be again.

The bottom drawer of Priam's mahogany desk caught for a moment as Paris pulled it open. Inside, lay the silver handgun. The streetlight from outside glinted across its polished surface as Paris pulled it from the drawer, holding it up to the window. He took a deep breath, feeling the blood pulsing through his fingers against the cool metal. *Hector will rest tonight,* Paris thought, feeling nothing at all. *And it will be because of* me.

That same night, Achilles pulled out a box of photographs. He had been avoiding them ever since... Patroclus had died. But sitting on his floor, facing the wall, he felt ready. He was ready to let go. A little, at least. As he laid the pictures out in front of him, he felt the tears pricking his eyes. Achilles was used to that now. Instead of letting the wall of grief suck him under, he smiled.

The first photo was one of him and Patroclus at camp, sitting on a log. When they were young. Patroclus looked like he had just done something horrible, his eyes wide, a smile pasted on his face that was more of a grimace. Achilles was sitting next to him, aggressively grinning, showing off his gap toothed smile.

Achilles laughed softly, letting the tears leap from his eyes as he went through the box. Patroclus didn't know about all the photos. And he never would. Achilles let out a forceful breath. That was okay. Patroclus would be fine. Maybe Achilles would be fine too.

A picture of Achilles holding his painted helmet. A picture of Achilles dumping a bucket of water on Patroclus. A picture of Achilles and Patroclus and Chiron, their camp counselor. A picture of a weird face made from sticks. A picture of Patroclus trying to waterski. Photograph after photograph... they all gave Achilles an aching sense of reality, but also a sense of hope. Memory might be enough. Maybe he could get back on track. That thought made him laugh. No. He'd never get back on track. He'd have to bushwhack an entirely new road if he wanted to keep going. But in that moment, he decided not to think about the future. Just about the past, and the beautiful boy who he would dedicate his life to. Achilles wiped his eyes with the back of his hand, smiling at the photo he pulled out. Briseis had taken it one night. He didn't know when. She had deleted it off her phone.

It was of him and Patroclus, asleep, curled against each other. Patroclus was smiling softly, and Achilles' own face was hidden by his hair. Achilles ran a soft finger along the picture, part of him longing for that sweeter, kinder time.

He didn't hear the door opening behind him. He was too wrapped up in the past to understand what was happening until it was too late. Paris, who had been driving for an hour, thinking through his decision. He had asked Helen, once, where Achilles lived, purely out of curiosity. He'd never known how useful that knowledge would be one day. Paris' hand shook as he held the gun. He stared at the back of the boy sitting in the middle of the floor. Achilles' shoulders were shaking, with laughter and tears and life. Paris hated him for it. He hated Achilles for ripping his family apart. For destroying his life. *This is Achilles' own fault, really*, Paris thought as he raised the weapon.

When the shots rang out, neither of them really comprehended it. Three, in quick succession.

*Bang.*

*Bang.*

*Bang.*

Achilles didn't feel the pain at first, but the loss of sensation made him pause. He felt heat, then noticed the blood. He pressed a hand to his stomach, his fingers coming away dark. Achilles laughed as he fell forwards, onto the photographs, his body spasming and giving up. Finally. *If only this had happened sooner*, he thought. And then: *I'm on my way, love.*

Paris didn't wait to see if Achilles died. As soon as he pulled the trigger for the last time, he turned and ran. Shouts followed him as he galloped down the stairs. Still, he felt nothing, except for the jolting of the steps he took. And the air, as he burst outside.

And the thundering of his heart. He was in his car and on the road before anyone thought to look for him.

The shots woke the residents through the entire building. It was a junior on the soccer team who ran into Achilles' room first. He actually almost crashed into Paris as he fled, but wouldn't understand that until much later. What he saw would haunt him for the rest of his life. Achilles, slumped forwards over blood splattered photographs, smiling into the ground. By the time the ambulance got there, it was far, far too late.

Achilles' funeral was a somber occasion. No one knew who killed him. Briseis was the only one who cried. Peleus didn't even show up. Thetis allowed Achilles and Patroclus' ashes to be mixed. What else could she do? It had been her first son's last request.

Pyrrhus, her second son, attended the funeral. He had never met Achilles, but he played for the Stallions in the divisional championship game, filling in for his half–brother. Odysseus came up with a brilliant play they used to defeat the Trojans once and for all, locking out their offense completely. Agamemnon and Odysseus had the idea to send the other team a box of... tampered doughnuts, like they had received at the beginning of the season. They went on to state championships, placing fourth out of sixteen private schools. They didn't make Nationals that year.

Paris came forwards after the football season finished, admitting to killing Achilles. Hecuba and Priam were devastated. Their only living son, a murderer. Paris didn't even try to explain himself. In court, he kept admitting what he did, no matter how the lawyers tried to convince the judge that he was lying. Hector would have confessed, so it was what Paris did. He had killed the boy who killed his brother, and he was happy with that.

Helen watched the entire trial, her face blank. She didn't understand how Paris came to the conclusion that murder was the appropriate response, but she knew it was also her fault. She had been the one to tell Paris where Achilles' dorm room was. She hadn't tried to talk to him when he shut her out. All she could think was, *at least Patroclus wasn't here to see all this.* It was a grim sort of conclusion, that Achilles should die. Of course, Helen didn't wish death on anyone, but Achilles without Patroclus was like rain without sun. She missed them. And all of her friends from Mycenae.

Paris got arrested the day after the trial, which he had lost, all by his own doing. Trying to be noble, like Hector. But when Hector had killed someone, he had let his parents pay off the bail. Helen couldn't stop noticing the irony. Now, all the friends she had made at Ilium were either dead, imprisoned, or... dropping out of school. Andromache had made that call last week. Hecuba and Priam had promised to support her through whatever she needed.

Aeneas didn't talk to Helen very much. He had disappeared for a week after Hector died. He was quieter now. They sat together at lunch, but that wasn't... really enough to make a friendship. Helen missed Paris. And his stupid sarcasm, and his stupid humor, and his stupid face.

After Paris' trial concluded, Helen caught up to Aphrodite and Aeneas. They were walking slowly down the hall together, even though Aeneas never talked to his mother.

"Miss Aphrodite?" Helen called, running to catch up to them.

The tall woman turned, took in Helen's disastrous state, and stopped. Whenever Helen wasn't wearing her school uniform, she wore sweatpants and a tank top. She didn't have the energy to dress herself with any kind of effort.

"What, Helen?" Aphrodite said, her face a perfect makeup job, as usual.

Aeneas sighed, looking between his mother and Helen, who clasped her hands together anxiously.

"I... need to go home," Helen said meekly, praying that the goddess of a woman would understand. "I have no one here. And I miss my friends. I'm so lonely, ma'am."

Aphrodite huffed. "Fine."

Helen's eyes bugged out of her face. "What?"

The blonde woman rolled her eyes. "I said, *fine.* Your boy just got arrested, so come with me. We'll get your stuff and I'll take you back to that Godsforsaken place, okay?"

Helen felt awful for smiling, but it was all she could do not to burst out laughing and dance. She was going home. Back to Menelaus and Mycenae and... it would be different. But she would be with her old friends.

"Thank you so much," she blurted, turning in a frenzied circle. "I–I'll just go thank Hecuba and Priam."

With that, she ran back down the hall, feeling lighter than she had in months. Hecuba and Priam didn't receive Helen's thanks very well, but she didn't expect them to. Their only living son had just admitted to murder and been taken away. But there was nothing Helen could do to fix that. The drive to the house with Aphrodite was awkward, but it was okay. Helen ran around, gathering all the things she had left in a big green duffel bag, not caring if she left some knicknacks behind.

The ride to Mycenae felt like it took hours. Helen bounced up and down for half the drive, until Aphrodite told her to cut it out. Instead, she tapped her toe on the floor, drumming anxiously on the edge of her seat. When the giant brick school came into view, Helen didn't even wait for the car to stop before tumbling out. She called another thank you over her shoulder as Aphrodite rolled her eyes and followed her into the main entrance.

Everyone was in the gym when Helen found them. An assembly, commemorating all the students from *both* schools who had died. She stood at the back of the gym, watching slideshows, and listening to teachers go on about the new safety measures that would be put in place.

Briseis and Iphis sat near the back, neither of them paying attention. Briseis couldn't believe that someone had actually broken in and killed Achilles. They said he was looking at photos when he died, and Briseis *hated* that. He was probably thinking about living *for* Patroclus instead of dying for him. He had even been getting a bit better. Started talking. Participating a little in classes. Even laughing once or twice. She couldn't believe that three people had died. Two of them had been her friends. Her luck... was horrible. Iphis gripped her hand tighter as Menelaus stepped up to the mic.

That was when someone came charging forwards, a huge bag smashing into a metal chair. The people around the noise flinched. Everyone was a little jumpy, ever since... Achilles.

"Menelaus!" the girl yelled, causing the red–head to look up from his speech cards. He was giving a shaky eulogy for Achilles, but he stopped.

Briseis watched as his face broke into a huge grin as the blonde girl in grey sweats, collided with him.

Menelaus couldn't believe it. Helen. Was here. In his arms. She had her face buried in his shoulder, laughing and crying at the same time. He couldn't remember the last time he saw her.

"I missed you," he whispered into her hair.

People started clapping. Cheering. He hardly even noticed.

# Epilogue

B RISEIS' EXCHANGE PROGRAM ENDED two weeks later. Iphis went with her. They both finished school in California, and dated halfway through university. They broke up in Briseis' second year after Iphis dropped out, because of the joint trauma they experienced in high school. They decided it would be better to stay friends and cope with their issues without the pressure of a relationship. The two of them remained close, and eventually decided it would be a good idea to get back together in their early thirties.

Helen and Menelaus reunited happily, much to the chagrin of Agamemnon. (That was the last time Menelaus talked to his brother.) The two of them never fought seriously again, and moved to L.A. after graduation. Helen became a marine biologist, and dragged Menelaus all over the world after her. (He didn't actually mind.) Eventually, they bought a small house off the coast, where they had three sons and a daughter. Helen and Paris talked every few months, over the phone. She even visited him once or twice.

Agamemnon graduated high school, and went to business school, where he met his wife, Clytemnestra. They lived in constant turmoil for many years, until Agamemnon went too far and cheated on her during a business trip. She found out, and murdered him when he got home. The lawyers never proved that she was the one who did it, and she lived out the rest of her days rich off her dead husband's money.

Odysseus became a travel writer, and got married to his girlfriend Penelope, who wasn't made up, contrary to popular belief. Antilochus and Automedon ended up playing college football. Ajax 1 made it all the way to the NFL, only to get a head injury that proved to be lethal. Ajax 2 followed him most of the way, but when Ajax 1 died at the young age of 28, he wrote a biography on his friend, excluding the high school drama.

Priam and Hecuba took Andromache with them across the States, looking for a way to escape the disaster their family had proved to be. They wanted to provide a safer place for their grandson. They moved into wonderful mansion in Montana, right near the Canadian border. When he was born, Astyanax, Hector and Andromache's child became the light of their lives. He was bright and kind, with a hunger to learn new things. His presence almost filled the void that Paris and Hector left. Andromache became a wonderful mother, and she eventually came to terms with how unfair life had been to her. She went back to school and got an English degree when she was twenty–seven.

Every year, they would go back home to visit Hector's grave. It was high on a hilltop, overlooking a patchwork of farmer's fields. Peaceful and grand, just like the man buried there.

Paris spent the rest of his life in prison, but he didn't mind. In his head, he had done the right thing, and that was enough. He and Helen talked often. She didn't cast him aside for what he had done, like his parents had. Ironically, she was the only family he had left.

Aeneas escaped his mother's sudden neediness and became a radio show host in Rome. Aphrodite… continued living however she pleased, without a care in the world for what she had spurred into motion. She never even realized that what had happened was her fault.

Pyrrhus, Achilles' half brother, under Thetis' guidance, became one of the best college football players of all time. Athena ended up helping to coach him. Apollo quit and moved to the Bahamas. Zeus kept up his oil empire, and continued choosing favorites between schools for many years to come. Hera remained unhappily by his side.

And back in that tiny town, Achilles and Patroclus rested peacefully in the Elysium Cemetery, in a far corner, away from the road underneath a May tree that bloomed every spring.

# Afterword

## (Notes, discussions, and me explaining my own jokes)

**Notes on the Text:**

Dᴜʀɪɴɢ ᴛʜᴇ 'Aᴄᴛᴜᴀʟ Iʟɪᴀᴅ' section, I tried to incorporate parts of the original story. Here's a brief guide to the insider scoop (and my insanity).

(These are before the Actual Iliad section. But I had to share my thoughts on it.)

**Helen and Menelaus (General note)**

One of my quarrels with many adaptations of this story is the portrayal of these two. When I first read the Iliad, I expected a wildly toxic situation. (I got plenty of those, but not from Helen and Menelaus.) Though we never see them together, Helen speaks fondly of her home and how much she misses her husband. In most translations, Helen has a monologue about being kidnapped by Aphrodite from a home she loved. Different writers from the time, like Euripides and Sappho both view Helen of Troy very differently than how she is portrayed in Homeric legend, so that's where the original variation comes in.

**Iphigenia (Chapters 6 – 7, *Before* section)**

Iphigenia, in the original text, is Agamemnon's daughter who he promises to Achilles, when he really just intends to sacrifice her to Artemis. The goddess is preventing the wind from taking the Greek ships to Troy without a sacrifice, because she doesn't want so much blood to be spilled, but Agamemnon, even though human sacrifice is Not Allowed Anymore ™, kills his own daughter and appeases the goddess. It would be weird if Agamemnon had a daughter in this version, so she is his younger sister.

**Chryseis and Chryses (Chapters 7 – 2, in *Before* and *(Actual) Iliad* sections)**

This is so confusing. The *SEIS* on the end of a woman's name, like Chry*seis*, or Bri*seis*, means daughter of *insert father's name here,* so Chryseis is the *daughter of* Chryses. Bri*seis* would be the daughter of Briseus. BUT. In the Iliad, Chryseis is the daughter of a priest of Apollo who Agamemnon kidnaps and refuses to return, bringing down a plague of Apollo upon the Greek army. (See ***Doughnuts.***)

**Doughnuts (Chapters 10 – 1, in *Before* and *(Actual) Iliad* sections)**

The laced doughnuts that the Stallions' receive before the beginning of the Actual Iliad section of this book are there in place of a disgusting plague Apollo looses on the Greek army after Agamemnon refuses to return Chryseis to her father. This incident leads to Achilles pulling out of the war, because Agamemnon #sux.

**Fake dating thing (Chapter 5, in *Before* section)**

In the Iliad, Briseis is literally Achilles' slave, and Iphis is *also* a slave that Achilles supposedly gave to Patroclus. Think whatever you want, but I chose to believe that relationships that started with abduction wouldn't necessarily be good ones. In this version, they're pretending to date because it can't be avoided, but their friendships matter the most. Also. Iphis and Briseis are together because... why not. I can add lesbians and bi folks if I *want*. Thank you for coming to my TED talk.

**Location (aka Rural Texas)**

I needed a way for Achilles and Patroclus to hide their relationship from everyone, so why not put it in the southern states, where all the terrifying bills are being passed? Also the attitudes of some of the characters around them would make it difficult to feel safe. Obviously, the entire population doesn't support the homophobic actions taken by the government. (Yay to the people protesting and fighting the system! Amazing humans! And also yay to the people who aren't fighting, but believe in equality and freedom!)

Okay this stuff is actually part of the 'Iliad' now.

**"The muses could sing of the rage mounting inside Achilles by the time he made it outside..." (Chapter 1, *(Actual) Iliad* section)**

Generally, the Iliad starts with some variation of this line. About how the goddess, or the muses, or some unnamed female deity could sing of the 'rage of the warrior, Achilles.'

**"...Stallions Team..." (Chapter 1, *(Actual) Iliad* section)**

The name of the Mycenaean team comes from the Trojan horse, which was an offering to Athena that the Greeks hid inside. They told the Trojans *not* to take it inside their city, which... they did anyways, and brought about their own downfall.

***"...oedipus'." (Chapter 1, *(Actual) Iliad* section)***

I personally thought it would be funny to add in some random greek references. Oedipus is a tragedy about a man who was destined to bring ruin to his family, essentially by killing his father. He ends up sleeping with his mother, who kills herself when she finds out. So Oedipus... in this context, is a nerdy way to say Mother–Fucker.

***Agamemnon's general horribleness* (Literally the entire book I dunno what to say)**

I HATE this character with a burning passion, in the Iliad and in this story. He's disgusting and gross and everything that's wrong with the world.

*and if we think about it, he's the kind of man who was in power back in ancient times. And many of the men in power nowadays aren't much better. Ironic, huh?

**"She had been an olympic swimmer..." (Chapter 1, *(Actual) Iliad* section)**

In the original, and the story of Achilles in general, Thetis is a water nymph. So obviously point A to B was making her a swimmer…?

**"By Jove…" (Chapter 1, *(Actual) Iliad* section)**

In Roman mythology, Zeus is called Jupiter or Jove. Essentially, what we're seeing here is Zeus swearing to himself. (This causes me unprecedented and unnecessary joy.)

***Anything about the Trojans and their storylines* (Helen and Priam scene: Chapter 3, *(Actual) Iliad* section) (Hector and Andromache scene: Chapter 6, *(Actual) Iliad* section)**

I made up most of the stuff about the Trojans because the focus of the Iliad is on the Greeks. (And a lot of graphic descriptions of death.) There are some sections between Hector and Andromache that're part of the original, along with scene between Helen and Priam, where she tells him the names of the Greek soldiers.

**'*Ant Men*' Group Chat (Chapter 3, *(Actual) Iliad* section)**

During the Trojan war, Achilles' men were called the *Myrmidons* because they were supposedly turned from ants into men and *Myrmex* means Ant in greek. Achilles brought 50 ships with 50 men on each of them to Ilium. The people who reply to Achilles' message on that group chat are the leaders of his battalions in the original story.

**"The Ilium ones were very purple." (Chapter 3, *(Actual) Iliad* section)**

Purple was actually a symbol of opulence because of the cost of the dye. Troy was known to be a rich city, and apparently purple was one of their colors

**"Hit 'em high! Hit 'em low! Hit 'em where the Trojans go!"
(Chapter 4, *(Actual) Iliad* section)**

Not related to Greek mythology at all, but funny story, my mom's high school team name was the Trojans, and this was one of their cheers.

**"I'm pregnant." (Chapter 6, *(Actual) Iliad* section)**

In the Iliad, Andromache and Hector already have a son and she doesn't want him to fight in the Trojan war so his child will always have a father. Also, their son gets dropped off the walls of Troy in the original story. (Not *in* the Iliad, but in the story.)

**"...the man–killing man..." (Chapter 7, *(Actual) Iliad* section)**

Hector has several titles throughout the Iliad, and 'Man–Killing Hector' is one of them. Just what you want to be called. What a man–killing icon.

**"He hadn't been expecting anything after Pandarus literally *shattered* the honor code." (Chapter 7, *(Actual) Iliad* section)**

Okay, the fixation with honor has been in the story the whole time, but I just thought I'd mention it. The Iliad is so obsessed with man's honor, and in a modern context, it feels a little weird. No one seems to know what honor is anymore, including me, honestly. It's very confusing.

**"As they traded blows, the red dust made the air thicker." (Chapter 7, *(Actual) Iliad* section)**

When Hector and Ajax fight, they fight all day on the dusty battlefield. A baseball diamond was the only place I could think of with readily accessible dirt.

**"That better, oh heavenly one?" (Chapter 8, *(Actual) Iliad* section)**

Poseidon says this to Zeus. This whole interaction. It sums up the Gods' relationships. Zeus is a horny idiot with a superiority complex, as demonstrated throughout the story.

**"... Hestia's bed and breakfast..." (Chapter 8, *(Actual) Iliad* section)**

Hestia is the goddess of home and hearth, so it seemed natural she'd have an Air BnB.

**Chapter nine**

This is one of my personal favorite chapters, this is where Agamemnon offers Achilles a *crap–ton* of stuff. Yes, he actually does offer Achilles one of his daughters to wed in the Iliad. I just... find it so hilarious. Achilles is so pissed off he turns down so much material wealth, just to spite his general. I took pieces of what Agamemnon offered and put it in there, as well as parts of how Achilles responds. It's so funny. So funny. The whole situation is just laugh out loud. No clue why. My sense of humor is dead.

**"...until Achilles went to get his guitar about an hour ago..." (Chapter 9, *(Actual) Iliad* section)**

In the Iliad, Achilles plays the Lyre. Green flag.

**Cleopatra story (Chapter 9, *(Actual) Iliad* section)**

In Madeline Miller's 'The Song of Achilles' (which. God. What a good book.) she points out how *Patroclus* and *Cleopatra* have very similar syllables, only reversed. I got super curious about this, and found that the name Cleopatra actually wasn't documented until after the Iliad was... shared. And written down. Both names mean 'the honor of the father,' as mentioned. It's possible that the name Cleopatra was literally made up by Homer or someone telling the Iliad, just for the purpose of Phoenix's story as he tries to convince Achilles to come back. Coincidence that Cleopatra is Meleager's wife? His *lover*? Hmm. I think not.

**"...Oikos Inn." (Chapter 10, *(Actual) Iliad* section)**

No, the hotel they stay at isn't intentionally named after the yogurt company. It means 'home' or 'household' in Greek.

**"...this Swedish thing on Netflix..." (Chapter 10, *(Actual)* *Iliad* section)**

Yes, Achilles was watching Young Royals.

**"Okay, plan," he said, staring at the house. "I'm going in to get the motorcycle keys, and when I get back, we're gonna ring the doorbell, drop... Dolon and then ride, okay?" (Chapter 10, *(Actual) Iliad* section)**

Originally, Odysseus and Diomedes murder Dolon. Then they go to Rhesus' camp outside the walls of Troy and murder all *his* men in their sleep. And *then* they go steal all Rhesus' famous horses. Aka, motorcycles...?

**"I don't think Achilles is human." (Chapter 11, *(Actual)* *Iliad* section)**

There's a comment about Achilles having *half a god-complex* somewhere in the *Before* section, and these two things are references to Achilles' demi-god status. In the Iliad, he's the son of a mortal man and the sea nymph Thetis. SHE DID NOT DIP HIM IN THE RIVER STYX. ACHILLES IS NOT IMMORTAL *OR* INVINCIBLE. THAT WAS ADDED ON LATER TO MAKE THE STORY MORE DRAMATIC>>>>

**Hector's character* (General note)**

All the movies I've seen about the Trojan war portray Hector differently than I personally interpreted his character. In the Iliad, he's actually a horrible person. I find it difficult to believe that Andromache would marry someone who's 100% awful, but then I remember that she's probably in an arranged marriage. So. In this story, I tried to make him have a disturbing side *and* a decent side, but that was. Difficult. I actually don't really like Hector, particularly in the Iliad. But that's a personal thing.

**"...pick six..." (Chapter 13, *(Actual) Iliad* section)**

Guys, I actually have no idea how to play football. My parents won't let me try out for the team. Which is fair. I *would*. But that... would admittedly be a bad idea. (Rookieroad.com saved my life. Football for dummies, essentially.)

**"There were puncture marks in the perfect shape of a cleat on his thigh..." (Chapter 14, *(Actual) Iliad* section)**

Greater Ajax gets stabbed with a spear in the Iliad and falls off the prow of a ship that the Trojans are trying to burn. Sadly this couldn't be that epic. RIP Greater Ajax's epicness. (Yes they are called Greater and Lesser Ajax in the Iliad. And Ajaces is used as a plural for these two characters, which is *so funny*.)

**"Be so kind and tell me how I can briefly seduce my husband to get back at him for something." (Chapter 14, *(Actual) Iliad* section)**

This is another hilarious scene in the Iliad where Hera seduces Zeus so Posiedon can help the Greeks. I just find it so funny that the only reason Hera wants anything to do with Zeus is so she can spite him. (Zeus hates Hera as well. Oh! Also. They're not siblings in this version. Incest is just... way less okay than it apparently was for the Greek gods.)

**"He blew past a giant player, somehow flipping him onto his back." (Chapter 16, *(Actual) Iliad* section)**

This giant player is Scarpedon, who Patroclus actually sort of accidentally, sort of on purpose kills in the Iliad.

**"That, is not Achilles Pelides." (Chapter 16, *(Actual) Iliad* section)**

In the original poem, Achilles bans Patroclus from pursuing any of the Trojans back to Ilium, but he does, deciding he's going to kill Hector himself. Eventually, he manages to climb the unclimbable walls of Troy, only to be thrown off by Apollo who guards the city. The god removes Achilles' armor from his body and pretty much lays him down for murder. Euphorbus stabs him first, and he's followed by Hector, who eventually murders Patroclus. Hector literally *knows* that Patroclus isn't Achilles because he's not wearing the armor. And this is why Hector isn't my favorite. He just kills Patroclus for no good reason. How rude.

**"Inside the room, ten minutes later..." (Chapter 17, *(Actual) Iliad* section)**

A weird thing about the written Iliad is how the verb tenses switch. A few times, when Homer talks about Patroclus or Menelaus, he speaks to them in second person, referring to them as *you* instead of by name. I tried to do something reminiscent when Patroclus died by changing it to present tense. (No one really knows why Homer did this. A theory is that he was talking to the more pure, good characters as if they were there with him, but. Just a theory.)

**The fight over Patroclus' body (Chapter 17, *(Actual) Iliad* section)**

Hector tries to steal Patroclus corpse in the Iliad, after removing the armor. The rest of the Greeks try to get it back, because they know how *important* he is to Achilles. They couldn't play tug–o–war with a body in the hospital so it had to be an argument.

**"Antilochus pinned Achilles' wrists to the floor..." (Chapter 18, *(Actual) Iliad* section)**

Achilles does, in fact, reach for his sword stab himself when he finds out Patroclus is dead, only to find that Patroclus took it to battle.

**"Briseis. Was sitting on the curb. Her face was in her hands..." (Chapter 17, *(Actual) Iliad* section)**

Briseis' only character development in the Iliad is her mourning the loss of Patroclus. It's also the only time she speaks. Yay women's rights.

***Fun Fact moment***

In the Iliad, Achilles cries so loudly that Thetis hears him from the *bottom of the sea* when Patroclus dies.

**"You can have her back!" (Chapter 18, *(Actual) Iliad* section)**

Just wanted to say a big screw you to Agamemnon. Pointing out how awful he is one more time.

**"He... yeah. That's my helmet." (Chapter 18, *(Actual) Iliad* section)**

Achilles' armor is a huge part of his personality in the Iliad. When Hector strips Patroclus of that armor, Achilles has a melt–down, and then Hephaestus creates him a new set that's far grander than the last. The description actually goes on for an entire chapter. Hector accidentally takes the helmet in this one because... it would be weird if he took Patroclus' clothes. I dunno.

**"...his newly shaved head." (Chapter 19, *(Actual) Iliad* section)**

Achilles chops off his hair and burns it with Patroclus' corpse. He also casually doesn't eat or sleep for a ridiculously long time. (The Gods sustain him with secret ambrosia and nectar, but that doesn't happen here.)

**"Hopefully no one else died." (Chapter 20, *(Actual) Iliad* section)**

Lol.

**"Achilles was up to his knees in the frigid water..." (Chapter 21, *(Actual) Iliad* section)**

Modern adaptation of Achilles fighting the river god. Running through the stream angstily.

**"I need your bike." (Chapter 22, *(Actual) Iliad* section)**

When Achilles goes to kill Hector, he hopes that Hector will kill him instead. When he doesn't, Achilles disgraces his body by dragging it behind his chariot and saying that he'll leave the body for the dogs. In this version, Achilles isn't *quite* so psychotic.

**"We're just celebrating how Hector tamed the fucking Stallions," he said with a wicked grin. "Killed one too." (Chapter 22, *(Actual) Iliad* section)**

One of Hector's other titles was, *Hector, tamer of horses.* And... god. Antenor. Hector. Euphorbus. Stop being so...ugh. (Yes, I wrote them, and yes, they are so out of line for this and I'm very upset with them. These characters. Agh, man, they're gonna be the end of me.)

**"He waited for Deiphobus to get on behind him..." (Chapter 22, *(Actual) Iliad* section)**

The only reason Hector decides to fight Achilles in the Iliad is because he hallucinates his brother. One of the Gods sends an image to convince Hector not to be a coward, only to leave him to die. The Gods are pretty uncool.

**"Elysium..." (Chapter 23, *(Actual) Iliad* section)**

Or, Ancient Greek heaven.

**"I thought flowers would be better than sacrificing people..." (Chapter 23, *(Actual) Iliad* section)**

Not Achilles sacrificing maidens and Trojan youths and dogs and horses and building a hundred by a hundred foot pyre for his friend. Sadly he couldn't do that here. So he bought flowers. And started the incinerator. Interesting fact: cremating someone on a pyre takes up to eight hours, while an incinerator only takes four. Who knew.

**"I just... I promise nothing will come of this. I just want to know what happened to my son." (Chapter 24, *(Actual) Iliad* section)**

In the Iliad, Priam goes to Achilles' camp, guided by Hermes and dressed as an old man. He's going back to get the literal body of his son, which... Achilles couldn't keep in his dorm without being psychotic. (In all honesty, this scene is heartbreaking in the poem.)

**"And so, they busied themselves with planning the funeral for Hector, tamer of Stallions." (Chapter 24, *(Actual) Iliad* section)**

Finishing off the Actual Iliad section, most translations end with some variation of this line. You'd think the Iliad went on for longer, but again, it's a weirdly short story. I'm convinced we're missing a bunch of books, because the Odyssey picks up at such a strange spot. But who knows. Maybe Homer was just... confusing. (What I wouldn't give to go BACK IN TIME AND ASK A BUNCH OF QUESTIONS—)

# Acknowledgements

First off, thanks for reading all the way here. This book. Has eaten my brain. So thank you for joining the madness.

Yayyyy for my parents who have put up with listening to me yap about this story for like. Five years now. The Iliad is my Roman Empire (that's a complete lie, I say pie is my roman empire. Or some random actor.) So thanks to them for listening and not shutting down my rampant creativity. Thanks to my brother for also being a Percy Jackson kid. It's nice to have someone else in the house who also Knows Their Greeks.

Thanks to that friend who's name has slipped my head, BUT they helped me realize that Iliad only has one L. That would've been super embarrassing.

I'm glad I have some friends. They're pretty cool. Yay for them!

And thanks to that one summer situationship who didn't laugh when I told him what this book was called.

I'm wildly, violently, incredibly grateful for everyone who's had a hand in shaping this story. And for everyone who's been a victim of my three hour Iliad talks, I'm only slightly sorry.

Lastly, to people fighting their own battles, at home, in their relationships, in their minds, at school... you guys are doing great. I believe in you. You're here and you're fighting. You've got this. Talk to someone if you feel safe. It helps. I promise.

# Further Reading

T HERE ARE PLENTY OF other things I could go into detail about, because again, I am so passionate about this story and the intricacies, BUT I'll just leave you with a list of other retellings and literary media that explores the Trojan war, ancient Greece, and mythology.

The Iliad – translated by Emily Wilson

The Iliad *and* The Odyssey – translated by Samuel Butler

A Thousand Ships – Natalie Hayes

Daughters of Sparta – Claire Heywood

The Song of Achilles – Madeline Miller

If Not, Winter: Fragments of Sappho – translated by Anne Carson

Helen *and* The Women of Troy – edited by Richmond Lattimore and Davie Grene

Troilus and Cressida – William Shakespeare (This is just a very entertaining retelling of the Trojan war with very little accuracy or substance.)

# About the author

Zoe Marlett was deterred from putting an absolutely absurd picture of themselves here. They've always loved Greek mythology, grew up as a Percy Jackson Kid TM, and has read nine or ten different translations of the Iliad. This book was written in the midst of high school and they are wildly grateful to be free of that environment. They would also really like a pizza, but it is very late.

*update: they got several pizzas the next day

photo credit: Rafal Wegiel